The reviews are in ...

Readers' Favorite 2023 Gold Medal winner for Fiction - New Adult.

First-place winner of 2022 Incipere Awards for Romance.

Finalist for Romance in the 2024 American Book Fest contest.

"With multilayered, intricate characters, expert pacing, and messy-but-beautiful romance, the novel makes for a must-read for lovers of New Adult romance."
—The Prairies Book Review

"Tricia LaRochelle understands what makes an effective romance story work. She doesn't just offer a girl-meets-boy setup. What she assembles is an interesting pair of characters with flaws that make them distinct, relatable, and utterly human. She handles Sara's traumatic past with sensitivity and keen atten-

tion to its emotional and psychological components, which makes Sara a convincing and fascinating case study in PTSD. "
    —Readers' Favorite

"Flickering Heart explores serious topics such as mental health and sexual assault, and the author handles these subjects delicately. LaRochelle also portrays college life skillfully. Readers will root for Sara."
    —blueink Review

This book has everything: a charming ingénue of a lead character, a blossoming love story that's impossible not to root for, a group of mean girls lurking in all the dark corners, and a mystery that evolves in a way that's both menacing and unpredictable. This is a promising debut that begs for a sequel!"
    —Kim Catanzarite, author of The Jovian Universe

Flickering Heart

Sara Browne Series Book 1

Tricia T. LaRochelle

FLAMING HEART PRESS

I dedicate this book to my husband, Bob, and two sons, Ryan and Sean, who have been there for me through thick and thin.

Flickering Heart

Contents

Chapter One

Sole survivor described me to a tee. *Soul* survivor, I was not. In fact, over the past six years since the accident, my *soul* was withering on the vine. I was surviving, yes, but I wasn't living. PTSD held me hostage, separating me from the people around me. Sorrow, nailing me inward. When your world crumbles into nothingness, the only family you've ever known gone forever, how do you rebuild? When you construct walls so high around your heart that no one can get in, how do you relate to people again?

I had no idea, but I was about to find out. In fact, I felt as though I were about to step off a cliff.

"Are you ready, Sara?"

The question had come from my new friend and suitemate, Amy, as we left our dorm.

"Yup," I said as I stuffed my keycard in the back pocket of my jean shorts with clammy hands and a racing heart. I was a freshman at Commonwealth University, which meant Charlottesville, Virginia, would be my new temporary home for the next four years.

Are you ready? While part of me wasn't even close to ready, another part of me was bursting at the seams to get out. Six years of solitude was long enough. Eighteen-year-old Sara Browne was moving on. Finally.

Outside, the sky was a pale blue, the birds chirped from the trees. Students were everywhere, populating the campus.

I took a breath and released it as blood pumped through my arteries like water through a fire hose. I was terrified and excited, nauseous and equally defiant to make this new chance at life work.

Amy and I snaked around two more dorms before my other new friend, Derek, came into view. Wearing a loose-fitted T-shirt and faded jeans, he waited by a bench near a large oak tree. Amy and I had met Derek at freshman orientation the day before when he was off by himself. Amy said he looked like a guy who could score some weed. I had laughed at the time, pretending I had experience with that sort of thing. After we chatted with him for a while, he convinced us to go to the football game the next day and the tailgate beforehand, which was our destination now. He'd said something about checking out some fraternities that he hoped would be there. Derek didn't look at all like a typical fraternity type, but who was I to judge?

The idea didn't impress Amy much, but Derek had promised he'd bring her beer, which was probably what was in the bag that dangled from his hand.

"Hi, Derek." I waved, enjoying the feeling of seeing a familiar face.

"Hey, Shag," Amy said as we approached. "There better be beer in that bag."

Shag? Did Amy just get Derek's name wrong?

I was about to correct her when Derek spoke.

"Shit yeah. I told you, I got ya covered." Derek paused, the corners of his eyes crinkling. "Wait ... what did you call me? Who the hell is Shag?"

"*You* are ... now." Amy scratched at one of her eyebrows that flashed a silver stud. She also had a small ring in her nostril. If you added in her spiky black hair, expressive makeup, and take-no-prisoners attitude, Amy was already the coolest person I had ever met. "You know *Scooby-Doo* don't you?" Amy didn't wait for Derek to answer. "You kinda got that Shaggy vibe going on." She smirked, her gaze traveling over Derek's outfit that hung from his lanky frame like a coat hanger.

"Huh?" Derek raked a few strands of long bangs away from his eyes as if that would cause Amy to come to her senses.

Derek *did* have the long hair, scruffy beard, and gangly body. He even wore a green T-shirt with the name "AC/DC" stamped across it, something I imagined Shaggy would also wear.

Amy shifted her stance. "I do nicknames, so deal with it." She didn't say it with an angry or annoyed voice, more matter-of-factly.

Derek's lips twitched their disapproval. He clearly didn't get it.

I stifled a giggle. These two were hillarious to watch.

Amy patted his shoulder. "It'll grow on you, dude." She cut her eyes, a vibrant shade of green, over at me next. "I haven't come up with one for *you* yet."

My smile faded. Considering they had called me "cave girl" at my last school since I rarely left my room, my bar was set pretty low. The thought of those years made my shoulders slouch, my confidence taking a nosedive.

That was then, this is now.

A cluster of students walked past, some with images of dogs drawn on their cheeks and others with "Go Hounds" written in magic marker on their shirts. Everyone was talking loudly or laughing. Two guys ran by barking and howling—their faces painted a collage of orange, black, and white. A few girls screamed, startled. The decorative clothing and face painting were tributes to the school football team, The Foxhounds. In the distance, loud music and voices drifted through the air where the football stadium loomed.

Letting go of the past, I bounced from foot to foot, wanting so badly to be part of this world—part of the living.

Derek set the bag on the ground. "Let's pregame before we hit the tailgate." He pulled out a beer and handed one to Amy, which she cracked right away, taking a long sip. When she lowered the can from her lips, she belched.

"Nice one," Derek said. "I could go for some weed right now."

Weed? I wasn't quite ready for *that* yet. I held my breath.

"Yeah, me, too," Amy said. "I was hoping you brought some."

I chewed my lower lip, wondering what I would say if they asked me to smoke, too.

Derek handed me a beer next. "I have some in my room, but I wasn't sure how strict the school is about that shit. Next time."

One crisis averted. I exhaled a shaky breath.

Having never partied before, I stared down at the chilled can in my hand, wary. I had tasted my dad's Irish whiskey once when I was ten. I thought my throat was going to melt. Even if beer tasted like a dead animal, I was still going to suck it down —at least a sip or two, enough that I didn't look like a complete dork. It was a beer, after all, not bungee jumping.

"I can't believe I'm going to a college tailgate." Amy shook her head. "Not my scene." Wearing an oversized black T-shirt —a wolf displayed on the front—Amy's "cool" rode past her shredded jean shorts all the way to her chunky black boots. She wasn't dressed for a preppy football game for sure, but she got my vote for best costume.

"Same." I gazed down at my plain white T-shirt, jean shorts, and flip-flops. Nothing risky, I was vanilla.

While Derek helped himself to his own beer and Amy took another sip of hers, I cracked my can and filled my mouth with a bitter taste that challenged my lips to grimace. Aside from the fizzy and acidic flavor, the next thing that came to mind was urine. Beer tasted like urine? Not that I knew what urine tasted like. How did people drink it? My father used to drink beer all the time. He was Irish, so it went with the territory—or so he said. I could almost hear him singing one of his Irish songs that prompted an eye roll from my mother and a snicker from me.

Don't go there. All at once, my heart sank the way it did every time I thought about them. I glanced around, uneasy, until my dad's voice rang in my ear. "Stiff upper lip." It was something he used to say whenever I was pouting or upset for no apparent reason.

I set my jaw and took his advice.

"So, where are you from, Derek?" I already knew Amy was from Connecticut. I took another sip of beer. The frothy liquid slid down my throat a bit easier this time. It wasn't as bad, but it wasn't great, either.

"Vinton, Virginia. It's just outside of Roanoke. Couple of hours from here."

I nodded as if I knew where that was. My third sip of beer caused my insides to heat up. I was boiling internally. A cool Vermont breeze was just what I needed, but it was August, and I was in Charlottesville, Virginia. Last time I checked my weather app, it was 92 degrees, the air dripping with humidity. I wiped my palms on my jean shorts, glad I'd doubled up on the deodorant. At least the can was somewhat cold and the sun was close to setting, hopefully, taking the day's heat with it.

"You?" Derek asked.

"I'm from Vermont. Middlebury, actually." I'd hardly been there in years. After my parents died, it took two weeks for me to grow tired of the sad faces and I'm-so-sorry-for-your-loss talk in my hometown. There was nothing left for me there, and I wanted out. Ignoring my mother's best friend, Abigail's, objections, I found a boarding school eight hours away and applied. I *had* to get away.

Turning inward, my breath hitched, and I hoped no one noticed.

"Connecticut," Amy said before Derek could ask her. "Farmington, just outside of Hartford."

Derek continued to pull from his beer. Then, he crunched the can, threw it in the bag, and took another one.

"Grab me one, too." Amy handed him her empty.

"How did you score the beer anyway? You know someone who's twenty-one?" Amy took another drink.

I had wondered the same thing as I took a sip and then burped. "Excuse me." I covered my lips with my fingers, my cheeks still burning like a wood stove in January.

Derek grinned and wiped his upper lip. "Nah. I'm twenty-one. I had to take some extra classes at the community college back home to get in here, and then I had to save up the money. I got a shit ton of financial aid, but still."

Amy and I nodded.

"Cool," she said. "You're becoming a very useful friend already."

"Yeah, that's great, Derek." I held back a hiccup. My body was literally flipping out on me.

Another cluster of students paraded past, this one a medley of funny hats, colored cheeks, and signs that read, "Go Hounds." One guy wore an orange Afro wig.

"Let's finish our beers and head out. I don't think they'll let us bring in open containers," Derek said.

Amy finished her beer while I struggled with mine. There was no way I was going to be able to finish it without barfing. Plus, my head was swimming, and I had this strong urge to pee. "Hey, do you mind if I run up to my room and use the bathroom before we go?"

"Sure," Amy said. "We'll wait."

With that, I jogged over to my dorm and up to my room, where I poured out the rest of my beer and emptied my bladder. A few minutes later, the three of us fell in line with everyone else on campus on their way to the tailgate. Excitement flooded my system until I squealed like a train whistle, "Yahoo," which earned me a sideways glance from Amy and Derek.

Yup, I was a dork.

A couple of minutes later, we reached a roped-off area, where a large man wearing a college polo shirt watched people enter. The man checked a few bags and coolers but didn't confiscate anything. The noise grew louder, the energy in the air abuzz. After the man gave Derek's bag a cursory glance, we passed through the entrance and into the fray, where country music butted up against hip-hop and rock and roll. Barbecue chicken, burgers, and roasted corn on the cob formed small clouds of tasty smells that coated the air and made my mouth water.

I followed Derek and Amy past all the banners, flags, and clusters of people, my pulse thrumming, my ears ringing. We rounded a corner where a group of guys played a game of cornhole, all of them holding red plastic cups. At the entrance to their area stood a flag with what looked like a coat of arms, the words *Phi Kappa Omega* printed across the bottom.

Derek stopped and eyed the banner. "Let's check it out," he said.

Amy thrust her palms up like two stop signs. "You're joking, right? You're not seriously interested in that superficial bullshit, are you?" Her brow lowered, judgment painted all over her face.

Derek leaned back a smidge. "I told you I wanted to ask around about frats. I may pledge."

Amy's mouth dropped open. "I thought you were kidding."

"Oh, come on." Derek nudged her. "It's not that bad. Here, have another beer. It's my last one."

While Derek handed Amy his last beer and tried to convince her to stay, my eyes took a tour of the small crowd, which mainly consisted of men. Wearing pastel-print Oxford shirts (sleeves rolled up to the elbows), khaki shorts, and loafers with no socks, a few of them looked like they just stepped out of an ad. As they threw beanbags into the cornhole board, drank, and carried on animated conversations with fist bumps and head bobs from the loud hip-hop music playing, they exemplified what I'd envisioned a typical fraternity would look like. One large guy with tree trunks for arms smashed a beer can into his forehead and guzzled the foamy fluid that spewed out. Another guy put his fingers to his mouth, kissed them, and yelled, "The taste when it hits your lips."

Amy and Derek looked at each other.

"*Old School*," they said in unison before they smiled, which made no sense to me.

A few girls were there, laughing with each other, hanging onto guys near them, or drinking. Everyone had a cell phone, which most of the women used to take selfies.

I needed to get myself acquainted with *my* cell phone and especially social media. I was basic when it came to technology. Then again, I was basic when it came to most things. Very lame

—unlike the girl who had just come to the party wearing a floral romper, wedge sandals, and large hoop earrings. Everything about her was stunning, from her long, shiny brown hair to her sleek body.

She approached a guy who had his back to me, placing her hand on his arm. He must've been six-three. His light-blue T-shirt hugged his muscular back and powerful arms, outlining a body that caught my attention and kept it. I liked his hair and the way his caramel curls danced in the late-day breeze. What did his face look like? As if he heard my question, he turned around and stared right at me.

I'd fallen off my bike once when I was a kid and knocked the wind out of myself. For a few agonizing seconds, I literally couldn't breathe. As I struggled to breathe now, my lungs reminded me of that moment.

While Amy continued to rib Derek, I caught sight of hot guy's strong jaw and perfectly proportioned face. The sun reflected off his baby blue eyes that were nothing short of stunning. The corners of his soft, plump lips curved upward into an enticing smile. *Enough already.* Before I started drooling, I tore my eyes away.

I'd thought about guys—obsessively—but I'd never dreamt up one who looked like him. The boarding school I went to was for girls, but if it had allowed guys, I imagined he and his romper girlfriend would have been king and queen of every prom. Picture perfect. And totally *not* for me. I was looking for chill, sweet, and cuddly. I didn't need a runway model or a guy who could audition for the next Marvel movie. No need to get crazy.

"Who might you be?" a guy with dark-brown hair and intense brown eyes asked. I hadn't seen him walk up. His sandy-haired friend stood next to him, grinning from ear to ear, neither too steady on their feet.

"We allow all babes in, but only if you have a drink in your hand." The dark-haired guy handed me a cup filled with beer.

Babes? That was a first for me.

"Thanks, and I'm Sara." I took a sip and looked away, taking several quick breaths.

"You new?" the dark-haired guy asked.

"Yeah, a freshman." I took another small sip, still not a fan of the flavor.

"Weeell, I'm Rick." Speaking in a long drawl, he faced his friend. "And this shithead is Kevin." He slapped his friend on the chest, which caused the beer in his friend's hand to spill. "Oh, fuck. Sorry, dude."

Kevin wiped his shirt with a clumsy hand. "Don't be wasting beer, man." He looked at me. "Don't worry, if he spills any on you, I can suck it off."

Both men laughed and swayed while my cheeks burst into flames, my toes curling.

"In fact, that white T-shirt would look even better wet." Kevin stared right at my boobs, his head teetering back and forth like a Tilt-A-Whirl. "What do you think, bro, freshman baptism?"

My feet melting into the pavement, I silently beckoned the earth to open and swallow me whole. Meeting boys excited me, but not drunk ones who were obnoxious. And what was the freshman baptism? I didn't want to know. The hand holding my beer started to shake as did my wobbling knees.

Rick put a hand on Kevin's shoulder and leaned so close that Kevin stumbled a step. "Don't be scaring off the babes, Kev."

Thankfully, Derek inched closer, his eyes wide and approachable. "Hey, dudes, cool party."

Rick looked at Derek and then at me. "He with you?" He scrunched his face as he said it.

"Uh-huh," I managed to let slip past my lips.

"No way this guy is your boyfriend—unless you want to shatter my image of you." Rick's gaze cut to Amy next. "You look more like his type." He took a long sip of his drink and then wagged his finger. "Then again, you may not do men at all."

Amy glared at Rick, her smirk brimming with sarcasm. "What's the matter? Lost a few to the other side?" She arched an eyebrow. "All you frat *boys* are the same. Big egos, small dicks." She flipped one hand in the air as if to say, "And *that*, is a fact."

Kevin and a few other guys within earshot laughed, hooted, and jeered Rick with "She just made you her bitch," and "Solid burn" comments.

Amy looked at Derek, her face tight and her eyes sharp. "These are the douchebags you want to hang with?"

Derek moved closer to Amy and whispered what sounded like, "He's just drunk."

He may have been right, but I was also tired of this scene. Something told me Rick and Kevin weren't very nice when they were sober. In one conversation, they'd managed to insult all three of us. "Yeah, guys, let's go," I said.

"No, no, no. Don't leave, Princess." Rick slammed into Derek next, almost knocking him over as well. "Derek, is it?"

Derek chuckled, his eyes tentative. "Yeah, man."

"Let's get you and your emo friend a beer." Rick swung his free arm over Derek's shoulders and dragged him toward a keg at the back of the party where the majority of the people were hanging. He peered over his shoulder. "You can't leave your friend now. Come on, ladies. Don't be shy."

"Humph," Amy said. "I've never been called *shy* in my life." She pursed her dark-colored lips. "If Derek pledges, this is going to be a short friendship. I never pegged him for a frat boy."

I agreed completely. "Once he gets a beer, let's see if we can talk him into leaving. We can head over to the game early."

Amy looked up at the sky for a moment and exhaled. "Fine. One beer, but they talk any more shit and I'm either leaving or kicking some balls—that is, if they have any."

I laughed. I'd never met anyone like Amy. She was bold and fearless. She was who I wanted to be. I felt stronger just being near her.

Together, we walked over to the crowd, where Amy finished the beer Derek had given her and took another full cup that sat on a table next to a bunch of others. The music was louder here and so was the chatter. I tried to talk with Amy, but it was difficult, so I went back into observation mode.

The flawless girl wearing the romper was talking with a bunch of other girls now, not the guy I'd seen her with before. Something about her slanted eyes and tight mouth reminded me of the "it" girls from the boarding school where I came from. Her clothes looked designer, and the way she popped her hip out, shoulders back, reeked of overconfidence. Where was her boyfriend? Two seconds later, I locked eyes with him about twenty feet away.

A jolt shot through my chest like a lightning strike. *Breathe.* I was light-headed and my heart pounded like two boxers in a ring.

This was the second time I'd caught him looking at me. Was it a coincidence? Like when you happen to glance over at someone when they happen to glance over at you? Once again, I pulled my eyes away, but then my gaze found him again. I couldn't seem to help myself. Yup, he was still staring right at me. My legs were as steady as two licorice sticks. And then he smiled—all the way to his eyes, showering me in something I couldn't describe. I felt like the Grinch when he was standing on that mountain near Whoville, discovering the sun.

Calm down.

Not realizing what I was doing, I gulped my beer. Big mistake. I almost spit it out, trying not to make a face.

Did he just laugh at me?

"Five more minutes and I'm outta here," Amy said inches from my ear, interrupting my unspoken exchange with hot guy.

Derek appeared on my right. He slid in between Amy and me. At the same time, someone grabbed my butt, hard.

I jumped, sending my full cup of beer through the air and onto the brown-haired girl wearing the romper.

She screamed in a pitch that was high enough to shatter glass. Then, her mouth dropped open as she stepped back and gasped.

"Holy shit," a guy nearby said as the crowd closed in.

"You've got to be fucking kidding me," the girl said. A second passed before she glared at me. "You bitch."

Her friends all shot me eye daggers.

The crowd parted like the Red Sea.

This was not a *vanilla* way to do things. My breath froze, my mouth so dry I could hardly swallow. Any butterflies roaming around my stomach had mutated into gut-eating moths.

Oh, God, what had I done?

Chapter Two

"What the hell?" Amy stared over at me. "Why did you chuck your beer?"

My windpipe so tight, I barely squeezed out the words "Someone grabbed my butt."

Amy's gaze roamed the area. "Really? Well, with this bunch of privileged assholes, I'm not surprised." She tipped her chin toward the girl I had just soaked. "You sure pissed her off."

I wanted to disappear. My heart battered, my palms clammy. Even my feet were sweating. "You saw that, right?" I asked Derek, in need of some serious back up.

"You throwing your beer? Yeah, I think everyone saw that," he said.

I clenched my jaw. "No. Someone grabbed me. Did you see *that?*"

Derek gave me a blank stare, and then he took a long drink from his cup. "Sorry. I wasn't looking. Hey, I'll be back. Need a refill."

Of course he hadn't seen it. No one had. This was my stupid luck.

Before I launched into my mega apology, I scanned the crowd again for an explanation, finding Kevin at the far edge, doubled over laughing. *Ugh.* Rick was next to him shaking his head and laughing, too. I knew it was one of them. I mashed my teeth together.

"Damn it. She even ruined my shoes." The brunette I had just rinsed in beer was still assessing the damage. She practically growled as she pulled at the material of her outfit and readjusted it.

As several people around her resumed their conversations and drifted away from the scene, three of her friends stayed close. One girl with short blond hair grabbed a napkin off of a nearby table and went to work blotting, although there was much more beer than there was napkin to soak it up.

The brunette batted her friend's hand away. "You're making it worse, Ava." Her eyes were flaming as they cornered me again. "Do you have any idea how much this outfit cost, bitch?"

Two of her friends slapped their hands on their hips and Ava crossed her arms over her chest. Their heads all tilted, they stared me down. The scene came right out of *Mean Girls* for sure.

"I'm so sorry. Someone grabbed me." I stepped forward on shaky feet, clasping and unclasping my hands. "Maybe I can find a towel or some soap and water." I wished a bucket of suds would suddenly appear. "My dorm isn't that far away or we can find a restroom to wash it out. Or I'd be happy to pay for any dry cleaning ..." I wasn't sure what else to say. I felt so bad about it.

The angry girl stepped closer. "It's Versace, you idiot, and it's ruined!" She looked me over from head to toe.

"It was an accident." A mini volcano was pumping heat into my chest. I was hot. I was nauseous.

"You sure about that?" She slapped a hand on her hip just like her friends had done. "Jealous much?"

My mouth dropped open. Was she serious? My guilty conscience was fading fast, my angry side taking over.

Amy stepped up next to me. "Oh, pleeease. Jealous of *what*, exactly?" She opened her mouth to say more when the girl's boyfriend, the hot blond, emerged from the crowd.

Oh, great, was he going to reprimand me next? I firmed my stance, ready. This wasn't my first go-round with the popular kids.

"Chill out, Rachael," he said as he fanned a hand in my direction. "She just said she was sorry and that it was an accident."

My muscles unclenched. Okay, so not what I had expected to hear, or what Rachael had expected, either, judging by her fallen expression. Her tone became much less diva. "It was one of my favorite outfits, Scott—"

Wow. She was practically whining.

"Yeah, we know. It's only beer. Just go change." Scott looked at me, his eyes reassuring. "Don't worry about it. It's fine."

Rachael's face went tighter than a balloon ready to explode. Her cheeks turned crimson. "Why are you worried about *her* feelings?" She swept one hand down in front of her. "She's not the one covered in beer right now."

Scott shook his head just before he pinched the bridge of his nose with his thumb and forefinger. He let his hand drop to his side and exhaled. "You're at a tailgate, Rachael. Wearing an expensive outfit probably wasn't a wise choice. Shit happens."

Rachael's lower lip bumped out. "I thought you'd like it."

Scott scratched at his temple, his eyes hesitant as if he wasn't sure what to say next. He took a sip from a cup he was holding, and then he looked back at me and rolled his eyes.

Like a tire losing air, tension leaked from my body, replaced with a flourish of giddiness and gratitude. I wasn't sure what to say. At the same time, I didn't want to get in the middle of their lovers' quarrel. Were they even a couple?

Rachael moved her lips as if she wanted to say more, but she didn't. Instead, she walked past me on her way out. "I'll repay the favor sometime," she said as she brushed by, her cronies following.

"Good riddance, bridezilla," Amy said in a booming voice everyone could hear.

I'd been at this school for five minutes, and I'd already made an enemy. I hoped Rachael would forget about this incident, but something in the back of my mind told me she wouldn't. Girls like her never did.

The party continued, but I wasn't into it anymore. The incident with Rachael was bothersome, but the fact that someone—most likely Kevin—had grabbed my butt was far worse. It wasn't a light grab, either—he really took hold. The more I thought about it, the madder I got, my chest tight as a drum. I was so upset I almost missed the fact that Scott was talking to me.

"I'm sorry, what did you say?" I asked with an edge that I didn't intend.

"I was just apologizing for Rachael. She's always been a bit ... uptight. Don't let it bother you. It was an accident." Scott smiled again, an adorable dimple winking at me from his left cheek.

"Well, I don't think *she* thinks it was an accident." I took a deep breath and released it, the muscles in my neck and shoulders trying to uncoil.

Scott touched my arm. "Don't let her get under your skin." He stared deep into my eyes, and for a moment I almost forgot what we were talking about. I'd never seen eyes so blue.

"I'm Scott, by the way." He put his hand out, and I shook it, appreciating the formality *and* the feel of his rugged palm.

"Always look out for a man who will take the time to treat you right, Sara," my mother used to say when I was growing up. My father never forgot to open a door for her or provide a back rub whenever she needed it. He also did the dishes, which she hated doing herself. In my mother's eyes that made him the perfect man.

"I'm Sara." I motioned at Amy next to me. "This is Amy."

Derek was MIA again.

"Hey, Amy."

Amy looked at Scott, her expression flat. "Hey." She bent closer to my ear. "I need to pee. You want to come, and then we can check out the game? Do you know what time it starts?"

"Eight," Scott said as he took another sip of his drink.

I pulled my phone out, which flashed 7:50 p.m. on the screen. Then the music stopped. Half the crowd at the tailgate had gone. I'd been so distracted, I hadn't noticed.

Scott looked off in the distance. "They have a row of Port-O-Lets just inside the entrance of the tailgate. The stadium restrooms are farther away. I'll stay with Sara if you want to go and come back."

"Yeah, go ahead, Amy, and then I think I'm going to head back to our dorm." I pulled my hair up off the back of my neck, wishing I had put it in a ponytail.

"Really? No football?" Amy wiped some of her black lipstick off the rim of her cup.

"Nope." I wasn't in the mood and hoped Amy wasn't, either.

"Cool. I didn't want to go anyway. I'll be right back." She dashed off, tossing her cup in a nearby trash can along the way.

A moment later, Derek appeared. Eyes glossy and red, he smelled of skunk.

"Where's Amy going?" Derek asked, looking after her.

"Bathroom." I released my hair, letting it fall around my shoulders.

Scott stared, his body pointed in my direction. "You have beautiful hair," he said in a purr, his hand brushing a few strands off my shoulder.

I'd blushed about a hundred times already, but this time my cheeks flared for a different reason. I was loving every minute of his attention.

"Did I hear you're not going to the game? Why not?" Derek glanced over at Scott a few times.

"This is Scott." I made a gesture with my hand. "Scott, this is my friend, Derek."

"What's up, man?" Scott took one last drink from his cup and tossed it into a trash can as if he were shooting a basketball into a hoop. Two points.

"Not much," Derek said. "Just hanging."

Any remaining people migrated toward the exit. Rick and Kevin rode the flow like two drunk inner tubes. They stopped when they saw us. "Aren't y'all headed to the game?" Rick's eyes were droopy and red, his smile exaggerated. "Shots in my room later." He let out a howl.

"Awesome," Derek said with a wide smile and a nod.

I glowered at them both, all the flattery I'd been feeling from Scott, turning to ice. "Well, *I'm* not going. And I don't appreciate what you did, Kevin." My chest filled with anger and heat. "It wasn't funny. You made me spill my beer on someone." I wanted to stomp my foot for emphasis.

Then something occurred to me, something I should have paid attention to long before now. I was surrounded by four men. Not one of them I knew very well, and two of whom, I couldn't stand. I should've gone with Amy.

Their complexions pasty, Rick and Kevin kept swaying this way and that.

"What did he do?" Scott looked at me and then at Rick and Kevin, his eyes full of questions.

I wasn't sure how to put it. "One of them ... grabbed me. I'm pretty sure it was Kevin." I huffed. "That's why I spilled my beer." I crossed and uncrossed my arms, unsure about this exchange. Scott had stuck up for me before, but now he was facing his frat brothers.

Kevin patted the air with magnified effort. "It was just a joke. You should be flattered." He half-belched from the corner of his mouth.

Flattered? Was this how guys flirted in college?

"That's right," Rick said in a boisterous voice to support his drunken friend.

"Right, Derek?" Kevin slapped his arm over *my* new friend's shoulders and jostled him. "You gotta have a sense of humor."

Derek rubbed his mouth, his gaze dropping to the ground.

I understood his timid reaction, sort of, but I also needed his support. I was outnumbered here.

"Bullshit." Scott took a step in front of me. "You two assholes are always pulling this shit. You want to go grab someone, grab each other." He widened his stance, his shoulders thick and protective.

What was happening? My guard wasn't sure whether to go up or down.

Kevin and Rick stopped slouching.

"Chill out, man. We were just joking around," Kevin said.

Scott gestured toward me. "Do you see her laughing?" He bugged his eyes at Rick and Kevin in a "Well, do ya?" sort of way.

Kevin spoke again. "Why so serious, Scott? She your girl?"

From my standpoint, one thing had nothing to do with the other. They had no right to violate anyone, regardless.

"What difference does that make, dipshit?"

I was so relieved Scott understood. Phew.

I took another measured breath.

Scott loomed over Kevin by three inches. He was also way bigger. If this confrontation went physical, Scott had a definite advantage. I took pride in that fact even though I didn't know Scott any more than I knew Rick, Kevin ... or even Derek, for that matter.

He moved closer to Kevin's face. "I'm going to say this slowly, so your pickled brain can understand it. You see that girl?" He pointed but didn't wait for Kevin to answer. "Keep your grimy hands off her and any other girl you see." He faced Rick. "You can't do whatever the fuck you want and expect *Daddy* to bail you out. Are you trying to get us suspended?"

Daddy? He sounded important.

I watched with rapt attention.

Rick's spine straightened as if Scott's comment had hit a nerve. He ran a hand over his face, his eyes showing more clarity than I'd seen yet.

Scott remained stationed, undaunted.

I wasn't sure what to do, so I did nothing.

"You only want her for yourself, dude." Rick pointed with the hand holding his cup, his face tensing up. "He may have been out of line, but don't act like you don't grab plenty of ass for yourself."

I hoped that wasn't true. Scott seemed so nice.

Again with the stares, both men waiting for the other to blink. I'd forgotten to blink myself. This was intense.

"Come on, man." Kevin finally nudged Rick. "Let it go. Scott's our brother, dude. This ain't worth it." He looked at Scott. "Sorry, man," he said as he stepped away.

I frowned, outraged. Sorry, *man?* What about sorry, *Sara?* Was I invisible?

"Let's hit the game, and then shot-skies." Kevin pulled on Rick's shoulder, trying to loosen his friend's feet from the pavement.

Rick took one last sip of his drink and then let go of the cup. It fell to the ground with a pathetic tap. Then, he blew out his lips and rubbed his eyes. "You're right, dude. Why am I wasting my time with this shit?" He peered around Scott at me and by doing so, stumbled. "Sorry, Princess. Didn't mean to *offend* you."

With that, both Kevin and Rick staggered off, dumb-and-dumber-style. When they reached the exit, Kevin turned around. "You comin', Derek?"

I looked at Derek, already knowing his answer.

"Do you mind? I'm sure he didn't mean anything. He's just shitfaced." His tone was friendly, his eyes hopeful.

Why was he cutting these guys so much slack?

Then I thought about what Derek had said about his struggles to get into college. He only wanted to fit in, just like the rest of us. I knew what it felt like to be an outsider. For years, I let my parents' death and the trauma from the accident separate me from everyone. I had created a barrier that was impenetrable. Except for my mom's best friend, Abigail, who had somehow chiseled her way into my heart.

I needed to ease up. "Sure, go ahead. Have fun."

Derek paused. "Want me to wait until Amy gets back?"

"I'll stay with her," Scott said. "Go ahead."

An unseen benefit. At least *some* frat guys proved to be human. Even though I was glad Amy wasn't back yet and I had a little more time with Scott, I was worried about her. My cell phone flashed eight o'clock. She'd been gone for ten minutes. If she didn't come back soon, I would have to go look for her.

When we were alone, I glanced up at Scott and smiled.

He smiled back, eyes and all.

Now my heart was bursting, my insides turning to jelly. Scott was a multifaceted hottie. Aside from his obvious good looks, I really appreciated him having my back just now. If he hadn't stepped in, I wasn't sure how the situation would've played out, especially since Amy wasn't with me and Derek was wimping out.

As the tailgate emptied, Scott and I walked to the edge of the parking lot where a road connected to the football stadium. The lampposts clicked on, inviting moths and mosquitos to dance in the light.

"Thank you, by the way," I said.

"No problem. Sorry the party was such a downer."

"It wasn't all bad. I got to meet you." I wished my dorky side would keep her mouth shut. How lame was *that* comment?

Scott stopped walking, his smile dazzling, his left dimple deep and precious. "I'm glad I got to meet you, too."

Once again, Scott had saved me, only this time from embarrassment.

We reached a stopping point under a large oak tree, where I tried *not* to focus on his impressive body or his hypnotic blue eyes. He even smelled nice: musky and fresh. "You don't have to stay with me. I'll be okay until Amy gets back." I was lying, of course, but didn't want to come off too needy.

"I'm happy to stay with you. Plus, I'm not really comfortable letting you stay by yourself."

Letting me? Did I need permission?

"Why not?"

Scott scratched the end of his nose. "It's just ... a girl went missing last year."

My overly cautious stomach did a flip-flop.

His comment sent my mind in a whole new direction. The

now-deserted parking lot took on an eerie aura. I was the girl in the horror movie who suddenly found herself alone, cue ominous fog and tall man wearing a hockey mask. Only I wasn't alone. I had a gorgeous stranger with me.

"That's terrible. Did you know her?" I asked.

Scott exhaled. "Not really, I only knew her name from the posters they plastered all over campus."

"What happened?" I scanned the area for Amy but didn't see any sign of her, so I sent her a text: "Where are you?"

Scott slid his hands into the front pockets of his khaki shorts. "Honestly, I don't know much more about it."

Amy texted right back: "I'm next in line."

A peaceful wind pushed through, reuniting Scott's spicy scent with my sinuses. *Stay focused*, I told myself.

I allowed myself one last question: "What was her name?" I didn't want to grill the guy. Well, I did, but I held back my obsessive compulsive brain.

Scott's phone alerted a few text messages from his pocket, but he didn't acknowledge it.

"Carrie Stevens. Her disappearance was on the news and in the papers every day for weeks. It got kind of crazy around here."

A shiver ran up my sweaty back. "I bet. Scary stuff."

Scott removed his hands from his pockets and relaxed his posture. "I know every inch of this campus. Anytime you need to walk somewhere at night, I'd be happy to go with you." He stared at me as if waiting for a reaction.

My heart sent off a round of fireworks at the thought of seeing Scott again. He said it so matter-of-fact, but it didn't feel that way to me. I could have been reading too much into it, and he may have just been being polite. Even though the story of the girl had me freaked out, I couldn't have felt safer with him. Didn't he have some other place he had to be? Friends waiting? His busy phone told me *someone* was trying to reach him.

"I don't remember seeing you here last year. Are you a freshman or a transfer?" he asked, breaking through my analysis.

"Freshman," I said. "How about you?"

"Junior." He leaned back against the trunk of the tree. "How do you like the school so far? Aside from the more questionable characters."

"It's nice. I mean, from what I've seen." I smiled, my upper lip catching on my teeth like a saber-toothed squirrel. No mistaking it, I was a dork.

Scott ran a hand through his loose, golden curls, causing his bicep to grow to the size of a grapefruit. To avoid gawking, I turned my eyes toward the setting sun and the veins of orange and yellow branched across the horizon. The moon had poked out, along with a few early stars, fighting to shine through a very humid sky. The distant glow of stadium lights and a cheering crowd competed with a few nearby crickets as another calm breeze sighed past my ears. It was a perfect summer evening. Although, something still nagged at me that I needed to clear up.

"So, Rachael's not your girlfriend then?" I felt a little possessive asking and hoped he didn't think I was being weird. Meeting guys was new to me, and I wasn't sure what this new me, the "dating Sara" me, was like.

Scott exhaled and shook his head. "God, no. I've never dated Rachael. She's not my type."

"Oh," I said, wondering what his type was.

"So, where are you from?" he asked, changing the subject.

"Vermont."

He nodded. "Cool. I've never been there, but I've heard they have some kick-ass skiing."

I laughed. *Nope.* My inner goofball was ready to mock.

Scott tilted his head. "Did I say something funny?" His eyes sparkled, the corners of his mouth inching upward.

"No, it's just ... I'm a terrible skier."

Scott waved me off. "I'm sure you're not *that* bad."

I cocked my head to the side and raised one eyebrow. "Well, let's see." I counted with my fingers for emphasis. "I fell off a chairlift once and hit a tree another time." I flipped the third finger. "Oh, and then there was the time I skied so far off the resort, my dad had to get the ski patrol to find me." I remembered the fear in my parents' eyes when they brought me back. They hugged me so hard and cried. At the time, I didn't understand what all the fuss was about. What I wouldn't give for one of those hugs now. My heart sank.

"Okay, you convinced me." Scott's face lit up. "You're not a good skier." More texts alerts from his pocket. "I've heard Burlington is a party city. I have an older cousin who used to go to the University of Vermont ..."

He went on about his cousin while I watched his mouth move and those soft, plump lips that I could stare at forever.

"I took a trip to upstate New York once when I was a kid. My parents brought my sister and me to Ausable Chasm ..."

The more Scott told me about himself, the more I wanted to learn. He spoke about his family and the traveling they had done throughout New England. He even told me about a few parties and concerts on campus that were coming up. The way he moved, leaning in and addressing me thoughtfully and attentively, always smiling as he spoke, his eyes never drifting, was captivating. And boy was he fun to look at. I realized that he had stopped talking, and I was still standing there awestruck.

I cleared my throat. "Where are *you* from?" I asked, hoping he hadn't told me already and I'd been too busy swooning to notice.

"Pennsylvania, a town called—"

"That fucking line was brutal," Amy said as she walked up. "I thought I was going to pee my goddamn pants. I think someone hurled in the porto next to mine. I could smell it." She crinkled her nose up. "Nasty."

"Gross," I said, glad I didn't go with her. With *my* luck, I would've been in that barf-ridden toilet.

Scott pushed away from the tree with his back. "Yeah, that happens. Lightweights."

Amy glanced at her cell and then steadied her gaze on me. "You ready?"

My soul had just discovered oxygen, and she wanted me to leave? Every fiber of my body objected. "Um."

"I was telling Sara about a girl who went missing from here last year. Why don't you ladies let me walk you back to your dorm?" Scott stared at Amy and waited.

Amy narrowed her defiant green eyes. "We don't need an escort. Or at least I don't." She looked at me for confirmation.

"I get that. I'd like to walk with you if you don't mind the company." His eyes found mine, reaching out with a gentle nudge. "Is that okay with you?"

Um, yes please.

"Sure." My heart jumped up and down in agreement.

Wearing miniskirts that barely covered their legs, long and lean, two girls sauntered up the quiet road with bodies that rivaled Barbie, platinum hair and all. Bronze skin and lashes so long, they couldn't be real, both girls spotted Scott and beelined. "Hey, stranger," one of them said, flashing a smile so bright you could read a book by it. "We heard you were over here."

Amy rolled her eyes while I experienced my first bout of jealousy. Who were they?

Scott turned. "Hey, Mindy. Hey, Charlene. What's up?" His voice dipped lower, less enthusiastic.

"We were looking all over for you," one of the girls said. "We wanted to know if you were ready for our annual welcome back party."

Annual? I exhaled, expelling all the delusional thoughts I'd been harboring about Scott from my body.

Scott raised his brow up and then down, his cheeks taking on a pink hue. "Sara and Amy, these are my friends Mindy and Charlene." He used his hand to point at each as he introduced them.

"Yeah, *friends*," Charlene said as she winked at Mindy. "We're all about being friendly."

The two of them giggled.

"Do you want to head back to your room or ours?" Mindy said with a glimmer of hope in her eyes.

Scott scratched his forehead, his gaze downcast. "I, uh, was planning to walk my new friends back to their dorm." The guy who seemed so confident a moment ago shuffled his feet back and forth, his brow forging a large wrinkle. He cleared his throat. "I'll catch up with you ladies another time."

Both Mindy and Charlene stared at Amy and me in such a way that I felt like a carcass on the side of the road, the two of them vultures picking us apart with their eyes.

Of course he was *that* guy: the one Rachael wore outfits for and who had sex parties with two women who could stop traffic. He was too perfect to be alone. I should have known better. Even more glaring: he wasn't mine, and he never would be. As much as I enjoyed his company, I didn't want any part of this scene. How would I compete with women like Rachael, Mindy, Charlene, and God knew who else, when I hadn't even kissed a guy? I wasn't willing to jump into the deep end of the dating pool. Not yet. I needed to learn to swim first.

"That's okay, Scott," I said as I took a step away. "It's still early, and Amy and I will be together. I'm sure we'll be plenty safe."

Scott's broad shoulders sagged, the light in his eyes dimming. "I'd really like to walk with you."

"Sounds like she's not interested. But *we'd* be happy to walk with you, teddy bear." Charlene batted her eyes at Scott, who ran a hand down his face and released a heavy sigh.

Teddy bear? This was really too much.

"We're good. Thanks anyway." I took another step away and looked at Amy. "You ready?"

Amy pinched her mouth into a smirk. "Yup." She grinned at Scott. "Have fun." Her tone was playful in a sarcastic sort of way.

I made tracks down the side of the road as fast as I could, Amy right beside me. Just as we hopped off the asphalt and onto the lawn leading to the walkway, I peered back at Scott, who was staring at me, his hands on his hips. While *he* stared at *me*, Mindy and Charlene stared at him. What was he doing, and why was he still standing there?

With Mindy and Charlene flanking Scott only a few feet back, the three of them formed a triangle—one that I wasn't about to get involved in.

Geometry was never my subject.

Chapter Three

On our walk back, I dragged my feet a little, unable to process or accept what had just happened.

Katydids, crickets, and cicadas filled the night air with their clicking percussion. The smell of must and stale earth supported the humidity that refused to relent. Above, the sky was a masterpiece of muted glimmer.

"That's weird about the missing girl," Amy said, glancing over at me.

"Yeah." That did bother me, and I kept my eyes peeled for any suspicious characters as we walked by darkened buildings and trees with thick trunks. All the shadowy areas were now suspect. My somber mood, however, was for a totally different reason, one I didn't understand.

"Are you still upset about that Rachael chick? Don't let Marie Antoinette get under your skin."

Good one, Amy. "Funny. No, she didn't bother me too much. I have a feeling I'll be hearing from her again, though."

Amy brushed her hand along the edge of a hedgerow that bordered the walkway. The thick leaves sounded like tinfoil against her fingers. "If she bothers you again, just let me know. I'd like nothing more than to put ole Marie in her place."

I touched Amy's arm as we walked along. "Thanks."

Amy shrugged. "I gotcha covered."

"I'm here for you, too. I hope Rick didn't offend you with what he said." I wasn't sure what Amy's sexual orientation was, not that it mattered to me either way. Whatever she identified with, I'd support her.

We approached our dorm. No kidnappers tonight. I swiped my keycard and opened the door for Amy. "After you," I said.

Together, we crossed the dorm lobby for the elevators. Our suite was on the third floor. A student volunteer who sat behind the welcome counter looked up from her book and smiled.

"So that woman who was here yesterday moving you in was your aunt?" Amy asked.

I thought back to Abigail and the moment when I introduced her to Amy. At the time, I referred to her as "Abigail" with no explanation as to her role in my life.

"No, she's my mother's best friend." Then I finally forced out the words I dreaded saying. "My parents died when I was twelve. They were in a car accident."

We loaded into the elevator, Amy going quiet. I had given her a lot to mull over. She didn't say much until we stepped out onto our floor. "Man. That sucks royally." She shook her head as she spoke.

I suddenly felt very tired. "Yeah, I haven't been home much since it happened. I went to a boarding school in Pennsylvania. I'm kinda used to being on my own. Not so ... social."

Amusement shined in Amy's eyes. "You mean you're not used to partying with wild and crazy college students?"

"Exactly," I said with gusto.

"You'll get used to it. Hey, do you want to hang out in my

room? I've got some vodka." She used her key to open the suite door. "I could make you a drink ... a weak one?"

"If you don't mind, I'm kinda tired. Raincheck?"

We passed through the living area furnished with some rather uncomfortable chairs and cheaply made side tables and our tiny kitchen that came with one small counter, a miniature stove, and a full-size fridge. Our building was new, equipped with singles and private bathrooms. Even though they cost more money and you had to apply through a lottery system, it was worth the effort. None of the roommates I had at The Bauer School for Girls were worthy of calling friends, and I wasn't willing to take a chance in college. My parents had left me a sizable inheritance that did nothing to salve the pain, but it did provide me with choices for my future.

"Are you all right?" Amy's eyes probed. "I didn't mean to make you talk about your parents."

"It's okay. No, I was just thinking about that guy Scott." My chin lowered. For a moment—just a moment—I had thought a real connection was happening between us. I was crushing big time. But to him, I was one of many.

All at once, the tension in Amy's face released. "Oh, I get it. You're hung up on pretty boy." She shook her head and grinned at me. "Yeah, I wouldn't waste too much time on him. He's what you'd call," she made air quotes, "a player." She tilted her head and smirked. "Plus, you don't have to worry about meeting guys. I mean, seriously. There was a reason Scott and all those scumbags were salivating over you." She sized me up with her eyes. "Don't tell me you don't know what you look like."

My mind went blank. "Huh?"

Amy got a disgusted look in her eyes. "*Come on,*" she said as if I were clueless. "Long blond hair, blue eyes, tiny waist, long legs. And I'm guessing those are real boobs." She crossed her arms. "You don't look any different than those girls at the party. In fact, I figured you were like *them*. At first. If you hadn't spoken to me, *I* wasn't going to reach out." Amy's face mellowed. "Turns out, you're kind of a nerd." She said it like that was a good thing.

Coming from the coolest friend I'd ever met, I took some comfort in her opinion. It wasn't as if I didn't know I was a nerd. I was well aware.

Amy tapped her lip with her finger. "I wasn't sure what your nickname was going to be until now."

Nerd girl?

Amy leaned against the wall between our doorways, her entire face eager. "Al—short for Alice of *Alice in Wonderland*." I let the name sink in as she fanned her hands out. "It's like you just stepped through the looking glass." Amy reached her door and keyed the lock. "It's perfect," she said as she disappeared through the doorway with a lift in her tone and her step. The words, "Goodnight, Al," trailed behind her.

I wasn't amped about the name but knew there was no arguing with her over it. *Alice.* I guess it was better than "nerd girl." I only hoped this school wouldn't include Mad Hatters and queens who wanted nothing more than to separate my head from my shoulders. I thought of Rachael.

I opened my eyes to the morning light, and the first thing I thought about was Scott. Okay, so not forgotten. Disgusted with myself, I climbed out of bed and then grabbed my favorite T-shirt along with a pair of black shorts on my way to the bathroom. After a long, hot shower, I texted Amy and by nine o'clock was outside her door. I knocked a few times and then gave up and headed back to my room. Maybe I'd go it alone this morning.

I had just keyed my lock when the suite door opened and closed. Voices and the smell of garlic and other yummy scents floated down the hallway. My stomach growled at me.

My suitemate Sue Anne and her friend, whom I hadn't met yet, emerged from the hallway. Wearing a pair of athletic pants and a spaghetti strap top that exposed the edges of her teal-colored sports bra, Sue Anne wore her hair pulled tight into a ponytail. She had the height of a basketball player, although her Asian friend was much shorter, barely reaching Sue Anne's shoulder. Both girls were carrying a take-out container.

"Oh, hey," Sue Anne said. "All unpacked?"

"Hey. Yup, I finally finished." I removed my key and stepped forward, glancing over at her friend. "Hi, I'm Sara."

"I'm your other suitemate, Mia." The petite girl with olive skin and delicate features raised her palm in a short wave before she handed her food container over to Sue Anne, who was next to the fridge. "I've gotta pee," she said and darted off into her room.

"Nice to meet you," I said to her back.

"Have you had breakfast? We're heading over to our prayer group. Want to join?" Sue Anne asked.

I had forgotten it was Sunday. "No, I haven't eaten yet, so I'll pass." Growing up, we hadn't gone to church much—other than on special occasions like Christmas or weddings. "You don't have to go to church to be a good person," my dad would always say. "In fact, what you do when no one else is looking says much more about a person." I wasn't particularly religious —more spiritual. I liked to think of my parents as my guardian angels.

Amy's door cracked open as she poked her head out, her eyes fighting the light. "What's up?" Her short raven hair spiked in all directions. Along with her smudged eyeliner, Amy was a rock star from the eighties.

"Sorry, I didn't mean to wake you. I sent you a text a few minutes ago. I was thinking of getting some breakfast and wondered if you wanted to join."

"Yeah." Amy's words caught in her throat until she cleared them with a grunt. "Just give me a minute to change and brush the grunge off my teeth." She closed her door.

Sue Anne made a cringey face as she placed her food along with Mia's in the fridge. "Great. *She* ought to be fun to live with."

As I headed back to my room to wait for Amy, I hoped Sue Anne's opinion would change. Religious devotees were living next door to new wave grunge. I kinda figured they wouldn't gel.

* * *

It was a quiet walk to the cafeteria at first. Amy glanced over a few times before she finally spoke.

"So, do you have any family that you're close to?" She kicked out her left foot and with it a small pebble from her Birkenstock sandal.

"My dad's family lives in Ireland, but I've never met them. My mother was an only child, and her parents passed away before I was born. I just have Abigail. She teaches at the same school my mom taught at."

Amy walked a little closer to me as she listened.

"She was my legal guardian until I turned eighteen last month." If it hadn't been for Abigail, I don't know what I would have done.

"So, Abigail still lives in Vermont?"

I nodded.

"Why didn't you just live with her?"

I hated these kinds of questions. "She asked me to. After we cleaned out my parents' house and sold it, I guess I wanted out." My throat thickened, emotions brewing.

"Yeah, but you've been home since then, right?"

"I took classes during the summer, but I went home for short breaks between the summer and fall semesters." What I didn't say was that I hadn't gone to the cemetery where my parents were buried. Not once. I was angry, and I was hurt—even though I knew I wasn't being fair. My heart felt hollow and sad.

Amy gave me a quizzical glance. "So, you were alone?"

"Not exactly. Abigail came to visit me plenty." I'd spent my first Christmas away from home crying into my pillow until Abigail showed up at my door, her arms loaded with gifts. "Since you won't come home, I had to come to you," she said. She stayed in town until after New Year's, making sure I was okay. We really bonded then. It was the first time I let her into the privacy of my broken world.

"Is Abigail married?" Amy's question pulled me back to the moment. She wore that same sad face I had grown to despise.

"She is now."

It was during the summer of my sophomore year when Abigail had brought me a surprise. His name was Joel, and he was the new principal at her school. I'll never forget the moment she introduced me to him. "Joel, this is my daughter, Sara." At first, it felt strange hearing that, like a betrayal. Over the years, I came to realize Abigail wasn't trying to replace my mother—she was happy to play runner-up. In fact, Abigail talked more about my mother than she did anyone else. She would reminisce about what my mom was like as a friend instead of a wife or a mother. I was grateful for that.

Amy cleared her throat, and I realized I had zoned out again.

"She's been married to a man named Joel for a couple of years now." I was tired of talking about me. "So, what's *your* family like?"

"Nuts." Amy smirked. "A little chaotic and strange, but whose family isn't?" She paused. "There were times when I was growing up that I would have loved to have been on my own." She laughed without much humor in her voice.

"Do you have any other siblings?"

"I have two younger sisters, Lydia and Abby, and one older brother, Griffin. He doesn't live at home anymore. Lydia likes to help herself to my shit. We used to share a room until Griffin moved out, and I took his room. Lydia still thinks what's mine is hers. I lock my door, but she picks the frigging lock."

The frustration in Amy's voice spoke volumes.

"Don't get me wrong, I love my family. My mother is a good person, but she has only one volume to her voice: loud. My father has gotten so good at zoning her out that he pretty much zones everyone out. When I told my parents I wanted to go to college, they were surprised that I even considered it." She peered up at the sky. "I just want to get a degree and make my own way. I'm sick of having to share everything in my life." She hissed through her teeth. "I can't even have a conversation in my house without everyone commenting on it."

I imagined myself in her shoes. To be surrounded by family was like a dream to me, but not for Amy. Funny how other people's lives seemed so much better, so much easier than our own. The grass was always greener.

I had only been in college for a short time, but already my perspective was changing. Instead of dwelling on my parents' death, I was remembering the good times—the special moments —like when my dad would brush his hand across my mom's cheek, or the way my mom would fold her body into his, inviting him to wrap his arms around her delicate frame, or the looks they would exchange with each other as if they were in on some private joke. It made me wonder what Scott was doing right now. Was he waking up alone?

I pushed the thought aside as we passed by "The Green," a two-acre field that yesterday had students lounging on the grass, throwing a ball or a Frisbee, or hanging with their friends. It was early, so not much happening today.

"So, which cafeteria do you want to go to?" I wondered what Sue Anne had in her container that had smelled so good.

"I don't care. How about the main cafeteria in the Student Union Building?" Amy examined her phone. "Shouldn't be crowded; it's still early."

We made a left onto an expansive walkway covered with brick pavers. The center of campus. Students roamed about chatting with friends while others looked confused. Two girls squealed and ran into each other's arms for what I assumed was a reunion. Amy rolled her eyes. Rows of colonial-style buildings boasting massive pillars, cupolas, domes, and an abundance of brick bordered the walkway. An array of flowerbeds, orange, black, and white to represent the school's colors, provided a nice contrast and a source of late-summer pollen for the hovering bees. Standing at the end of the walkway, the Student Union Building watched over the campus like a den mother. An enormous gold dome rested above a circle of Palladian windows, like a crown. Home to the main cafeteria, the student mailroom, several ballrooms, a gift shop, a pizzeria, and a coffee shop, the Student Union Building was always bustling.

"Do you want to walk around campus later to figure out where our classes are?"

Amy didn't answer me. She stared at a small group of guys who had gathered up ahead. Standing next to a large fountain, the guys chatted and listened to music, some wearing oversize beanie caps and dark T-shirts, exposing a tattoo here and there.

"Amy?"

"Uh, yeah, we can do that." Her gaze remained fixed.

"Do you know those guys?" I asked.

Amy glanced at her phone. "No, I thought one was *interesting*."

"Which one?" I was beyond curious and eyed each of them carefully.

Amy arched a brow at me. "I'm sure *you* think they're all nasty. You like that beefcake look."

I had to laugh at that one. Up until yesterday I hadn't had a preference, but I had to admit after meeting Scott, it was hard to see anyone else the same. Not that I would admit to anything. "No, I don't. Which one?"

"Shut up. He's looking over." Amy stared down at her phone again. It gave me a chance to see which guy had caught her eye. Light-brown hair spilling out from under his cap and a small patch of hair under his lip, the one man paying attention to us was attractive. He had a kind face and a lanky body that towered over his friends. Sort of an easygoing vibe. As we drew closer, I nudged Amy's arm so she would glance up. When she did, a broad smile radiated from the guy's face.

"He's smiling at you."

From the corner of her mouth, Amy spat the words, "Cut the shit."

As we passed by them, she raised her hand in a half-wave. "Hey." Amy sounded so nonchalant.

"Hey." The guy's tone held much more promise.

Once we were clear, I snuck another peek. He hadn't taken his eyes off her. I couldn't blame him. Underneath her thick and expressive makeup was a striking girl. Amy's vibrant green eyes, high cheekbones, and full lips would make any man turn his head—any man with taste.

As she covered her mouth, Amy released a fake cough, which turned out to be a warning. "I'm going to kick your ass if you look back there again."

Laughter bubbled up like seltzer water in my throat. I enjoyed witnessing this very unusual side of my cool, confident friend. When it came to guys, we were all a hot mess.

We reached the Student Union Building, where I opened the heavy glass door with a wide smile on my face. "I guess I'm not the only one who's getting attention around here."

Amy wagged her finger at me. "You better watch yourself, *Al.*"

Touché.

The aroma from the cafeteria found my nose long before we reached the entrance. Bacon, garlic, and a flurry of sweet scents had my stomach screaming and my feet practically running ahead. I wasted no time filling my tray with pancakes, scrambled eggs, bacon, roasted potatoes, toast, and a large unsweetened tea to wash it all down, ready to satisfy the hunger demons.

"Gee, are you hungry?" Amy judged my tray with round eyes. She led the way across the cafeteria in search of a table. "So, you're the size of a toothpick, but you can eat like a bear. I hate you."

I sat across from her. "Yeah, like you're any bigger."

We dove into our food and chatted until Derek, carrying a full tray of food in his hands, plopped down in the seat next to mine. I was surprised he was up so early.

He grabbed a large cup of water from his tray. After he guzzled the entire cup dry, he took a few gasps of air. "Man, what a night." He wiped his mouth with the back of his hand.

Amy stabbed a pile of scrambled eggs with her fork. "Get wasted, did ya?"

"Hell yeah." Derek looked at me with bloodshot eyes and exhaled—a stale odor escaping from his mouth.

I wanted to gag.

"Those frat bros were dope. We did shots and got stoned." He blew out a long breath. "That Rick dude can really party. He has a shitload of alcohol in his room. He mentioned *you* a few times." He glanced my way. "His father is a senator, you know."

"So?" I said, incredulous. Did he expect me to be impressed? Obviously, *he* was. I buttered my toast, annoyed, then stuffed it in my mouth.

"He said he might be able to get my dad a job."

I swallowed. "Why? Is your dad out of work?"

"He's about to be laid off. Sucks." That was all Derek said before he shoveled food into his mouth as fast as physics would allow.

"Wow, you even eat like Shaggy," I said before I did the same, although, not with quite the same velocity.

Derek gave me a side glance that made me smirk.

I expected Amy to join in on the jeering, but she peered over her shoulder instead. "I need some more brain juice."

I looked down at Amy's full cup of coffee.

Huh? And then I saw him. Hat guy was there at the coffee station.

I smiled in full tease mode. "Well, you better go get some, then."

Amy wrinkled her face at me. "You're sick."

After gulping down a large sip, Amy made her way over to the coffee station where hat guy took notice. He said a few words to her, and within a short time, they laughed like old friends. I couldn't wait to hear about it—every word.

More laughter hit my ears as Rick, Kevin, and a few other people I didn't know descended upon our table like a frat monsoon. *What is the deal with these early-morning people?* Derek perked up and I scowled, as Rick took the seat across from him.

"Sup, bro? Feelin' okay this morning?" Rick's sweet-smelling cologne blanketed our table. He also didn't have a hair out of place. How was that possible?

Derek snickered. "Holding it together." He put his hand out in front of him, showing a slight tremor. "Feelin' pretty shaky though."

Rick's dark, hooded eyes panned over to me next. "Good morning, Princess."

Not only did I hate the nickname, but I also hated the way he said it, so sarcastically. I scowled back, not saying a word.

"Sorry about my behavior last night." Rick's tone was welcoming, his eyes less edgy. "I had way too many shots and beers and vaguely remember acting like a total dick."

Did I wake up in an alternate universe?

He speared an elbow into Kevin's side, who flinched. "And this shithead wanted to say something."

Kevin made brief eye contact with me. "Sorry." His voice lagged in the way a child's would when forced to apologize for something he didn't think he did wrong.

"Hey, did you invite Sara to go with us today?" Rick asked Derek before taking a sip from his mug.

"No, man. I just sat down." Derek faced me. "We're going to the reservoir to cliff dive and swim this morning. Want to come?"

That explained the early breakfast.

"I can't," I said quickly, hoping there wouldn't be an argument, and then I took a long sip of tea, using my cup to hide behind.

Rick stared at me. "Why not? It's going to be a beautiful day. Classes don't start till tomorrow."

"I know, but I'm busy today." *Doing anything but that.* My eyes shifted over to Amy and hat guy. Would it be lame of me to go join them? Third wheel.

"Come on, Sara. It'll be fun." Derek bumped me with his shoulder.

"Yeah, and bathing suits are optional." The comment came from a burly guy who sat a few seats away. His camo tank and crew cut hair suggested a military background. The men next to him responded with fist bumps. Kevin almost choked on his egg sandwich.

Here we go again.

Rick glared at them. "Shut up, Owen."

So, now Rick had my back? What the heck was going on?

"Don't listen to him." Rick put his hand over his heart. "We'll be on our best behavior." He flashed me a photogenic smile, his teeth as bright as Mindy and Charlene's were. "I won't take no for an answer."

My chest filled with heat and apprehension. This was *not* how I wanted to spend my morning. Yes, Rick wasn't as bad as I had originally thought, but there was no way I was going to some water hole with a bunch of strange men. It was time to find an excuse to get out of here.

"She can't go," a male voice called out. "She already has plans ... with me."

Chapter Four

My first thought was, *what now?*

And then he spoke again.

"We're going hiking after breakfast." My eyes found Scott at the end of our table.

Dormant butterflies sprang to life in my stomach, ready to rile up the rest of my insides. Scott was as hot as I had remembered him, maybe even more so.

Rick looked over at Scott, his smile fading. "Oh, hey, dude." He sounded about as enthused as a golf commentator.

"That's right." Blood pumped into my cheeks, my heart going spastic.

Scott spoke across the table. "Why don't you bring your breakfast, and I'll fill you in on where we're going?"

I took my tray into my now restless hands and got to my feet. "Thanks for the invite, and have a good time today." I walked toward Scott, trying not to trip or faint.

We were halfway across the cafeteria when Amy rushed over. "What are you doing?" She held a brimming cup of java in her hands. My nose sensed hazelnut.

Scott continued walking until he realized I wasn't behind him. When I put my finger up for him to wait, he looked at Amy and nodded.

"It was getting crowded over there, so I'm going to sit with Scott." After what Amy had said about Scott last night, I wasn't sure how she'd feel about it *or* react.

A few feet away, Derek, Rick, Kevin, and crew were laughing and carrying on.

"Oh, I see. So, you won't mind if I sit with Luke then?" She peered over her shoulder at her new friend, who stood tall like a happy tree.

"Luke, huh?" I so loved this side of Amy—the crushing-on-a-guy side.

As if she wasn't listening, her eyes went vacant. "Doesn't he kinda look like a young *and tall* Luke Skywalker? I think I'll call him Sky."

Does everyone have a nickname? I couldn't help but giggle. "It sounds like Luke, I mean Sky, might be sticking around?"

Amy twisted her mouth at me. "Well, what about you, Al? What's *your* deal?"

Good question. What *was* I doing? Falling for the hottest guy I'd ever seen, that's what. I hoped it wasn't a mistake. "Well, have fun." I took a step away.

"Cool. Catch you later." She pointed at me. "Remember what I said last night."

For a second, I was worried she was going to finish with, "He's a player." Thank God she didn't.

When I caught up to Scott, he cleared his throat. "Is everything okay?" His voice hinted concern, his eyes tense.

"Oh, yeah, everything's fine." I sure hoped it was.

Scott raised his chin toward a vacant area by a row of windows. "Let's sit over there."

I followed him over to the table and took a seat across from him, pleased my new location offered a view of the courtyard. Beams of sunlight blanketed our table with an abundance of solar energy. The table was warm against my palms, the chair against my back.

"This will work." Scott smiled.

"I guess I should thank you a second time for having my back. I wasn't really comfortable sitting there anymore." I flattened out my napkin on my lap.

"I hope no one grabbed you again." Scott's serious face came out but just for an instant. "I might have to slap some heads together."

"Nah. It wasn't like that. They were nicer today."

"They may be my frat brothers, but we aren't all best buds." Scott peered over his shoulder before shifting his brilliant blue eyes back to me.

For a moment, my mind went blank all over again.

"So, you do realize you have to go on this hike with me. Otherwise, people will know you were lying." His eyes filled with fun as he picked up his coffee mug and took a sip, his breakfast nearly eaten already.

"I can hide in my room." Fumbling with nervous energy, I arranged and rearranged my utensils.

"I can't go back to the frat house now. They'll know. I'll have to hide there with you."

The image of Scott in my room sent my stomach into a frenzy, blood rushing to my chest and face. I set my utensils down and rested my elbows on the table, taking several quick breaths. Once my heart settled down, I was able to speak.

"Okay, I'll go."

Scott put his mug down and cupped a hand behind his right ear. "What? Did I hear you correctly?" That left dimple laughed at me from his cheek.

"Yup, you did." I lifted my chin and pursed my lips at him, trying to show resolve.

"Well, all right, then." Scott's gaze drifted down to my half-full tray of food. "Finish your breakfast, and I'll tell you about where we're going."

I grabbed my fork, ready to fill up. Nervous or not, it was going to be a busy day, and I needed the fuel.

"There's a beautiful place not far from here called 'Lookout Rock.' I've hiked there several times. It's got the best view in town. Do you have good sneakers?"

I nodded and then swallowed. "I have hiking boots."

As a child, my parents and I would hike on all sorts of mountainous trails. Camel's Hump, named after its distinctive shape, was one of our faves. My mother would pack a picnic lunch, which we enjoyed from what felt like the top of the world. Without knowing it, Scott was opening a door to some of my fondest memories.

"Cool. You're all set then."

Scott's phone rang, which he pulled from his pocket. "It's my sister. Do you mind?"

"No, not at all. Go ahead." At least it wasn't another girl.

"Hey, Kelse. What's up?"

Kelse? Short for Kelsey?

I took a bite of bacon, enjoying the smoky flavor on my tongue. While I consumed my breakfast and Scott chatted with his sister, I watched him while trying not to be obvious about it. When he wasn't discussing anything serious, Scott had a way of smiling when he spoke as if a joke was waiting to get out. It made everything he said feel light and fun. He ran a hand through his hair, and I wondered what it felt like to touch those soft curls. Stretching across very broad shoulders, his gray T-shirt hugged his chest and arms in such a way that I envied the material. Putting all of that aside, I decided on my favorite feature. Reminding me of a perfect Vermont sky, Scott's eyes carried warmth and a flicker of adventure. For me, it was like gazing into an oasis after spending years in the desert.

Scott finished his call and returned his phone to the pocket of his Bermuda shorts just as a storm cloud named Rachael blocked out the sun.

"Hey, Scott." She stood at the edge of our table with a few of her friends—the same girls from the night before.

"It's Sara, right?" Her tone brisk, invisible lightning bolts shot from her eyes.

I nodded as though I was about to be scolded.

"Well, you two seem to be hitting it off. Should I be jealous?" Wearing another flashy outfit, Rachael represented entitlement and privilege. She smiled, but the rest of her face didn't get the memo.

Scott secured his jaw and steadied his eyes with mine. "Are you finished?"

"Yes." I wiped the corners of my mouth and then draped my napkin over my empty plate.

"We were just leaving." Scott got to his feet and grabbed his tray. I followed his lead.

"Well, I need those muscles of yours to help me move some furniture later." Rachael placed her hand on Scott's arm.

Fuming, I wanted to slap her hand away.

"I can't. Sara and I have plans." Scott kept his tone clipped and to the point.

"Well, I guess I'll have to ask someone else." Rachael scanned Scott's face, I assumed for a reaction. She didn't get one—not that I could see, anyway.

"Sorry. Catch you later." Scott led the way in the direction of the garbage cans.

As I walked alongside him, I peered back at Rachael, who mouthed the words *you bitch* at me as if it was *my* fault Scott wasn't interested. I just arrived at this school, so I knew that wasn't true. That girl needed to stock up on chill pills.

We stepped out into the blazing sunshine and a campus even more populated with students. A custodian drove by on his lawnmower, releasing the scent of freshly cut grass into the air. As the sun climbed higher in the sky, so did the temperature. It was going to be another scorcher.

"It's a great day for a hike." Scott looked up, his tone hopeful.

"I agree," I said, trying to stifle my perma-grin. "Do you hike a lot?"

Scott pulled a pair of sunglasses off the neck of his T-shirt and put them on. I wished I had remembered mine. "As much as I can. It's nice to get away from here once in a while."

As we ventured across campus, it seemed like every person we passed acknowledged Scott in some way. The men offered "hey, bros" or fist bumps while the women smiled or flirted with their eyelashes and smiles. His phone continued to ding in texts from his pocket. Busy guy. I felt like I was walking with the mayor.

"Hey, did you hear that we won the football game last night?"

"No, I didn't. That's great." I was happy to hear that he was at the game and not in his room with Mindy and Charlene—at their welcome back party.

"Yeah, it was a close one ..."

I smiled and listened. Off to the right and about a hundred feet away, a woman caught my eye. Mostly because she was so fixated on Scott. It was either Mindy or Charlene, but I couldn't tell which one. She blew Scott a kiss from afar. *Great.*

"The quarterback escaped a sack when he ran the ball into the end zone ..."

Was she thanking Scott for a night of passion? Images

invaded my mind that brought my feet back down to earth. *He's a player.*

"I don't know who they got for a field goal kicker, but he sucks. ..."

I spotted my dorm and quickened my pace. "I think a migraine may be coming on (named Mindy and Charlene). Can I take a raincheck on the hike?"

Scott jogged up beside me. "What? When?"

"Just now. I guess I just don't feel well." I touched my forehead.

"You guess?" Scott took my arm to stop me from walking, his eyes probing.

One thing my parents had always told me was I was a terrible liar. For that reason, I never got away with anything.

"Do you really not feel well, or is something else wrong?"

"Um." I felt like an idiot acting this way. *You have so many girlfriends, and I'm not prepared to deal with that?* I should've said no right off the bat. Then again, Rick had been pressuring me to go cliff diving.

Wearing a stony expression, Scott continued to eye me. "What's going on? Is it Rachael? I'm not dating her or anyone right now." For a moment, he didn't blink.

What did *dating* mean to Scott? Did it mean he still slept around with every woman who would have him—which was pretty much anyone—or did it mean he was not seeing *anyone?* Did he consider a welcome-back party with Mindy and Charlene dating? It was all so confusing.

The truth was, I already felt drawn to Scott and didn't want to get hung up on a guy who would forget me when the next shiny "someone" came along.

I had to find a way to tell him this. It was too important. "I'm very different from you, Scott." *I'm cave girl, and you're McDreamy.* "You seem like someone who is used to having a lot of women in his life." *And I don't want to be your fling of the week.*

Scott released a long breath as if weighing his response. "Has it occurred to you that the fact that you are different is one of the things I like most about you?" His blue eyes made their best effort to show his sincerity. "Look, we're getting way ahead of ourselves. Just go on this hike with me. I'm asking you as a friend."

I sighed. When it came down to it, he was right. I *was* being way too possessive. Plus, I really wanted to go. Hiking was my thing. "You're right. Sorry, but I need to change and get my hiking boots first."

"No problem. I'll follow you up." He quirked an eyebrow in a way that told me he wasn't taking any chances on leaving me alone to change my mind.

* * *

While Scott waited in the living room of my suite, I changed into a pair of tan shorts and a light-pink tank. After I had put my hair up in a ponytail and was lacing my hiking books, my phone dinged.

It was Abigail texting. "College is going to be great! I'm so proud of you."

I typed, "Thank you," which I sent with a heart symbol.

She had been coaching me via texts and phone calls often.

Five minutes later, I reached the living room where Scott *and* Amy were in a stare down. Eyes narrowed, jaws set, they faced each other like Scott and Rick had the night before. What was going on?

When Scott spotted me, the cords in his neck released and his face tried to smile. "Are you ready?" Without waiting for my answer, he headed straight for the door, and a second later, he was gone.

I was dumbfounded. "How was your breakfast with Luke?" I asked Amy. "I mean Sky."

"Good. I'll fill you in later."

Amy stared at me. Before she turned and headed down the hallway, she whispered the words, "Be careful."

What did *that* mean? Something was up.

Chapter Five

On the way toward the parking lot, Scott's phone dinged and rang a few times, but he continued to ignore it. I kept wondering what had happened between him and Amy. It was difficult to think of anything else, especially since I was going off campus *and* on a hike with a man I barely knew. Once we left the suite, he opened every door for me. My mom would've liked that.

Eventually, he cleared his throat. "Are you ready for your classes tomorrow?" He slid his sunglasses on again. Mine were still in my room.

Other than a few billowy clouds skidding across the sky, it was relatively clear, the blue a tad hazy. Humidity was back in play.

"I guess so."

"You'll do fine. Freshmen classes aren't hard. What's your major, anyway, or are you undecided?"

"Education." My mom was a teacher and somehow choosing this major made me feel closer to her.

"That's cool." Scott tapped my arm when we reached a fork

in the path, steering me to the left. "I had to park in your dorm lot last night because my lot was full."

I had noticed that the lots around here filled up rather quickly and made a mental note of it.

"Do you have any friends who go here?"

"No, not really." Then I thought again. "Well, I know Amy and Derek a little, but no one else." I gave Scott a sideways glance. "*You* seem to have a lot of friends here."

He was more like a celebrity who knew everyone.

A smile played at the corners of his lips. "Well, my best friend, Jason, goes here, and I've made a few friends along the way."

A few, huh? I couldn't help but wonder how many women he'd slept with. Not that it was any of my business.

When we arrived at the parking lot, Scott pointed out his car. "I'm the jeep over there."

It was a red jeep with large off-road tires, a sport bar with full padding, and chrome accents. Vermont's roadways were loaded with trucks and jeeps with enormous tires. One thing I knew about jeeps was that they rolled over easily. *Not good.*

I bit my lower lip.

"Since it's such a nice day, I was thinking about keeping the top off. I won't if you don't want too much wind on you, though." Scott fished his keys from his shorts pocket.

"Sure, that's fine."

I scanned the car's visible safety features: steel body, seat belts, roll bars. Scott even had a spare tire mounted on the back —a soccer ball emblem on its cover.

"We're not going off-road, are we?" If he said yes, it would be the end of our date. I was willing to step out of my comfort zone, but ...

"I wasn't planning on it." Scott raised an eyebrow. "Did you *want* to go off-road?"

"Oh, no. I'm happy to stay on pavement." I exhaled, relieved.

Scott opened the passenger-side door and smiled. "Your chariot awaits."

As I approached him, his entire face beamed, his eyes practically glowing. He was so open, so accepting, and so beautiful.

"It's a high step. Let me help you up." He placed his hands around my waist and boosted me up as if I were made of air.

I pulled the seat belt over my shoulder as Scott crossed the front of the jeep. His phone rang from his pocket. This time, he took it out and read the screen.

Like he was Tarzan swinging on a vine, Scott jumped into the driver's seat and placed his cell phone facedown in the cupholder behind the shifter. "Don't worry; I turned my ringer off." He gave me a reassuring grin. "No more interruptions."

As we pulled out of the parking lot, a warm draft caught Scott's spicy scent—it was fast becoming my new favorite smell.

"Is something wrong with your seat belt?" Scott looked over, shoulders and all. He slowed the jeep.

I let go of the seat belt I'd been testing too many times. "No. I just didn't hear it click." A few habits had stayed with me since the accident. This was one of them. Driving extremely slow was another.

Scott pulled his visor down and accelerated. "You're gonna love the view. The climb can be a bit challenging, but it's worth it." He shifted into second gear, the campus fading in my side mirror.

"I can't wait." Wisps of hair escaped from my ponytail, dancing around my head, an abundance of fresh air flogging my face.

The speed of the jeep made it difficult to talk for a while. Scott took a scenic route, which allowed me to enjoy the Charlottesville countryside. We passed by several horse ranches and a few orchards. We were slowing down for an upcoming inter-section when a deer darted across the road.

My stomach lurched. "Look out!" Fearing the worst, I grabbed my head, flung my chest over my knees, and readied myself for the crash. I thought my heart was going to burst from my ribcage.

Only there was no crash.

The jeep slowed until we came to a complete stop.

When I looked up, Scott slid his sunglasses down, his eyebrows squishing together. "It's okay. I didn't hit it."

I sat up and took several shallow breaths, trying to slow my pulse. With a shaky hand, I brushed a few strands of hair off my forehead.

"Some people think I'm a pretty good driver." He said it jokingly, his tone light.

I shouldn't have come. This was a mistake. My head spun like a blender on full speed.

Scott touched my shoulder. "It's okay."

But it wasn't okay, not for me. "I'm sorry. I saw the deer and thought ..." My voice shook as I held back tears. PTSD wasn't pretty when it reared its ugly head.

"I understand. I know some people who have hit a deer. They can do some serious damage."

My body quaked. If he only knew. It took one second—one —before my father's truck skidded across a patch of black ice, destroying an innocent deer, right along with my parents, my home, and my life.

Scott pushed his sunglasses back in place and accelerated again, slowly this time. "I'll keep an extra-close eye out." He was being way too nice about it.

My hands trembled, my heart hammered. Just when I thought I had it together, I unraveled into a complete basket case. If Scott hadn't regretted asking me to go on this hike before, I was sure he did now.

"Did you know that Thomas Jefferson's home isn't far from here?"

"Huh?"

"Yeah, it's called Monticello." He rested his wrist on top of the steering wheel, keeping his body angled my way.

His calm demeanor encouraged me to relax as if he knew I needed that. *Thank you, Scott.*

"My friend Jason is a huge history buff, so he's dragged me to all the major spots. George Washington's home is a couple of hours away and so is Colonial Williamsburg." Before long, I thought more about Virginia and less about me, my pulse returning to normal.

"I'm terrible at remembering facts or events." I sat back, letting the last of the adrenaline float off my skin.

"Same. But I have Jason to remind me."

The wind played with Scott's lustrous curls, and I found myself staring.

"So, you and Jason decided to go to school together?" Every time I spoke, a wisp of *my* hair was determined to force its way into my mouth. I kept trying to grab it.

"I got a soccer scholarship, which made the choice easy for me. Jason was going to another school, but then he found out about Commonwealth's connection to D.C. That changed his mind."

Soccer scholarship? "Wow, you must be good at soccer." A loud screeching brought my eyes to a rotation of hawks flying overhead.

"You'll have to come watch me play sometime." Scott shifted into a higher gear. "Jason and his girlfriend, Heather, come a lot." His voice grew louder, competing with the wind and the road noise. "You could all sit together. The team has been here practicing since July."

"I'd love to come," I said, flattered that he wanted me there, especially after what had just happened.

When we reached another intersection, Scott kept his speed slow, his eyes on full alert.

I cringed.

No animals in sight. Once the wind had died down, I collected all the loose strands of my hair and redid my ponytail, mainly to keep my bumbling hands busy.

"Do you like to go to the beach?" Scott fed the jeep gas, followed by another shifting routine.

I imagined Scott in a bathing suit. It brought my heart rate up again but for another reason. "Yes, but I haven't been in years. I went with my parents to Maine when I was a little girl." I stared out into the thicket as it blurred by, thinking about sandcastles from the past, roasted marshmallows, and lobster bibs. What I remembered most about Maine was how cold the water was. Even in July, it felt like a tub filled with ice cubes— enough to make your toes throb.

"Well, the beach is only a few hours away, along with a few amusement and theme parks." He smiled. "I get bored here in the summer."

We pulled off the highway and followed a dirt road to its end. When we parked, Scott jumped out of the driver's seat and bounded over to the passenger side in time to take my hand as I jumped down. I didn't need the help but appreciated the gesture—so would Mom.

"I usually have bottles of water in the back. Let me see if I can find some." Scott stepped onto the back bumper and rummaged through a pile of rope, soccer balls, backpacks, and dirt-covered sneakers until he came up with a small cooler, looking like he had struck gold. He pulled out a few bottles, dumped out one of the backpacks, and then put the bottles inside of the backpack. Then he grabbed a pair of hiking boots wedged behind the driver's seat, plus a pair of wadded-up socks to accompany them.

While he worked, I remained off to the side. I closed my eyes and found my center—something a counselor had taught me to do. I meditated on the birds chirping idle conversations across the branches, some louder than others. I always wondered what they were saying to one another. The scents of damp earth and pine pitch found my nose, which invited in more childhood memories: hide-and-seek behind the trees, scavenger hunts, and the alphabet game (nature edition). I really missed home.

"The path is just up ahead."

I opened my eyes to Scott standing in front of me, his boots on, his backpack slung over his shoulder, and his smile as welcoming as the sun. "Ready to go?"

"Sure, I was just taking it all in."

He winked. "Trust me, it gets better."

The first leg of the hike was more like a gravel road, and the vegetation was thin. It made it easy to peer deep into the wooded areas.

After a few minutes of awkward silence, Scott raised one finger. "So, you're from Vermont, but you don't ski." He let his comment linger, and I sensed he was waiting for more.

"Yes, Middlebury, actually. It's a small town in the center of the state." I bent over and picked up a long stick, catching Scott's eyes sliding down my butt and legs.

He looked away when I noticed.

"It's awesome, especially in the fall. The leaves get so vibrant; it's like they're on fire." I imagined what autumn would look like here. "So, what part of Pennsylvania are you from?"

Scott perked up at my question. "Good memory. Phoenixville. It's about—"

"I know where it is." I was amazed at the coincidence. Phoenixville, a typical American town with an artsy feel, was located just over an hour from where I had spent the past six years of my life. "I mean, I've been there before. Our school took a few trips there to check out the farmers market and hit some of the restaurants." I tapped at the trees with my stick thinking: small world.

"I thought you said you were from Vermont."

Crap. Did I want to get into this now?

"I am. I went to a private school in Pennsylvania."

Scott tipped his head as if surprised by my comment. "Oh. Fancy. I wish I'd seen you around. My dad owns a car dealership in town. I work for him all the time, so I may have been in some of those restaurants." He lifted his voice. "I would have remembered *you*."

There was no short supply of flattery with Scott. I wasn't used to it, but I loved it just the same.

We passed a sign that read, "Foot traffic welcome."

"Sounds like you come from a successful family." I hoped my comment would encourage him to say more.

"Yeah, well, my dad's kind of a high achiever. He could sell just about anything he sets his mind to. He certainly has made a good living at it." His voice carried an edge, but I wasn't sure why. "What do *your* parents do?"

It had been a long time since anyone had been interested in my life—past or present. Amy was the first.

"My dad worked at Middlebury College as the lead custodian, and my mom taught high school ... special needs children."

Scott grew quiet. I assumed it was because I had referred to my parents in the past tense. If I hadn't, it would've been a lie. He didn't say anything about it, so neither did I.

The higher we climbed, the denser the vegetation and the rougher the terrain. The canopy consisted of maple, oak, and a few ash trees, while fern growth blanketed the forest floor. A breeze had picked up, carrying with it rich scents of berries, juniper, and a slew of other organic aromas. As the path narrowed, Scott gestured for me to go ahead of him. I took a few more steps and turned my head to catch him staring at the back of my neck, right where that gross-looking three-inch scar lived —another remnant from the crash. It was the reason I kept my hair long.

"Will you take over your dad's dealership someday?"

"Um." He looked away. "I know my father would like that. I work for him whenever I'm home from school. I'm not much of a salesman. I'm more interested in architecture, but I've been taking a double major to satisfy him anyway." His face went rigid. "My dad and I aren't always on the best of terms."

That explained the tension in his voice and the bad vibe.

"He seems to think he can run my life. My dad has always been good at business but not so much at family life. When his dealership was taking off, I was young. My mother quit her job and took care of my sister, Kelsey, and me." Scott huffed a little. "Any time my sister or I won an award, though, he'd sure love to brag about it. As though he had anything to do with it. Half the time he didn't even know what grade either of us was in."

I listened, appreciating his honesty but saddened by his struggle. My parents had always been so attentive.

A squirrel scampered across our path and up a tree with lightning speed, causing me to yelp and stumble backward.

From behind me, Scott gripped my waist. "Are you all right?" His eyebrows shot up.

I put a hand to my chest and smiled. "Yeah, it just startled me." I made sure to keep my voice steady this time.

Scott let go of my waist and exhaled. After the deer incident, he was probably expecting a full-on meltdown.

Squirrels I could handle. I should have given Scott a checklist.

As we kept walking, a cardinal caught my attention as it flew from one tree to the next, its red feathers electric against the green foliage. "The scenery is amazing up here. It reminds me so much of home. I used to go hiking a lot with my parents." I needed to tell him the truth about them, but I wasn't ready.

Baby steps.

"Wow, look at that." I pointed at a large monarch butterfly, its gold-and-black pattern like stained glass. It landed on a cluster of flowers with purplish domes that drooped downward. "Pretty flowers. I've never seen them before."

Scott looked up and said, "You mean bellflowers? I'm surprised. They tend to grow in colder climates, like where you're from."

I smiled, impressed. *You know flowers?*

"Oh, really." A few feet up the path, I pointed to a collection of plants resembling giant pipe cleaners.

"And what kind of flower is that?" I glanced back at him, my wiggling eyebrows offering a challenge.

"Blazing stars."

Blazing what?

He didn't even hesitate. Scott was full of surprises.

"My mother is really into flowers and used to teach me about them. When I was younger, she planted small beds of wildflowers all over our property. It was her hobby. Every year she'd add more to her collection. Now our yard is filled with them. It looks nice." I loved the way Scott's face softened when he talked about his mom.

"It sounds incredible." We were heading into steeper territory, so I tossed my stick into the brush.

"Yeah. When our backyard was full, she filled terra-cotta pots along our driveway. I helped her do it." He spoke with such pride. "There's some Queen Anne's lace." Scott pointed at the white, umbrella-shaped flowers soaking up the last of the summer sun.

That one I knew, but I nodded anyway.

A moment later, Scott moved ahead and took my hand to help me over a fallen log. When our hands touched, an intense feeling slid through me, a longing I didn't know was there. Until he cut the power and let go.

I pointed. "I bet you can't tell me what *they* are."

Scott followed my eyes to a small tree with yellow, thread-like flowers. It looked like something you'd see at the bottom of the ocean. No way would he know that one.

"Witch hazel."

"Wow, you do know your plants."

Scott's eyes sparkled with joy, his smile satisfied. "I told you." He gave me a light nudge.

We continued to climb until we reached an enormous rock near the summit.

"Let's go to the left." Scott watched my every step. "It's a little steeper, but it has better footholds. Don't worry. I'll stay close behind in case you need help. The view is worth the effort."

I flipped my hand. "Oh, I've hiked worse than this before." And I had, but when Scott's shoulders drooped like the bell-flowers below, I offered a counter. "Just in case, you better stay close."

"I'll be right behind you," he said, a ray of light returning to his eyes.

Remembering everything my parents had taught me, I

watched for strong footholds and places to grip my hands as I navigated the steep climb. "Take your time, munchkin," my father coached me from the past. Scott stayed so close his breath tickled the back of my legs. When I reached the top, my mouth fell open while I did a three-sixty to take in the panoramic view. The tips of the Blue Ridge Mountains expanded in all directions while puffy, white clouds cast large, shaded patterns on the green vegetation below. The air was lighter, refreshing, and liberating. "Amazing."

Getting to his feet, Scott stood beside me. "I told you it was one of the best views in Virginia." His chest rose and fell as he wiped a sheen of sweat from his brow. I was sweating as well.

Then he reached into his backpack and handed me a bottle of water.

"Thanks." I took the bottle, unscrewed the top, and guzzled. Scott did the same.

Once we were hydrated, Scott tipped his chin. "Let's sit for a minute." He gestured toward a flat area near the edge. As I followed him over, his foot skidded on a wet spot. "It looks like it may have rained recently. Be careful." He reached his hand out to me again, and I was eager to take it.

I sat next to him and gazed out at the vast scenery. "I love it." I felt so free, so inspired, like I could float with the clouds, not a worry in the world.

"It's my favorite spot. I come here to clear my head. You're the first person I've shared it with." His tender smile made me believe it was true.

"Really?" I was touched.

"Yeah." His smile holding, Scott stared at me for several seconds until he blinked and turned away. "Want a mint?" He reached into his front pocket and pulled out a roll of peppermint Life Savers. He peeled off the wrapper.

"Sure." I took a mint and popped it in my mouth. The

sensation of the peppermint on my tongue was invigorating. Then again, *everything* about this day was topping the charts.

Scott focused on my lips, until he straightened up and unlocked his gaze.

"You're not like the people around here," he said.

"What do you mean?" *I* knew I was different, but what did *he* see?

His gaze fell to his water bottle, which he turned over in his hands. "I'm still trying to figure that one out." When he lifted his chin and stared at me, the sun reflected off his eyes, making them even bluer. *How is this possible?* He hooked a few strands of loose hair behind my ear, his fingers gentle and caring.

I almost melted right off the edge of the cliff.

"Putting aside your obvious dislike for beer—" His lips curled as I remembered the tailgate when he had laughed at me about it. "—it's refreshing to be around a girl who eats real food, climbs rocks like Spider-Man, and shares funny stories about her skiing debacles." He inched a little closer, his eyes filled with intention. "You're funny, honest, and unbelievably gorgeous." The timbre in his voice was deep and buttery, especially when he said that last part. "What's not to like? I have a whole new appreciation for Vermonters."

Gorgeous? It was hard for me to look away, but I forced myself. I wanted to be real with him. He had to know the truth: I was a girl with a lot of baggage.

I prepared myself and then locked eyes with him again. "I think I've always felt separate from most of the people around me. It hasn't been easy for me to fit in."

His hand found my arm. "You don't need to fit in. That's what's great about you."

"You don't understand. I'm different but not in a good way. I was in a car accident six years ago. It was winter, and a deer ran out in the middle of the road." My words felt heavy, my heart begging me to stop. "My dad's truck skidded sideways and then rolled over and down an embankment. My father went through the windshield, and my mom was crushed. Neither one of them were wearing their seat belts."

The reason they weren't wearing them was because my mom had just scooted over next to my dad so she could snuggle in close. The truck's heater never worked right, and she was cold. The only person who wore their seat belt that night was me. The lone survivor. "I'm still messed up about it."

Scott's head dropped before he looked up at me again. "Wow. I'm so sorry. That's terrible. No wonder you were upset about the deer in the road."

I fanned my hands out. "That's what I mean."

He rested his hand on my shoulder before he trailed his fingers around to the nape of my neck, raising a few goose bumps along the way.

I knew where he was going.

The pads of his fingers touched the scar just below my hair-line. "Is that what this is from?"

"Yes." I struggled to keep it together. It had been a long time since I had opened this vault. I hadn't even told Amy this much.

Scott removed his hand and blinked. "That's intense." He draped his arm around my shoulders and pulled me closer. For a second, I let my head rest against him. Part of me hated his pity, yet another part of me yearned for it.

I still had more to say, so I pulled back, even though I didn't want to. "Don't get me wrong I do have good people in my life. My mother had a best friend named Abigail. She teaches at the same high school my mom taught at. She's really been there for me." I stared into his concerned eyes and sensed he understood somehow. "Meeting people and going to parties is all new to me. They called me 'cave girl' at my last school, if that gives you any idea of what I was like." A lump bobbed in my throat.

Scott stayed close, his aura reaching out to me. "People can be assholes." He made a pfft sound. "My dad can be a dick sometimes, but I can't imagine our family without him. You're a strong person."

I took another sip of water. "You're giving me too much credit. I hid away for six years. That's hardly strong."

He made a noise in his throat. "Most people would have given up, but you didn't. And don't worry about college." Scott screwed and unscrewed the top of his water bottle. "You'll get used to college life."

Funny how much Amy and Scott sounded alike. I wasn't sure Amy would appreciate the comparison.

"Whatever you need, I'm here." As he spoke, the edges of his irises seemed darker, more vibrant. "Thank you for coming today and for sharing that with me. Trust me when I tell you, this has been one of the best days I've had in a long time."

I tried not to get swept up in his words, but how could I not? He was medicine for my soul. Whether I was ready for it or not, I was already falling for this guy—and hard.

We sat for a while longer, being still and listening to the leaves rustling in the breeze, the birds, and the Earth.

"Do you want to head back?" Scott finally said.

"Sure." That was a lie. Part of me wished we could stay here forever.

As we ventured across the large boulder, a loud flapping noise brought my eyes up just as an enormous bird landed on one of the dwarfed tree limbs in front of me. It was big enough to carry off a small child. My pulsed ramped up.

"What in the world is that? It's huge." I pointed while peering over my shoulder.

"That's a turkey buzzard. They're big fuckers, aren't they?"

I was about to ask Scott if they were dangerous when my foot slipped on a wet spot near a small pool of rainwater. I squealed, my arms flailing. My water bottle sailed through the air as Scott dropped his and grabbed hold of me.

"Are you alright?" He pulled me into his chiseled abdomen, his breath grazing my forehead, his heart thumping with the power of a locomotive.

The proximity of my body with his had me scrambling with too many emotions to keep track of. My lungs were running a marathon with my heart.

"I'm okay." *Aside from the fact that I'm about to pass out from being this close to you.* "I should have watched where I was going. Being graceful isn't one of my strong suits."

"You're not hurt, are you?" His eyes showed concern.

"No, just a little embarrassed."

That brought a smile to his face. "Don't be. You made my day." He lifted my chin, locking my eyes with his. "I would really like to kiss you right now." He caressed the sides of my face with the backs of his fingers.

"Okay," I said, and then I wondered if it was possible to kiss wrong. I tried to stay chill about it.

With a feathery touch, he swept the loose hairs away from my face and then brushed his soft lips over my cheek and the bridge of my nose. When he found my mouth, he started with tender kisses before pressing his lips hard against mine. The only word to describe him was delicious. I'd been admiring him from afar, soaking in the sight of him, and now I was able to taste him, touch him. The peppermint on his breath, the bristle of his sprouting stubble tickling against my cheek, and the combination of his spicy cologne mixed in with sweat from our hike had my senses reeling. He opened his mouth a little, brushing the tip of his velvety tongue against my lips.

My reflexes told me to open my mouth, too. If he was asking, my answer was yes.

Our mouths connected, our tongues intertwining. Scott lowered his arms, wrapping them around my waist and drawing me close, his heartbeat drumming in perfect rhythm with mine. We explored each other in a way I had never experienced before—didn't even know was possible.

It had taken eighteen years for my first kiss, but it was worth the wait. When he pulled away, I almost thanked him. I swallowed the urge instead. It was no wonder women sought him out. *What else can you do?*

Onto my lips, Scott whispered, "This is definitely the best part of my day, maybe my year."

"I bet you say that to all the girls." I made it sound light, but it wasn't. Not to me. He had cast a spell on me, and I didn't want to share.

Something vibrated against my hip, interrupting our private moment. Scott stepped back before pulling out his phone and gazing at it. For a few seconds, he studied the screen while I studied him. When he put the phone back in his pocket, he confronted me with his eyes.

"I'm going to be honest with you, Sara. If you knew me better, then you'd understand how unusual this is for me to say. I like you." He took a breath. "I know this is sudden, but I'd like to go out with you more. A lot more."

"Aren't you seeing other girls?" I knew it was a loaded question, but I had to ask.

Scott scratched at his eyebrow, his face bordering sheepish. "Sounds like you've been told a few things about my reputation."

Not really. I've seen it for myself, Scott.

"And I won't deny that any of it is true." He came closer.

"But I have no interest in dating anyone else. You can trust me." His strong hands found my upper arms.

My cautious side took over, pulling my emotional reins back. "I like you, too, but can we take this slow and see where it goes?" This was all happening so fast. I had a hard time believing it was real.

Scott backed up, his eyes going distant, then he offered a faint nod.

I was sure a guy like him wasn't used to hearing words like "Can we take this slow?" from women. Maybe that was a deal-breaker for him.

He straightened himself up as if he was rebooting. "We can definitely take things slow. I wouldn't want it any other way." His dimple appeared right before the flash of his winning smile. "I know your name is Sara. Is there a last name to go with it?"

Finally, an easy topic.

"Browne. And you?"

"Williams."

I rolled this surreal moment around in my mind. Was it really happening? I was standing on a mountain with a guy who was kind, considerate, and hotter than anyone I had ever seen. Best of all, he was into me, and I was into him. Did I dare to hope that my dark days were behind me? Everything felt so right.

Chapter Six

Once we returned to campus and while we were still sitting in his jeep, Scott asked for my phone number, which I gave him right away. Actually, I let him punch his number into my phone, but he wasn't as willing to let me do the same with *his* cell phone. I suspected there may have been some recent texts on his screen that he didn't want me to read. It was probably why he always placed his cell phone screen down. Coincidence? Maybe. "You can trust me," he'd said. Trust wasn't an easy one for me. When you trusted people, you let your guard down. Before the accident, my heart was wide open. Afterward, I was a different person—one who always waited for the next boot to drop, the next fissure to crack open beneath my feet.

We were walking to my dorm when I contemplated taking his hand—a bold move for someone like me. We'd held hands on the ride back to campus, Scott brushing his thumb over my knuckles. However, since the phone number exchange, Scott didn't seem as attentive as he was before. He had also grown quiet. Maybe he thought I was upset about his cautious cell phone behavior, but I wasn't. Not yet, anyway. I'd known him for all of five minutes. Then again, maybe his change in mood had something to do with the fact that we were back on campus, where prying eyes could see. It was too soon to get all spun up over something I wasn't sure about, so I just put it away for now. I was good at compartmentalizing—at one point it became my way of life.

"If you want, I can show you around campus. You should let me see your schedule in case I need to warn you about any strict or weird professors."

I was relieved to hear him talking again and wanting to spend more time together, too. In fact, I loved the idea, but I had already asked Amy to tour the campus with me, and I wasn't about to blow her off—not even for Scott.

"I'd like that. I had asked Amy to go with me to look around. Would you mind if she went with us?" Not only did Scott's face harden at my suggestion, I wasn't sure Amy would agree, anyway.

We reached the entrance of my dorm, where we came face-to-face.

"I don't mind, but I don't think your friend would be too happy about it."

Why not? What happened between you two?

I was about to ask him those very questions when someone yelling Scott's name stopped me. The voice was male.

"Hey, man, where ya been?"

Scott turned his head. "Oh, hey, bro." He gave his friend an informal handshake.

Of medium build and average height, Scott's friend had the warmest coffee-colored eyes I had ever seen. The August sunlight brought out the natural copper, toffee, and amber highlights in his brown hair.

"This is Sara." Scott motioned with his hand. "Sara, this is Jason."

Jason? The best friend? I smiled at him with renewed interest.

"It's nice to meet you, Jason." I shook his hand. "I've heard a lot about you."

"Nice to meet you, too." Jason's gaze shifted between Scott and me. "You guys met at the tailgate last night, right?" He scratched behind his ear. "Sorry I missed it."

So, Scott told him about me? "Yes, that's right," I said.

"Good luck with this loser." Jason hooked his arm around Scott's neck, trying to pull him down into a headlock. Given Scott's physical advantage, he didn't get far.

"You're just jealous." Scott pushed Jason back, shaking his head and casting him a half-grimace, half-smile. They reminded me more of brothers than of friends.

Once Jason stopped goofing around, he stepped back and pointed at Scott. "Hey, there's a touch football game starting up. You interested?"

"Uh, I was going to show Sara around campus." Scott dangled his soccer ball keychain from his fingers.

"You go ahead. It will give me a chance to check with Amy." I was happy for the opportunity to talk to her about Scott. "If she wants to join, we'll come get you. If she doesn't, I'll either come alone, or I'll text you, and we can meet up after your game."

Scott stared at me for a few seconds. He made a *hmmm* noise in his throat. "Are you sure? I don't mind waiting." His brow pulled in, his eyes all serious. It reminded me of a moment at the tailgate when I'd left him with Mindy and Charlene.

"That's okay. I need to get changed anyway."

"Come on, man." Jason punched Scott on the arm. "We need ya, bro."

Scott handed his keys over to Jason. "Go grab my cleats and meet me at the field."

"Sure, man."

Once Jason was gone, Scott put his hands on my waist and gazed deep into my eyes. The intensity of his stare made my heart flutter. "So, you'll come to the field and get me, right? Do you know where the football stadium is?"

"Yes, I walked by it yesterday. Don't worry." I fiddled with the elastic band holding my ponytail. Was he going to kiss me again?

"I don't dare let you out of my sight." Scott pulled me closer. "Some other guy may try to snatch you up."

Not a chance.

Then he pressed his luscious lips against mine. Prying eyes be damned. I dissolved into his arms.

When two girls walked past us and into my dorm, both of them giggling, I pulled away and stepped back, taking out my keycard. "See you in a few minutes."

I entered my dorm and bounded up the stairs to my suite in one of the best moods I could remember. I opened the suite door, ready to find Amy and tell her all about my day. Whatever had happened between them, we'd work it out. We had to.

"I was wondering when you were coming back."

I spun around and then my smile flattened—mainly because sitting on the couch in my suite living room was the last person I wanted to see.

"How did you get in here?" I said through clenched teeth.

"One of your suitemates let me in."

Mia peered around the corner, her gaze swiveling between Rick and me. "I hope that was okay."

No, it wasn't, Mia.

She disappeared before I could answer, not that I would have.

Rick lifted himself from the couch and took a step forward, a bouquet clutched in his hands. "I wanted to bring you a peace offering—to make up for my behavior last night." Sunglasses propped on his head, his shirt pressed, and his shorts tailored, he handed me the bouquet and smiled, his aroma expensive, or so I assumed. "I figured you didn't have a vase, so I got you one."

It was a full arrangement of white daisies, pink roses, and greenery. "Thanks," I said, my voice deadpan. This was not what I had expected *or* wanted.

"Look, I bullshit a lot, but I don't mean anything by it." He paused. "And I made sure Kevin knew he was out of line. Let me take you to dinner and apologize properly." He pulled his sunglasses off his head and twirled them with his thumb and forefinger. "I know some decent places that are far better than this shit cafeteria food."

Appearing confident and bold, Rick was the kind of guy who probably sailed through life with all the doors *and* opportunities open to him. I suspected he didn't have to work for much. He was good looking, but he lacked something—a layer of empathy—or maybe it was sincerity that only happened when a person had to sacrifice or struggle. Even though Scott was just as popular, I sensed he understood the underbelly of life. His issues with his dad may have contributed to that.

"I can't. I've got plans." I was living a déjà vu moment from breakfast.

"Are your plans with Scott?" Rick's voice probed, his dark eyes judgy. "Don't waste your time with him unless you want to get dumped. He never stays with one woman ... ever. Love 'em and leave 'em." His crisp tone matched his crisp collar.

"It's none of your business, and my plans are with several

people." I bit down on the inside of my cheek, wanting this moment to end.

Rick lowered his brow like a window shade, darkening the mood even more. "If you don't believe me, ask anyone. Scott makes an art form out of juggling women. You ladies think he's hot, but he's not what he seems." He stayed close, relentless.

I hated the way he was trying so hard to make his point. He was like a needle set on popping my good mood bubble. I didn't need this right now.

"Well, thank you for the flowers. I gotta go." I gazed down the hallway, wishing a strong wind would whisk Rick away, along with his lamo flowers.

"Okay, I'll back off. If you get tired of the playboy, I'll be around." He hung his sunglasses over the top button of his shirt and headed for the door. "As a friend, I can't warn you enough about Scott." He put his hand on the knob and pulled the door open. "If you continue to see him, be prepared for the female wrath that will come after you. I've seen more than a few catfights over that dude. Some crazy shit." He shook his head and disappeared through the door.

I thought about Rachael, Mindy, and Charlene. Were there others?

Deflated, I schlepped back to my room, put the vase on my desk, and then collapsed onto my bed. If I could sum up the past six years of my life in one word, it would be *miserable*. Meeting a friend like Amy was more than I had expected. Finding Scott was far beyond that. What difference did it make what Scott was like before? Maybe he'd changed. My alter ego —the one who was waiting for that next boot to drop—wasn't convinced. I stared down at my hands, sad and unsure. Whether Scott was being sincere or not, how would I know any different? Especially someone like me with no dating experience. I needed advice. I needed Amy.

"Hey," Amy said when she opened her door a few seconds later. "How was your date? Did he try to get in your pants yet?" Then she looked at my face, and her smiled faded. "Are you okay?"

I released a breath and frowned. "Can I come in?"

"Sure."

I crossed the room and sat on the edge of Amy's bed while she dragged her desk chair over, taking a seat in front of me. Tie-dyed fabric hung loosely on her walls. Draped over the material were several strands of string lights along with a few dream catchers, giving the room a bohemian feel. All I had were a few covered bridge and outdoor scenery posters, all from Abigail.

"So, I'm taking it the date sucked." She paused, probably for me to confirm her suspicions.

What she didn't say was what had happened between her and Scott, not yet anyway.

"It was great, actually." My lips said one thing, my face said another.

"Yeah, I can tell." Amy's flat tone and narrowed eyes told me she wasn't convinced.

"No, it was. I just really like him." My shoulders sagged under the weight of my situation.

"And the problem is?" Amy angled her head, trying to figure me out.

"I've seen him with the girls around here. Rick was probably right. He juggles women."

Amy sat forward. "Wait. What? When did you speak to Rick?"

"When I got back from our hike, Rick was waiting in the living room. He brought me a bouquet. I guess he was trying to apologize for the tailgate. Anyway, he warned me about Scott."

Amy turned her head toward the door. "Oh, I wouldn't

listen to what that loser has to say." Her eyebrows shot up. "He's trying to make Scott look bad so *he* can fuck you."

"Yeah, but you don't like Scott, either. I can tell." I leveled my eyes with Amy's, hoping for the truth ... yet a smidge afraid of it. "I noticed the two of you before the hike, and you looked mad at each other. Then you told me to be careful. Why?"

As she fiddled with the stud in her earlobe, I prepared myself for what she might say next. "I was just ... I can't say I don't like *him*. I just know his type. That frat-boy crap makes me want to lose my shit." Tightening her jaw, she looked away.

"Did you say something to him?" *Come on, Amy, spill it.*

"Yeah. I wanted to ruffle his feathers a little and see what he'd do." She sprang to her feet and crossed the room. "I told him that if he was only interested in getting laid, then he should find another sucker." She grabbed a hooded sweatshirt from her laundry basket and pulled it over her head. "Are they trying to freeze us out here? I could store meat in this fucking place."

She was right. The air-conditioning pumped more cold air than necessary. Amped up on anxiety and worry, it actually felt good to me.

"What did he say?" Too anxious to sit, I rose.

"Captain America assured me I was wrong about him."

"Did you believe him?" I held my breath and waited for validation or a revelation or *something* that would tell me what to do.

Amy flung her arms up. "Shit. I don't know, Sara. You need to be careful; that's all." She spotted her cell phone on her desk and went to it. "If he's looking to get laid, then don't give him anything. He'll lose interest if that's his deal."

Not giving my body to Scott was the easy part. Giving my heart to him was another matter. The fact that this upset me so much told me I was already in over my head.

After Amy checked her cell phone, she sat at her desk and opened her laptop, her back doing a good impression of a brick wall. Tapping my hand against my leg, I watched her.

"He offered to show me around campus."

"Yeah." Amy palmed her mouse, opening what appeared to be her email.

I blurted out the words: "I told Scott you were coming with us."

Amy spun around in her seat, her face outraged. "No way. I'm not tagging along with you two. I'm no one's goddamn chaperone." She slapped her laptop closed and bolted into the bathroom.

I followed her in. "I need you there. If Scott's not being sincere, you'll know." I didn't trust my own instincts, but I did trust Amy. Things had already gone too far between him and me. *That kiss.*

She unzipped her makeup bag and pulled out a stick of black eyeliner. As she applied a new layer to her already made-up eyes, I leaned against the doorjamb, watching her work.

"Why do you care what I think anyway?" she asked.

I picked at a clump of dried paint breaking free of the door casing. "Because you're my friend, and I trust you."

She exhaled. Her determined mind was weakening.

"You could even invite Luke."

That brought a spark to her eyes. "He's busy today. We're having lunch tomorrow." She lowered her eyeliner pencil. "Are you sure you want my opinion? You may not like what I have to say."

I flung my shoulders back like a soldier ready to salute her commanding officer. "Yes. I'm sure."

A few seconds passed while Amy moved on from her eyeliner to her mascara. "Okay." She pointed with the hand holding the mascara brush. "But if you two make me feel like a third wheel, I'm gone."

"Deal." Before she had a chance to change her mind, I made a quick exit.

* * *

I'd told Scott I'd be there within a few minutes, but between convincing Amy to come with me, giving myself a quick sponge bath, and changing my clothes multiple times (I decided on khaki shorts, a white tank, and flip-flops), I'd already wasted at least half an hour.

I texted Amy when I was ready and met her out in the hall. "Don't forget your schedule," I said, holding mine up like a flag.

Amy patted the back pocket of her jean shorts. "Got it."

When we left the dorm, I slipped on my sunglasses—the ones I finally remembered—to shield my eyes against the hot sun. "Hey, let me see your schedule. Wouldn't it be awesome if we had a class together?"

"Uh-huh." Amy handed it over, which I examined as I followed a path under a line of oak trees that provided just enough shade to see the wording.

I let out a yelp. "We *do* have a class together: Art Design." I pointed as Amy peered over.

"Cool," she said before she took her schedule, folded it, and returned it to her back pocket. I did the same with mine.

We continued along, our destination the northwest end of campus where all the athletic fields were located. Given the ninety-degree temperature, the breeze felt more like gusts from a hair dryer on the hot setting. Once again, I'd doubled up on the deodorant to keep my pits dry. My thighs felt weak from the hike—or maybe they were just nervous about seeing Scott again. His eyes, his lips, his rockin' body.

"Where is Scott?" Amy peered over her large sunglasses, pulling me from my sexy image.

"He's at the football field, playing with some friends."

"Of course he is." She wrinkled her face at me, her tone snide.

As though applauding Amy's comment, cicadas clicked from the branches above like a band of guiros.

We passed by the parking lot that yesterday had been filled with cars at the tailgate and approached what appeared to be a soccer field on our right, judging by the netted goalposts on each end. Just past a line of tall oaks, the football stadium waited patiently, the faint sound of male voices touching my ears. We were close. My stomach went nuts.

On one end of the soccer field, a tall, slender woman with auburn hair and a preteen girl were kicking a ball. On the opposite side, two guys were throwing a Frisbee. I stopped for a moment to watch the girl, letting another memory play out in my mind.

"What are we doing?" Amy asked.

"Remember when I told you my mother had taught high school?"

"Yeah."

"Well, she taught special needs kids."

Wearing thick glasses under a full crop of dark, wavy hair, the young girl attempted to kick a soccer ball in the woman's direction numerous times. Her coordination was off as was her timing, and she tired easily, falling to the ground in an animated way. Every time the ball went in another direction, the woman ran to retrieve it and the girl giggled.

"Some of her students had mild to severe cases of autism." I lifted my chin toward the field. "Others had Down syndrome."

What I remembered most was how relatable and accepting those kids were. They were by far the most enjoyable people in that school. Any students who tutored for class credit couldn't help but fall in love with them—I could tell by the way they behaved in their presence. In my mind, special needs meant brave because that's what those kids were. Braver than anyone I'd ever met. I was so excited to tutor for them, which my mom would talk about often. Unfortunately, fate had other plans.

A thought occurred to me. "I wonder if I could tutor at one of the local schools." Just as I said those words, the girl kicked the ball again, only this time it went sideways. The auburn-haired woman chased the ball into the far end of the field to retrieve it. At the same time, one of the guys threw his Frisbee to his friend, who missed the catch, allowing the disc to go sailing past the edge of the field and into the road— the same road that stretched to the football stadium ahead of us.

The young girl yelled out, "I'll get it," and ran to get the Frisbee. That would've been fine except a car was coming from the direction of the football stadium, toward her and us.

I expected the Frisbee-throwing college students to stop the girl, but they didn't. They just laughed as if it was funny to watch a girl with special needs running on their behalf. *Jerks.*

My blood pressure shot up. My sunglasses came off.

Maybe the car would stop when whoever was behind the wheel would see the Frisbee or the young girl closing in. There wasn't a lot of time to waste or distance to cross.

When neither the driver nor the young girl slowed, I kicked off my flip-flops, dropped my sunglasses, and ran as fast as I could. The problem was, I was about fifty yards away, and the girl was at least half that distance ahead of me.

"Stop! Don't get that," I said as loud as I could. "I'll get it. There's a car coming!"

The girl kept going as if she didn't hear me, and so did the car, the gap between them narrowing.

Who was driving? A teacher? A student? I waved my arms, trying to get their attention. "Hey, watch out!"

Through the windshield the driver, a girl, was staring at her phone.

"Put your phone down, you dumbass," Amy said in my tailwind.

The young girl kept going, the distance closing fast. She was slower than me, but still several yards ahead. "Wait. Stop. There's a car coming!"

The girl turned her head a fraction and giggled as though a game were underway. Was that what she thought was happening? Was I making her run faster? Her feet stomped across the grass, *thump, thump, thump*.

I pushed myself faster, my muscles burning, my pores spewing moisture. I huffed and puffed, using my arms to help advance me forward. Amy fell back, her breathing heavy.

A shot of hot air slammed into me, but I refused to relent. I continued to wave my arms over my head at the car, at the girl, at the idiot Frisbee-throwing college kids who caused this scene, at anyone who would pay attention. "Stop!"

Seconds ticked away, the situation growing more dire. I'd witnessed enough death and tragedy to last me a lifetime; I wasn't going to let this girl become another victim. No more grieving families. No more loss.

Like a windshield wiper on high speed, my gaze swiped back and forth between her and the car. Even the Frisbee guys were now trying to help, one of them yelling "Stop!" right along with me.

As the girl stepped off the curb and onto the road, I closed in on her. Thrusting my body forward and reaching my hand out, I grabbed her arm and yanked the girl back just as the car sped past, the driver staring at us with dazed eyes and an open mouth. Crunch went the Frisbee. *Was that Rachael?* That random thought flew from my mind as we both fell to the ground, my knee scuffing the curb and my shoulder harnessing the weight of my body. I caught my breath and then pushed myself up to face the girl's tearing eyes.

"Why did you do that?" she asked as she sat up, grief-stricken.

"You were running into the road and a car was coming." I could barely get the words out, my lungs fighting for oxygen. I kept my tone friendly, even though I wanted to shake her. *You should watch where you are going.* She'd scared me half to death.

The girl's lower lip wiggled, her eyes spilling tears.

"I'm so sorry. Did I hurt you?" I climbed to my feet and helped her up.

Amy was off to the side, hunched over and panting. "Jesus. That was a close one."

The Frisbee guys came closer, one with his hand over his mouth, the other just as dazed looking as the driver had been.

Footsteps thumped against the grass before the auburn-haired woman ran up to us. I hoped she didn't think I was hurting her daughter, or student, or whoever this girl was to her.

"Oh my lord, Gwen," the woman said. "You should never run into the road like that. We always check both ways, remember?" Gasping for oxygen and with the same wide eyes, the woman stared at me. "Thank heaven this girl stopped you. Thank you so much." She grabbed hold of my forearm and then let go.

"I don't know why that driver didn't stop," I said exasperated.

The car was gone, nowhere in sight. The model was expensive, like a BMW or a Mercedes. It could've been Rachael, but I was too worried about Gwen to know for sure.

"Because the dumbass was busy staring at her phone," Amy said.

"She said a bad word." Gwen pointed.

Amy smiled back, her tone gentle. "My bad, little lady."

More feet came bounding up the blacktopped road, just before Scott grabbed me, his face beet red, his breathing rapid. "Holy shit. Are you okay?"

Another coin for Gwen's swear jar.

* * *

"Ouch."

Scott cringed outwardly. "Sorry." He blew on my wounded knee—the one he had just dabbed clean of gravel and loose dirt, using one of my washcloths. I felt like a five-year-old. My shoulder was sore, but nothing major. Even my knee wasn't that bad—just a large scrape that burned a little. What was crazy cool about the whole deal was the six-foot-three blond who knelt before me acting as my nurse while I sat on the closed toilet lid in my bathroom.

"Are you sure you're able to walk around campus? We can go another time if you want."

Opening my first-aid kit (the one I always had on hand), he peeled the wrapper off two good-size bandages and covered the scrape. His strong hands worked gently.

"Oh, yeah. It's not that bad. I'll survive."

Scott looked up at me and shook his head. "You never stop surprising me."

"Is she going to make it?" Amy poked her head in through the bathroom door. "Has the *big guy* got you all bandaged up?" She sounded different, her tone lighter. Her change in attitude could've been due to the fact that once Scott had arrived at the scene of the almost accident, he jumped to my aid—or it could've been the fact that Scott practically carried me back to my dorm, telling me how awesome I was for helping that girl. He said he left the football game to see where I was and saw the whole thing happen. "I ran my ass off to get to you in time."

I wanted to tell him it may have been Rachael behind the wheel and ask if she was at the football field watching them play, but I didn't. I wasn't sure it was Rachael since it had all happened so fast, and there was no need to act petty about whether or not she was there. What difference would that make, anyway? Scott had made it perfectly clear how he felt about me.

Gwen's care person introduced herself as Candice. I also discovered that Gwen's school did in fact hire tutors, and since I'd saved Gwen's life, Candice was all too happy to encourage me to sign up. She said I could work with her on campus from time to time.

"I'll send you the link," she said after we exchanged phone numbers. "I think I can even get you assigned to Gwen since her last tutor graduated last year."

I was thrilled, but I wasn't sure Gwen, who still didn't grasp the situation, was. In her eyes, I had grabbed and yanked her to the ground for no apparent reason—which she kept going on about in her own way. I had some work to do to earn her trust, and I was okay with that. I felt so empowered by what had happened—like I had made a difference in someone's life.

Scott stood and faced Amy, a smile nudging at his lips. "Yup. Wonder Woman is all bandaged up." He winked at me.

"Okay, Big Guy. I'll take your word for it."

There it was again. The nickname. Did this mean what I thought it meant?

"Big Guy, huh?" I said, hoping to find out.

"Yup. If he's going to be hanging around, he needs a nickname." Amy leaned against the door casing and crossed her arms.

Scott's brow shot up. "And 'Big Guy' is the best you can do?"

I placed a firm hand on Scott's shoulder. "Don't bother challenging her." Whatever test Amy had given him, Scott had passed. The nickname was proof. And that was good enough for me.

Chapter Seven

On a wet Monday morning, I used one hand to hold my hood in place as I dashed across campus toward Lexington Hall, the home of Arts and Humanities. I blinked a few persistent raindrops off my eyelids while inhaling an earthy fragrance. A gentle rain always reminded me of home—that pattering that prompted my mom and me to cuddle on the couch with a warm blanket and a fun movie. I used to love the sound of the rain as it dripped off the leaves near my bedroom window.

I had been missing home a lot lately. For so long, I had focused on the bad things that had happened—memories of me standing in my childhood home devoid of furniture, warmth, and my family, the walls echoing with memories long lost and future opportunities never experienced. My thoughts had shifted, allowing those precious moments to capture my heart instead of my gut.

I splashed through a puddle as I neared Lexington Hall, an ominous-looking structure with four gigantic columns on each end and a clock tower at its center. It looked like something right out of a movie set.

Through the lobby I dashed, my wet sneakers squeaking against the marble floors. When I arrived at my classroom, a crowd clogged up the doorway. I joined the fray, edging my way inside. The classroom was larger than I had expected, with a drop-down screen in the front and stadium-style seating. Creative Writing was a popular course, or at least a required one. I ventured up the wide steps until I found a seat at the back of the room. It was like climbing a hill to get there. When I found a spot, I took a seat and pulled out my laptop. A note sat waiting, stuck to my screen. "Good luck on your first day, beautiful."

I smiled and touched my lips as I thought of Scott. He had come to my room last night and we had talked for several hours, a few moments of kissing mixed in between. Every time his lips joined with mine, the world faded away for me and it was just us—nothing else existed or mattered. I lost myself in the tenderness of his touch, the spicy scent of his skin, and the radiance of his eyes. My insides pulsed and moistened, ripening and ready for more. Kissing Scott Williams was all I wanted to do anymore.

The sensation that someone was staring at me, forced me to look down a couple of rows at Scott's so-called friends, Mindy and Charlene. *Oh, great.* Given the higher elevation of my seat, I felt like a flag blowing in the wind. I wondered if they knew about Scott and me dating. Was this going to be a problem? I booted up my laptop and decided it didn't matter. Scott had probably dated lots of women on campus, and if I wanted to be with him, I had to accept that fact.

The sound of whispering brought my eyes around the screen. Mindy was showing Charlene an image on her cell phone, or maybe it was a text. Something in the way both women kept glancing back at me felt purposeful. What were they looking at, naked pictures of Scott?

Charlene nudged Mindy's arm. "Text him to come by our room later."

Mindy typed, making a *tap, tap, tap* sound with her acrylic nails. It had always impressed me how women could type with those long nails. Now, it was just annoying.

If she was texting Scott about a possible hookup, he would surely tell her no. I had to believe that.

"Hello, ladies." A guy with a sturdy frame and a shaved head took the seat next to Charlene. He was handsome with ebony skin and deep-brown eyes. "I thought this class was going to be boring as hell, but not with you two here." His eyes twinkled, his smile wide.

Charlene pinched his chin. "Aren't you sweet, Christian."

After pulling his backpack off his shoulder, Christian sat sideways in his seat, engaging both women, his eyes drawn to their enormous chests. They continued to talk with each other until a short woman with wavy brown hair entered through the doorway below. Dressed in a white ruffled top and black dress pants, the woman crossed the room to where she plunked her briefcase down on a small table next to a podium.

"Good morning, class," she said with a welcoming tone. "I'm Dr. Alicia Baker. Welcome to Creative Writing." She pulled out a stack of papers from her briefcase and handed them to a male student in the front row. "Take one and pass it along." Her eyes took in the class. "The course syllabus is being passed around." She pointed to the drop-down screen, already illuminated with a website address. "I assume you are all familiar with Clipboard?" She waited for a few nodding heads. "The syllabus, along with all the class assignments, my office hours, contact information, and anything else pertaining to this class will be posted there." She lowered her hand. "Once you all have a hard copy, I'll go over the highlights with you. While we are waiting, let's go around the room and introduce ourselves. State your name, where you're from, and what you're hoping to gain from this class."

Charlene and Mindy looked at each other and rolled their eyes.

Dr. Baker advanced toward the same front row of students but walked to the opposite end this time. "Let's start with you." She pointed to a girl with short blond hair.

By the time the introductions had come around to Mindy, her answer to the question of what she hoped to gain from the class was college credit. Charlene's answer wasn't any better: "to write creatively."

Dr. Baker exhaled.

When my turn came around, my heart pounded so loudly, I was convinced everyone could hear it. I had never been good at public speaking. In fact, the last time I had spoken to a crowd was at my parent's funeral. Not a fond memory for me. What would I say now? I wiped my palms on my shorts and forced the required words from my lips. "My name is Sara Browne, and I'm from Middlebury, Vermont." I swallowed. "I've always loved reading books. I'm in awe of people who can turn a phrase or introduce characters that linger in my thoughts long after the story has ended. What I'd like to learn from this class is how to improve my own level of writing. I don't expect to be an author."

Mindy and Charlene giggled.

"But I'd like to improve as best I can. I'd also like—"

Charlene groaned. "Is she for real?"

A few chuckles and murmurs floated around my head.

That was all it took. My mind went totally blank. What was I talking about? The room went silent—until Dr. Baker rescued me. "Thank you, Sara." Her eyes shifted to my right, where a guy with curly brown hair sat next to me.

"My name is Isaac ..."

* * *

By eleven o'clock, my stomach growled and my mind wandered. I had just left my Western Civilizations class, which was smaller than Creative Writing and to my relief didn't include Mindy and Charlene. I dashed into the Student Union building and grabbed a slice of pizza, which I ate on my trek back to my dorm. When I got there, a bouquet sat waiting in front of my door. *Uh-oh.* Not another one. To avoid any unnecessary questions from Scott, I had placed Rick's bouquet in the suite living room. Where would this one go?

The note accompanying the arrangement set my mind at ease. "Congratulations on your first day of college. Text me when you get this, Scott." I texted him a thank-you right away.

"You're welcome. Glad you like them," he texted back.

We'd exchanged a few texts all morning, but Scott never mentioned anything about a surprise. I buried my nose in a cluster of daisies while imagining Scott leaving them for me.

Wearing a pair of army boots with socks midcalf, jean shorts, a black T-shirt with the word "Nirvana" printed across the front, and a thin flannel shirt rolled up at the elbows, Amy came shuffling down the hallway. As I admired her outfit, I almost missed the scowl on her face.

"Nice outfit," I said. "How's your morning going?"

Amy's shoulders sagged, enough that her backpack shifted on her shoulder. "It sucked. My math teacher looks like a bundle of fun. A guy made a math joke in his class, and I thought he was going to kick him out."

As she grabbed her backpack strap, Amy's gaze drifted

92

down to the bouquet in my hands. "Are those from Rick again?"

"No. They're from Scott. Wasn't that nice?"

"Yeah." Amy dragged her feet over to her door, where she inserted her key into the lock. "Give me a minute and we can walk to class together."

Our next class was Art Design, which started at noon. I was excited to have a friend in this one, although poor Amy didn't look too enthused.

Outside, the rain had let up but thick clouds hung low. "I was just in Lexington Hall this morning," I said. "You'll never guess who was in my Creative Writing class."

"Who? Anyone good?"

I smoothed my hair back. "Not really. Do you remember those two platinum-blond women who were at the tailgate the other night?"

Amy's phone dinged in a message. After she examined the screen, she faced me with an impassive face. "Huh?"

I broke eye contact with her. "Never mind. It's not important." And it wasn't—or at least it shouldn't have been. I just had to work past it.

Westminster chimes floated through the air as the clock tower sang its quarter-hour warning.

"Our class is on the third floor, right?" Amy asked, looking up at the enormous clock.

"Yup."

"Let's take the elevator." She yawned. "I'm too tired to walk up three flights of stairs."

The acrid smell of paint, oil, and charcoal spilled out from the art room as we entered through the doorway. Student artwork covered the pale yellow walls, the flat filing cabinets, the windowsills, and the shelving. Drying racks, a light table, and a multitude of easels added to the chaotic decor.

Wearing a tweed blazer and khaki pants, our teacher, Dr. Adams, stood at the front of the room next to a desk piled high with folders, art supplies, and books, stroking his full beard while reading from a sheet of paper in his hand. His thick, dark-brown hair tickled against the collar of his shirt.

"Let's sit over there." I nudged Amy toward one of the counter-height tables at the back of the room.

Students filed in behind us while others called out greetings from the doorway as they passed by. With every greeting, Dr. Adams lifted his eyes from his paper, addressing each student with a kind gesture or comment.

After I pulled out my laptop, my eyes traveled the room. "What do you think that means?" I pointed to a quote on the whiteboard behind Dr. Adam's desk. It said something about a rug complimenting a room that I didn't understand.

No rug in sight, just high-grade linoleum speckled with paint.

Amy smirked. "It's from *The Big Lebowski.*" She shook her head, amused. "Looks like our art teacher may have a sense of humor."

"The big what?" I stared at her, perplexed.

Amy pulled out her laptop. "It's a classic movie. I'll tell you about it later."

Dr. Adams cleared his throat. "I hope you all had a nice summer ..."

* * *

By six o'clock that evening, I was crossing campus again, but this time, it wasn't for a class. I was joining Scott for dinner. Since Greek Village was across the complex, I told him I'd meet him halfway. It gave me another chance to orient myself with the layout of the university grounds. When I reached the

Student Union building, I went left, venturing north, past the library in search of a second, smaller cafeteria called Campus Creations. A full head taller than most of the people around him, Scott was easy to spot, talking on his cell phone not twenty feet away from me. That wasn't what caught my eye, though. It was the way he was gripping his phone: as if he wanted to crush it. My ears picked up his harsh tone just as he flailed one hand in the air.

"Yes. I heard you. I'll take care of it." He was practically screaming. "How many times are you going to tell me that?"

Who was he talking to? I slowed my pace at the same time that Scott turned his head in my direction, his body rigid. The moment he spotted me, his eyes widened. "Look. I've gotta go."

He ended the call and shoved his cell phone into the front pocket of his shorts. Then he swiped a hand down his face and smiled. "Hey, there."

Before I could ask if everything was okay, he gave me a quick hug and escorted me through a throng of students and up to the dining hall entrance, where he opened the door for me. Once inside, I grabbed a tray, on which I placed a prepackaged sub sandwich, a side salad, and an iced tea. Scott filled his tray with two burgers, a large fry, some onion rings, and two large bottles of water. Just before we reached the register, he noticed my salad and grabbed one for himself.

We found an empty table in the corner and sat next to each other. As I tore the wrapper off my straw, I took a moment to enjoy his spicy scent. My new essential oil.

Before he touched his food, Scott moved closer and kissed me on the lips. He always tasted of fresh peppermint. Life Savers. From what I'd seen, he never went without. "So, you had a good day?" He rubbed my back for a moment, his fingers easing into my muscles.

"Yes, and thank you again for the flowers." I stuck my straw in my drink before placing my napkin in my lap. "That was so nice of you." I unwrapped my sandwich and took a large bite. Roasted turkey, Swiss cheese, and a ranch-flavored dressing agreed with my taste buds right away.

"Today was a big day. You deserved it. I had to wait for one of your suitemates to let me in."

Since Amy hadn't known about the flowers, it must've been Mia or Sue Anne. I hadn't spent much, if any, time with either of them. It seemed they were always coming when I was going. They were nice enough but not on my wavelength. Plus, they always curled their lips at Amy whenever she was around as though she were a dreg of society, and I didn't like it much.

Scott took a sizable bite of his burger. As he chewed, two muscle-bound guys came strolling by, one wearing a baseball cap backward. "Hey, man," the guy with the hat said to Scott. He carried a large Gatorade. Both men wore nylon gym shorts and tanks covered in sweat stains. A pungent odor tagged along for the ride.

Scott swallowed—his Adam's apple bobbing. "What's up, guys?" He took a sip from his water bottle.

"So, tell me about your day." Scott took another bite of his burger.

His cell phone screen flashed from the table, but he ignored it.

"It was good. I love my art class. Our professor is funny. Amy is in that one. What about you?" I took a bite of my sandwich.

"Cool. I'm pretty stoked about my architecture class. I almost didn't take it because of ... never mind." Scott shook his head and exhaled through his nose.

"Your father?" I touched his arm.

His jaw flexed.

"Is he that rigid?"

Scott pulled a long face. "You have no idea." His voice was coarse, as if loaded with bad memories.

Was that who he had been talking with on his cell phone? His dad?

As though answering my question, his phone flashed again. This time he read the screen from afar.

"I signed up for tutoring at the middle school. I did it after my last class today. Candice told me I may be able to tutor Gwen on campus once in a while. She said she brings Gwen here often," I said. "You remember Gwen, right? She was the girl on the soccer field?"

Scott swallowed another bite. "How could I forget? The girl who was almost run over—" He kissed me again, leaving the scent of his burger salty on my lips. "—until my badass girlfriend saved her."

I picked up my iced tea and sipped from the straw, my shoulder's stacked with pride

"I meant to tell you, I have a scrimmage at the end of the week against a team from Northern Virginia. If you're free, I'd love to have you come. Jason and Heather should be there. I'd like you to meet Heather; you'd like her." Scott took a bite from his second burger.

"I'd like to meet her, too," I said, glad he wanted me there. "When is the scrimmage?"

More activity came from Scott's phone. "It's okay if you need to answer it." It was difficult to ignore.

Scott waved his hand. "It's nothing important. And the game is Thursday at four-thirty."

I searched my mind. "I think I'm free, but let me check my schedule to be sure. I'll text you later and let you know." Since Scott had first told me he was a soccer player, I had been anxious to see him play in a game. Was he an aggressive player or calculating? Either way, I was sure no other player could look better in a tight uniform.

"Hey, did you get caught up in that downpour this morning?" Using his napkin, Scott wiped ketchup from the corner of his mouth.

"No, I must've been in class. It was raining when I went out, but it was light." I pulled the lid off my salad, opened my ranch dressing packet, which I drizzled all over the vegetables, and speared a cherry tomato with my fork. "Did you?"

"I got soaked. I went out for a run, and the sky just opened." His face lit up. "It was actually kind of refreshing."

Unable to get his attention, Scott's phone continued to flash incoming messages. My phone had fewer messages in one week than Scott's had in one meal.

"I usually go for a run on most mornings. You're welcome to join me if you want." He guzzled more water down.

"Sure." I had always enjoyed running and found it helped clear my head. "What time do you go?" After I had swallowed my last bite of sandwich, I stirred the remnants of my salad with my fork and then took another bite.

Scott had just tucked a few French fries into his mouth, which he chewed fast and then swallowed down with more water. "I don't have any morning classes, so I usually go then." He moved in, touching my head with his. "One thing you'll learn about college is not to schedule any early-morning classes. They suck."

I made a mental note. Monday, Wednesday, and Friday were out since my schedule was loaded on those days. "I could go this Thursday and on most Tuesdays and Thursdays. Just promise me that if I'm too slow, you will leave me behind. I don't want to slow you down."

Scott stopped eating and angled his entire body at me, his eyes fixed. "I would never leave you behind." The weight of his words and the sincerity in his eyes gave me chills, but in a good way.

As I concentrated on not turning eight shades of red, Derek came out from behind the food-service counter. When he spotted us, he rushed over to our table.

"Hey, guys." He pointed his thumb over his shoulder. "I just got a job here." Derek sat across from Scott. "I'm stoked. I needed some cash." He used his hands to drum a few beats on the surface of the table.

"That's great, Derek." I took one last bite of salad.

Scott still hadn't tried his.

"Awesome, dude." Scott's phone illuminated for the nth time. He picked it up and stared at the screen. "Hey, I've got a frat meeting soon." He brushed a swath of hair from my shoulder.

I loved the way he touched me, so casually, as though we had known each other for years.

"Are you finished? Want me to walk you back to your dorm?" Scott asked.

I looked at Derek. "Are you free right now?"

"Yeah, I was just going to get something to eat."

I faced Scott. "I think I'll stay and chat with Derek for a few minutes." I crumpled the parchment paper from my sandwich into a ball and gathered up my trash, piling it all on my tray.

"Be right back." Derek dashed away for the food counter.

"I'll get that." Scott got up, handed me my drink, and then picked up my tray along with his. He put his unopened salad on the table. "Maybe Derek will want this. Hey, have they loaded you down with too much homework yet?"

"Not yet. Just some reading for my writing class. Your friends Mindy and Charlene are in that one."

"Who?" Scott's forehead wrinkled.

"You know. The girls you introduced me to at the tailgate." *As if you don't know.*

"Oh." Scott's enthusiasm fell like a rock sinking to the bottom of a lake.

My stomach hardened at his reaction. Had I said something wrong?

An awkward silence followed, until he took our trays to the trash. I wanted to tell him not to worry about it. Mindy and Charlene were his past. I was his future. Well, maybe *future* was a tad overconfident. Then I thought about something Charlene had said to Mindy in class earlier. "Text him to come by our room later." She had said it loud enough that I could easily hear. *Even if she did text Scott, he would say no, right?*

I hated this side of me. The suspicious side. I didn't want to be one of *those* girls. I also didn't want to be the girl who was duped.

When Scott returned to our table, he bent down to kiss me, touching my jaw with his fingers. "I'll call you later."

"Okay."

After he was gone, and while I waited for Derek, I pulled out my phone to send a text to Amy, but she had already beaten me to it.

"What are you up to? I fell asleep, and now I feel like total shit," she wrote.

I giggled to myself and typed, "I'm at the smaller dining hall, Campus Creations. Scott just left, and Derek is here. Want to join? It's right next to the library."

A few minutes later, a message came rolling in: "On my way."

Derek approached, his tray piled high with similar menu choices as Scott. He took the seat across from me. I moved my bag out of the way to make room for him.

"Amy is on her way. Want Scott's salad?" I slid the salad over next to his tray.

"Sure. I'm starved." Derek wasn't kidding. He ate so fast, he had to stop and take breaths. Meanwhile, I scrolled through my phone, listening to my inner coach about Scott. *He said he had a fraternity meeting. He's not with Mindy or Charlene.*

"So, you and Scott are dating now?" Derek had stopped chewing, his tray nearly empty.

Wow, that was some fast eating. "I guess so. I mean, I just met him two days ago." I took another sip of my drink, realizing how surreal that sounded. Two days ago, I hadn't even known Scott existed. Now, my life centered around him, or at least my thoughts did.

"You do know Scott dates a lot of girls, right?"

Oh, great. Another skeptic. "Dated. Past tense. And yeah, so?" I didn't expect this from Derek of all people.

"School just started. Why tie yourself down so soon? Plus ..."

Why was he pausing?

"What?" This conversation was getting über weird. He was really throwing me some curveballs.

"I've heard a lot of shit about him with women. He's like, legendary."

"Heard from who?" My stomach twisted, the sandwich turning into a rock.

"Hey." With sleepy eyes and a pasty complexion, Amy dropped her small leather bag on the table and fell into the seat next to mine, rescuing me from Derek's "Scott" protest. "My advice ... don't fall asleep in the middle of the day." She yawned. "How's the grub here?"

"Good," Derek said. He cleared his throat. "Rick said he's psyched about me joining his fraternity. Freshmen can't pledge during their first semester, but I'll be ready for it this winter."

He rolled his straw paper into a tiny ball, which he threw onto his plate. "Rick's the kind of person who can make things happen. You oughta get to know him better."

"Who, me?" I asked.

Amy rolled her eyes. "Well, he sure as shit isn't talking to me. If he were, I'd say *that* idea sucks ass."

"Never mind." Cheeks flaring, Derek cleared his throat. "Listen, I've gotta head. Thanks for keeping me company, Sara." He tapped Amy on the shoulder on his way out. "Hope you feel better."

Amy lifted her chin. "Yeah, see ya, Shag."

Once Derek was gone, Amy hit the food counter, returning a few minutes later with a bowl of chicken noodle soup, a roll, and some coffee. With each rotation of her spoon, ribbons of gray steam floated from the surface of her soup. "Did I hear you saying something about the big guy?"

"Well, Derek was asking about whether we were dating or not." I tipped my cup up to enjoy the last few drops of my diluted iced tea.

"Oh." Amy blew on a spoonful of soup before tucking it into her mouth. The scents of chicken stock, garlic, and spices floated past my nose. "Hey, I gotta hit the clinic after dinner. They're open until seven. I need some more birth control pills. You might want to grab some for yourself."

I stared at Amy, trying to stop my jaw from hitting the floor. *Birth control?* A few days ago, I hadn't even kissed a guy. Now, I was supposed to be thinking about sex? It wasn't as if I hadn't thought about sex before—I had—but not as though it could actually happen. "W-what are you saying?" My mind tangled with possibilities. Sex was a big deal—the biggest.

"Don't look so worried." Amy studied me. "I know you just met the big guy, but it's been my experience that things can move quickly when it comes to relationships." She got a twinkle in her eyes. "I've never gone longer than a week before hooking up with a guy... or a girl." She tore apart a dinner roll and buttered the inside. "I'm just sayin'. If you want to join, I'm going there after this."

A week? I was thinking more like months. Time to prepare, both mentally *and* medically. What was Scott's normal waiting period? Hours? Minutes? I agreed to go with Amy, thinking I'd better keep my bases covered, but my head was still swirling like a Creemee machine.

We sat in the clinic thirty minutes later waiting for a nurse to call on us. At least they weren't busy. Amy went in first while I stared at posters about pregnancy prevention, counseling services, and signs of drug addiction that blemished the walls, my mind overthinking every aspect of this new idea. I crossed and then uncrossed my legs, shifting in my seat. Kissing was a big deal for me—how was I going to handle something as complicated as sex? What if I was bad at it? What if I did something totally embarrassing? Then there was the biggest fear of all: *What if I got pregnant?* I could barely handle myself, much less another person ... of course, that was why we were here. Then, a comforting thought hit my brainwaves: my first kiss and how epic it had been. This was Scott I was worrying about —the guy who took me on hikes, nursed my scraped knee, and brought me flowers and love notes. I thought of what he had said to me before our hike up the mountain. "Has it occurred to you that the fact that you are different is one of the things I like most about you?" He appreciated me on a level that no one had since my parents had died. He saw me. Amy was right to bring me here. This wasn't a bad thing. It was a way to stay safe. When the time was right, I wanted to be ready.

* * *

I warmed the bench with Jason and Heather, cheering on Scott's team. With long, shiny black hair, olive skin, and distinctive brown eyes, Heather looked like a Hawaiian native. She was also incredibly nice. So was Jason, who sat next to her, engrossed in the game. When Scott scored a goal, Heather grabbed my arm. We all jumped to our feet, and I cheered until my throat strained. When we returned to our bench, Heather scooted closer to me.

"So, you and Scott are together now?" She spoke loudly to compete with the crowd around us. "Jason said he's pretty psyched about it."

At least she didn't feel the need to warn me about Scott like Derek, Rick, or even Amy had, although Amy had come around.

"Scott has talked a lot about you and Jason. He thinks the world of both of you," I said as one of our players threw the ball to Scott, who kicked it downfield before attempting another goal—this time unsuccessfully.

"I've known Scottie since we were in high school." She spoke with a sense of pride. "He's usually pretty chill when it comes to girls." Her gaze shifted to the field, where a player from the other team had kicked the ball out of bounds.

Heather knew Scott in a way that I didn't. I wished I could ask her about his past. Derek had called it legendary. Was that true? Given the newness of our relationship, it felt too soon to start grilling his friends.

During the second half of the game, the competition grew more intense. None of us spoke, absorbed by the action. Scott and his teammates manipulated the soccer ball as though it were an extension of their bodies. I couldn't do with my hands what they were doing with their feet.

At the end of the game, our team achieved victory, 2-0, with Scott scoring one of the two winning goals. I walked with

Jason and Heather to the exit, where they peeled off for the dorms and I detoured for the locker rooms. I couldn't wait to congratulate Scott on his win. How exciting it was to watch a game like that, especially since I knew one of the players. I was a huge fan already.

"Waiting for Scott?" I turned toward Rachael, who shot me a look that could peel paint off the walls. I had never been a popular person, but she stared at me as though I belonged nailed to a stake over an open fire. What was *she* doing by the locker room?

Since she knew I was waiting for Scott—she had to—I didn't bother to answer. Instead, I searched through my phone. Social media my distraction.

Rachael cackled. "What a joke." She regarded her friends, then me. "Girl, you are way out of your league. Seriously."

Her friends gobbled their support like a flock of turkeys. At least, that's what it sounded like to me. Luckily, that was all she said as she sauntered past.

A few minutes later, three solid-looking men, who I assumed were on the team, came bursting through the locker room door, a cloud of fresh soap accompanying them. The three of them wandered off, pushing each other and laughing.

Another five minutes passed, and I was about to ask a bystander if there was another exit to the locker room when Mindy and Charlene strolled by. What was this? A Scott Williams's exes parade? Shoulders back, boobs forward, both women walked along as though they owned the sidewalk, letting the sun glimmer off their long, tanned legs.

Were they also looking for Scott?

Mindy spoke. "Make sure you give his muscles a good rubdown. He likes that after a game." Wearing a catlike grin, Charlene nodded. With a flip of her hand, she and Mindy continued on their way as though I were a gnat she had just swatted off her acrylic nail.

I swallowed what felt like a brick. Who was coming next? The cheerleading squad? By the time Scott came strolling out with wet hair, smelling of fresh cologne, I was close to fuming.

"Hey, babe. I'm so glad you were able to come. That was the best game I've had in a long time." Holding a gym bag in one hand, Scott wrapped his arm around my waist with the other, pulling me closer. "My best girl was at my best game." He touched his lips against mine. It was just what I needed in that moment.

* * *

The following day, I headed to the library to work on a paper I had to write for my Western Civilization class. I needed to use their printer. I passed by Derek and Rick on my way in. They were really chumming it up lately. Rick acted especially happy to see me, but I wasn't sure why.

"Where are you off to?" Rick asked.

"Oh, hi, Rick. Hey, Derek. Library. I've gotta print some stuff off."

Rick reached into the back pocket of his pastel shorts. "I've got a huge credit on my student card if you want to use it." He opened his wallet.

I put my hand up. "No. That's okay. I just funded mine ... but thanks anyway."

He put his wallet back. "I also have a decent printer in my room if you ever need to use it."

I took a step closer to the library door. "Okay, thanks."

"I'll text you and Amy later," Derek said as the two of them wandered off.

The library housed a small café where you could get Starbucks if you wanted. Rachael was standing in line when I passed by. I wasn't in the mood for one of her snide comments, so I walked fast so she wouldn't see me.

I found a study area, sat, and opened my laptop. There was another note waiting for me from Scott: "Thinking about you."

I sent him a quick text. "I got your note. Thinking about you, too, handsome." If Amy could have a nickname for everyone, so could I. My mother had often referred to my father as handsome, so it seemed fitting.

An hour of writing, and I hadn't made much progress, although I had at least put together an outline for my paper, which was due on Monday. I chose the topic: Influence of Classical Greece on the Foundation of Western Civilization. Mind blown. History had never been my subject, but it was part of my core curriculum. Scott had bragged about Jason being a history genius, and I wondered if he had any tips that could help me remember this stuff. I took a bottle of water out of my backpack to quench my thirst while thinking about it. I screwed the top back on my water bottle and sent my file to the printer. As I crossed the library, I thought about Rick's offer. Did he honestly think I would go to his room to print a document? I swiped my student card and then went through the process of printing my stuff.

When I returned to my study area, my laptop was off, the screen blank. It wouldn't power up, either. *Battery?* No, I had just charged it right before I left my dorm. My water bottle was three-quarters full when I had left it a few minutes ago. Now it was empty. A few droplets beaded on the keyboard. I picked up the now empty bottle, which was still upright, not tipped over, its cap secured in place. Had someone opened my bottle, tipped it over, and put the cap back on? *What the?* I looked around. Nothing about this situation made sense. The first thing that came to mind was sabotage—the second, Rachael.

"I'll return the favor," she had vowed at the tailgate. Was this payback for the spilled-beer incident? Was a laptop worth the same as a Versace outfit?

That night, I walked to my car to do a grocery run. When I got there, my windows were marred with pink marker, the words "Watch your back," in all caps. The windshield, the side windows, and the back. They were all covered. I used the hand wipes in my car to clean it off.

It seemed ruining my laptop wasn't enough; Rachael was on the warpath. If not her, then someone else, which worried me beyond words. Considering my hypersensitivity to dangerous situations, it was like throwing gasoline on the tinderbox that was my PTSD. No one knew me here. And after running the situation through my mind, the only reason I could come up with, aside from Rachael's ruined outfit, was my new relationship with Scott. Either Rachael was jealous or someone else was. Mindy and Charlene came to mind. Needless to say, I didn't sleep a wink that night.

Chapter Eight

I had to move past the pranks and the laptop sabotage, mainly because I had a new obstacle to overcome: Abigail.

"It seems like you have an awful lot to adjust to, with college and everything. I just want you to be careful." For ten long minutes, I had been pacing my room while Abigail lectured me on the other end of the line. The subject: my new relationship with Scott.

She had witnessed me at the lowest point in my life. Falling for an upperclassman seemed like an impulsive thing to do. *To her.* It didn't seem that way to me. I'd spent six years lonely and depressed.

"I will. Wait till you meet him. He's a really nice guy." I sounded hopeful. "He even passed my friend Amy's test, and she's a tough nut to crack."

"I'm sure he is, but you haven't been around boys for a long time. I'm not sure you're ready for a relationship so soon. Just take things slow."

More pacing. "I will."

A long silence followed.

Abigail sighed through the phone. "Joel and I will be there next weekend for parents' weekend." Her tone lightened. "I can't wait to see you." The slight tremor in her voice told me how much. "I realize you missed your teenage years, and I'm glad you're enjoying them now. Once we meet Scott, I'm sure we'll agree with you."

"Don't worry, Abigail. I'll be careful. Hey, I gotta run. Love you."

I got off the phone, grabbed a bottle of water, and took a few long sips. The call had been more stressful than I had expected. There was the possibility that Abigail was right. Could I handle a relationship so soon? We'd been seeing each other for a few weeks now, and my attraction for Scott had only intensified. When we weren't together, due to his busy schedule or mine, I missed him like crazy. It was scary to need another person so much.

The strums of an acoustic guitar floated through the wall, telling me Luke was visiting Amy. They had been spending as much time together as Scott and I had. I liked Luke. He was as mellow as Amy was bold. She'd tried to rile him a few times, but so far he'd kept his cool—in fact, I think he enjoyed the challenge *and* the attention.

It was late Friday afternoon, and I hadn't seen Scott since Wednesday. He'd invited me to an impromptu party at his fraternity house later, so I was excited about that—and nervous.

While I waited for Scott, I took a shower and then picked out a loose-fitting, long-sleeved white top and a pair of skinny jeans. After I had finished getting dressed, drying my hair, and putting on my makeup, I grew impatient.

I opened my *new* laptop since my old one suffered from water damage—something I had confirmed with a techie at the school help desk. However it had happened, Rachael or otherwise, I was determined to keep this one protected. Another handwritten note was waiting for me. "Missing you," it said, with a heart drawn around it. Leaving sweet notes was Scott's thing, and I loved it—to the point where I found myself searching for them as if I was on a treasure hunt. Yesterday, I had found one in my math folder that said "Have a great day, babe," and last week, in my wallet, "You're the most beautiful girl in the world." My favorite was "I'm so lucky to be with you." I had found that one stuck to my bathroom mirror.

A light knock on my door had my feet sprinting across the room and my hands flinging the door open—so my eyes could drink in my gorgeous boyfriend.

"Hey, babe. Are you ready to go?" he asked bending down to kiss me.

"Yup. I just have to put my shoes on." I searched for my wedge sandals, which were by my wardrobe. Scott grabbed my hand and pulled me back like I was a rubber band.

The way he looked at me—that naughty spark in his eyes—told me he was full of mischief. "We don't have to rush, you know." He closed the door, wrapped his arms around my waist, and lifted me up to meet his mouth. "I've missed you." He whispered the words, his lips tiptoeing down my neck.

I tilted my head back and let my hands roam the stiff cords of Scott's back. Since my visit to the clinic, I had thought a lot about what my first sexual experience with Scott would be like. I imagined his muscular body hovering over mine, those hypnotic blue eyes reaching into my soul. I wanted it to be epic —just like my first kiss had been. The way Scott nuzzled my neck made me wonder if that moment had arrived.

Before I could think any more lustful thoughts about it, my phone dinged. I snapped out of my trance and read the screen on my desk.

It was Abigail: "I do trust your judgment, Sara. JUST TAKE THINGS SLOW."

All the way from Vermont, Abigail had managed to parent me from afar. I envisioned her standing there, arms crossed, eyes judging.

Okay, Abigail, you win.

I took a step back from Scott.

He leaned forward as though I had been holding him up.

"I'm starving." My stomach gurgled its support. "Could we grab dinner before we go?" I threw on my shoes and snatched my jacket off my chair.

Scott ran a hand down his face as though trying to adjust to this new development. "Um, yeah, I could eat."

* * *

After a quick dinner at a local pizza joint, we'd arrived at Scott's room, moments ago.

"I'm sorry I haven't had you here sooner. I kind of let things go over the summer."

"It's okay. It looks nice now."

"That's because I cleaned. Just for you." He leaned in and nuzzled on my neck, his hands everywhere.

"Wait, I want to check out your room." I pushed him back, using a little extra force.

His eyebrows slanted downward like two lightning bolts, telling me he didn't like it much. I wished he'd chill out. I loved the affection but needed a minute. It may have been the intensity of his eyes or maybe it was the fact that I was in *his* territory now—or it could have been the fact that a rowdy party was going on just a few feet away—one that we had squeezed through to get here. Regardless, I was on edge. For our first time, I'd imagined a romantic evening, Scott patient and ready to ease me into this new stage of our relationship, not pepperoni pizza burps and loud music vibrating the walls. Okay, maybe this wasn't the perfect scenario, but I could work with what I had—a gorgeous man who had gone to great effort to clean his room. *That's something, right?*

My eyes took a tour of his "man cave," which was much bigger than my room, enough that he could house a full-size futon, which he probably used for the PlayStation sitting in front of it atop a beat up old coffee table. A good-size TV rested on his dresser against the wall. Two floor-to-ceiling windows, vinyl blinds covering them, provided ample amounts of natural light. His sport car and soccer posters, along with the enormous American flag that hung proudly on the wall above his queen-sized bed, reeked of maleness. What didn't reek of maleness was the strawberry scent lingering in the air.

"Wow. You have your own bathroom."

"One of the perks of being an officer in the frat."

"And it smells nice in here." *Not like a locker room, thank God.*

Scott scratched his head, smirking. "Okay, I'll admit I bought a few air fresheners." He came up from behind me and peeled my jacket from my shoulders, draping it over his chair.

Not quite ready to get all hot and heavy, I drifted around the room, feeling his eyes following me. To hide behind my jitters, I did what I often did when I was nervous: I babbled. "Oh, did I tell you about the art teacher Amy and I have?"

"Uh, I think so." Scott followed along in my shadow.

"Professor Adams is cool. You don't even realize you're learning in his class. I wish all my teachers were like him." I picked up a PlayStation FIFA game from his coffee table.

"Cool," Scott said.

Shouting and laughter filtered through the door, along with a continuous stream of loud music. "Is Derek coming to the party?" I put the game back down.

"He's planning on pledging, so he better come."

"If he pledges, I'm glad you'll be here to watch out for him." I opened the door to the bathroom, peered inside, and then closed it again.

"He doesn't need a babysitter, babe." Scott gave me a side-look and cleared his throat. "Does my bathroom pass your inspection?" A playful smirk spread across his face.

"Yup."

As he narrowed the gap between us, he placed his hands on my shoulders, giving them a tender massage. The warmth from his fingers helped to ease my tight shoulders.

"Things haven't come easily for Derek. He told me it took him three years to afford his tuition to come here."

"I'll look out for him. Don't worry, babe." Scott worked his fingers farther down my back. "You're so tense."

He was right. I was tense. When it came to sex, I had no idea what to do. Kissing required little skill. This was different.

I rested my head back against Scott's firm chest, my muscles feeling like soft dough beneath his touch. My mind drifted, and then Scott spoke.

"You've missed the most important part of my room." He stopped the massage and took my hand, leading me across the room to his bedside.

On the nightstand sat an eight-by-ten framed photo of the two of us. Jason had taken the picture a week ago at one of Scott's soccer games. I was kissing Scott's cheek while he flashed his perfect smile for the camera. I hadn't realized he'd gotten the pic developed.

I picked up the frame and traced my fingers over the frozen image. "I love it."

Scott took the frame from my hands and placed it back in its rightful place. "See, I have you next to me when I go to bed at night." He tapped my nose.

I peered deep into Scott's blue eyes. The edges of his irises were darker tonight, more vibrant. I'd seen that raw passion before when we were on the mountain.

"It's much better having you here in person." After placing a few short, tender kisses on my lips, he put my hand against his chest and held it there. Underneath a solid wall of muscles, his heart pounded. "You are always with me in here."

Awww. I melted.

He sat on his bed, covered by a blue-and-white-striped comforter, and guided me down to join him. Reaching up, he cupped my jaw and stroked my cheek with his thumb. I closed my eyes as his lips grazed over my earlobe and then my neck, his breath fresh and his lips, supple and needy. Caught up in the moment, I ran my fingers through his loose curls and inhaled, drinking in his spicy scent. As his mouth ventured along my neckline, I leaned my face closer, inviting him to find my lips, my body feverish—for him. With his velvety tongue, he explored my mouth for several minutes while I explored his. His hand, warm and adventurous, roamed underneath my blouse. With nimble fingers, he glided up and down my back until, *pop*, my bra went slack. His hand came around to the front, where he touched my nipples in a way that caused a yearning so powerful it devoured all my other senses. I didn't want him to stop. Okay, so sex may be easier than I thought. Inside, my body pulsed and moistened, ready for more. I was just about to put his hand between my legs when the door swung open.

I recoiled, yanking Scott's hand away and my shirt down. I braced my hand against my chest and swallowed, trying to catch my breath.

Scott bared his teeth. "Jesus Christ. Don't you knock?!"

With shoulder-length, shaggy blond hair and a body as thin as a rail, Willy, one of Scott's housemates, appeared in the doorway in board shorts and a tank. I'd seen him with Scott a few times around campus.

"Oh, shit." He shielded his eyes as if we were naked which we weren't, thank God. "I didn't get a text, dude."

Had Willy seen anything? My cheeks sizzling, I wanted to cover my head with Scott's comforter.

Scott barked at his friend, revealing a side of him I had never seen before. "Get the fuck out of here!"

Geez, Scott.

Willy bolted out the door as though he were on fire, and for a moment I was tempted to go with him. The situation was far more embarrassing for me than it was for Scott.

Once the blood had drained from Scott's cheeks, he said, "I'm sorry, babe. Where were we?" He moved closer for a second round, but I wasn't having it. Not here. Not now.

"This has been great, but ..." How was I going to say this? *Sex is a big deal for me, and this situation is too cringey for me.*

"I'll lock the door." Scott rose until I grabbed his arm.

"That's okay." I chewed on the inside of my cheek. "I mean, maybe this isn't the best time for this."

Scott's face went flat, like I had just told him the worst news. For several uncomfortable seconds, he stared at me with vacant eyes. Without saying a word, he got up and went into his bathroom. As soon as the sink turned on, I hooked my bra and straightened my blouse. A few moments later, Scott reappeared, wiping his face with a towel.

"Let's go join the party, then." He threw the towel onto the futon like a quarterback would pass a football. A sharpness had replaced the sweetness in his voice, his eyes unfriendly.

"Are you okay?" I rose and met him by the door.

Without looking at me, he said, "I'm fine. Let's go." His speech was clipped and the muscles in his jaw flexed. With his brow bearing down, it was clear to me he wasn't fine.

As soon as Scott opened the door, music and chatter amplified down the hallway. I laced my fingers inside of his hand, feeling a distance between us I hadn't felt before. I wasn't saying I *never* wanted to have sex with him, just not right now. And I didn't appreciate him making me feel bad about it.

When we reached the kitchen, Scott released my hand to greet several of his fraternity brothers with their usual bro handshakes and shoulder bumps. Several women were filling their beers or mixing drinks while chatting with each other. Not one of them acknowledged me, nor did I expect them to.

Amidst the rowdy voices and music, Willy approached Scott, his shoulders hunched, his eyes timid. They visited for a few minutes, and then they walked out of the room together. Was I supposed to follow?

A few feet away a girl with shoulder-length blond hair moved to the music with her friend. In fact, most of the girls around me were swaying in one way or another. Everyone had a friend, a drink, or a guy, except for me. I was the loner ... again.

And there I remained, stiff as a new pair of shoes and just as uncomfortable ... until I decided to do something about it. On my way out of the kitchen in search of Scott, I ran into a familiar face, and yet not so familiar. It was Derek, though new and improved.

"Hey, there," I said, happy to see him. "Not working tonight?" With wide eyes, I scanned over his new haircut, clean-shaven skin, and outfit. Shaggy had grown up. "Wow. You look nice." I straightened the collar of his polo where it had flipped up. He even smelled nice.

Derek took a sip from his red cup. "Yeah, Rick set me up.

He knows a guy who owns a men's store over at the mall. He got me all this for cheap. You like my new look?"

I was nostalgic for the old version, but I said yes anyway.

An attractive girl with shiny brown hair gave Derek the once-over on her way into the kitchen. "Hi, Derek," she said before she hugged one of her friends.

"Oh, hey, Zoe."

Derek's smile stretched wider.

He deserved a leg up, and Rick was giving him one. I was happy for him.

"Have you seen Scott?" I couldn't believe Scott had just up and left me. He knew I didn't know anyone.

"Yeah." Derek tipped his head back. "He's at the bar."

I peered around him to find Scott in the room that housed a tiki bar, enjoying the company of his friends and not me. Where was the guy who had been so attentive over the past several weeks? This person didn't seem to care.

I hooked my arm inside of Derek's. "Come on."

The two of us made our way over to the tiki bar, where Scott, Willy, Kevin, and a guy named Owen were all talking sports. Rick was behind the bar, pouring drinks.

I placed my hand on Scott's lower back. "Did you forget me?"

Instead of answering me, Scott said, "Who's up for shots?"

Willy piped in first. "Uh, hell yeah."

"Bring it on," Owen, the military-looking guy, screamed.

Kevin slapped his hand down on the bar as hoots and hollers swirled around him. "Line 'em up, boss man."

After lining the bar with shot glasses, Rick poured a syrupy liquid into each of them. Cinnamon wafted past my nose.

Scott tipped his head back and downed the shot, as did the rest of the group.

Derek reached for the shot glass closest to him when Kevin patted his shoulder. "Pledges don't get shots, dude."

My forehead tensed as Derek pulled his hand away.

"Chill out, man," Rick said. "He's not pledging yet." Rick slid a full shot over to Derek. "Go ahead, dude. Drink up."

Kevin pulled back, eyeing Rick. "Since when do *you* give pledges shots?" He opened his mouth to say something, but then stopped short. "Oh, wait. I remember."

What? That he is trying to be nice?

Rick's nostrils flared. "I paid for this bar and all the liquor behind it, so why don't you shut the fuck up?" He stared Kevin down, and I worried he was going to punch him.

Weren't they like best friends?

Kevin was the first to unlock his gaze. He stared at Derek, who was holding the shot in question. "Drink up, dude. When pledging comes around, you'll be cleaning up my puke."

"*Jesus*, dude." This time Scott glared at Kevin. "What crawled up your ass? Chill out, man." He patted Derek's shoulder, then spoke to Rick. "Let's give our man Derek a real welcome." He swirled his index finger in the air, motioning for another round, which Rick seemed all too happy to provide.

Holding a full beer in his hand, Kevin shook his head and then wandered off, taking the tension with him.

Rick refilled the tiny glasses. "Would you like one?" he asked me. "It's Fireball."

"No thanks."

While Scott downed his second shot, Rick disappeared into the kitchen, returning a moment later with a glass bottle in his hand. A picture of an apple decorated its label. "Here, try this." He poured the yellowish liquid into a plastic cup. "It's hard cider, made locally."

The scent of apple hit me immediately. "Thanks." I slid the

cup under my nose before taking a small sip. Not bad. Definitely better than beer.

I leaned closer to the bar. "Derek looks great." I mouthed the words *thank you* to Rick.

Scott's head angled in my direction, his ears perked.

Oh, so you do know I'm here.

Rick used a towel to wipe up a few small droplets from the bar. "No problem. He deserves it."

While I sipped on my drink, Scott and his friends continued to discuss sports. Every time I snuggled into Scott's side, he edged himself away from me. At one point, he even glared in a leave-me-alone type of way, enough that I removed my hand from his back. More shots followed. The whole situation was fast becoming a hard pass for me.

I remembered seeing a game room to the left of the foyer when I had first arrived. "Want to play some darts?" I said into Derek's ear. I hoped it was available.

"Sure."

"I'll be back," I said to Scott, who was debating Owen over the skills of two quarterbacks I had never heard of. When he didn't acknowledge me, I took off through the living room and into the foyer.

Derek followed.

Scott stayed where he was.

Like everywhere else within the walls of the Kappa house, the game room was a flood of energy. I passed by two guys spinning the knobs on the foosball table at a frantic pace on my way toward the dartboard waiting vacant at the back of the room. Derek and I set our drinks on a small table and then collected the darts from a case mounted against the wall. Tiny holes speckled the walls and the ceiling. I felt like making a few new holes myself.

"Ladies first." Derek stepped back and motioned with his hand.

The muscles between my shoulder blades burned with tension as I took my spot on an X taped to the floor. *If Scott liked me, then what did it matter when our first time happened?* I took aim. My first shot was a fifteen pointer, my second shot hit the double-ring on the twenty-point section, and my third shot hit the bull's-eye. *Was this how all guys behaved about sex?* In total, my one turn had compiled over a hundred points. I stared at the board, wondering if I was seeing things.

Derek furrowed his brow. "Do you play darts a lot?"

"Not really." I was amazed at my accuracy. "Just beginner's luck," I said, retrieving the darts and then using a tiny piece of chalk to record my score on the miniature chalkboard.

Derek closed one eye and threw his first dart, penetrating the outer edge of the board. Zero points. "Where's Amy tonight?"

"She's hanging with Luke and his friends."

Derek's second shot bounced off the wall and fell to the floor, but his third dart hit the seventeen-point section. I was relieved he had at least scored *some* points. He collected the darts.

I readied myself to make my next shot when someone squealed in the other room. Derek and I both craned our heads in the direction of the foyer, where two girls hugged each other. Dressed like exotic dancers in form-fitting dresses, Mindy and Charlene were, once again, the center of attention. I rolled my eyes, watching all the males ignite with testosterone.

"Your turn." Derek's prompt returned my mind to better things.

My feet found the X, where I made my next three shots, scoring another sixty points. *Wow.* Poor Derek fell way behind.

"Jesus, your aim is spot on." Derek kept looking at me as if I were really a world darts champion and I had kept it from him.

I retrieved the darts and recorded my score. It seemed frustration toward Scott had improved my accuracy. "You're getting better," I said in a hopeful tone.

"Well, well, well. Look who's here."

Great. The Barbie twins had found me.

Chapter Nine

I pretended I didn't hear them—at least for a few seconds, so I could prepare myself. When I turned around, Mindy and Charlene were standing next to Derek. His eyes looked like they were going to pop out of their sockets, his cheeks red.

What do you want?

"We have a very important question for you.'" Slurring her words, Charlene pointed her acrylic fingernail at me.

"What would that be?" I figured there was no chance it was about our Creative Writing class. It was bad enough I had to tolerate them every Monday, Wednesday, and Friday.

"We were just wondering when you plan on returning our boy toy to us." With a seductive sway, Mindy put her hand on her hip.

My cringe factor shot through the roof, the darts cutting into my clenched hands.

"That's up to Scott, not me." I swallowed, wondering how the night could get any worse.

Both girls looked at each other, grins cunning.

My stomach lurched into my throat.

"*Sara*, is it?" Charlene said, her apathy bold and obvious. "We'll be waiting when our man wants a little *fun* back in his life."

Mean girls. This school was full of them. Petty, immature women, who couldn't stand losing. Especially the one claiming that Scott was *her* man now. The edges of the darts cut deeper into my fists as I held back the urge to throw them all at their heads. I hated to think about what the three of them had experienced together. The fact that Scott was already upset with me about *not* performing sexually for him only made matters worse. My stomach was a vat of acid.

"I'll be sure to let him know." I kept my tone sugary sweet but with a bite.

"Come on, ladies, play nice. Pull your claws in," Rick said as he sauntered over. "Scott's got a special lady now. Don't be jealous."

If only Scott were here defending our relationship instead of Rick.

Both girls glared at Rick as he gave Derek a bro handshake.

"Just look at her." Rick held his hand out in front of him. "He's found the hottest girl at *this* school." He winked at me.

"Jealous? You don't know shit." Mindy looked at Charlene, her lips tight, her chin high.

"I know that much." Rick took a sip from his cup, unfazed.

"Only if you like that poor-me orphan-girl routine." Mindy stuck her finger in her mouth and pretended to gag.

Who told them? If it was Scott, we were going to have another problem.

"We know what Scott wants, and it's not 'Drab Queen' over there." Charlene spun on her heel and took off, her clone by her side.

I looked down at my outfit. Drab Queen? That was a new

one. After they were gone, I rolled my eyes at Rick. "Thanks." I felt like a cartoon character with steam billowing out of my ears.

"No problem. They don't lose well." Rick read the scoreboard. "Looks like you're crushing Derek."

"More like destroying me." Derek closed one eye and readied his next shot. "My aim sucks." A moment later, he was pulling his darts out of the paneling.

Rick and I tried not to laugh. It was easy for me since I wasn't enjoying much about this night anyway. If Scott had dated women like Mindy and Charlene, then what was he doing with me? I was nothing like them, nor would I ever be. I thought we had a connection that went beyond sex. Not that I didn't *want* to have sex with him. Why else was I on birth control? I wasn't going to let him pressure me.

"Did you guys hear about that drunk dude who ran naked through the farmer's market last weekend?" Rick took another sip from his cup. "The market off of Water Street."

"No." I returned to the X taped to the floor.

"What happened?" Derek grabbed his drink off the table, eyebrows raised.

"From what I heard, he was a big burly dude with a long beard." Rick rubbed big circles over his abdomen. "Beer belly and all."

He had me curious. "Really?"

"Oh, yeah, I guess he was hammered and ran through the farmer's market looking for his car. The idiot ran into a woman who screamed and flung something into the air—I think it was a bag of apples—that hit the windshield of another car driving by." Rick became more animated as he spoke. "Then *that* fucking car veered off the road and plowed into a telephone pole." He laughed and flung a hand up. "Mass chaos in Charlottesville, Virginia." He took a sip from his cup.

Funny story. Although I worried about the driver of the car.

Rick set his drink down and stared at the dartboard. "Hey, have you guys ever played beer darts before? …"

I sipped on my cider and continued my game with Derek while Rick told us about the various dart games one could play for drinks.

I kept glancing in the direction of the foyer, hoping Scott would appear. The lights dimmed in the other room, and the music changed tempo. Several girls whoo-hooed, waving their hands in the air and forming a small train as they danced out of the game room and across the foyer.

I had just thrown my last dart, which sealed poor Derek's fate. His aim was as bad as mine was good.

"Let's check things out." Rick tipped his head toward the other room.

"Okay." I nudged Derek, who rattled his head, as if trying to recover from the landslide dart game. Together, we followed Rick.

Several people, mostly girls, had gathered in the center of the living room and moved to the music. Anyone who wasn't dancing took to the perimeter to watch. I located Scott. He was standing in the doorway near the tiki bar room facing us. When I waved, he didn't wave back. To be fair, I wasn't sure he could see me from across the way and through all the gyrating bodies.

"I see Scott. I'm going over." Both Derek and Rick nodded and followed me.

When I reached him, I tugged on his arm and tipped my head up, hoping for a kiss. The lights reflected off his glassy eyes as he stared down at me, offering nothing more than a blink. He also reeked of alcohol.

"Everything okay?"

He shrugged.

I knew what was wrong but didn't want to believe it. He

expected sex from me at this party, without caring about what *I* wanted. I grew less sheepish and more annoyed with each passing second.

I turned around and thought about what to do next. On the outer edge of the dance floor—literally ten feet in front of us—Mindy and Charlene were moving their bodies seductively to the beat. They were staring at Scott, who rewarded them by staring right back at them. Then came the beckoning fingers. *Come join us, teddy bear.*

I wanted to throw up.

What did Scott do? Nothing. He just remained there transfixed. Between the loud music, the stagnant air, and the humiliating dance display, I grew queasy. One song ended and another started, but it made no difference to me. The invisible interaction between Scott and his *girls* had soured my stomach and my mood. My fears about Scott's past were front and center.

Someone tapped me on the shoulder, and I just about jumped out of my skin.

"Sorry." Rick smiled. "I didn't mean to scare you. Would you like to dance?" He looked up at Scott. "Mind, bro?"

The statue formerly known as Scott didn't answer, so I did instead.

"I'd *love* to dance." I had never danced in public, but I was willing to try anything at this point.

Rick led me through the animated crowd, far away from Scott and his women. Disco lights floated over the walls and ceiling. I found a beat and moved my body to it as unassumingly as possible, trying to blend in. When it came to dancing, I was a total spaz. Rick took hold of my hands and guided me through several dance moves, swiveling and spinning me around. I must have stepped on his feet at least a dozen times. Whether he didn't notice or he was too polite to acknowledge it, he never said anything or even flinched. Just when I found my rhythm, the song ended abruptly.

"Thank you for the dance." I fanned my cheeks with my hand. "Sorry I was such a klutz."

"You were fine. And anytime."

An irate Kevin came stumbling over. "Owen is taking over your bar. He's mixing all sorts of shit together."

Rick rolled his eyes and firmed his jaw. "Dickweed." He put his hand out for me to go first, and together we made our way back over to Scott. Derek was nearby chatting with a cute redhead when I got there. Neither Scott's feet nor his eyes had moved an inch.

"I gotta head back to the bar. Catch you all later." Rick patted my shoulder and then left. "Get your slimy fuckin' hands off my liquor, asshole, unless you're planning on paying for it."

Now what? If Scott expected me to stand next to him while he fantasized over two women who had less depth than a mud puddle, he was mistaken. I returned to the dartboard area where I had left my drink. Thankfully, Derek had followed me over.

"You want to play another game?" He picked up his drink and took a sip. "Clean slate?"

"No, maybe later." Another idea came to mind. "Let's dance, Derek." I grabbed his hand and dragged him out of the game room.

"Oooookay."

When we reached the living room, Mindy and Charlene were gone, and I half expected Scott to be gone with them. He was in the same exact spot wearing that same exact expression: deadpan.

It took me all of two seconds to realize that Derek was about as comfortable with dancing as I was. At least the fear of looking like a complete dork helped distract me. When the fast-paced song ended and one with a much slower tempo replaced it, the floor cleared out, leaving couples and a few drunk girls left behind. I draped my arms over Derek's shoulders, tethering him in place. I didn't want to be alone right now.

"What's up with Scott? He barely spoke to me," Derek said. "Is he upset about something?"

I tried not to scowl. "Who knows?"

We swayed in place for several minutes until my mountain of a boyfriend decided to take notice.

Derek stopped dancing. He removed his hands from my waist and looked up at Scott.

"Can I cut in?" Scott asked.

Derek backed up. "Sure, dude."

"No thanks," I said before crossing through the foyer and over to the dartboard area, leaving both men behind.

Scott was right on my tail. "What's your problem?" he asked when we got there, his tone snide.

I spun around. "That's a funny question coming from you."

His eyes flared. "What the fuck is that supposed to mean?"

I stared at him in wonder. Was he really acting this way?

"Look, Scott. If you want to go play with your *dolls*, go right ahead. No one is stopping you." Anger boiled the acids roaming my gut.

"Dolls?" He looked at me as if he had no idea what I was talking about.

"Oh, please. Do I look that dumb?"

"Whatever. I'll be at the bar." Scott shook his head and took off, leaving me alone for a second time, something he told me he would never do. No discussion, no apology.

Turning my back to the crowd at the foosball and poker tables, I took a moment to chill out, gripping the small table that still held my drink. This was the first time Scott and I had argued. He said he liked that I was different, but tonight he made me feel wrong about it. What I needed him to understand was how foreign this was to me. I was already way out of my comfort zone. I was in a fraternity house stuffed with a bunch of drunk people, and I couldn't have felt more alone. It was just as it used to be. Whether he meant to or not, Scott had demoralized me as a person. I felt unimportant—and worse, dispensable.

I wasn't a fan of walking back to my dorm alone, but the thought of seeking Scott out was worse in my mind, and I didn't want to keep bugging Derek. Still, walking alone at night. The missing girl. Not a smart thing to do. I swallowed my pride and searched for my supportive and loving boyfriend. *Not.* We didn't have to talk. We could just walk and see what happened.

Standing in the foyer and holding a plastic cup in her hand while chatting with her friends was Rachael. When did she get here? My night just kept getting better and better.

One last obstacle to get by. I clamped my jaw so tightly the tension shot right into my temples. I was just about to sweep past Rachael when she spun around, her full cup of beer hitting me like a smelly tidal wave. I was soaked. *Payback ... again.*

"Oh, I'm so sorry. I didn't see you there." Her entire face mocked.

While her friends made feeble attempts to hide their amusement, I stepped back and gasped from the cold, icky shower. I wanted to scream at her or find another beer to throw back. What made matters worse was how everyone gawked, their eyes wide, their mouths open. Some of them laughed. I was dizzy, a tornado of emotions swirling in my head—Scott, Mindy, Charlene, and Rachael—all flashing by like debris. Before I lost control of myself, I bolted out the door as fast as my feet would carry me.

"Hey, wait up."

Whoever was calling to me, it wasn't Scott, and I *wasn't* stopping.

Tears streamed down my cheeks as I took off down the sidewalk. And I would've kept going except for Rick, who reached out and grabbed my arm.

"Hey, wait a second." He took a step back, his mouth forming an O. "Oh, shit. What happened?"

I couldn't talk, not without exploding.

"Want me to get Scott?"

"No!"

Rick tore off his Hawaiian shirt and handed it over to me. He wore a white undershirt underneath.

"I'm fine." My lip quivered and my body shivered.

"It's getting chilly. Just put it on, and I'll walk you back to your dorm. You can give it back to me when we get there." He put his hands in his pockets and took a step down the walkway.

I draped the colorful shirt over my shoulders and joined Rick. His sweet-smelling *and* strong cologne overpowered the beer.

"You want to talk about it?"

My mind reeled. So many things had gone wrong tonight; it was difficult to separate them all. When I didn't answer, Rick kept me company in silence. For a time.

"Hey, tomorrow I'm coaching some first graders in a flag football game. Why don't you come with me? It's a lot of fun, and the kids are cute as hell."

"I've got some things I need to do." I appreciated Rick's offer, but I wasn't in the mood for this.

"Derek's coming. He could use the community service hours. The kids have a way of making you forget your problems." His tone was light and airy. "The organization doesn't have much money, so my family donates the uniforms and the snacks."

I kicked at small stones in front of me, imagining they were Rachael's head, then Scott's, then Mindy's and Charlene's.

"Just as friends, and I'm sure Derek would love to have you there. I can even get you a community service form if you need the hours." When I didn't answer, Rick rambled on about the kids and all the work he had done for them. He didn't seem to mind the one-sided conversation. My first encounter with Rick had given me an impression, a wrong one. I now understood what Derek was trying to tell me.

I finally blurted out, "I'll think about it. If I change my mind, I'll text Derek in the morning, okay?"

"Sure. No pressure."

When we reached my dorm, I took off his shirt and handed it back to him. The beer had bled onto the material.

"I'm so sorry. I tried to keep it away from the stain." A second wave of emotions erupted in my chest.

The warmth of Rick's hand found my shoulder. "It's a cheap shirt. Don't worry about it. Are you going to be okay?" His eyes prodded.

Lip quivering, I wasn't sure.

"I'm sorry Scott was such an asshole to you. I thought he was going to be different with you, but that's the way he always treats girls."

Great. Another confirmation that I had put my faith in the wrong guy. I opened my mouth to speak until Rick raised a palm.

"I know he's your boyfriend, so I won't say anything else."

Boyfriend? I wasn't sure anymore. He was Ken on team Barbie.

"Don't forget to text Derek." He took a few steps backward. "I'm leaving at nine o'clock."

"Thanks for walking me back, Rick." I swiped my keycard

and bolted up the stairs to my room, ready for an emotional outburst—the kind I only did in private.

By the time I had peeled off my shirt, which now reeked of beer *and* Rick's cologne, I was sobbing and fuming at the same time. My cell phone dinged with a few text messages, *ping, ping, ping,* until it rang. Scott's name shot on the display. I shut it off.

Not happening.

* * *

I stepped out of a much-needed shower to someone banging on my door. I threw on my robe and peered through the peephole at Scott with his hands propped up against the casing. When I opened the door, he backed up a step and barged into my room like a bull ready to charge.

"What the hell, Sara. You just leave the party and don't tell me?" He threw my jacket onto my bed. I was surprised he remembered that I'd left it in his room.

I closed the door and continued to wipe my hair with a towel.

"Like you would have noticed," I said. "I don't know why you even invited me to that stupid party. Was it so you could watch all your women fighting over you?"

Scott glared at me with fire in his eyes and a brewery on his breath. "My what?" The veins in his neck matched the Hulk.

I made my own mad face. "I'm not in the mood for your games. If you want to sleep with other women, then go right ahead." I tossed the dampened towel onto my bed. "All you did was ignore me."

Scott leaned over and gripped the back of my desk chair, his knuckles white and threatening. "I didn't ignore you. I was just hanging out. Jesus. *You* were the one who couldn't wait to get to the party. And if you're referring to Mindy and Charlene, I never even spoke to either one of them tonight."

No, you just salivated over them as they danced for you. What I didn't say was how Mindy, Charlene, and Rachael had been treating me. Deep down, I could handle the girls, but not this. "You know what I think?" I asked. "I think you like all these women fighting over you." I grabbed a comb and tugged on the snarls. "Rachael, Mindy, and Charlene act like they own you. Like you're their property."

"Own me?" Scott straightened his spine. "Oh, that's rich. Now you're making shit up."

"No I'm not. You should see the way—"

"No one owns me. Not even *you!*" His cheeks flared, right along with his eyes. "You're so good at pointing fingers, well, what about you? You take off with Rick? I thought you couldn't stand him. You should've gotten me. How do you think it looks, having my girlfriend take off with one of my brothers? He's playing you, Sara."

"I was coming to find you when Rachael—"

"Oh my God." He threw his arms up. "Now you're back on Rachael again?"

This was impossible. We were getting nowhere. Anything I said now would sound petty.

"Look, Scott. I am not the girl you think I am. And I'm never going to be *that* girl." I wiped a drop of water off the side of my eye. "It's clear to me that you still want that life. So, have at it. No one's stopping you." I swept one arm toward the door.

No, Sara. I don't want that life. I want you.

I wished he had said *those* words and not, "Maybe I will," before he bolted out of my room with "I don't need this shit," in his dust.

As the door clicked shut, so did my heart. All the joy I'd felt over the past few weeks abandoned me, too. I was sick. I was lonely. I realized I'd set myself up for failure with Scott. He wasn't the guy for me. Scott had pulled the plug, and for no good reason. Abigail was right. I couldn't handle this.

At least we hadn't said, "I love you," yet, I tried to reassure myself, tears streaming, my gut wrenching.

Yeah, right. Whether I'd say those words or not, the heart felt what the heart felt.

Chapter Ten

I'd hardly slept. All I could think about was what Scott did after he left me—or more accurately, who he did.

Because I wouldn't have sex with him the first time he asked—and it *was* the first time, really—he had bailed. He'd summed up our relationship in one superfluous moment.

As much as his rejection hurt me, I was glad I hadn't gone all the way. If that was a test and I'd failed in his eyes, what would the next one be? Scott expected things from his women —and from what I could see, they delivered. *Delivered?* They craved him. The problem was ... so did I.

What happened to that nice guy who had swept me off my feet? Just last week when we had been watching a movie in my room, Scott had paused the movie and said, "You know, I always used to envy Jason and Heather's relationship. I never thought I'd find someone like you."

His words refreshed my soul like a glass of ice-cold lemonade on a hot summer day. "I know exactly what you mean. You're an amazing person, Scott. I'm so glad I met you, too."

He got all serious for a moment. "I just don't want to turn into my dad. I don't know how my mother has put up with his bullshit all these years."

"You won't." I sounded confident because I was.

"I won't because I have you." He kissed my hand and then my forehead. "You've changed all that for me, Sara. I don't envy anyone anymore. But they sure as shit envy me now." At the time, I thought most guys already did envy Scott, but I understood what he was saying. We had something special, unique.

That so-called special memory got slapped aside by Amy's earlier advice. "If he's looking to get laid, then don't give him anything. He'll lose interest if that's his deal." She had called it.

Who was Scott Williams? Did I even know the real *him*?

After a quick shower, I put on a pair of coral-colored cotton shorts and a white T-shirt with a sunflower on the front, convinced I was better off. My mind knew this, but my heart was still crying about it. My instincts told me to withdraw and isolate. Go back to being cave girl. My inner voice disagreed. *You didn't come to this school to fail.*

Tired of living inside my head, I decided to take Rick up on his offer. At eight o'clock, I powered up my phone and texted Derek: "If it's not 2 late I'd like to join u and Rick."

My inbox had exploded with a plethora of missed calls and voice mails from Scott. No texts. I started to listen to one but heard the anger in his voice and shut it off. My tired brain wasn't ready. He had sent me ten voice mails. How many times did he need to make his point? *I don't need this ... I don't need you.*

A message dinged in from Derek: "Not 2 late ... b at your dorm parking lot at 9."

I chewed on a protein bar as I texted Amy next: "R u up?"

A response came back: "Yes."

I stepped into a pair of flip-flops and headed next door.

"Is Luke here?" I asked when she opened her door a crack.

"No, he left for work already." Amy rubbed one eye. "What's up?"

My throat ached from holding back emotions that threatened to tear me in two.

Amy's squinty eyes grew round. "What happened?" She grabbed my arm and ushered me into her room. "Give me a sec." She clicked on her lamp and then pulled her bedspread up over her pillow. "Here, sit down." The scent of sandalwood clung to her bedding and walls.

Then the dam broke. Through tears, I gave Amy an emotional recount of the events from the night before.

"What a prick." She sat close, her support like a crutch. "And those skanks are unbelievable. Jesus, they act like he's the only guy on earth. Get a life. Move on."

The clock on her nightstand warned that my time was running out. "I've only got a few minutes before I have to meet Derek and Rick in the parking lot."

With sleepy eyes and lopsided hair, Amy asked, "Why? Where are you going?"

"We're coaching some first graders in a flag football game today." I didn't want to go, but it was better than hanging around here.

"Really, with Rick?" Amy's eyebrows tensed and then released.

"And Derek," I said, reminding her. "You were right about Scott." I sucked in a shuttering breath and wiped my eyes.

"Guys can be so weird about sex." Amy stretched her arms up over her head and yawned as she spoke. "If we're not quick to put out, they take it so personally."

"Is Luke like that?"

Amy tipped her head to one side, taking a long blink. "Well. No. But he's the first."

I brought a hand to my forehead. "Well, I'm sure Scott's not frustrated about it anymore. You should have seen the way he looked at those girls. I'm sure they all hooked up." I stared at the floor as Amy patted my back, my heart too heavy to hold up.

"You don't know he cheated on you." She fought back another yawn. "I'm not saying he didn't, but you don't know for sure. It's a good idea to get away for a few hours. We can talk when you get back." Poor Amy looked as tired as I felt.

"Speaking of which, I need to get going." I headed for the door. "I'm sorry about unloading all this on you."

Amy waved me off. "It's fine. I'm sure I'll be ranting about Sky soon enough." She pulled back her comforter, ready to slide into the sheets.

"Thanks, Amy. I'll call you later."

I pushed my way out of the dorm, my feet dragging against the pavers. The sun was bright, the birds were chirping, and I could care less. When I arrived at the parking lot, Rick's shiny black SUV, tinted windows and all, sat idling. I opened the door to the back seat and was surprised to find Derek already there.

"You can ride up front." Derek patted the headrest.

I slid my glasses down and pleaded with my eyes. "Really, why? I don't mind sitting in the back."

Part of me wanted to call the whole thing off.

"I won't bite," Rick said from the front seat. "Come on. We better get going."

Holding his grin, Derek closed the door.

I slid my glasses back into place, trying not to bare my teeth as I opened the passenger-side door to climb aboard.

Rick wore his typical flashy grin. "Good morning."

"Morning," I muttered, doing my best impression of Oscar the Grouch.

The industrial smell and the immaculate interior made me wonder if Rick had driven here straight from the dealership. I could almost see my reflection in the wood trim.

"I've just got to punch in the address." Rick pushed some buttons on his cell phone, which he'd plugged into the navigation system.

"Don't you go there regularly?"

"The location changes every week." His gaze volleyed between a small sheet of paper in his hand and his cell.

I sat back, allowing my body to conform to the contoured leather seats, which offered my sore back needed support. A night of tossing and turning had left my ribs and back feeling like a shirt just out of the spin cycle.

When Rick was finished working, he put the car in drive and glanced my way. "Derek said you like tea, so I got you a chai latte."

A large cup sat in the holder closest to me.

"Thank you." I picked up the cup, opened the lid, and blew on the tea, releasing a strong cinnamon scent into the air.

Derek scooted forward in between the seats. "Hey, what was the deal with Scott last night?" The inflection in his voice made me leery.

"I don't know or care." I bit down on my lower lip and peered out the window, trying to gain mental footing.

"He was a little out of control. That's why I asked." Derek's words added salt to my wounded soul.

Out of control? Was he celebrating his new independence?

Sorrow, anger, and desperation were no stranger to me, but this was different. "I don't need to hear about it." I gulped down a sip of tea way too hot for a human mouth. Great. Now I had a scorched mouth to match my scorched heart.

Derek patted my shoulder and then sat back in his seat just as Rick cleared his throat.

"Are you cool enough?" Rick adjusted the dual-zone temperature controls.

Huh? I looked over at him, my mind vacant, until his question finally sunk in. "I'm fine."

The car grew silent, and I was happy to keep it that way. The less talk the better.

Rick sipped from his cup, a hint of vanilla competing with my cinnamon. "Today should be a lot of fun." He tipped his head. "There are a few cases of snacks and water in the back."

I gazed into the far back of the SUV to see enough snacks and drinks to supply a small army. *A few cases?*

"Wow, how many kids are on the team?" I stared back at him.

A smile curved Rick's lips. "Most of these kids don't have much at home. I bring extra supplies for them to take back with them."

Rick reminded me all over again how wrong I had been about him. At the tailgate, he had acted obnoxious, but in reality, he was just drunk. As far as Scott was concerned, I had let a pair of dazzling blue eyes hypnotize me like a strong narcotic. My observation skills needed work.

As Derek and Rick discussed fraternity events, I spent the remainder of the trip gazing out the window, the landscape a blur.

We were the first to arrive at the field, which appeared to be a community center, neglected over the years. A gray cinder block structure with one door and no windows marked the edge of the field. The dirt parking lot, covered in potholes, splashed muddy water onto Rick's pristine vehicle. It didn't seem to faze him any.

Rick shifted the vehicle into park and then pushed a button to open the tailgate. We all climbed out and made our way around to the back, where Rick pulled out a large green canvas bag, dropped it on the ground, and unzipped it. Owen's name dominated its side in black marker.

"Sara, can you put these cones on the corners and edges of the field? Also, put two where the end zones are supposed to be." He held up a small stack of orange cones for me to take.

"Sure, but I have no idea how wide the end zones should be." I took the cones from his hands.

Rick's face lightened. "These are five- and six-year-olds. They don't care where the end zones are. Most of them are chasing butterflies instead of the person with the ball anyway. I'll adjust it later."

"Derek, I need you to set this table up over there." After pulling out a foldable table, Rick pointed halfway down the sideline. "I've got a couple of folding chairs for you guys to sit on while you keep score."

Derek and I got busy with our duties, which gave my mind something else to focus on. Given the height of the overgrown grass, which obscured the painted sidelines, I understood the need for the cones. By the time we had all the cones out, tables set up, and equipment organized, the parents had arrived. A man with short reddish-brown hair and gray sideburns walked over to Rick. He wore a whistle around his neck and a white T-shirt with the word *Coach* printed across the back. The coach faced Rick with his hands on his hips, listening to him. After a few minutes, he shook Rick's hand and then walked over to the table where Derek and I sat.

"I understand you two will be keeping score? I'm Coach Brady, but you can call me Ed." Derek and I shook the coach's hand.

"I'm Derek, and this is Sara. Yeah, we'll keep score."

The coach handed me a book with lines and numbers all over it. "If you could put down the names of the players and each of their jersey numbers that would be helpful. Don't worry about substitutions or stats, only the score and which player did it." He spoke like a man who had done this a hundred times before. "Here's our roster, and I'll get one from the other team in a few minutes." He handed me a handwritten list of names.

I nodded and did as he asked.

"How about you handle the scoreboard?" His gaze drifted to Derek as he handed him a flip scoreboard.

"We gotcha covered." Derek sounded so psyched.

I wished I felt the same, but I didn't.

As soon as the game was underway, parents who weren't standing, cheered and clapped from their lawn chairs or blankets on the sidelines. I had played soccer for the YMCA when I was little. Mom and Dad came to every game, cheering and coaching me on. Afterward, they'd take me out for ice cream to celebrate my win or console me over my loss. I enjoyed the fond memory—until Derek spoke.

"Scott's got a *bad* temper, you know." He flipped a point for the opposing team.

My smile faded.

"Just between us, he threatened Rick last night when he found out he walked you back to your dorm."

My stomach turned. "What did Scott say to him?"

Coach Brady's whistle cut through the air as he attempted to guide the young players on the field.

Rick stayed off to the side, observing.

"I don't know exactly what he said, but he warned Rick to stay away from you." Careful to keep his eyes on the field, Derek delivered the unpleasant news from the corner of his mouth.

It wasn't a big surprise. Scott had told me himself how much my leaving with Rick had bothered him—and for all the wrong reasons: "How do you think it looks?" The night Scott had told Amy and me about that missing girl, he had acted so concerned about our safety. Instead of threatening Rick, he should have been thanking him. Yet again, Scott's ego meant more to him than I did.

The morning sun migrated toward midday as Derek and I worked diligently. When our team won an hour later, the miniature athletes jumped up and down and screamed with joy. They were adorable little munchkins.

Coach Brady took the team aside to say a few words, and then Rick made an announcement about the snacks. The parents and the kids followed Rick over to his SUV, where he and Coach Brady distributed the food and water to the crowd. Derek packed up the table and chairs while I collected the cones. He and I reached the SUV just as Rick had handed out the last case of water.

"I'll carry that for you." Derek sprang forward to take a heavy load from one of the mom's hands.

In Derek's absence, Coach Brady and I helped Rick load up the rest of the equipment.

"Thanks for all your help today." Coach Brady clapped Rick on the shoulder. "If you ever want to assist in coaching again, call me. We're not used to all these extras."

Didn't he know Rick?

"Anytime, man." Rick shook the coach's hand.

"You've done a better job in one game than Owen has all season." Coach Brady gave Rick a two-fingered salute before walking away. "Tell Owen if he blows off another game, he's out."

Once he was gone, Rick pushed a button to close the tailgate. "All set?"

"Yes." I scanned the area for Derek, then made a mad dash for the back seat, Rick watching me the entire time. It wasn't that I didn't want to sit next to Rick. I just needed space. I hoped he understood.

On our drive back to campus, Derek scanned through the radio stations while Rick navigated us back onto Interstate 64.

"What did the coach mean about Owen? I thought you were the other coach." I examined the expansive back seat, wishing I could stretch out. How weird would that look?

"We both are." Rick sped up, merging into ongoing traffic.

"Oh, it sounded like this was your first game."

"Well, Coach Brady isn't always there. These organizations have a bunch of different coaches. To be honest, it's the first time I've met him." He glanced at Derek. "That's a good station, man."

In my YMCA days, we had always had the same coach, sometimes an assistant. My hometown ran things differently. To me, it would be difficult to adjust to a new person every week. I wondered how well it worked here. It didn't seem like a good system to me, although the kids responded to Coach Brady well enough—at least from my standpoint. Maybe he'd coached them during a previous season?

Rick adjusted his rearview mirror to catch my eye. "Did you enjoy yourself today?"

It was difficult to enjoy much of anything, but I did like seeing the kids. Plus, I didn't want to spoil the mood or the effort Rick had put into this event. "I did. Thank you so much." It was a friendly lie, so no harm.

A tickle in my nose prompted a sneeze, then another. "Excuse me."

"Good, we enjoyed having you." Rick reached into the back pocket of his golf shorts, the kind my dad would wear once in a millennia. "Here." He pulled out a white handkerchief and handed it over to me, the letters RBS embroidered on one corner. The brushed cotton was thick with quality.

I sneezed again, only this time into the hanky. "Thanks." When I was finished, I wasn't sure what to do with the soiled cloth. I'd have to wash it somehow.

Rick caught my eyes through the mirror again. "Keep it; I've got a million of those."

You have a million embroidered handkerchiefs? This was a new one.

He opened the sunroof, sending fresh air throughout the cabin. The wind mixed with the soft rock playing on the radio had a relaxing effect on me, and my eyes grew heavy. Random scenes played out in my mind. Most of them filled with conflict and frustration, like me trying to get somewhere but unable to move. At one point, I was sitting in a classroom in my underwear taking a test that I didn't understand.

"I'm starving." Rick's voice jolted me awake. "Why don't you both let me take you out to lunch to thank you for your help today?"

I wiped the corner of my mouth and gazed out the window, realizing how close we had gotten to campus.

"I could eat. Sounds good to me," Derek said full of vigor.

Just the thought of food made my stomach rumble, but I had other issues to deal with first—one being those voice mails from Scott. I had left my phone in my room to avoid him, but now I wanted closure. It was easier than admitting I just wanted to hear the sound of his voice.

Rick stared from the mirror.

I sat up straighter and used my hand to wipe the fatigue from my face. "I appreciate the offer, but I should get back to school."

"Come on, Sara." Derek turned in his seat, his eyes compelling me. "What's so important that you have to get right back?"

Argh. Now I had to come up with a plausible excuse.

"It's okay. We can bring you back." Rick lowered his gaze to the road.

"I'm sorry. I didn't sleep well, and it's been a long day."

"I understand," Rick said.

A few minutes later, we arrived at my dorm parking lot. I was glad to be back.

"It meant a lot to me that you came today." Rick shifted the car into park and then sat sideways in his seat. "Maybe we can grab a coffee sometime ... or a tea." He smirked.

"Um, sure." I kept my hand on the door handle.

"You know, as friends." Rick blinked, doing his best to be chill about it. "I'll get your number from Derek."

Rick had these intense brown eyes, bordering on black that always carried a seriousness about them, even when he was joking around. Rather intimidating, really. Today, however, I saw a different side of him, a warmer more generous side.

"Thank you again for bringing me along." I climbed out of the vehicle and smiled back at him. "You did good today."

As I was walking away, Derek rolled his window down. Had I forgotten something? Then I remembered that I hadn't brought anything with me, other than my key card, which was in my hand.

Derek opened his mouth once and then twice before he cleared his throat. "I saw Mindy and Charlene in Scott's room last night." He offered a sad blink. "I just thought you should know."

It felt like a meteor had just shot out of the sky and landed in my stomach, which burned like a fuse all the way to my aching heart.

Chapter Eleven

Feeling as if I'd just been run over by a truck named Scott, I entered through the dorm entrance to find him standing there waiting for me. *What?* Shock sent my heart into defibrillation and my lungs into spasm. What was *he* doing here?

I headed for the stairwell, trying not to freak. What I really needed was a paper bag to breathe.

Scott rushed forward. "Can we talk?"

Can we talk? I spun around to face his drooping shoulders and sad eyes. He looked like he hadn't slept. "About what? You made yourself perfectly clear last night."

"I am so sorry about that. If you give me a chance, I'd like to explain myself."

I let out a huff. What kind of explanation could possibly absolve him from cheating on me?

"Some things are unforgivable, Scott. Please leave." My insides whimpered as I took a step away.

"Please! Can we just go to your room and talk?" Scott sounded desperate. I wasn't used to hearing him this way.

"After you let me explain, if you still want me to go, then I promise I'll leave you alone. You have my word."

Whatever I had envisioned about my next confrontation with Scott, it hadn't included the pale, distressed expression sketched over his face. His pleading bloodshot eyes were the worst. *Remorse?* Was he like those husbands who cheated and then begged their wives to take them back? That was *not* me.

Still, I wanted to hear what he had to say. "Fine." I kept two steps ahead of him as I led the way to the stairwell.

After I keyed my lock and we were inside of my room, I sat on my bed, crossed my arms, and waited for him to speak. It didn't help matters that he looked irresistible. I scolded myself for how much I ached for his touch.

Scott sat in my desk chair, leaned forward, and propped his hands on his knees.

He pulled in a deep breath. "I'm not used to being the insecure one, Sara. I've never fallen for anyone like you." He straightened up, his eyes emphatic. "I'm madly in love with you, goddamn it."

"I can't listen to this." I jumped to my feet. "How can you say that to me?" The trembling in my body bounded for my lips. I clamped my mouth shut, doing my best to hold back the words *I love you, too.* This was agony.

Scott lifted a cautionary hand. "Please let me explain." He stared at me, his eyes begging. "Just give me another minute longer."

I wasn't sure I had the strength for another minute. After a few seconds, I returned to the edge of my bed and crossed my arms again. I was holding myself together by a thread.

"I think a part of me has loved you since the moment I met you. Our day on the mountain was incredible. I'd never felt drawn to anyone like that before. I'm so attracted to you; I have trouble controlling my fucked-up emotions. I know you haven't had any experience, and I don't want to pressure you." He hissed through his teeth. "I let my emotions take over last night. I wanted you so badly I couldn't see straight. When you pulled away, I felt rejected, like you didn't want me—not like I wanted you." He bowed his head in what appeared to be self-loathing. "I was wrong, and I'm ashamed of myself. I know this is hard for you to believe, but it's not just about sex for me, Sara." He leveled his eyes with mine. "I should have been supportive and there for you, but I failed miserably." His gaze fell to his hands.

"What else did you do last night?" I asked in a disparaging tone.

Scott lifted his chin, his brow tightening. "What do you mean? After I left you, I went to my room for the rest of the night." He tilted his head and shot me a look of confusion.

"Who went with you?" I refused to blink.

Scott's eyes rode upward as though trying to remember something. I wasn't buying it.

"Also, there's no need to threaten people who were trying to help."

Scott flinched, shaking his head in disbelief. "I don't know what you've been told, but I didn't threaten anyone. And the only person who came to my room last night was Jason, to talk to me." He rubbed his eyes with the heels of his hands. Then his shoulders sank. "Well, that's not entirely true."

I gripped my comforter, preparing myself for the verbal bullet.

"Mindy and Charlene came to my door, but I turned them away." He lengthened his spine, reaching a hand out. "You can ask Jason if you don't believe me. He was there."

It was obvious Scott wasn't going to own up to his behavior. I huffed and then sprang to my feet. "Are you finished?"

Scott rose and walked closer.

I thrust my hands out like a traffic guard.

"Sara, I would never cheat on you. If I wanted girls like them in my life, then I would have them in my life. I don't. I want you. You are the first girl I have ever really loved."

Why didn't you say that last night? It's too late now.

Scott took another step forward and gripped my shoulders. "Look into my eyes." With his strong hands, he held me in place.

As if they had a mind of their own, my eyes traveled upward. I'd never been this angry with someone I loved so much. I wasn't sure what to do. I was a Jenga game, and Scott was pulling me apart, piece by piece.

"You can ask anyone who was at that party. You can even ask those girls. I didn't sleep with them. I would never pull that shit on you." He gripped me tighter. "I'll go with you, right now, and we can ask anyone who was there."

That seemed a little extreme, although I considered it. "I don't know what to think."

Scott pulled me into his arms and bear-hugged me. His heartbeat pounded against my ear. "I'm so sorry. I wish I could go back and be the boyfriend you needed me to be." Every part of him screamed with regret. "There hasn't been a moment since I met you that I have even thought about another woman."

Wait a minute. I pulled away. "That's not true. I watched you when those girls were dancing for you. You were staring right at them." My cheeks refueled with anger.

Scott brushed a few strands of hair away from my face. "Sara, I wasn't looking at *them*. I wasn't looking at anyone. I was too caught up in my own dumbass head."

"But I was right there. And later when I told you to go back to that life, you said maybe you would." I peered deep into his blue eyes, searching for some semblance of the truth.

Scott's voice grew heavy. "I was an asshole. I'm used to

being the one in control, but since I met you, I've been a head case."

That resonated since I had the same affliction.

Scott took out his phone and dialed someone's number. He put the cell to his ear and waited. "Hey, bro. Can you meet me at Sara's dorm? ... It's important. If you're free, now would work." He listened. "Okay, text me when you get here." He ended the call and returned the phone to his pocket. "To prove what I'm saying is true, will you talk to Jason?"

I took a moment to consider it. Whatever the outcome of the situation, I had to know the truth. There *was* the possibility that he'd already spoken to Jason to get his story straight. Would Scott be that cunning? I doubted it.

I agreed for the sake of my sanity. "Okay."

I followed Scott to the lobby, where we waited in silence. To say it was awkward would be putting it mildly. There was no way small talk would help, so I didn't even try. I let the silence hang between us.

When the three of us got back to my suite, Scott faced his best friend. "Go with Sara." He said it as a demand, not a question.

"Why, what's going on?" A list of unanswered questions flitted across Jason's face.

Scott motioned with one hand. "Just go with her. She'll explain."

Jason took a slow step, his eyes wary. "Um. Alright ... I guess."

I led Jason to my room while Scott sat in the living room and waited. It was beyond weird.

"I'm so embarrassed, Jason." I closed my door. "I heard some things about last night that I need to ask you about."

Jason cringed a little. "What kinds of things?"

"I was told Mindy and Charlene were in Scott's room last night. Is that true?" I motioned toward my desk chair.

Jason sat at my desk and picked up one of my pens, which he clicked continuously. It was distracting. "Well, when I got to the party last night, Scott was in his room. The girls came to his door about a half hour after I arrived. The way Scott shot over to the door, I'm pretty sure he thought it was you. From what I could hear, he told them he was busy." He dropped the pen and lifted his eyes. "I don't know what's going on between you two, but I knew some shit was going down. I kept asking him what happened, and he just said that he'd fucked up big time."

The stories matched, sort of. Enough that it mattered.

"Is there anything else you want to know?" Jason rested his arm on my desk, allowing his new focus to become a paper clip, which he first straightened and then bent beyond recognition.

"We had a fight last night, and it made me wonder if we're right for each other." I hated this feeling of uncertainty.

Jason put the paper clip down next to the abandoned pen and sat forward. "I get that. You have to understand Scott's led a very different lifestyle."

My eyes grew wide. "Yeah, I know. That's what worries me."

"I think you guys may run into some challenges, but he seems to care about you. He was a real mess last night." He shook his head in amazement. "I've never seen him so fucked up over a girl." He grew sheepish. "Sorry."

I patted the air. "No worries."

Jason twisted his mouth a little. "I never thought Scott would fall this hard or this quickly for anyone. He's had relationships, but he's never been this ... into anyone." He sat back and scratched the end of his nose. "And if you want proof, well, here it is." He spread his hands out wide. "I'm sitting in your room vouching for him. I can honestly say I've never done *that* before."

If Jason was telling the truth, then Derek must have seen those girls at Scott's door and assumed they went in. Could Derek have also misunderstood what had happened between Scott and Rick? Mindy, Charlene, and Rachael were ridiculous, but they acted on their own behalf. What had Scott really done? He'd pouted, and for that he was sorrier than I ever imagined he could be.

Jason rose to his feet, took his phone from his pocket, and examined it. "Do you have any other questions? Heather is waiting for me."

"No, but thank you. You must think I'm crazy. I'm sorry about all of this." I took a swipe across my forehead, removing a thin layer of tension sweat.

"It's cool. I get it." Jason patted my arm. "Scott can be a stubborn son of a bitch, but I've known him since we were kids, and he's a good guy."

I opened the door. "I appreciate that. And tell Heather I said hi."

"I will."

When we reached the living room, Jason beelined for the door.

"Thanks, man," Scott said.

"Anytime, bro."

After the door had closed, Scott faced me, his eyes drooping. He reached out, but then pulled his hand back. "Is there anything else I can do to convince you I'm telling the truth?" He didn't seem at all concerned with what Jason had said to me. "I told you once that you could trust me. You can."

"Let's go back to my room and talk." I didn't need my suitemates or Amy bursting through the door.

Back in my room, I finally allowed myself to fully acknowledge what was going on. I gazed into Scott's responsive blue eyes, feeling silly but also redeemed on some level. "You also told me once that you liked that I was different."

"I remember, and I meant it."

"When I first met you, what I liked most about *you*, aside from your hot body and sexy looks," I said with a grin, "was how you stuck up for me. You really had my back."

Scott opened his mouth, but I motioned for him to wait. I needed to get this out.

"One thing I've grown to understand about life is that it doesn't always go the way you want it to or the way you think it might. I want to be with someone who will be there for me, not just when things are great but when things aren't." Anchored by his eyes, I took a step forward. "Are you going to be *that* guy?"

Scott firmed his posture. "Yes, I *am*. I know I fucked up, but I love you, Sara, and I want this to work."

I love you, Sara. I took a moment to savor the significance of his statement. My heart was ready to sprout wings ... if I let it. "Are you sure?"

Scott bridged what little gap remained, taking my face in his hands. "Oh, yeah. I realize my past doesn't exactly instill your trust in me, but it's *because* of my past that I know."

"Well, I love you, too." The words tumbled out of my mouth. It felt good, as if I'd finally admitted something that I'd been harboring for some time now.

I didn't think it was possible for Scott to look more intense, but he did. He took me in his arms and kissed me in a way that left nothing to chance. It was loving, it was passionate, and it was hot.

"You love me?" he asked, his voice hitching.

"I do." It surprised me how much.

"I know I'm an asshole and I don't deserve it, but you've

just made me a happy asshole. I won't pressure you again. I promise." I could feel the truth in his words and in the way he said them. "We can wait for as long as you want."

I was safe, but I no longer wanted to be. We'd crossed a threshold and things were different now. I was different. I wanted to rip my clothes off and find out what I'd been missing. I was a ripe tomato, ready to fall off the vine.

"I want you to make love to me." I said it without hesitation.

I suspected a feather could have knocked Scott over. His eyes bugged, his face flushed, his mouth hinged open in a did-she-just-say-what-I-thought-she-said kind of way. "Are you sure? I don't want to—"

"I'm sure." To show my resolve, I pulled the waist of my T-shirt up.

"Wait. Let me do that. If you're sure about this. I want it to be special for you ... and for me. Let *me* unwrap you."

My spine tingled. "Unwrap me?"

"You're a gift. The best kind, and that's what you do with gifts." He stepped forward, his eyes taking me in.

I raised my arms overhead, inviting him to slide the T-shirt free and toss it aside.

He kissed my exposed shoulder, his lips and fingers trickling down my arm. "Citrus and coconut. I love the way you smell. If I could bottle that shit, I would." He came to the front and tipped my chin upward, rewarding my mouth with his lips and his tongue. His hands wandered to the waistband of my shorts, and then he pulled back and looked at me, a question lingering in his eyes.

"Yes," I said knowing I was standing at a crossroad.

My shorts came off and then my bra and silk panties. That was the moment when Scott moved back a step and surveyed. "Christ. You're unbelievably beautiful." His words sang to me, his eyes dancing with passion and love.

"Your turn."

Scott peeled his clothes away much faster than he did mine. Now it was my chance to gawk. His soft yet firm pecs merged with a layer of rolling bumps carved into his abdomen —a mogul field of flesh that traveled all the way up to his broad shoulders. His skin was like smooth caramel, touched by the sun. His arms and legs bulged with muscles. But that wasn't the bulge I was paying attention to at that moment. I was impressed by the size of him—*and* intimidated.

Scott came to me. "You don't have to worry. I won't do anything that will hurt you." His hand slid to the back of my neck as he kissed me, his fingers lacing through my hair. "And if you want to stop," he touched his forehead to mine, "we'll stop." The corners of his mouth lifted. "It may just kill me, but we'll stop." He took my hand and walked me to my bed, where he explored my body with his fingers and mouth. His hands wandered over my breasts, and they hardened to his touch. He kissed me long and hard before his mouth surrounded my nipple.

I grabbed a handful of sheet and moaned, my eyes closing from sensations vibrating up and down my body. Scott's hand followed the line of my hip, his face sinking lower, his eyes watching me with delight. Between my legs, his tongue grazed and caressed. I lost myself, my back arching, my mind taken away by a flood of sexual adrenaline. *Oh God.* I cried out.

Urges to touch, to kiss, and to lick came over me. I pushed Scott down on the mattress and roamed his body the same way he had just roamed mine. His breath grew heavy, his eyes rolling. I devoured him with everything I had.

"Are you ready?" he whispered.

"Yes."

He rolled me onto the mattress and hovered over me. I felt him between my legs as he pushed himself deeper inside me. It was tight, and I looked at him, wondering if it was normal. His eyes told me it was. "I'm being careful. It will get better," he said, and it did. Much better. Scott moved his hips in perfect rhythm to mine. I climaxed right before Scott did. Seeing his eyes glow and hearing his breath catch, the moans of ecstasy escaping from his lips gave me such a feeling of pride. I never knew I could make someone feel that way.

As we lay there in each other's arms, I celebrated the love between us. He was mine and I was his. It wasn't a possessive thought; it was something I had longed for but never believed possible. For the first time in many years, I was part of someone else's life. Scott and I were building something together—our future—and my world would never be the same.

Chapter Twelve

I awoke to a pair of expressive blue eyes staring back at me. Propped on his side, Scott wore nothing more than a bright smile, my blanket barely covering his robust body. On my twin mattress, he was a giant, sandwiched between the wall and me. I drank in his scent, my soul giddy.

"Good morning, gorgeous." He traced the bridge of my nose with his finger.

"Morning." I stretched and yawned, welcoming the images of last night's lovemaking.

"You don't have any regrets, do you?" Scott's finger continued its trail down the length of my jawbone.

Regrets? Was he kidding? Being so close to him had my insides begging for more.

"How could I regret the best night of my life? I can understand why you like sex so much." I flipped onto my side, letting my fingers brush down the length of his chiseled abdomen. He was mine, and yet I wasn't the only girl who had enjoyed him. Out of nowhere, jealous thoughts sabotaged my elated mood.

"I know I'm not experienced and not as good as some of the

other women you've been with." Overcome with emotion, I stared off. My eyes welled. What was happening?

Scott placed his hand behind my neck and eased my face closer. "Sara, I may have been with other women, but this experience was completely different for me. All those other girls were just sex—what you and I did was make love. It would be like comparing the light of a match to a fireworks display." He kissed my nose. "It was the best night of *my* life. No one compares to you. You feed my body *and* my soul."

"So, I'm your firework?" I fought back a tear, feeling like a complete idiot.

"You're more than that. You're my grand finale, babe." Scott pressed his lips to mine. How yummy he was, and addicting.

"I've never experienced anything like this before." I let out a girlish giggle. "My body is still tingling."

Scott combed his fingers through my hair. "I'm so thankful I met you, Sara."

I teased with my eyes. "I *think* I'm thankful, too, but I need more of what you did to me last night to decide for sure."

Scott came closer, his dimple loving the challenge. "Looks like I've created a monster."

He was right. I *was* a monster, one who couldn't get enough of him.

"Well, then. I better get busy." He ran his tongue along the side of my neck before tugging at my earlobe with his teeth. My body quivered, knowing what was coming next.

* * *

"Are you feeling okay, Sara?" At the front of my Creative Writing class, Professor Baker eyed me. It was Monday morning, and I was still reeling from the weekend. Scott and I had spent all day Sunday together, making love with shorter lengths of eating and homework mixed in between.

"Yes, I'm sorry. Did you ask me something?" I sat up and snapped myself out of my euphoric cloud, which wasn't easy considering Scott's cologne still lingered on my skin.

The students sitting next to me offered quizzical glances. My palms grew clammy. Mindy and Charlene were there, but somewhere behind me. Not that I cared. Not anymore.

"I asked you to read pages thirty-eight through fifty."

I was quick to locate the pages and comply.

* * *

I managed to get through Creative Writing relatively unscathed, and then Western Civilizations that followed it. With my free hour, I ventured over to the counseling office in the Student Union Building to fill out some forms and finish a training tutorial, even though I'd been tutoring for weeks now. It took longer than I had expected. By the time I left, I was in dire need of caffeine. The best weekend of my life had not been a restful one. After purchasing a large black tea at the Starbucks counter, I sat on a bench out front of the building, drifting in and out of fantasyland: Scott on top of me, Scott below me, Scott licking my—

"Helloooooo. Earth to Sara." Amy nudged my arm and huffed. "Didn't you hear me yelling your name?"

"Oh, sorry." I stood, forcing my mind back to earth. "How's your day been?"

"Great. Other than my math teacher needs to remove the stick that's permanently wedged up his ass," Amy said with zeal. Her trigonometry teacher was often a topic of discussion on Mondays, Wednesdays, and Fridays.

"I'm glad I don't have that class," I said before taking a big gulp of tea.

It had been cloudy all day with the threat of rain. As we walked along, the sky grew dark, transforming natural daylight into a surreal twilight. Another swift breeze punched the air, scattering dead leaves and debris into a dust storm. I squinted against the tiny particles pinging against my skin.

"It looks like it's going to storm." I tossed my cup away in a nearby trash can, even though it wasn't empty, and tugged on the hood from my raincoat.

Thunder clapped, causing both of us to flinch. A few large drops splashed down on the pavers, releasing a dusty scent, and then the sky opened. I tore off my rain jacket and covered both of our heads as we sprinted toward the entrance of Lexington Hall.

Once inside, the air-conditioning against my damp skin had my body covered in gooseflesh.

"Thanks for the hood." Amy wiped the excess rainwater from her head. When she was finished, she probed me with her eyes. "So, where have you been? I called you and knocked on your door several times yesterday." She arched a brow. "What have you been up to, Al?"

"Well, I worked things out with Scott." I shook out my jacket, avoiding her dismantling eyes.

"I already figured that. I heard his voice through the wall ... last night *and* this morning. I heard a few *other* noises as well." She made a come-here motion with her fingers. "Details, please."

Nothing escaped Amy, my overly observant friend.

"It's a long story, but Scott wasn't with those girls. Jason was in his room when they came by."

"The girls he was watching dance?" Amy inched her head closer, trying to understand. "They went to his room?"

I rubbed the area between my eyebrows. She hadn't heard the latest in my soap opera podcast.

"Oh, sorry. I guess I need to catch you up." I explained the series of events while Amy kept her ear tipped in my direction. "Derek must have seen the girls at his door and assumed they went in."

I laced my coat through the handle of my backpack and then slung it over my shoulder as we continued down a long corridor for the elevators, the walls lined with student artwork. Amy stayed way too quiet. I wondered what she was thinking.

"Do you believe him?" she finally asked.

"I do. Scott shared a lot with me about his feelings. I could tell it wasn't easy for him." I chewed on my lower lip. "I love him, Amy. And he loves me."

"Cool," she said, as if it was no big deal. Then, she looked at her cell phone. "Shit. We better hurry, or we'll be late for class."

* * *

After another class where Dr. Adams kept us in stitches, I sent a quick text to Scott while Amy loaded her backpack.

"Where r u?"

I knew Scott was in class but couldn't remember which one. An instant later, my phone dinged.

"I'm in my drafting class, thinking of u. I'll come 2 ur dorm when it's over. All I can picture is ur naked body. It's driving me mad." A few crazy-face emojis followed.

I stared at my phone and laughed, thinking about *his* body just as much.

Amy rolled her eyes as she made a clicking sound with her tongue. "You two aren't gonna get sickening now, are you? I thought you were sappy before."

"I'll try to contain myself," I said, putting my phone in my jacket pocket, my grin unwavering.

"So. Are you going to tell me about the *sex* or what?" Amy said overly loud.

A wave of heat shot into my cheeks while Amy sauntered out of the classroom, her shoulders back. She was such a brat.

I stepped out into the hall behind her, noticing a small crowd gathered by the elevators. The last thing I needed was Amy giving me the third degree amidst a group of listening ears.

"Let's take the stairs." I sprang through the door and bounded down three flights of stairs, Amy keeping up the entire way. When we reached the bottom, she asked, "So, how was he? And does he live up to his nickname?"

"Huh?"

"You know—*Big Guy?*" She gave me a what-else-would-it-be look, her hands motioning the same message.

Stairs were definitely the right choice.

I was tongue-tied. How was I going to respond to *that?*

Amy prodded. "Come on, Sara. That's half the fun about your first time. Telling your best friend about it."

I pushed through the door to the lobby and speed-walked in the exit's direction. If I had to answer that question, it wasn't going to be in the middle of the human traffic venturing through the hallways. Outside, the rain had stopped, leaving a thick wall of moisture hanging in the air.

"You never talked about Luke." I lowered my voice, my eyes scanning the area.

Amy had moved on to her cell, although my comment captured her attention. "Yeah, well. You were a virgin, and I was afraid I'd scare you. Ask me anything you want. Positions. Locations."

I grabbed her wrist and pulled her off the walkway. When the coast was clear, I spoke. "I don't have anything to compare him to, but he's *built* everywhere. In fact—" My armpits were moist for all kinds of reasons. I wanted to talk about it but wasn't sure how much to divulge. Things had gotten pretty hot and heavy between Scott and me.

"What? He's huge?" Amy got so close she was inches from giving me a kiss.

"Well, it was a bit intimidating at first." I gave her a sheepish glance.

"The first time can be uncomfortable. It will get better." Chin raised, Amy spoke with authority. "Aren't you glad I made you get on the pill now?"

"Yes, and thank you, but Scott used protection anyway. It was a little uncomfortable, but he did things to my body that ..." My eyes drifted all over the place to avoid Amy. How was I going to say this?

"Scott's been around, Sara. I'm sure he knew what he was doing."

Her comment brought up another issue I was struggling with. I knew how special last night was for me, and I had to assume it was also special for the women who had been with Scott before me. How could Scott have shared his body with them and not his heart? And who was *his* first sexual encounter? Was she still important to him? For the second time that day, my emotions got the best of me.

Amy scrunched her face. "Don't be so sensitive. Aren't you glad Scott knew what he was doing?"

Not really. It was like being in love with a Hollywood star that everyone knew and adored. I wanted Scott for myself. Unable to say that, I fiddled with my backpack strap. "I guess. I wish it had been his first time, too."

She grinned in a you're-being-silly sort of way. "Well, if that had been the case, then you definitely wouldn't have enjoyed it. Look, you can't get hung up on shit like that." She pushed on my arm. "From what you've told me, he obviously loves you."

I knew she was right, so why was I such a basket case?

Amy's phone dinged in a message. "Shag just got to work. Let's go harass the shit out of him."

A walk was just what I needed. It would give me time to process. By the time we had reached the snack bar, I decided that Scott's past, however unpleasant, was what had proved to him how he felt about me. He had said so himself.

We found Derek wiping down tables when we arrived at Campus Creations. Over his cotton shorts and polo (no more AC/DC T-shirts), he wore a not-so-white apron that had been stained many times over. A paper hat crowned his head like a cherry on a sundae.

"Hey, Shag. Working hard?" Amy patted his paper hat flat, ready to harass.

A pink shade burned Derek's cheeks. "Hell yeah."

We dropped our backpacks and bags on the table and took a seat next to him.

Derek puffed his hat back out, his gaze finding me. "So, did you ever talk to Scott?"

"Yes. He wasn't with those girls. They went to his door, but they didn't go in. He sent them away." I was happy to set the record straight.

Derek's eyebrows lowered, his tone incredulous. "So, you're back together?" He said it like it was the worst thing in the world.

What was his deal? I knew he didn't like Scott much, and I wasn't sure why. Well, I kinda knew why: because Rick didn't like him. Plus, he probably didn't think much of the Mindy and Charlene incident.

"I never said we were broken up. We had a fight." I crossed my arms, agitated.

"Well, I *did* see them at his room." Derek resumed his table-cleaning duties, leaving me defensive and bothered.

"I know, but they didn't go in," I said, hoping he would understand how much Scott meant to me. "Jason was in Scott's room when they came by, and he told me the same thing."

"Just be careful with him, Sara. It's a shame. I think Rick would be a better guy for you."

There it was. He was trying to set me up with Rick.

Derek stopped working, his eyes wide. "But don't tell Scott I said so."

I could accept him not liking Scott, but being afraid of him was another issue altogether. A bitter taste formed in my mouth. This conversation was going downhill fast.

Amy's eyes sparked to life. "Are you playing matchmaker now, Shag?"

I put my hand on his arm to stop him from working.

"Derek, I'm not interested in Rick." I said it firmly and with conviction. "I'll admit he's a much nicer guy than I thought he was, and I'd like to be his friend. And you don't have to worry about Scott."

Derek slunk out of my grasp. "Rick's a lot nicer than people give him credit for. My dad is starting a new job next week, thanks to him." He made a few more passes with the rag and then straightened up. "I gotta get back to the kitchen." He dropped the wet rag into the soapy bucket, causing pieces of foam to fly out. To say he sounded annoyed would be an understatement.

"Catch you guys later."

I spun in my seat, flustered. "Are you upset with me?"

Derek stopped. He peered over his shoulder, the angst melting away from his face. "Nah. I get what you're sayin'. It's all good."

Was it?

Once he was gone, Amy raised her eyebrows at me. "You can't blame him. From what you told me, Scott did act like an asshole." Amy sat back in her chair and stared at her cell.

"Yeah, but it wasn't as bad as I had thought." I felt awful about their opinion of Scott. Especially since I was the one who had blathered on about him—to Amy, anyway.

Amy got up. "I'll be right back. I'm gonna run over to the Student Union Building to check my mail. Want to come?"

"No, I checked mine earlier."

"Wait for me, and then we can walk back to the dorm." After fishing out her mailbox key, she dropped her bag on the table and darted off.

I grabbed a bottle of water from my backpack and took several long sips. I wasn't used to having friends—much less friends who worried about me. I had to remind myself it was a good thing.

The sound of a girl giggling caused my eyes to drift upward. At a table across the room sat Gwen and her care person, Candice. Since the almost-accident, I'd tutored Gwen a few times already—twice at her school and once at the counseling center on campus. Thankfully, she didn't hold a grudge about me throwing her to the ground to avoid that oncoming car. In fact, we worked well together.

I rose and crossed the room. "Well, hello, Gwen."

Gwen jumped to her feet and wrapped her arms around my waist. "Hi, Miss Sara."

Candice smiled. "What a nice surprise. How are you today, Sara?"

I wrapped my arms around Gwen's warm body and patted her back. "I'm good." I pulled back from Gwen and stared at her. "Have you been doing your reading?"

Gwen nodded and returned to her seat. She picked up a half-eaten bag of potato chips and resumed eating.

"I made up a quiz for you to take." I wagged a playful finger. "So, you better make sure you read that next chapter."

Gwen chewed on her chips. *Crunch, crunch, crunch.*

"Her reading has improved," Candice said with a spring in her voice. "We took a vocabulary test yesterday, and she did very well."

Gwen's improvement with reading had nothing to do with anything I had done, but I was proud of her anyway.

"I'm impressed with Gwen's reading. I'm hoping after winter break we can bump her up to the next level." I bent closer to Gwen. "I'll pick something fun."

Gwen sat up a little taller as she listened. If teaching was as rewarding as tutoring students like Gwen was, then I had chosen my dream job.

Through the window, I saw Amy approach the cafeteria entrance. She had a few letters in her hand.

"Well, enjoy your snacks. It was nice seeing you both." I patted Gwen's shoulder. "I'll see you tomorrow."

I returned to my table just as Amy got there.

"You ready?" She grabbed her leather bag and stuffed her mail inside of it.

"Yes." As we headed out, I glanced over at Gwen and Candice. "I love working with her." I slung my backpack over my shoulder and pushed through the door.

"Yeah, she's sweet. Did I tell you I got a job in town?"

We stepped outside to find the clouds had receded, exposing large patches of blue sky and the promise of better weather. The air was lighter, less congested with humidity.

"No, but that's great. Where?"

"Mike's Diner. A waitressing job." Amy pulled out a stick of lip balm from her utility-jacket pocket and coated her lips. A hint of watermelon sailed past my nose. "I've been waitressing for years. Should be an easy gig." She put her lip balm back in her pocket. "I can't believe Shag thought you and Rick would make a good couple. Was he high?"

I opened my mouth, astonished. "I know. I was a little surprised myself. Not that Rick isn't a nice guy and all."

Amy raised an eyebrow. "He's a jackass."

I pursed my lips. "He was drunk the night you saw him. He's a much nicer person than that." I hooked a few stray hairs behind my ear. "You wouldn't believe all the nice things he did for those kids."

Amy offered a blank stare. "What kids?"

I recounted the day with the flag football team.

"Hmph," was all Amy had to say. "He only did that to impress you."

I cocked my head. "He asked me to tag along because he felt sorry for me," I argued, but she was probably right, especially after Derek's latest comment. "I'm just happy he's helping Derek out."

Amy continued to roll her eyes and make dismissive hand gestures until I gave up trying to convince her that Rick wasn't the devil incarnate.

A long arm, covered in red-and-black flannel reached around Amy's neck. She stopped short and fell back into Luke's chest. "How's my wildcat doing today?" he asked before kissing the top of her spiky head.

Luke was as tall as Scott, but with half the body mass. With hazel-colored, puppy dog eyes, long hair, and relaxed clothing, a light amount of scruff on his jaw, Luke personified folk singer.

My parents' love of music made me think of Jackson Browne, although Amy had thought of Star Wars.

"Hi, Luke."

"Hey, Sara. Are you keeping my wildcat out of trouble?" He nudged his lips into her neck before looking up. "After her last text, I expected to find her math teacher hanging out the window by his balls."

Amy thrust her elbow into Luke's abdomen.

He winced and then laughed. "I've gotta make a run over to Rainbow Guitar. Want to come with me?" He kissed Amy's ear, his lips lingering on one of her lobes.

Amy quivered as though a chill had slid through her. "I guess so."

I enjoyed seeing the two of them together. "Let me take your backpack, and then you won't have to carry it." I reached out for it.

As Luke removed his arm, Amy pulled her pack from her shoulder and handed it over to me. "Thanks, Al. Catch you later."

The two of them walked away, Luke's arm across Amy's shoulders and Amy's hand buried deep in the back pocket of Luke's loose-fitting jeans. New romances were blossoming all over campus.

In my room, I kicked off my shoes and collapsed on my bed, my mind plummeting into a deep well of sleep. It was during the most delightful dream that a knock on my door forced my eyelids to flutter open. Seconds later, the hunky man who had just ravished me in my dreams was standing in my room.

"You've ruined me." Scott pulled me into his arms, landing several kisses on my lips and neck.

I molded my body against his, breathing him in. "How did I do that?"

Scott lifted his head off my neck. "I went to the wrong class-room, ran into a closed door, and forgot I had a frat meeting this afternoon. All I can think about is your sexy body." He hoisted me up by my hips while I wrapped my legs around his waist.

My mind was whisking up all sorts of luscious thoughts.

"I've been hard all day." He carried me over to the bed. "If I don't make love to you right now, I'll go insane."

Chapter Thirteen

For me, autumn meant colorful landscapes, warm sweaters on a crisp fall night, candy apples, pumpkins, black cats, and my favorite holiday: Halloween. This year, the autumn leaves brought changes in the weather along with changes in my attitude. I felt like a bird that had just learned to fly, and I was soaring. I had come to this school to try new things, learn more, and laugh every chance I got. And that was what I did. No longer sex deprived, I was sex crazed. I spoke up more in class and stopped worrying about what other people thought of me.

Amy got frustrated with me for not getting any of Dr. Adam's movie references to *The Big Lebowski*, so she forced me to watch the flick one weekend to educate myself. I was happy to spend more time bonding with her. Plus, the movie was hilarious. I almost peed my pants several times.

* * *

Abigail called me on the first Sunday in October. "I sent you a care package full of goodies. Let me know when you get it."

"That was so nice of you. What did you send me?" Abigail knew I loved treats and had been sending them to me at the boarding school for years.

"You'll see," she teased. "How are things going? Are you still seeing Scott?"

"Wow, a whole fifteen seconds before you asked," I said, serving up a heavy dose of sarcasm. "Yes, I'm still seeing him."

"I'm only asking." Abigail sounded defensive, but just a little. "He certainly is cute."

During parents' weekend, Abigail and Joel had finally gotten to meet Scott. It happened during a soccer tournament, so their time was brief. One thing that stuck out in my memory was what Scott had said to Abigail: "You have a very special daughter. She's the most remarkable person I've ever met."

I smiled thinking about it until Abigail spoke again.

"So, you promise you'll come home for Christmas break, right?"

I had only been home a handful of times over the years, and I was determined to change that. I even planned to visit the cemetery. No more cowering. It was time to face the past.

"I remember. Don't worry. I haven't changed my mind."

"Good," Abigail said. "Don't forget to call me when you get your package. Love you."

"I won't forget, and love you, too."

Excited to get mail other than the regular campus clutter, I visited my mailbox every day of the following week. It was Friday when the package finally arrived, along with another letter. I carried them both back to my dorm and tore into the box as if I were nine years old. Keeping with tradition, Abigail had sent me a bunch of cookies, chocolates, granola, chips, maple nuts, and teas—all made in Vermont, of course. She'd never let me forget home.

A note rested at the bottom. "Enjoy. Can't wait to see you over Christmas break. Love, Abigail and Joel."

I sat on my bed and sampled the treats while I opened the second piece of mail I had received that day. The envelope, heavier than most, included my first name only—in a gothic typeface, no less. *Fancy.* I pried open the flap, pulled out a thick sheet of paper, and frowned. Someone had cut words out of a magazine and pasted them on the paper to create a message:

"STAY AWAY FROM HIM OR SUFFER THE CONSE-QUENCES."

"What the ..." I'd thought, or maybe I'd hoped, that since the laptop fiasco and the graffiti on my car windows, Rachael, Mindy, Charlene, or whoever was doing these things had moved on. No such luck.

Why couldn't they just leave us alone? Amy was right. They needed to get a life.

When Scott came to my room later, he read my face before I could tell him about it. "You look upset."

"I am. I got something in the mail today." I pulled the envelope from my desk drawer. "Here." I held the envelope out.

Scott gripped the piece, his eyes tight. "What's this?"

I tipped my chin up. "Open it."

He opened the envelope and then the letter. Then he turned the paper over and then back again. "What the fuck?" His jaw flexed, his eyes clouded in confusion.

"I don't know exactly who it's from, although I have my guesses, but I assume it's an angry girl from your past." The words *your past* permeated the air like a foul odor. "I didn't mention this, but someone wrote nasty words on my car windshield, and I think someone even sabotaged my laptop."

Scott looked at me, his eyes outraged. "What? When did this happen?"

"A couple of months ago," I said sheepish. "They act like they own you."

For a moment, Scott looked down, his gaze wandering.

"I've taken you off the market, and it's made one of them angry."

"You should have told me about your car and your laptop. You never said why you got a new one. Don't keep these things from me." His voice was firm.

Old habits. I was used to handling things on my own.

"And even if it *is* some psycho girl, you need to be careful until we find out who's doing these things." Scott fanned the letter out to punctuate his words.

I'd spent years worrying about every possible disaster. Jealous ex-girlfriends were not on my list. Part of me wanted to freak out—and then I thought about Amy. She wouldn't cower, and neither would I.

I stepped closer and stretched my arms around his neck, threading my fingers through his satiny blond curls. "Remember when you offered to escort me around? I might need a bodyguard." I rose up on my tiptoes and tapped several small kisses on his lips.

Scott's forehead remained furrowed. "We're not done talking about this. Someone is targeting you, and I don't want anything to happen to you. We should bring this to campus security."

I nodded. "Good idea. I think if whoever this is wanted to hurt me, they would have done so by now, don't you?"

He released a heavy sigh and rubbed his forehead. "I don't know what to think."

I caressed his arm. "Well, I'll be careful. I won't go

anywhere alone, and I'll keep my guard up." That was easy for me. I'd lived my life that way.

Scott stared down at me with unconvinced eyes.

"I promise."

Finally, a subtle nod. "I'm worried about you. Who would do something like this?"

I had my list, but for now, I chose not to accuse anyone until I knew for sure.

"I honestly think someone is trying to scare me off. I won't let them do that, Scott." I'd spent too many years hiding behind tragedy. Cautious I could do. Running away, I could not.

He took me in his arms and rubbed my back. "I know. You're probably right. Just promise me you'll be careful."

"I will, but for now, let's get some dinner. And don't forget, we talked about shopping for our costumes later."

In two weeks, Scott's fraternity was hosting a Halloween party off campus. It was one of many parties he had mentioned when we'd first met. From what I heard, the fraternity had spared no expense in renting an old, abandoned mansion for the event.

"Oh, I almost forgot. I told our fraternity president, Christian, I'd make a trip over to the house to take measurements. Come with me?"

Christian was in my Creative Writing class. I'd forgotten.

"Sure. Let's go over there before it gets dark. We can grab dinner afterward." I was looking forward to the party, although the letter had dampened my costume-wearing enthusiasm.

✱ ✱ ✱

After we visited campus security, who told me they'd start a file but couldn't do much else, unless the culprit made contact, we arrived at the old Victorian mansion an hour later. My eyes drifted over the complicated asymmetrical shapes, the faded gray wood siding, and the porch. Any trim that wasn't broken or missing looked elaborate. Steep, pointed rooflines and a small tower lent a spooky ambiance to the place. It was perfect for a Halloween party. We climbed out of Scott's jeep and walked past a yard overgrown with dead weeds—some taller than I was.

"We hired a guy to clear the yard, and then we're gonna put tombstones all over the place." Scott's gaze roamed the terrain.

"Wow, that's cool. Where will you get the tombstones?"

"One of our frat brothers works in the drama department. He said he's got it covered, along with a few fog machines." At the front of the house, Scott bent down and peered under the porch. "They should fit under there nicely."

"Be careful. You don't know what's living under there." I imagined snakes and rodents of all kinds ready to attack at any moment.

Scott raised his head and gave me a look most men would give an overprotective spouse. He straightened up and took my hand. Together we climbed the porch steps, each one sagging under the weight of our feet. The chipped paint and rotted wood made the expansive front porch sad.

"Boy, if someone wanted to put some time and money into this place, it could be really nice." I imagined the building in its youthful state. It must've been striking.

Scott quirked a brow. "You'd need a magic wand."

He inserted the key into a tarnished lock and swung the door open. The hinges groaned from atrophy. I covered my mouth and nose. Old wallpaper stained with black-and-brown mold, decorated the walls, telling me where the musty smell came from. Several windows were broken and replaced with boards, allowing streams of light to invade the dilapidated manor. If ghosts lingered about, the creaky floorboards were sure to alert them of our presence.

"Who owns this place?" My eyes took it all in.

"Rick's family, I think." Scott shrugged. "He scored it for us, anyway. His mother is a real estate agent."

After we had finished surveying the first floor, Scott grabbed me by the waist and pulled me toward him. "Have I ever told you how haunted houses make me horny?" His lips parted as he moved his face closer to mine.

I shook my head, ready for fun. "No, you didn't. But doesn't *everything* make you horny?" I pushed him away and dashed out of the room. When Scott caught up to me, he waltzed me over to the cleanest wall possible and then edged me up against it. Bending, he unbuckled my jeans and then pulled them down along with my panties, his hand going to work between my legs.

I gasped with excitement.

His kiss was deep before he tugged at my lower lip with his teeth. "Did you hear that?" His gaze danced around the room. "The spirits like what they see."

"Oh, they do, do they?" I said, panting. "Well, then. Let's give them a show."

I unbuckled Scott's jeans and lowered them. No surprise he was hard and ready to satisfy.

Using the wall to stabilize us, Scott lifted me up and that was where he kept me as he planted himself inside of me. Something about the situation added a new layer of naughty, and I was really getting into it. With slow but intentional motion, he moved me up and down doing the lion's share of the work. I reached out and grabbed a tarnished wall sconce, tethering myself to the world around me. Moans floated around our heads. Not ghosts or specters of any kind, just two live humans lusting after each other.

* * *

We had dinner in town and then purchased our costumes, which consisted of a swashbuckler pirate for Scott and a pirate maiden for me. I threw the bags into the back of Scott's jeep and climbed into the passenger seat. He was waiting, wearing a full-on grin.

"We'll have to break these costumes in before we go." He faced me, his dimple telling me he wanted more adult playtime.

"What am I going to do with you?" I shook my head, still trying to recover from our last sexual encounter.

Scott leaned over and kissed me. "Just love me, babe."

Chapter Fourteen

bigail called me the following day, her voice bursting with energy. "A last-minute training seminar opened up that I've been hoping to take for my certification. It's optional, but when I heard where it's located, I signed up right away."

"Where is it?" I pressed the phone closer to my ear.

"Newport News, Virginia. I've already searched Google Maps. It's just over two hours from you. I'm staying at the Marriott at City Center. You *have* to come and stay with me." Her voice squeaked with excitement. "It won't cost you a penny, and you can shop and look around while I'm in class. We can go out to dinner and spend some time together. Just the girls."

"Absolutely. I'd love to come. When is it?"

"Two weeks from today. As I said, it's all last minute. I've already booked my plane ticket. Plus—"

"Wait. When did you say it was?" My eyes drifted over to the Vermont scenery calendar on my wall—another gift from Abigail.

When she repeated the date, I didn't have the guts to tell her it conflicted with Scott's Halloween party. Not that it would've done any good. Abigail was talking so fast it was difficult to get a word in edgewise.

"I've gotta run. Talk later."

"Wait." It was too late. She'd hung up. I thought about sending her a follow-up text, but I struggled with what to say.

As soon as Scott finished with his Saturday soccer practice, he came by my room. The minute he walked through the door, his face froze. "Has something else happened?" Somehow, he'd grown proficient at reading my face, an area my parents had also been skilled in, which made it tough to hide things. "Did you get another letter?"

"No, not at all. Abigail called me earlier ..."

Once I had finished explaining the situation, Scott looked at me as though he would have preferred the letter option. Although I hadn't said I was going to see Abigail, Scott scowled anyway. "Are you going? I was looking forward to the party and *you* being there."

I took his hand and swung it back and forth. "I know. I don't want to miss the party either, but Abigail was so excited. I couldn't even get a word in to tell her about the Halloween party."

Scott's jaw flexed. "Well, how long will you be gone?"

I stepped closer and placed my cheek against his chest. His lungs filled and emptied in a comforting rhythm—my happy place. "I think she'd like me to stay for the weekend, but I'm sure it would be okay if I went on Saturday and then came back on Sunday."

Scott eased my shoulders back. "That's great except the party *is* on Saturday."

Out came my lower lip. "I know. But ... Abigail has done so much for me, Scott."

For years *she* had always come to *me.* She never gave up on me. I stared at the floor, my brain wrapped in conflict. I thought of all the holidays and birthdays she had spent in a hotel room —all to accommodate me. Yes, I loved Halloween, but there would be more parties. This felt like a rare opportunity for me to give something back to a woman who had saved my life—in more ways than one.

For several long and arduous seconds, neither one of us spoke. Then Scott adjusted. "It's okay."

My head sprang up. "Really?"

Scott made a "tsking" sound. "Well, don't sound so psyched about it."

I rewrapped my arms around his thick waist. "I'm not *that* happy, handsome. I'm just glad you understand. Besides, I would rather be with you. Always."

* * *

On the last Friday in October, I packed a small suitcase for my trip to Newport News while Scott was still in class. As the sun slid below the horizon, we had dinner in town and then returned to Scott's room for the night. He stretched out on his bed to channel surf while I went into his bathroom. I opened the cabinet under the sink and pulled out, from the back, a surprise I had been hiding for days.

Several minutes later, his voice came drifting through the door. "Are you okay in there?" The cheering crowd from the sporting event he was watching on TV went mute. "Did that Italian dish make you sick?"

"I'll be right out." I dabbed my lips with one last layer of lip gloss, then puckered for the mirror.

With teased hair, dark eye makeup (borrowed from Amy), and a pirate maiden costume that left little room for my ribs

183

much less my breasts, I gazed into the mirror assessing my disguise. For the next several hours I was no longer Sara Browne, college student, I was Sara the morally corrupt and slutty pirate girl.

I opened the door and walked out, my bare feet kissing the floor.

Scott glanced over before his neck jerked back in my direction. "Wow!" His eyes were huge. "What's all this?"

"You said we should break in our costumes, remember?"

I glided across the room as Scott sat up against his headboard, his curiosity rising—along with another part of his anatomy. When I reached the bed, I climbed up beside him, straddled his body, and then gave him a luscious kiss, leaving nothing to the imagination.

Speechless, Scott's hands crawled up my thighs until he made another discovery.

"I didn't realize pirate girls went pantyless." His breathing was labored, his cheeks ruddy.

I grinned and licked my glossy lips. "Well, I'm a bad pirate girl. I think you need to give me forty licks, captain." I cupped my hands around my breasts and leaned my head back, imagining what Scott was going to do to me. A low moan vibrated from my throat.

Scott buried his face between my breasts and kissed them generously.

"I love the feeling of your tits against my face."

Eager for more, he attempted to unlace my peasant blouse.

I lifted his hand away and wagged my finger back and forth. "I only let pirates do that to me."

Scott's eyes shined with dirty intentions. "Well, don't start without me." He lifted my body gently off him and sprang from his bed to change. When Captain Scott Williams returned to the bed, he showed me just how naughty pirates could be.

* * *

After breakfast the next morning, Scott escorted me to my car. Our kinky night of role-playing had my hips lopsided—or at least they felt that way. I did my best to walk normally.

Scott opened the door to my back seat and placed my small suitcase, along with my backpack, inside. When he closed the door, he faced me. "I'll miss you, babe." He blinked slowly.

"I'll miss you, too. Have fun tonight." I scrunched my face and pointed my index finger. "But not too much fun."

Scott grabbed my waist, burying his face in my neck. He inhaled before lifting his head away. "You don't have to worry." He grazed his finger across my lips. "I'll be thinking about my pirate maiden from last night." Pressed up against me, his erection backed his words. He was insatiable.

My cheeks flushed as I stepped back and blew him a kiss.

I drove out of the parking lot, glancing at Scott in my rearview. It was our first separation, and my eyes watered. Yup, I was still crushing.

* * *

I arrived in Newport News at one o'clock just missing Abigail for lunch. She had left a key for me at the front desk. I opened the door to our room, the sweet aroma of lavender—Abigail's signature scent—brought nostalgia to my heart. A small note sat waiting on the nightstand: "Make yourself comfortable. I'll be back at five to take you to dinner. Can't wait to see you."

I sent a quick text to Scott informing him I had arrived, removed my shoes, then took out some books to study for an upcoming Creative Writing test. It wasn't long before my eyes grew heavy.

The sound of the lock mechanism on the door made me

realize I had dozed off. I sat up and rubbed my eyes as Abigail came waltzing in.

"You fell asleep?" She smiled, her tone sympathetic. "How was your drive here?"

I yawned and stretched. "Long."

"I was starting to worry until I got your text." Abigail carried a canvas bag full of papers and folders over to a table in the corner of the room, where she set it down. "How long did it take you to get here?"

I stretched out a few more cramped muscles. "Three-and-a-quarter hours." The route would normally take someone two and a half. I was a turtle.

"Wow." Then Abigail looked at me with eyes that had known me forever.

"Well, splash some water on your face, and let's go to Williamsburg. I heard about a great restaurant there. There's also a large outlet mall, so we can shop afterward. I'll drive." She puttered around the room, getting herself ready.

We had dinner at a family-owned restaurant where I ordered the best tenderloin salad I had ever tasted. The honey-mustard dressing was scrumptious, although Abigail picked at her food.

As we walked out of the restaurant, I asked, "Did you not like your meal?"

"It was good. Just trying to shed a few pounds before the holidays." From her driver's side door, she stared at me from across the roof. "Ready to shop till you drop?"

"Oh, yeah."

We visited half a dozen stores where I purchased a light-blue chenille sweater, a pair of jeans, and a black fleece jacket. With the temperatures getting cooler, I felt the need for more outerwear. Just like with dinner, Abigail insisted on paying.

"I don't get many chances to spoil you, young lady, so let me have this." Credit card in hand, she was insistent.

We arrived back at the hotel a half hour later. My phone dinged in a text from Scott. He'd sent so many I'd lost count. I loved knowing how much he missed me.

His latest text read, "I was going to blow off the party, but Jason shamed me into it. I'm wearing my soccer uniform. Only you get to see the pirate. Every time I think of last night, I'm rock hard for you, baby. I'm apologizing now for any drunken or perverted texts you may get later. Love you."

I texted back: "Lol. Have fun ... but be careful. Love you, too, handsome."

After changing into our pajamas, Abigail and I watched a remake of the movie *Ghostbusters* in honor of Halloween. When the movie was over, we brushed our teeth and climbed into our beds. I snuggled into my sheets as Abigail clicked off the light. A small gap between the drapes allowed light to spill in from the street below.

"So ..." Abigail rolled over to face me. She hugged her pillow under her neck and ear. "You and Scott are pretty serious, huh?"

I flipped onto my side to see her across the three-foot gap between our queen-size beds. "Yeah. You could say that."

Abigail cleared her throat. "So, should we have the birth control talk? Or is it a little too early for that?"

I gulped. Of all the questions I had expected her to ask me, that was *not* one of them.

"Well . . ." Scott and I had been together for ten weeks, and intimate for seven. I was sure Abigail wouldn't approve. She was the closest thing I had to a mother, and her opinion of me meant a lot. Would she be ashamed of me?

"I see." She released a breath. "Dare I ask how long this has been going on?"

I pulled a hand out of my blanket to rub my left eye. "Well, let me put your mind at ease. I am on birth control, and I was when the time came. Scott has also been attentive about that. Plus, it was *my* decision, not his." I swallowed. "I love him, Abigail, and he loves me. We talk about the future all the time. Scott wants to be an architect, you know." I fell onto my back and stared up at the ceiling. "I have these dreams of us living together—him telling me about his day at the office as we sip our wine and make dinner together in our tiny apartment. And then I tell him about a student who did something funny in my classroom." I sighed. "Sometimes, I swear I can almost smell the spaghetti sauce cooking on the stove."

Abigail grew silent for a moment. "You sound just like your mom did when she would talk about your dad." She reached her hand out to me as I did the same. "I had never seen two people more in love than your parents. Do you remember how they would dance around the kitchen?"

An image of Daddy's arms wrapped around my mom, her head rested against his chest came to mind. "I do."

"From watching them," she said, "I learned for myself what I wanted in a relationship. Before I met your mother, I had only known jerks."

"I'm so sorry, Abigail."

She let go of my hand, waving me off. "Oh, it's not that bad. It's just that watching them showed me what was possible." She snuggled her pillow tighter. "And now I have Joel."

"Yes, you do. And he's great."

Abigail yawned. "And you have Scott." She rolled onto her back. "Maybe your parents had a hand in that, too."

I thought about how thankful I was for my life. If my parents had anything to do with it, I was grateful, which I told them in a silent prayer.

Chapter Fifteen

I waited for Abigail to finish her last seminar the following day. We had a late lunch before she drove my car to the Norfolk airport.

"There's no need to get parking." She pulled up to the curb and shifted the car into park. "Will you be okay driving back to school?"

I put my hand on the door latch. "I'll be fine. I'm getting better at driving, and I'll take my time. I may try to reach Scott again. Hopefully, he can keep me company."

Unlike yesterday's flurry of texts, he was MIA. I had seen firsthand how those parties went, and this *was* Halloween, after all. The party was probably an all-nighter. If my predictions were right, Scott was sleeping the day away.

Once Abigail had retrieved her suitcase from the trunk, we shared a long embrace. "I can't wait to see you at Christmas." Her eyes glimmered with tears. "I'll have a whole month to spoil you." She backed up a few steps.

"I'm looking forward to it, too. Love you." I waved as she turned and disappeared through the airport entrance.

I tried to reach Scott several times on the road. Still no answer.

Don't worry, he's fine.

I managed three hours on my return trip, not three and a quarter. Progress.

* * *

It was dark when I arrived on campus. A crescent moon shone high above, like a purse for the thousands of cosmic diamonds now scattered across the autumn sky. Unable to reach Scott by phone, I drove to his dorm parking lot and dashed over to his room, eager to see him.

Halloween had exploded inside the walls of the frat house: decorations they had carted back from the old, abandoned mansion. The air was stale and tired. Fraternity guys, along with a few girls, lounged on the couches, the recliners, and the floor. A football game played on a large TV, several blank stares aimed in its direction. As I stepped with caution over the battle-field of bodies, Owen and Kevin offered a passing wave.

In the kitchen, Rick sat at the table with a blond girl whom I didn't recognize. *New girlfriend?* They were examining pictures from the party on a laptop in front of them.

"How was the party?" I craned my neck, curious.

Rick's normally pristine hair was matted to one side, and his complexion matched those of the people in the living room.

"Rough."

"Is Scott in his room?" I asked, grateful to have missed the event.

"I think so. Be gentle with him," Rick said.

Did Scott look worse than these people did? I ventured down the hallway, concerned. How crazy did things get?

I found Scott lying face down on his bed and snoring like a

polar bear in hibernation. I locked the door, undressed, and snuggled in next to him. Rubbing my body against his had me so worked up, I came close to climaxing on my own. I ran my hands over his tight butt and back, planting a few tender kisses on his neck. No reaction. Judging by his deep, rhythmic breathing, he must've been tired. I chose not to wake him and drifted off to sleep.

* * *

A hand brushed across my cheek causing my eyes to flutter open. The sun filtering through the vinyl blinds brought new light and energy to the room. I couldn't wait to make love to Scott. What a great way to welcome me back.

"Good morning, sunshine." Scott sounded like he had been gargling with gravel.

I rolled over to face bloodshot eyes, dark-purple rings, and the complexion of a ghost.

"You look horrible." I rubbed my eyes and stared again. "I mean, are you okay?"

Scott flopped onto his back and blew out his lungs.

"Scott?"

"I'm fine. The party just kicked my ass a little." His voice was thick and raspy.

"The party was two days ago." I sat up, worried. "How much did you drink?"

Scott sat up and swung his feet over the side of the bed, his back providing a perfect barrier. "Too much." He combed his fingers through his hair and let out an extended yawn, his head sagging.

I caressed his back while trying to peer around him.

"I missed you, babe." He made it to his feet and, with stiff movements, walked into his bathroom.

No morning cuddles?

A few seconds later, the shower turned on. This was not the reception I had envisioned. Where was my insatiable boyfriend? After several minutes, I dressed in my clothes from the night before. When I was finished, I cracked the door open and peered into the steam-filled bathroom.

"I've got a nine o'clock class, so I'm gonna run back to my room and get showered and changed." I was hoping for another option. "Unless there's room in there for two."

No response, until Scott cleared his throat.

"I'm almost done, babe, and I've got a meeting with one of my professors. Can I take a rain check?" He sounded so different, his voice hollow and weak.

"Sure." I closed the door and pouted. A two-day hangover? It must've been a wild night.

With my lower lip protruding, I gathered my things together and left the room, experiencing my first bout of sexual frustration. Scott *had* created a monster.

* * *

After a quick bite at the snack bar, I found my regular seat in the front row of Creative Writing and prepared myself for class. The stench of Mindy's perfume arrived just before she took the seat next to mine. Charlene sat next to her.

"How's Scott feeling?" Mindy batted her long lashes at me, her shiny lips forming a plastic smile.

"Fine." Why did *she* want to know? "Class is about to start. Dr. Baker likes to call on the front row a lot." *In other words, get lost.* "Did you read the material?"

When Mindy didn't answer, I glanced over, apprehensive. A snarky grin remained spread across her superficial face. "I was just wondering how our teddy bear was feeling. He sure felt good the other night."

My skin crawled.

After dropping her verbal bombshell, she sauntered off, as did her body double, Charlene.

I was about to follow and confront her when Dr. Baker entered the room.

"Good morning, class. I hope you all had a nice weekend."

Giggles drifted through the air from behind me. *Ignore it*, I told myself. *Nothing happened. They are just trying to get to you.* I had to believe I was right.

Dr. Baker's gaze scanned over the class. "I hope you all finished reading, *The Old Man and the Sea*, because I'm giving you a pop quiz."

I made a beeline for the café where Derek worked. Maybe he could tell me more about the party. I grabbed a fruit smoothie and walked up in line to find him handling the register.

"How was your trip?" He punched a few keys on the register to ring up my purchase.

"Good. Can you take a break?"

"Um. Yeah, I came in early to prep, so I'm due for a break anyway." Derek signaled to a co-worker in the back of the kitchen. "Give me a couple of minutes."

I found an open table and waited until Derek came out with a tray full of food. He was always hungry. "I've got fifteen minutes." He sat next to me.

"I was surprised to see Scott still pretty sick this morning," I said, eager to grill him. "How was he at the party? Did he drink a lot?"

Derek cocked his head and swallowed. "Sara, we *all* drank a lot."

Did he cheat on me?

"I actually hung out with Scott until around ten or so. We shot the shit. After that, I had to refill the fog juice and prop up a few tombstones that had fallen over in the yard." He held his sandwich out in front of him, grinning. "A cute girl named Penny wasn't feeling well, so I stayed outside with her. I think she might like me."

I was happy to hear that he'd met a girl he liked. I wanted to ask him more about her, but after that comment from Mindy, I had other things on my mind. I kept reminding myself about the last time I had suspected Scott of cheating *and* how much those girls enjoyed getting under my skin.

Derek cleared his throat. "Anyway, I guess I didn't see much of Scott after that. Did you say he's still sick?" He dumped his French fries onto his tray and grabbed a handful.

"He's not horrible or anything, but he doesn't look well."

I finally mustered the nerve to ask the question that had been burning in my throat. "Were any girls trying to hook up with him?" *Like Mindy and Charlene?*

Derek had just stuffed what remained of his chicken sandwich into his mouth. With his cheeks protruding, he motioned with his finger for me to wait. I found myself counting the seconds. After he had swallowed the sizeable bite, he chased it with a brief sip of his drink.

"If you keep asking me questions, I'm never gonna get to eat." He looked up while trying to recall the night. "No, I didn't see him with anyone. Am I safe to keep eating?" He paused.

"Go ahead." I felt like a complete dork. A paranoid one.

"Why are you so worried?" Amy had materialized next to me with her backpack slung over her shoulder. She had a way of sneaking up.

"Mindy and Charlene said some crap to me in English class." I had been keeping Amy informed on all the prior drama.

"Again? Man, those bitches are relentless. Don't let them get to you. Scott came clean on them, right?" Amy sat on the opposite side of the table, rummaging through her bag.

"Yeah, sort of." I took a sip from my drink, the taste of strawberry and kiwi bursting on my taste buds.

"They're just trying to mind-fuck you. Don't let them."

Amy was right. I bowed my head, disgusted with myself. I had spent the past six years of my life waiting for the next bomb to go off. Why couldn't I accept a good life that was staring me right in the face? In my mind, there had to be a weak spot or a crack in the dam—or a cheating boyfriend.

Amy stopped searching through her backpack and looked up. She patted the table to get my attention. "Stop worrying about it. I'm sure the big guy fought off all the female demons."

I imagined a flock dancing around him.

"So, it was a wild party, huh?" Amy looked over to Derek.

"Oh, most definitely. A rager. I found this one guy outside drunk off his ass talking to a tombstone like it was his long-lost buddy. Another guy kept hiding in a coffin Rick had brought for the living room. He kept jumping out at cute girls until one of them barfed all over him." Derek continued to entertain us with his stories. Apparently, several people vomited in the bushes as well, and a few more of the windows got shattered. The late-night crowd got so rowdy the cops came. Before I could ask, Derek assured me Scott wasn't around by then.

While Derek devoured what was left of his meal, Amy checked her phone. "We need to get to class, Al. Don't forget. We have to study for our art test. I heard the history part is really fucking hard." She rose from her chair. "I'm going to the library after class if you want to join."

I took one last sip of smoothie. "Sure, that would be great."

Derek finished his meal, crumpled the wrappers into a ball, and then stood, taking his tray in his hands. "I gotta head back to work anyway. Thanks for the company, and tell Scott I said hi."

"I will." It was nice to hear him talk about Scott that way. I really wanted them to get along.

After art class and two hours of studying with Amy, I texted Scott: "How are you feeling?"

A few seconds later, a response came back: "Better. Want me to come by your room when I get out of statistics?"

I typed, "Is the sky blue?" A winking emoji followed.

When Scott showed up at my door forty-five minutes later, I felt like a champagne bottle ready to pop its cork. Combustible, sexual energy filled every inch of my body.

"I've been missing you. A lot." I yanked him through the doorway before planting numerous kisses on his lips, face, and shirt.

"Wow, I guess so." Scott ran his hands up and down my back.

He still looked gray, but I didn't let it stop me. I peeled his jacket off and then worked on the buttons of his shirt. A huge grin spread across his face. "I like where this is going."

In less than thirty seconds, we were naked.

* * *

While my insides settled down, I rested my head on Scott's chest, listening to the sounds of his lungs and heart. I loved it when we lay naked together, skin touching skin.

"I missed you so much." I brushed my fingers over his left nipple, making it stiffen.

Scott gazed down at me. He twirled a few locks of my hair around his finger. "I missed you more, babe."

I reached up to graze his cheek. The stubble tickled the pads of my fingers. Scott shaved regularly, but I enjoyed the new rugged look. "You're becoming more like a pirate every day."

He rubbed his chin. "Yeah, I know I need to shave."

"I don't mind it." I rested my chin on his chest and stared up at him. "So, Derek said the party was a wild night."

"I guess so. I left pretty early."

"Well, what did I miss? I'm dying to hear all about it."

"Not much to tell."

I nudged him. "Well, tell me anyway."

Scott exhaled—loudly—then slid me off him and sat up. He got out of bed and put on his boxer briefs. Was he leaving? Normally, he'd be ready for round two.

"Scott?" I swung my feet over the side of the bed while wrapping a blanket over my shoulders. "Why are you getting dressed?"

Keeping his eyes downcast, he shook out his jeans and stepped into the legs.

"Are you going somewhere?"

He didn't answer me right away. Instead, he finished putting his jeans on.

What was happening?

He rubbed the back of his neck. "Yeah, I gotta go. I got a ... meeting." He didn't sound convincing—at all. In fact, he sounded like someone who had just made up an excuse to leave.

I walked over to him. "Is everything okay? Did something happen at the party that you need to tell me about?"

Scott looked away. "No, of course not."

Again, not convincing.

Then why won't you look at me?

"Something's wrong; I can tell. Did you hook up with someone?" My gut wrenched at the thought. *Was it Mindy and Charlene? Rachael? Please say no.*

Scott swiped a hand down his face and exhaled. "No. The truth is, I got really drunk and threw up all over the place. My stomach still feels kind of fucked up from it. I won't be drinking any more shots for a while." He put on his shirt but left it unbuttoned.

I remembered what Derek had told me, although he'd never mentioned Scott being sick.

"Jason had to bring me back to my room. I'm a little embarrassed for making such an ass out of myself."

The knots in my stomach loosened, but only a notch. "Well, you shouldn't feel so bad. From what Derek said, a lot of people got sick. He even told me the cops were called at the end of the night."

"I heard." Scott buttoned his shirt, put on his socks and shoes, and then grabbed his backpack and coat. "Listen, babe, I've gotta run."

Out the door he went, no kiss goodbye, leaving me suspicious and worried.

Chapter Sixteen

The next day brought unseasonably warm temperatures. Since Gwen was on campus, I told her we should do her required reading at a picnic table out on the Great Lawn next to the Student Union Building, which I cleared with Candice first. Gwen was all for it. We sat at a table, the sunshine warm on our backs.

"Then—we—walled." Gwen caught herself. "Then—we—walked—across—the—classroom—to—where—a—hamburger—sat—in—a—cage." She giggled.

I tapped her arm. "Let's try that word again. We can sound it out together." I pointed to the word *hamster* and mouthed the word with her.

Gwen said, "Hamburger," and giggled some more. The fresh air was making her silly.

I held back my own laughter. "Now, does that make any sense? Would a hamburger be in a cage?" I anticipated her answer long before Gwen nodded emphatically.

I pointed to the word again. "Let's try that first syllable." I used my finger to block the *ster* portion of the word.

Before Gwen could respond, a voice came hurling through the air at me like a snowball. "I was surprised you weren't at the Halloween party."

Rachael was five feet away with three of her friends. Did she ever travel alone?

I ground my teeth and firmed my face, ready for whatever she wanted to dish out.

One of Rachael's friends spotted someone she knew and walked off. Her other friends followed. "Did you really think he was going to change for you?" With her hand poised on her hip, Rachael glanced down at her cell, and then her icy gaze found me again.

"Is there something you want, Rachael?" I sat up straighter, my meal from earlier curdling in my stomach. "I'm working right now. And even if I weren't, I wouldn't waste an ounce of my breath on someone like you."

Rachael rolled her eyes. "Whatever."

"Let's go back inside, Gwen." I got up and urged Gwen to do the same.

Mindy, Charlene, and Rachael were on the prowl, and I had to keep my guard up. They knew I hadn't been at the party, so they were using it to make me doubt Scott.

My week didn't improve much after that. Scott was moody, impatient, and distracted. When I mentioned Rachael, he came close to barking at me. "She's a bitch, Sara. Don't let her get to you." A few times, I'd catch him staring off into space, his shoulders like two stiff boulders. Whatever was upsetting him, he wasn't willing to tell me about it. And that bothered me more than anything else did.

* * *

"I have a surprise for you," Scott said, beaming.

It was Wednesday afternoon and we had decided to stay on campus for Thanksgiving weekend. Since I was going home for Christmas break, Abigail didn't argue. "There's a nice resort called the Tortoise Inn that's not far from here. I made reservations for us. What do you think about sleeping in and ordering room service?" A glimmer of excitement returned to Scott's eyes.

It was a relief to see him coming out of his funk.

"We can drive around and check out what's left of the foliage season or go for another hike. Plus, on their website they show a massive Thanksgiving buffet with carving stations and tons of food."

I missed the foliage season back home and was psyched about the idea of leaf-peeping with him. "Count me in."

We spent the next hour packing our bags and then hit the road. As we drove along Route 250, I soaked in the mountainous scenery, letting my mind wander back to my childhood. Middlebury was a beautiful place to grow up, regardless of the time of year, but in the fall the explosion of color was nothing short of magical. Mountains of candy, I used to say. On a clear day, the crisp blue sky provided a perfect backdrop for the brilliant shades of yellow, orange, and red. My mother and I would collect the best-looking leaves and press them into a book. If she were here, I imagined she'd love Charlottesville in the fall—not to mention my fetching boyfriend. I laced my fingers inside of Scott's hand while enjoying the sentimental moment.

As we traveled up the long driveway of the inn, I admired the country estate nestled at the base of the Blue Ridge Mountains.

Guests moved about as we walked through a stone archway and into a lobby decorated with shiny dark woods, soft lighting, and an abundance of country charm, the scent of cinnamon and cloves in the air. I couldn't wait to see our room.

An antique-looking four-poster bed, an armoire, a desk, and a beautiful stone fireplace, along with the aroma of fresh linens, welcomed me at the door to our room. I imagined us making love in front of a crackling fire. In the corner of the room sat a cream-colored oversized armchair that I couldn't resist plunging into.

"Wow, this place is amazing."

"I'm glad you like it," Scott said with a boost in his tone.

Scott set our bags on the floor and then crossed the room to where I was sitting in the chair. He took my hands in his and pulled me up, flinging me over his shoulder like a sack of horse grain. I squealed as he carried me over to the bed, his shoulders vibrating with laughter.

"Can we make a fire first?" Lying on our bed, I ran my fingers down the side of his cheek.

"Of course." He drifted over to the fireplace, glancing back every few seconds with hungry eyes.

While he worked on layering the logs and kindling, I decided to change into a sexy black negligee I had purchased in town.

"I'm going to freshen up."

On his knees, Scott stopped and glanced over his shoulder. "You can't improve on perfection, babe."

After I had put on my negligee, brushed out my hair, and sprayed a smidge of perfume between my breasts, I examined myself in front of the bathroom mirror. A memory sprang to life of me sitting on the floor watching my mother primp before date night with Daddy. The way she hummed and carried her shoulders, the sparkle in her eyes as she applied her lipstick. She was in love, and so was I.

I came out of the bathroom and posed with my hand pressed against the doorjamb. "It's not a pirate girl costume, but I hope you like it."

"You're sexy as hell, woman." Scott's eyes never left me as I crossed the room and slid an afghan off the back of the over-sized chair, which I dragged behind me.

While I spread the blanket out in front of the fireplace, Scott undressed in record time. He grabbed a pillow off the king-size bed and scooted across the room to join me.

With the whispering hisses and pops from the burning embers in my ears, I gazed up into Scott's wanting eyes.

"I've been waiting all day to get you naked." With his teeth, Scott pulled the strap of my slip down before his lips found my shoulder. He ran his fingers up my leg and hip, igniting a burning need in their wake. Sensing his urge and my own, I raised my arms over my head and arched my back, allowing him to pull the slip over my head. My pulse roared as he kissed my neck and wandered past my collarbone, finding my breasts. He always started there. His tongue grazed over my nipples, prompting a whimper from my lips. I ran my hands down his strapping back and cupped his firm butt before I moved to the front, embracing his massive erection. Scott breathed deep, his eyes blinking in slow motion. With our mouths and our hands, we explored each other's bodies for several minutes until I couldn't wait any longer. I pushed him over onto his back and straddled him. With each lift of my hips, I enjoyed the pulsing sensation of him inside me. As our bodies moved to satisfy one another, I lost myself in everything primal. Scott brought me to heights that consumed my every desire. I cried out several times, unable to contain myself and unaware of anyone who could possibly hear.

After we made love, I stretched out on my side facing the fire, Scott's solid frame twined around me like a giant beanstalk. Between the light snaps of the fire and the sensation of Scott's fingers brushing up and down the contour of my side, I grew sleepy.

"Oh, I have another surprise for you."

I jolted.

"I'm sorry, babe. I didn't mean to wake you." He kissed the top of my head. "It can wait."

Surprise? Wait? Yeah, right.

"No, it's okay. You have a surprise?" I rolled up onto my hip and rubbed my eyes.

Like a jack-in-the-box, Scott sprang from the floor and crossed the room to where his overnight bag sat waiting. He returned to the floor and propped himself up on one elbow.

"I bought you a present."

"You did?" I sounded like I'd been sucking helium.

"I hope you like it." He handed me a velvet box, light blue in color and the size of a small picture frame.

I gazed at the box and then back up at Scott.

"Open it." His eyes wide, he tipped his chin.

I opened the box to reveal a necklace. The firelight made the white gold pendant, comprised of two dainty hearts intertwined and studded in small diamond studs, gleam. I covered my mouth, amazed.

"It's an early Christmas present." He pointed at the pendant. "Those two hearts are you and me." He lifted my hand to kiss my knuckle. "Every day with you is like winning the mother of all lotteries. You are my heart and soul, Sara. I'm so glad I have you in my life." He removed the necklace and placed it around my neck, making sure the clasp was tight.

Tears welled. "I love it, Scott, and I feel the same way about you." I stared into his warm eyes, my heart ready to burst. "Life was so hard for me after my parents died. I felt so alone and different from everyone else."

Scott stayed close, his hand caressing my back, his eyes receptive.

"There were times when I just wanted to give up. I never

imagined that I'd meet someone like you—or that I'd ever be this happy."

Scott wiped a tear from my eye as I smiled and touched his leg. "I mean, I smile all the time ... and it's because I have you in my life."

All at once, his face went slack, his eyes dimming.

Did I say something wrong?

"I know I'm not perfect, Sara, and I know I fuck up." His shoulders sagged, and his head drooped. "But don't lose faith in me."

I cupped his strong jaw in my hands and stared deep into his eyes. "I won't." When that didn't perk him up, I spent the next hour letting my body do the convincing.

* * *

On the drive back to school on Sunday afternoon, I stared over at Scott, feeling so fortunate for my life. I'd been doing that a lot lately.

I leaned over and kissed his cheek. "I was just thinking about how lucky I am to be with you."

"*I'm* the lucky one." He reached over and rubbed the muscles at the back of my neck. I rested my head against the headrest and enjoyed the massage.

"Our fraternity is hosting a holiday formal in a few weeks, right before winter break." Scott pulled his hand back. "Would you like to go?"

"Um. Yes!" I lifted my head and pulled the mirror down to apply lip gloss to my parched lips. "I've never been to a prom." I slapped the mirror closed while raising the visor back into position.

"I'll make sure it's a special night, then," he said.

I enjoyed the perkiness in Scott's voice. Whatever had been

dragging him down was over. What a relief.

"I'll make reservations for dinner at the Tortoise Inn."

A dark cloud moved aside, allowing a ray of sunlight to beam down on my pendant, traveling through the lattice of stones and making it sparkle against the dash like a kaleidoscope. I held it between my fingers, reveling in the moment when he gave it to me.

"You'll have to buy a dress." Scott gave me a once-over.

I let go of the pendant. "What types of dresses do the girls typically wear?"

Scott rested his hand atop the steering wheel and made subtle motions as he spoke. "The girls usually wear formal gowns. Some guys rent tuxes, others wear suits." His gaze traveled all over me again as though he had something in mind. "For you, I suggest something strapless—lots of cleavage." His lips curved upward. "And extremely short would be nice."

"Where do you want me to purchase this dress? Victoria's Secret?" I asked sarcastically.

Scott's face lit up as though I had just made a genius suggestion. "That's perfect. I'll even go shopping with you."

I slapped him on the arm. "I don't think so." If I wanted a respectable dress, Scott would *not* be the one picking it out.

We talked a bit more about the party before we switched to the topic of when we'd see each other over winter break. I planned to ask Abigail if Scott could come visit for New Year's Eve. As I thought about all the fun we were going to have, an unexpected cold front crashed into Scott's mood. It happened when we reached campus. He slammed on the horn, a few expletives flying from his mouth, when another driver hesitated at a stop sign in front of us for one millisecond too long. It wasn't that big a deal, but Scott was definitely making it one. When we passed through the intersection, his clenched jaw and tight shoulders remained intact. As we unloaded our bags, his face was so tight I thought a blood vessel was going to burst in his forehead.

Aside from our weekend getaway, he'd been this way since the Halloween party. My fear was that he'd cheated, but I trusted that he wouldn't do that. I had to. He was my everything, and I needed to believe in him.

Chapter Seventeen

It took some persuading, but I managed to convince Amy to go to the mall with me a couple of weeks later.

"First you want my opinion about the big guy, and now you want fashion advice? I don't get you, Al." Amy rode in the passenger seat of my Subaru. "We have different tastes." She fluffed her spiky hair as she spoke.

She was right, of course, but I knew she had my best interests at heart. That counted for something. "You're great at picking out clothes and blending colors."

Amy shrugged one shoulder and tipped her head as if to say, "Well, that's true." She sat looking out her side window until she shouted, "Jesus, could you speed up? I could walk faster."

Startled, I tapped the gas a little harder, but not enough to appease her. It took us a while, but we managed to reach the mall, despite Amy's grumbling.

After passing through three levels of a parking garage, I found a vacant spot on the roof.

An angry early December wind confronted me as I stepped

out of my car, cutting all the way to my bones. I shivered, pulling my coat tighter.

Together, we hustled across the windy lot and into the elevator, where I pushed the button on the panel for the first floor.

"Where do you want to go first?" Amy blew warm air onto her fists.

"Let's try Macy's, and then we can hit Dillard's." I rubbed my hands together, hoping to start a fire.

A moment later, the doors sprang open to Christmastime at the mall. Stressed-out shoppers, shrieking children, and bored husbands scuttled past us. Teenage girls walked in clusters, enthralled with their cell phones. Salesclerks standing at various kiosks pushed everything from colorful scarves to sunglasses. I slipped through the throngs of people in search of an anchor store.

"It's over there." Amy pointed at a large Macy's sign hanging over the store's entrance.

We walked through the Macy's men's department and rode the escalator up to the second floor, where we found women's formal wear.

"I'm gonna look for dresses *I* think would look good on you." Amy attacked a rack full of gowns, determination riding on her shoulders.

"Sounds good." I took the rack next to her.

I felt like a child standing in my mother's closet ready to play dress-up. Every gown with shiny sequins, frilly chiffon, and silky satin fabrics, dazzled me. I wanted them all.

A few short minutes later, I threw one last gown over my arm, which was starting to sag. "I've picked out a few already. I'm going to try these on."

Amy peered over her shoulder. "Holy shit, you work fast. Are they even in your size?"

I examined the bundle in my arms, my voice wavering. "I think so?"

Amy shook her head, her eyes laughing. "I can see this is going to take some time. Okay, I'll keep looking, and if I find anything, I'll bring it in to you. You're a size four, right?"

I nodded and then walked past two three-way mirrors, where a heavyset female attendant guarded the dressing room entrance. Going by the piles of discarded clothes she was sorting through, I assumed it had been a busy morning.

Next to the dressing rooms was a small lounge area where two men sat scrolling through their cell phones.

The slightly pale saleswoman examined the stack of dresses in my arms. "All the dressing rooms are full, but it shouldn't be a long wait. How many items do you have?"

I checked. "Six."

Just as the attendant handed me a small plastic sign, a voice said, "I can't believe they don't even have a Saks here." Rachael came strolling out wearing a tight black dress that hugged every curve of her slender body. My excitement plummeted like an elevator losing its cables. As she sauntered over to one of many mirrors as if she were walking a runway, I was amazed at her pretention. She twisted her body back and forth, her hands running down the fabric while one of her friends stayed close, offering her opinion.

"Do you think he'll like it?" Through the mirror, Rachael looked right at me when she asked the question.

Did she want *my* opinion? *Weirdo.* I focused on the dresses in my arms to avoid finding out.

A few seconds later, she found me again. "Where did you get those, off the clearance rack?" She crinkled her lip as she catwalked past me on her way back into the dressing room. A burst of laughter rode down the carpet behind her.

"I feel sorry for the poor bastard who's taking her out," Amy said, coming up from behind me.

"Yup." Blowing out my lips, I handed the saleswoman back the small plastic sign. "I've changed my mind." I faced Amy. "Time to find another store."

"Don't let her scare you off. She's nothing but a skank." With her brow pulled down, Amy's voice blared—loud enough to make the salesclerk flinch. I was sure Rachael could hear her as well. Not that that bothered me any.

I headed for the dress rack, Amy close behind. "I'm not leaving because I'm afraid of her." There were a lot of things that frightened me, but Rachael wasn't one of them. "This was supposed to be fun, and I don't want her ruining our day. She's not worth it."

Even though the day hadn't started off well, things improved when we found another store and the perfect dress for me to wear.

"You look hot, Al." Amy's face opened up as she stared at the sleeveless, floor-length, crabapple-red chiffon gown that fit me so well it seemed designed for my body alone.

"You don't think it's too revealing?" I twirled in front of my reflection, admiring the halter bodice that embraced me like a second skin. It wasn't as short as Scott had requested, but I figured the thigh-high slit down the front was a nice compromise.

"Who gives a shit? You should buy it and make all those snobby bitches jealous." I loved Amy's righteous attitude. "Their boyfriends won't be able to keep their eyes off you."

Inspired, I purchased the dress along with a pair of black, opened-toed, high-heeled sandals to match.

"Now let's get you some makeup." With a spring in her step and a glint in her eye, Amy tugged me along to the makeup counter. An invisible mist of various perfumes dominated the airspace as a brunette saleswoman, whose face looked painted on, suggested appropriate shades.

"We're good. I got this." Amy swiveled a stool in my direction. It was obvious, she was not about to let some salesclerk do her job for her.

I sat on a cushioned stool and let Amy perform her magic. Ready to go to work, she leaned in, her tongue protruding from the corner of her mouth. With her spiky black hair, she was a mad scientist, and I was her experiment. The only thing missing was her white lab coat.

"This pink champagne lipstick is perfect." As she bit her lower lip, Amy applied the color with a miniature paintbrush. When she was finished, she stepped back and waved a hand out in front of her as though she had just created a masterpiece. "There. You look perfect, Al."

I stared at my reflection in the mirror, amazed. The combination of gold and brown shadows really accentuated my blue eyes. Amy was truly an artist. Even the saleswoman was impressed, offering her support.

Once we had checked out, I showed my appreciation by taking her to lunch. She deserved it.

* * *

"I want to see it."

I had just stepped out of the shower when Scott showed up at my door. I had told him about the dress and was now regretting it.

"No way." The opaque garment bag hung off my wardrobe, hiding the surprise. "You'll see it when you pick me up for the party."

Scott put his hands on his hips, releasing a small huff. "Well, can you at least tell me what color it is?"

"Why?" I tied the belt of my robe.

"Because I rented a tux and want to get a tie to match." With adventurous eyes and a grin stretching from ear to ear, Scott was my very own Cheshire cat.

"Crabapple red." I wagged my index finger at him. "And that's all I'm telling you." I turned an invisible key over my lips.

Scott moved closer and wrapped his arms around my waist. "It's going to be a long two weeks." He bent down to whisper in my ear. "I may have to peek when you're not looking."

I poked him in the ribs, making him wince. "You better not, or I won't wear it."

"Then you're going to have to give me something else to think about." He knelt in front of me, opened my robe, and placed several warm kisses on my stomach. My inner thighs twitched with excitement as his palms glided up the inside of my legs. I ran my fingers through his blond hair, and within minutes I had forgotten all about the dress and the party.

I fell asleep in the warmth of Scott's arms until I realized he had spoken. "What did you say?" I yawned.

Scott cleared his throat. "I said I have a meeting to go to next Saturday night. It's a fraternity obligation. I wish you could go with me, but it's not allowed."

I lifted my head. "No problem. I'll use the time to study."

* * *

I checked my mailbox in the Student Union Building the following day only to find another one of those strange envelopes—gothic typeface intact. The hairs on my neck rose.

After my last class, I returned to my room with a dreadful feeling in my gut and an unwanted guest in my backpack. I sat at my desk staring at the envelope for several minutes before mustering the nerve to open it, only to have my fears amplified.

213

Just like before, someone had cut out words from a magazine. This time, the words were scattered all over the page, forming a collage.

"IGNORANT, NAÏVE, DENSE, OBLIVIOUS, UNSUSPECTING, THICKHEADED, IDIOT"

One word—much bigger—stood out from the rest: "BLIND."

I gulped. The graffiti on my car windows and even the sabotage of my laptop screamed of Rachael, but not this. This took planning and calculation, something Rachael didn't strike me has having the patience for. And yet, all of the incidents felt connected. What did that mean?

I wanted to text Scott, but he'd only recently risen out of the irate mood he'd been in, and I thought better of it.

I texted Amy and Derek instead: "Come 2 my room as soon as you can."

Amy showed up thirty minutes later and Derek soon after. By then, my nerves were battered, my mind on high alert.

"What's up?" Amy dropped her backpack on the floor.

I handed her the sheet of paper. "I got another note." I'd already told her and Derek about the other one.

Amy's brow lowered as she scanned over the sheet. Derek read it over her shoulder.

"We should have it dusted for fingerprints," Derek said.

Amy shot him a look. "How the fuck are we supposed to do that?"

Derek shrugged.

Feeling a dull headache coming on, I plopped down in my desk chair. "I can't believe anyone would be stupid enough to leave their prints."

"It's probably that Rachael bitch. She's been a pain in the ass on several occasions." Amy's canines came out. "Don't forget what happened to your laptop."

I agreed, for the most part. "That's true, but the twins, Mindy and Charlene, have also been on my back." I had to wonder if there was someone else out there I hadn't even thought of.

"The twins. That's funny." Derek cracked up and then caught himself when Amy shot him another look. He cleared his throat. "What does Scott think?"

"I haven't told him yet. He's been so stressed lately. I don't want to worry him."

Amy examined the envelope. "The postmark is local. You should show it to the campus police."

I pulled up a pic of the last letter on my phone, something I suspected would come in handy later on. "STAY AWAY FROM HIM OR SUFFER THE CONSEQUENCES," the first letter read.

Options limited, I revisited campus security that day. With no solid leads or a suspect, they put the letter in their "file" and told me to keep them posted if anything else happened. Yeah, as long as the "other thing that happened" wasn't me getting murdered. I took some comfort in knowing that at least they were aware of the situation.

* * *

As time passed, another less-threatening phenomenon washed over the campus like a dense fog: final exams. Quiet and contemplative students now replaced the chatty and effervescent campus crowd. Most students had a distracted look in their eyes, as though they had just forgotten something or were trying to remember ten other things they still needed to do. Scott was no different. He was restless, distracted, and overall miserable. Most of the time, our conversations were one-sided—me doing all the talking—and at night, he did nothing but toss and turn. No sex, either. By Friday, his insomnia had robbed us both of a full week's rest.

On Saturday, we signed out a room in the library to study. I had gotten little sleep in more days than I could count, and my tired eyes struggled to focus on the textbook pages in front of me. Unaware I was doing it, I caught myself counting the number of times Scott sighed, shifted in his seat, or shuffled from one textbook to another.

"What time does your meeting start again?" My hollow stomach made me ask.

Scott gave me a blank stare before he slapped his textbook closed so hard it caused a small gust to send a few loose papers flying. "Not till seven. Why? Are you hungry?"

I bent over to pick up the sheets from the floor. "You seem really out of sorts."

Scott stood and arched his back. "Sorry. I'm just a little stressed about my engineering class."

A little stressed? It was like describing the sinking of the *Titanic* as a fender bender. I put the papers back on the table.

"Well, I'll go get you some coffee, and you can stay here and study." I needed a caffeine fix anyway. Maybe it would stave off my hunger.

"No, I'll go with you." Scott rubbed a knuckle under his nose, then gathered his books together.

On our way over to the coffee shop, Scott continued to sigh. I put my arm around the small of his back, which was now as hard as stone.

"Don't worry. I'm sure you'll do fine on your tests." I kneaded his muscles until my fingers burned. "I'd be happy to quiz you if that would help."

Scott let out a jaw-cracking yawn, which prompted one from my own mouth. "I'm sure I'll do fine." He bent sideways, and without looking, kissed the air above my head.

Distracted much?

* * *

After finishing a large cup of black tea, I sat across the table from Scott watching him pick his napkin into a pile of confetti. Starving, I purchased a muffin and suggested we go back to my room, where I attempted a full-body massage on him, but considering Scott wouldn't sit still for more than thirty seconds, it was like trying to pin down a jackrabbit. By six-thirty, a deep crease had forged across his forehead, his eyes red and his mood volatile. What was happening to my boyfriend?

"Are you sure you're okay? You seem so stressed out."

"I'm fine." His growly voice and corded neck said otherwise. He made for the door.

"Why don't you tell them you can't go tonight? I'm sure your fraternity brothers will understand. That way, you can study some more."

"I can't. We have to discuss some housing issues we're having next semester." He opened the door. "I have to go, I'm an officer."

"No, you don't. Just tell them—"

"I told you! I have to go!" His hands flew up, his eyes flaring.

What is going on with you? He'd missed meetings before. This was ridiculous. "Well, excuse me for trying to help." My patience was wearing thin. He wasn't the only one who was tired.

Scott mellowed his tone and rubbed his eyes. "I'm sorry, babe. I just want to get this fucking thing over with."

"What thing? The meeting?"

Instead of answering me, he shook his head and exhaled loudly on his path down the hallway. I made a mean face

217

behind his back. He was making me feel like an idiot, and I didn't appreciate it much.

With a new sense of freedom, I closed my door and took a moment to appreciate the time alone, without Ebenezer Scrooge around. Once Scott had told me he would be busy tonight, I had made plans to visit Amy at her work, but I needed a catnap first. Craving rest, I set the alarm on my cell for an hour later and collapsed onto my pillow. Within seconds, I was out.

* * *

Roused by an annoying cell phone alarm, I pried my eyes open. It seemed as though the past hour had flown by in an instant. I felt worse than I did before the nap. I splashed water on my face and slugged my way to the parking lot while checking my cell for the directions Amy had sent me. The promise of free French fries and a killer milkshake kept me motivated as I drove down the road. I would need another large cup of tea as well *and* a juicy burger. My mouth watered thinking about it.

"You can't miss it," Amy had said about the sign for Mike's Diner. She wasn't kidding—on the roof of a modest-looking restaurant stood a sign that must've been thirty feet tall. I pulled into the parking lot and cut the engine.

My phone dinged in a text message.

It was Scott: "I'm sorry, babe. I miss you."

I smiled and exhaled, ready to forgive. Poor guy was so worried about his grades. He said his father was strict, and it was wearing on him.

I typed: "I miss you 2, handsome." When I hit send, my phone rang.

It was Abigail. "Just two more weeks, Sara. I can't wait to see you," she said.

"Me, too." I wanted to share in her joy, but I was dog-tired.

"Do you mind if I run a few details by you?"

"What kind of details?" I yawned as I spoke.

"Oh, just plans for the holidays. Joel's sister lives in Rutland, and she wants to have us over for dinner one night. Plus, there's a show in Burlington at the Flynn Theater. ..."

As I listened to Abigail, my eyes drifted across a manicured three-foot hedge to the fancy Omni Hotel next door. Enormous wreaths and strands of garland intermixed with lights decorated the portico entrance. Men in hats and formal uniforms helped guests collect their luggage while valets parked cars. Within the chaos, a limousine pulled up to the entrance. Two young couples dressed in formal wear exited the vehicle and disappeared into the lobby. An idea popped into my head—a surprise for Scott. He'd certainly surprised *me* enough. He needed a lift.

"Sara, are you listening to me?" Abigail's voice broke through my plan.

"Yes, you said Joel's mother might come over for Christmas Eve." *Thank God I caught that.*

Soon, I ended my call with Abigail and jumped out of the car.

The original limo had driven away, although another one had pulled up. This one had a company logo on the license plate. Trying to seize the opportunity, I slipped through a gap in the hedge to get a closer look. As the chauffeur walked around to the passenger-side door, I typed the name *Jefferson Limousine* into my phone. I was about to walk back through the hedge when Rachael climbed out of the limo, wearing the same black dress she had tried on at the mall. What were the odds? She waited for someone to join her. I knew Amy would want to know who the unlucky victim was, so I waited with anticipation.

As the tall, blond-haired man emerged from the limo and rebuttoned his suit coat, my heart stopped, my lungs refusing to breathe.

Rachael glanced up at him with adoring eyes as she laced her arm through his. Together they disappeared into the hotel, looking like the perfect couple.

This can't be happening.

Chapter Eighteen

Sitting on the curb with my head between my knees, I spent the next several minutes trying to force air into my lungs. Why was Scott here ... and with her? I really was *Alice in Wonderland,* and I'd just fallen through the rabbit hole. When I found the strength to lift my head, I took out my cell.

I fumbled with the keys to type: "How's the meeting going?"

Scott's response was prompt: "Boring!"

Liar! Underdressed in a hooded sweatshirt, jeans, and sneakers, I darted into the Omni and crossed the polished marble floor, passing several decadent Christmas trees in search of a concierge desk. I had to find out what was going on. Another couple of about the same age, came strolling through the entrance, also dressed formally. I'd seen the girl before on campus. *So, it was a school event?* Scott had said it was a fraternity meeting.

I followed them, venturing up a wide staircase to a mezzanine level and then down a long corridor. Beyond several closed ballrooms, a door sat open from which music and colorful lights spilled into the hallway. I struggled with every step, my body trembling and weak.

A woman with shiny black hair, styled in a shoulder-length bob, wearing a red dress and silk scarf with a holiday pattern on it, patrolled the entrance. She greeted the young couple I'd been following with a polished smile. After showing her a piece of paper and saying a few words, the young couple disappeared inside.

"Can I help you?" the woman asked as her gaze found me next.

Speak. "Yes, I've been trying to reach my brother, and I just wanted to check and see if he's here." I swallowed, trying not to choke on her pungent perfume or my own sorrow.

"I'm sorry, but this is a private sorority event. Unless you have an invitation, I'm afraid I can't let you in." She pulled a folded sheet of paper from her blazer pocket. "What is your brother's name?"

Sorority? This was Rachael's party?

Her eyes shifted over to another couple who was closing in and who also looked familiar.

"Happy holidays." The woman sounded so welcoming and kind. "Don't you two look nice." A smudge of red lipstick flashed from one of her front teeth.

While the woman examined the couple's invitation, I thrust my head inside the door, scoping the room as fast as my eyes would allow. Through the streamers, garlands of lights, and hordes of people, I found Rachael. And standing right next to her, drinking a beer and chatting with his friends, was Scott. Why I needed to see this, I wasn't sure. I just did.

I braced my hands against the wall, feeling as if a cannon-ball had clobbered me in the gut.

"Miss, what is your brother's name?" the woman asked, a hint of annoyance in her voice.

With my organs in full spasm, I mumbled, "Never mind," and headed for the lobby, my hand sliding down the wall for support.

I earned a few honks from irate drivers on my way back to campus. If it weren't for that, I'd have had no recollection of getting there. I collapsed onto my bed and cried until my throat ached. An image of Rachael standing at the dressing room mirror seared into my brain—her smug expression intact. She knew. Scott wasn't only cheating on me; he was cheating on me with my sworn enemy.

My phone dinged in a text. It was Amy: "R U coming???"

I'd forgotten all about her.

Through blurry eyes, I typed: "Something's come up. Can't make it."

A moment later she texted, "Bummer, I was looking forward 2 the company. I'm staying with Sky 2nite. Catch u tomorrow then."

While sobbing into my pillow, I considered how far Scott's betrayal went. "I was just wondering how our teddy bear was feeling. He sure felt good the other night." Mindy had been so confident when she spoke to me. I sat up and wiped my cheeks. My pendant, which I never took off, swung forward. The necklace was a symbol of what—a way to keep me loyal while Scott continued to play the field? Was Scott another nightmare I would have to survive? How could this happen? Everything I knew about him felt ... fake. I broke out in a sweat, my heart tortured.

At 11:15 p.m., a knock on my door rattled my nerves. As I wiped the remaining dampness from my cheeks, I crept the door open.

Wearing the same blue jeans and sweater he'd had on from

before, Scott's face was relaxed, his smile wide. The strain was gone. Something else was different about him. He was a liar and a cheat—a stranger. My puffy eyes and I backed up, letting him enter my room. One glance at my face and he knew.

"What's wrong?"

Something told me I didn't need to spell it out for him, but I did anyway. "I was wondering how your date went." A sharp pain shot through my chest. I pushed my fingers against my breastbone to stave it.

Scott dropped his head and shoulders like a puppet without its strings. "Sara, let me explain." He lifted his chin.

As he took a step forward, I took a step back.

"Don't bother. You lied to me. I guess you didn't consider that the Omni Hotel is right next door to where Amy works. You told me you had a fraternity function, and you were at a party with her ... *her!*" My cheeks smoldered, my pulse sprinting a hundred-yard dash. "Did you get a room there, too?" I was sick to my stomach over the thought of it.

Scott shook his head, frantic. "No, absolutely not. I owed her a favor."

Shaking my head, I let out an ungratified laugh. "Wow." Did he expect me to buy that excuse?

"She helped me pass a difficult class last year, and I told her back then I would take her to this function." His voice wavered. "I didn't even know you then."

"Well, you know me now." I crossed my arms like a vice.

Scott kept his voice slow and measured. "I had forgotten all about it, and then a couple of weeks ago she reminded me. I had assumed, since you and I were together, she would find another date." He cleared his throat while scraping a hand through his hair, which was still slightly wet. "She said she hadn't gotten another date and that I owed her. I told her I would only take her as a friend. I didn't tell you because I knew how you felt about her." The signs were there: rapid blinking, flushed cheeks, and a forehead beaded with sweat. The most obvious sign of his lying came from those blue eyes of his, which refused to look at me.

"Why do I feel that way, *Scott?*" A wildfire spread through my chest like a tinderbox. "Oh, that's right." I let my arms fall, slapping them against my thighs. "Because she threw a beer at me and may have ruined my laptop and ... she's been obnoxious to me since I arrived at this school—all because she's jealous." I leaned forward. "Why is she jealous, you ask?"

Scott swallowed visibly. I could almost hear the gulp.

"Because she wants *you*," I said, answering my own question. "Well, she didn't need to be jealous. She got you anyway—on the side."

"She threw a beer at you? And I thought you didn't know who fucked with your laptop." Scott finally looked at me, his eyes pleading. "She doesn't have me, Sara. I didn't kiss her. I treated her the same way I would treat a friend. I swear to you."

He reached his hand out again, but I swatted it away as though it were a mosquito. "Really? So, you walk arm-in-arm with your friends? And you rent tuxedos and limos for your friends?" Every part of me pointed him toward the door. "I have nothing more to say to you. Get out."

"She got the limo, and I wore an old suit. Sara, please. I love you. I—"

"Would never cheat on you?'" My words burst through his lies like a missile.

Scott rubbed the back of his neck and stared at the floor. "I knew this was a mistake. I wish I had told you about it. Whether you believe me or not, I love you and would never be with another woman."

His words carried no weight or credibility. I'd been duped.

"So, you're telling me you would never be with another

woman—right after you get back from a date with another woman? You must think I'm blind."

My breath hitched. Those strange letters. The graffiti: Watch your back, BLIND. Either it was Rachael or someone was trying to warn me. Then, why the laptop? My head hurt, trying to process it all.

I stormed over to the door and swung it open. "Please leave."

Scott walked out into the hallway, looking like a wilted plant. He stopped and turned. "I'm going to prove to you I wasn't unfaithful. I love you, Sara, and I won't lose you over this."

I slammed the door shut, refusing to believe another word his lying mouth had to say. All those years of playing it safe, and I'd managed to shatter my life all over again. *Nice job, Sara.*

Chapter Nineteen

When I wasn't watching the clock, cringeworthy images plagued me all night of Scott and Rachael. I had tossed and turned so much that by morning my sheets and blankets were in a huddled mess, my muscles ransacked. What ached most was the space that once held my heart. My love for Scott had been a source of strength for me, and without him, I felt ... lost.

I carried my tired body over to my desk, grabbed my cell, and powered it up. My voice mailbox was full of messages from Scott. I listened to a few—all of him professing his love—before powering my phone off again. Even if I chose to believe his lame explanation, which I didn't, it wasn't as though Rachael had saved his life or anything. Yes, Scott worried about his grades, but there were many other options for thanking her. He could have given Rachael gift certificates, or flowers, even. Jason had helped me several times with my Western Civilizations class, but I hadn't repaid him with dates. More important, Rachael didn't strike me as an academic genius. And I couldn't imagine her helping anyone. It was all lies. He knew what she wanted from him. All he had to do was say no.

I jolted when someone knocked on my door. Was Scott waiting out there? I straightened my hair and then searched for my robe. With blood pumping into my ears, I peered through the peephole at Amy.

I lowered my shoulders and opened the door.

"Hey." I practically coughed my greeting at Amy who strolled in, giving my room, and then my appearance a once-over.

"Why didn't you make it last night?" She narrowed her eyes. "What's going on with you?"

I closed the door and propped my back against it.

"Let's see. When I went to visit you at work, I saw Scott and Rachael going into the Omni Hotel next door. They were *together*." Having to admit that was like swallowing poison. "Remember the dress she was trying on at the mall?"

Amy nodded in slow-mo, her eyes dazed.

"Well, apparently she was buying it for her date with Scott."

"You're shitting me." Her eyes bugged, her mouth hinged open. "I can't believe that." She looked away, scratching her head.

You can't believe it? I was knocked off my axis.

"There was a party there for her sorority." My head sunk into my shoulders.

Her expression vacant, Amy found her way to my bed. I pulled my messy hair into a ponytail and joined her. It was comforting to have her here. I needed someone to talk to.

"I was sitting in the parking lot at your work, talking to Abigail on my cell ..." I verbally vomited the hot mess of a story.

Amy had three words. "What a dick."

I rubbed my temples, hoping to stave off another tension

headache. Eight hours of crying had my tear ducts screaming for hydration.

"He's sent me a ton of texts and voice mails, but why bother? It's over." I was blind and an idiot, just like that nasty letter had said. Everything had worked out so well for Rachael, as I was sure most things always did.

I crossed the room and grabbed a bottle of water from a small case that sat next to my hamper. While I downed a few sips, Amy ventured into my bathroom and returned with a roll of toilet paper.

"Looks like you're out of tissues." She handed me the roll while her eyes drifted from my empty tissue box to the wads of white fluff decorating my floor like a garden of cotton candy.

I unrolled a few sheets, then sat on my bed and blew my nose.

Amy stayed close. "So, he said he didn't sleep with her, but he took her out on a date?"

This was the second time Amy and I had analyzed Scott's possible infidelity. I was living in the movie *Groundhog Day*—only this version was *Groundhog Day* with cheating partners.

"Yup, but I don't believe him anymore. I can't even wrap my mind around why he would do this. And either Rachael sent me those letters or someone is trying to warn me."

"She is a fucking nut job, that girl. How would ruining your laptop be warning you?"

I fell back onto my mattress. "Maybe they were separate incidents. I have no idea."

Amy planted her hands on her hips, her mental wheels turning. "What I can't figure out is how he found time to cheat. You two are always together."

I sat up, my brain wobbly. "Well, clearly not." I thought about all the times I couldn't reach Scott or we were apart: soccer practice, so-called fraternity meetings, classes. "You know, he was so anxious last week, and I couldn't figure out why. He didn't sleep well, and he was distracted and edgy." A stress hiccup bounded up my throat. "He acted the same way after that Halloween party. I wonder if he cheated on me then, as well." I brushed my hand over my forehead. "The Monday after the Halloween party, Mindy made a point to ask me how Scott was feeling. She said he was feeling pretty good to her on that night. She called him her teddy bear. A few days later, Rachael also mocked me about Scott." I gripped a wad of sodden tissues in my palm. "Has Scott been cheating on me all along?"

I'd heard stories about men who had secret families hidden all over the country. Was I dating one? What a horrifying reality.

"Maybe we should talk to Shag." Amy moved a thin gold chain back and forth across her neck. *A gift from Luke?* "He was at that party. Maybe he saw something."

"I've already asked him, and he told me Scott was fine." I balled up the wad of tissues and walked over to the trash can, picking up a few strays along the way.

"Well, let's ask him again, and this time we'll tell him the reason. Shag will be straight with us." Amy pulled out her cell and typed a message. When she was finished, she firmed up her face. "We have another problem."

From inside of my water-balloon head, I stared at her. "What now?"

Amy gave her eyes a half roll. "The big guy has set up camp in the living room."

"What?! What do you mean?" It felt as if the floor had shifted beneath my feet.

"He's been out there all night." She walked over to my desk and sat on the edge. "You know the small sofa?"

I nodded.

"Well, he slept on it, and he's out there right now." She crossed her arms. "Do you want me to get rid of him?"

My gaze floated around the room as I readjusted my thinking. Even though I wasn't prepared to deal with Scott, a piece of me was relieved to know where he was.

"No, I'll talk to him on my way out." With a new surge of energy, I searched my room for yoga pants and a sweatshirt to throw on, then sneakers.

Amy's phone dinged, seeking her attention. "Shag's working this morning and said to come by the snack bar." She tapped a reply.

"Why don't you go ahead of me?" I made for my door. "And please don't say anything to Scott. I'll handle this."

Amy made a *pfft* sound as she strolled past.

I reached out and grabbed her arm. "Please, Amy."

She made a rumbling noise in her throat. "Okay, okay."

After she left, I brushed my hair in front of the mirror. Between the red streaks in my eyes and the dark rings under them, I was an older version of myself. I wasn't ready to face Scott, yet I was desperate for a glimpse of him. Man, I never thought I would be so pathetic over a guy.

My nose caught the scent of his musky cologne before my eyes found him in the living room. It was comforting and equally tormenting. Donning bloodshot eyes, dark rings, and a scruffy chin, he rose when he saw me.

"Scott, what are you doing here?" I pushed the words from my scratchy throat.

He leveled his murky eyes with mine. "I wanted you to know where I was. Sara, I'm so sorry ..." He pursed his lips as though realizing the futility of his words.

"I can't get into this right now. I have to go." Worn out, I was having trouble keeping my mind focused. *Snack bar ... Derek.*

"Then I'll be here every night until you're ready to talk. I made a bad judgment call, but I promise I didn't cheat on you." Scott dropped his chin. "I mean I didn't kiss her or touch her in any way. I give you my word."

What difference did *that* make? The trouble with catching Scott in a lie of this magnitude was that it made it near impossible to believe him again—something I wanted so badly to do.

"I can't talk right now." My body wavered.

Scott took a step closer.

"Please." I shook my head while I fought against a deluge of tears.

"I'm so sorry, babe. The last thing I ever wanted to do was hurt you."

I bristled. "How could you go out with Rachael and think it wouldn't hurt me? Or maybe you planned to keep this lie forever." It was the *lie*—the deception—that had hurt me the most. "I have to go." Without looking into the trap of his entrancing blue eyes, I walked away.

When I reached the snack bar, Derek and Amy were sitting at a table with their heads bent in huddled positions. Along with his standard apron and paper hat, Derek wore a sorrowful expression.

Amy just looked mad.

I plopped myself into a chair across the table from them both, willing oxygen into my lungs as best I could.

Amy pushed a cup of hot tea over to me.

"Thanks." I hugged the warm cup for comfort.

"Amy filled me in." Derek pursed his lips. "I *knew* something was up."

My forehead tensed. "How did you know that?" I fought the urge to leap across the table and grab him by the shirt collar.

"Because I saw Scott last night, and he looked like he'd just lost his best friend. I wondered if something bad had happened to his family, so I asked Jason about it. He only said it was personal."

I wilted. "I need to know what happened at that Halloween party." I kept my eyes locked on Derek.

He shook his head, fanning his hands out. "Nothing happened. Scott was fine. I don't know why he took Rachael to that party. You can't let her destroy your relationship. She's not worth it. And you and Scott have something special. I know I didn't believe it before, but I do now." He looked away, his mouth opening a notch and then closing.

I gripped my tea mug tighter. "What aren't you telling me? I need to know, Derek. I trust you."

He crossed and then uncrossed his arms before clearing his throat. "I'm telling you Scott loves you, Sara. Don't let other people come between you." He bowed his head. "There are forces out there that would like nothing better than to destroy your relationship."

I reached my hands out across the table. "What do you mean? Does this have anything to do with those letters? Do you know who's sending them? Was it Rachael?" I slapped my hands on the Formica table, trying to force eye contact.

Derek's eyes refused to comply. He blew out his cheeks, which were growing redder by the second. "No. I don't know who's sending them, but it seems pretty clear, don't you think?"

Amy put her hand on Derek's forearm. "Dude, don't hold out on us."

"I'm not holding out on anyone. I've witnessed firsthand how the girls behave around Scott and Sara. I know all the same shit you know." He huffed as though his answer should have been obvious. "This isn't anything new." He rubbed his fingers back and forth over the edge of the table. "Scott doesn't have feelings for Rachael—of that I can assure you."

I took a sip of tea and thought hard about what he said. It

did make me angry that Rachael could get the better of me, but it wasn't Rachael who had betrayed me. It was Scott.

"I love him, Derek, and I want nothing more than to forgive him, but this is so messed up. What would stop him from doing it again? I can't live my life that way."

Amy nodded, her eyes firm.

Round and round the conversation went until Derek threw his hands up and said he had to get back to work. After he was gone, Amy and I sat in silence finishing our hot beverages.

My mind wandered.

Finally, Amy tapped her hands on the table. "Let's go for a walk." She pushed her chair back, stood, and crossed the room to put our mugs on a cart that held dirty dishes.

I walked around campus alongside Amy, trying to pull answers from the air that weren't there. With each scenario I played out in my head, I always came up with the same conclusion. No matter what his reasons were, betrayal was betrayal—and there was no excuse for that.

Eventually, we made it back to our dorm. As I lifted my keycard, my hand froze midair. *What if Scott's up there?*

Amy put her hand over mine. "Let *me* go up. If he's still there, we can go to the library for a while. I'll grab your books." She was so in tune with my feelings.

"I *am* behind in my studying." My voice sounded as weak as my knees felt.

Amy's face brightened. "Okay then, we can sign out a room in the library to study if we need to."

"Okay."

"Wait around the corner, and I'll text you in a few seconds." She shot through the door.

Less than a minute later, a text came in: "Clear."

I dashed up the stairs, ready to pass out by the time I had

reached the second floor. My feet were loaded with imaginary sand.

Once inside my room, Amy touched my arm. "Want me to stay with you?"

"No, but thank you." I gave her my sad smile. "I need to study."

"Sky's coming over later, but if you need me, I'll be right next door." She pointed at her room before giving me a small hug and leaving.

Trying to study for my finals was like trying to sleep on a trampoline with a group of children jumping on it. My mind raced—my thoughts random and unpleasant.

At six o'clock, a light knock startled me. Through the peephole stood a man looking disheveled, distressed, and mournful.

If he felt that bad, why did he do it?

"I wanted to let you know I'm here if you want to talk. I love you."

I clung to those last words as if they were my life vest in a treacherous sea.

A few times that night, exhaustion took over, forcing my mind to sink into a fitful slumber. I was in a bathroom—the bathroom from my childhood—yet somehow completely different. A massive-sized ceramic tub overflowed with baby toys and water. I turned off the faucet and realized the toys were car parts. Unconscious, a baby bobbed to the surface of the now-soiled water like a buoy in the ocean. I pulled the baby out. She had no eye sockets, and she wasn't breathing. I pushed on her delicate chest, terrified I was going to hurt her. She didn't move. I cried out for help. No one came. I shrieked, my eyes flying open.

Monday morning had arrived unwarranted.

With the horrible dream chipping away at my thoughts, I threw on a sweatshirt, a pair of yoga pants, and sneakers—my new staples. I gathered up my books and then schlepped out the door.

Scott wasn't in the suite, but a few of his personal belongings remained, along with a note that sat on the couch.

"I love you, babe. Please give me a chance."

I wrapped my arms around my chest and allowed a few tears to spill. Was there any scenario where I could forgive him? I didn't know anymore.

* * *

Amy met me for lunch. "I can't wait to get the hell out of here for a few weeks." She spoke between the bites of her Caesar salad. "No more asshole professors to piss me off. ..."

Ignoring my sandwich, I stared off into space, hearing bits and pieces of her conversation.

"I guess my mother has been on a painting binge ..."

I was so tired my body was vibrating, my eyes unable to fully focus.

"My little shit of a sister got a job in town ... hopefully that will keep her out of my hair ... and my room."

When Amy grew silent, I looked over.

"It will be good for you to get away from here, too." She held a forkful of salad near her mouth.

"I don't know what to do, Amy." I was exasperated. "I can't forgive him, but ..."

Amy lowered her fork to her plate. "You don't need to forgive him."

But how can I live without him? He was my future ... part of my DNA ... my soul mate.

"Just take it slow. It's raw right now." Amy took her last bite of food and picked up her tray. "Listen, I've gotta check my mail. Want me to grab yours?"

I handed her my mailbox key.

It seemed like only a minute later, Amy had returned, although I knew that wasn't true. Time had lost all measure. She dropped a large manila envelope on the table in front of me. "This was all you had."

I picked up the envelope.

"I have to work tonight. Why don't you come visit me, and I'll treat you to dinner." As Amy gathered up her things, I cringed at the thought of being anywhere near that Omni Hotel. She took the wrapped sandwich off my tray and stuffed it into my backpack, then slid it over for me to take.

I added the envelope to my backpack, zipped it closed, and rose, my joints beyond stiff. "I appreciate that, but I need to study. I've gotta get to my next class. See you later." I walked away, trying not to trip over my own feet.

At the end of a very long day, I returned to my suite to find Scott waiting there. He was sitting on the couch with a textbook in his hands. When I came in the door, he got up from the couch, his movements slow, his eyes cautious.

"Could we talk?" Shoulders hunched over, he rubbed a finger down his nose.

One word rammed its way up my throat. "Maybe."

Scott froze.

"I need to unload my backpack and take a few minutes, and then you can come to my room."

"Thanks, Sara. Take as much time as you need."

I ambled my way down the hall with a disturbing sense of relief. The past forty-eight hours had been a nightmare, and I knew I had to move forward. Maybe if I hashed things out with Scott, a resolution would come for both of us. My reluctance to face him was making the situation worse for him and for me.

While unloading my backpack, I handled the manila envelope Amy had collected from my mailbox. No address label hinted at college material. I opened the flap and pulled out a small stack of eight-by-ten photos. *Oh, I don't need this.* Another violent blow shot through my entire system like a nuclear bomb as I stared at a pile of graphic images of Mindy and Charlene having sex with my boyfriend. I could only stomach the sight of one: Scott sitting up with his face buried deep in Charlene's bare breasts. Mindy was behind him kissing his back. Who took the picture? Another girl? Was it a four-some ... an orgy? *Gross.* A date was on the photo, adding another punch to my abdomen. My suspicions had been correct all along. Scott *had* cheated on me at the Halloween party. Resting at the bottom of the grotesque peep show was another magazine-sponsored note:

"HE DOESN'T BELONG TO YOU. HE NEVER DID."

So, not a warning. This was an ambush.

As the blood drained from my head and my veins turned to ice, I staggered over to my bed, convinced I was having a stroke. For several minutes, I clutched my knees to my chest, trying to stay alive. "He felt pretty good to me." Mindy had said flaunting her affair in front of me. Rachael had done the same. I was nothing more than a joke. A stooge. I really was "duped girl."

"Sara?" Scott tapped on the door, his voice cutting through a wall of heartache. "Do you still want to talk?"

What kind of man was he?

On my way toward the door, I grabbed a photo from the scattered mess on the floor.

"Sara, are you in there?" Scott continued tapping on the wood.

I opened the door and stared at the con artist who had destroyed my life. Like before, Scott's warm smile melted into a grimace as he peered deep into my seething eyes.

Why me, Scott?

"Are you okay?" His face contorted with strain. "What's happened?"

I slammed the photo hard against his chest.

Scott stumbled backward, struggling to grasp the photo in his hand so that he could get a better look at it. When he did, all color drained from his cheeks.

"How are you going to deny this one?" I spoke through my teeth. "What favor did you owe *them?*"

I yanked the necklace from my neck and threw it at him. "I don't ever want to speak to you again. You are a sick person, and I'm glad I found out who you really are."

Three words drifted from Scott's lips: "Oh my God."

Chapter Twenty

Someone was knocking, but I didn't have the strength to lift my head, much less answer my door. Amy was with me and took care of it. My eyes burned as though grains of sand were grinding under my lids. I was lost in another dimension—sorrow and despair my new reality. I knew this place well.

Amy kept her voice low as she advanced on my bed. "Sara, Jason and Heather are here to see you."

Why? Laying on my side, I faced the wall, unwilling to move. "I can't talk to anyone." The words came out in a hoarse whisper.

A few seconds later, Amy opened the door a crack and spoke in a low voice. "This isn't a good time."

Jason murmured something indistinguishable. The inaudible exchange continued until my ears picked up footsteps and the sweep of the door closing.

"Sara, I know you don't want to talk, but can you just listen to me for a few minutes?" It was Jason.

I shook my head no.

Jason released a heavy sigh. "I was there and saw what happened." He cleared his throat. "In fact, I was with Scott at the Halloween party for most of the night. He was doing fine, and other than small talk, never spoke to any girls there. I left him at ten o'clock to drive Heather to her dorm and was gone for maybe an hour. When I returned to the party, Scott was nowhere around. Owen told me Scott felt dizzy when he was moving a keg. He said he helped him get upstairs to lie down. Rachael was standing right next to me and heard the conversation."

Hearing Rachael's name caused my intestines to cramp up. I curled into a tight ball, hoping it would pass.

"When I walked into the room upstairs, Charlene and Mindy were there with him."

I gagged on my own saliva.

"Don't tell me any more of this. I can't hear it, Jason. Please go." Why was he putting me through this?

"Let me finish, please. Scott *was* there, but not completely naked. He had his soccer shorts on. I swear to you. I'm almost certain he didn't have sex with either one of them. Scott was totally out of it. I had a hard time getting him down the stairs and into my car. When we got back on campus, I had to call a frat brother from the football team to help me carry him back to his room. And the only reason he took Rachael to that party was because she threatened to tell you about it if he didn't take her."

I turned over and focused on his face. It was like staring through glass covered in dust and grime.

"Please go, Jason."

Amy opened the door while Heather took hold of Jason's arm. He looked at Heather, and then his troubled gaze shifted over to me.

When he spoke, he stepped closer. "I've known Scott for

most of my life, and I've seen him drink a fair amount of alcohol. But I've never seen him in that condition before ... never." Heather nudged his arm, causing Jason to acknowledge her. "He doesn't even remember what happened." His voice pitched higher.

I sat up, my breath shuddering. "I know he's your friend and you would do anything for him."

Jason waved his hand. "No, Sara. It's not like that."

"I can't." I raised a palm. "Please go, Jason." I repositioned myself against the wall, my focal point that covered-bridge poster Abigail had sent me.

"Come on, she's too upset to talk right now." Heather's tone was gentle as she urged Jason out the door.

The group walked out of the room, leaving me alone in the deafening silence. Those pictures said it all. They were not what Jason had described. Scott may have regretted his actions, but he had no one to blame but himself, and sending his friend to lie for him for a second time was pathetic. The truth of the matter was I had fallen for someone deceitful, manipulative, and narcissistic. Another gush of water trickled down my cheeks and onto my wet sponge of a pillow.

A few seconds later, Amy returned. The mattress sank under her weight as she lowered herself onto my bed.

"I don't blame you for not forgiving him." She brushed a few strands of hair away from my face. "What a scumbag."

I waved my hand out behind me.

"Please, Amy. I need to be alone."

She paused. "Okay."

After she left, I buried my head in my pillow. How could Scott do something so horrible to me? Every time I imagined one of those girls touching his body, my insides burned, and I thought I might throw up. While part of me didn't want to know what had happened, the darker recesses of my mind struggled to imagine every detail. It was a sickness, a plague on my psyche, and I prayed for it to end. "Sara, I would never cheat on you." *Clearly you would.*

By morning, I pried my eyes open, surprised I was still in one piece. My room sure wasn't. I had no notion of what I was going to do next. As though she could sense my struggle, Amy forced me out of bed and into the shower.

"You need to go to class, and then you need to eat. I'm not going to let you make yourself sick over this." She tugged me along as a mother would an inept toddler.

I showed up late for my Creative Writing class, looking like I had used a balloon to comb my hair, and mentally prepared myself for an exam I wasn't equipped to take. My ears hummed and my eyes strained with fatigue. Mindy and Charlene were there in the *far* back, a place they never sat. They didn't look up or acknowledge me. If I had heard so much as a giggle from them, I would've lost it. The gloves were off now.

After handing in my test, I skulked out of class and went to the snack bar. Derek was checking out a customer when I walked up in line. Once he had finished handing back change to a fellow student, he leveled his eyes with mine.

"Hey. Amy told me what happened. I'm so sorry, Sara." Derek's right eye appeared more slanted than the other. *Swollen?*

"It's not your fault."

His shoulders sunk. "I swear to you. I didn't see Scott with those girls."

He shook a layer of bangs out of his eyes, exposing a small cut near the swollen eye.

"Are you okay?" I pointed.

He pushed my money away. "It's nothing. Your coffee is on the house." He sounded so depressed—so somber—so much like me.

I looked down at my hands. I didn't even like coffee.

"Thank you." With heavy limbs, I took the coffee and dragged my somber body in search of a place to drink it.

To avoid any further interactions, I found an area near a wall of windows where the sill was wide enough for me to sit on. I set my cup on the floor, rested my head against the glass, and let the sun's rays blanket me in warmth. It was soothing. My mind drifted to images of me driving down a mountainous road. I sped past trees, barely missing them while rocks flew from the tires. Not a road at all, I was driving down the mountain itself—my speed much faster than I was comfortable with. Adding to the challenge, people shot out in front of my car repeatedly. Every time I slammed on the brakes, a squealing noise vibrated in my ears.

As the sound grew louder and more pronounced, my eyes fluttered open. Someone was dragging a chair across the tiled floor in my direction.

I straightened up and rubbed my face.

Rick turned his chair backward and straddled it, draping his arms over the back. "Derek told me what happened. He's worried and asked me to check on you. Are you okay?"

"I can't talk about it right now. I appreciate you checking on me, but it's not a good time." I picked up my coffee cup from the floor and took a sip, tempted to spit it back out. Hot coffee had never been my favorite, but cold coffee was disgusting.

Rick lowered his head to my level. "I know this is hard. And I'm here if you need me." His tone was kind. "As your friend."

I peered past Rick to Derek standing at the register, his brow gnarled.

"If you need to get away, I have some fun events coming up." The corners of Rick's lips tugged upward as he dipped his head even lower to catch my gaze. "It might be a nice distraction."

Given my appearance and current state of mind, I was surprised anyone would want my company.

Rick gave me a long stare. "I just don't want you to think you're alone. I've always thought you were a nice person, Sara, and I care about you as a friend." Rising to his feet, he stepped forward and patted my arm. "Hang in there." After returning the chair to the table he had retrieved it from, Rick walked away.

Chapter Twenty-One

Friday afternoon arrived. Each day passed longer than the last. I planned to spend the weekend in my flannels, finishing a paper, catching up on my latest novel, and watching a movie or two. Winter break started on Tuesday, and I was looking forward to getting away. I had expected gloating from Mindy, Charlene, and Rachael, but when I saw them on campus, each of them avoided eye contact as if I had the plague. No gloating of any kind—very atypical of them.

Amy and Derek brought me food and checked on me regularly, and now a new friend had taken up the charge: Rick. It was kind of them, but I grew tired of their constant monitoring. I hadn't had a full night's sleep in so long my immune system had weakened. As a result, I had spent the past week blowing my nose and coughing through the night.

I popped a cough drop in my mouth and collapsed on my bed. A few minutes later, my cell dinged. I rolled onto my side and grabbed my phone off the nightstand, hoping it was Scott and then hating myself for it.

"R U feeling any btr?" It was Rick. "What r u doing?"

The outer layers of the honey and eucalyptus cough drop coated my throat. "A little and hanging in my room," I typed.

It was strange having regular conversations with Rick. He had joined me for lunch once and even helped me study for a test in the library. I appreciated the company but, at the same time, didn't want to lead him on. Every time I brought up the subject of our friendship, Rick assured me he wasn't looking for anything more. "You know, I have a lot of friends who are women, and I've never had a problem with it before." He kept his tone cavalier. "If I had thought Scott could have handled it, I would have contacted you sooner."

My phone dinged again: "My dad is hosting a holiday gala tomorrow night. My date bailed on me, and everyone I've asked can't go. Could you do a friend a favor? It's good food, music, and I'll even sneak you a couple of drinks."

I rubbed my itchy nose and peered over at the dress still hanging from my wardrobe door. It had a presence in my room —a reminder that true love didn't exist. Not for me.

"I don't have a dress to wear."

A few seconds later, another message came back: "It's not until tomorrow night. Can you get one? I'll buy."

I typed, "I don't want to get you sick."

Another message dinged back: "Don't worry. I'll keep a safe distance. You're running out of excuses!"

What was the harm? How long was I going to obsess over Scott? I needed a break. If I didn't do something soon, I was going to go crazy. "Okay, I'll get a dress with my friend Amy. What time do you want to pick me up, buddy?"

His response was prompt: "8:00. Pal." Smile emoji included.

* * *

"You're going to love the selection there. It's vintage. It's much nicer than what you'll find at that crappy mall." Amy's silver 2001 Volvo Wagon rumbled down the road. We were on our way to a store in Charlottesville that she had discovered. Amy didn't care for Rick, but considering I had spent every waking moment outside of class in my room sulking, she seemed pleased I was back in the land of the living. "What did you do with your other dress?"

"It's still in my room. I can't bring myself to return it." I fiddled with the zipper on my coat. "Weird, huh?"

Amy tipped one shoulder. "It's a hot dress. Keep it, and maybe someday you'll wear it. Just don't wear it for Rick the—" She bit her lower lip.

I tilted my head and quirked an eyebrow, causing her to chuckle.

"So, you don't think Rick's trying to make a move on you?" Amy turned down the visor to shield her eyes from the angle of the December sun.

It was a cool day with gusts of wind pushing up against the car like a rhino. Any leaves that remained on the trees were now blowing like confetti in a holiday parade. Solar heat amplified the warmth pouring from Amy's heater, causing her crystal keychain made of rose quartz to swing back and forth. She claimed it contained Reiki healing powers, but I wasn't sure.

"No, I've made it clear I don't feel that way about him."

"Good girl." After stopping for a light, she flipped on her turn signal and made a right onto the ramp for I-64. "So, are you feeling any better?" She craned her neck while merging into traffic.

"A little. I can breathe through my nose now, and my cough is better."

Once we were riding along with the flow of interstate traffic, Amy gave me a sideways glance. "That's *not* what I meant." She cramped her face.

"I know." The emptiness and sense of longing I had been pushing down floated up into my chest. "I miss him." I sunk into my seat. "Do you think he even thinks about me?" Sniffing, I wiped my nose.

"I'm sure he does."

While I searched my purse for a tissue, Amy adjusted the radio dial.

"I think Scott loved you, but he's not the right guy for you. You need to be with someone you can trust."

A song came on the radio that spoke to me. It was all about loss and the sting of it. While Amy sang to the lyrics, I held back the urge to burst into tears.

"Who sings this?" I choked out.

"Lord Huron. It's called 'The Night We Met,' I think."

Funny how just the right song could encompass your pain. This one really resonated with me. Thankfully, Amy kept talking to keep me from blubbering all over her car.

"I've had a few dickheads cheat on me, and it sucks royally." Amy adjusted her rearview mirror.

"Can you tell me about some of them?" As the song ended, I buried my nose in a tissue, blowing like a trumpet. "I could use a survivor story."

Amy sniggered. "I wouldn't exactly call them survival stories." She tipped her head, her eyes amused. "Although they're lucky *they* survived."

I loved listening to Amy. She made me feel so much better about things.

Radio music played while Amy snacked on her trail mix. She rambled on about a few guys and one girl who had ditched her in the past. The nicknames she assigned them were an added bonus.

"One guy even asked me for gas money," She spat out. "I called him 'T.W.' for tight-wad."

I giggled.

We turned off the exit and drove another ten minutes before parking in front of a store called The Real Deal. Floor-to-ceiling windows displayed mannequins of yesteryear, wearing dresses that fell just below the knee. A bell rang above our heads as we entered through an etched-glass door, alerting the staff, or at least the young woman sitting behind a display case. Dressed in an antique-white top with lace edging and wearing several strands of beads around her neck, the female clerk flipped through a magazine while chewing gum, her lips coated in crimson lipstick.

"Let me know if you need any help." Not taking her eyes off her magazine, she sat on a stool twirling her beads around one finger.

The smell of mothballs and old wood reminded me of my attic back home. I loved that smell. It was comforting and told me my nose was starting to work again. I counted six clothing racks scattered across the wooden floor, each holding every-thing from cocktail dresses to full poodle skirts.

Halfway through the rack, I found a champagne-colored tulle and sequin party dress that I liked. It was strapless but not revealing.

After examining it with scrutiny, I said, "I'm gonna try this one on."

* * *

"I wish I could have found something." Amy pulled her Volvo away from the curb. "Sky wants to visit me over break, and I thought we could go out for New Year's Eve."

Jealousy zapped me like a bug catcher. What could be

better than spending New Year's Eve with the man you love? As a matter of fact, I had the same plan. I gazed into the back seat of her car at the dress I had purchased, wishing my life could be different.

"What time is Rick picking you up?"

Amy's question distracted me. "Eight."

While adjusting the heater to full blast, she glanced over in a consoling way. "You'll have a good time." She opened her mouth to say something, but then stopped.

"What?"

"Oh, nothing, it's just that I've seen Scott a few times around campus."

That was the second time she'd called Scott by his real name. *He'd lost Amy's nickname, right along with her faith in him.*

"He looks like shit."

Sadness turned my stomach while I detached my mind from the image of Scott's partying lifestyle, something I imagined regularly. I wanted to believe he was as destroyed as I was, but I knew better.

Once the car's heater was pumping out a sufficient amount of warm air, Amy turned it down. "Sorry. I'll change the subject." Amy kept her eyes on the road. "Derek's eye is looking a lot better."

"Did he tell you how it happened?" I kept wondering about that.

"At first I thought someone had punched him. But, he said he slipped on some wet tiles in the kitchen at work. Plus, who would be mad at *Shag*?" Amy peered over her shoulder as she merged into another lane. "Move out of the way, dipshit."

"Wow, he's lucky he didn't damage his eye." I craned my head, trying to see the driver who had earned Amy's contempt.

"I love this song." Amy turned up a song by The Cranberries and moved her shoulders to the music.

My parents had liked these bands—at least my mom had—so I enjoyed the music right along with her. "I like it, too, what's this song called again?"

"Zombie." She tapped the steering wheel to the slow beat.

I laughed to myself—how appropriate for my life these days.

* * *

By eight o'clock, I was dressed and ready for my night out. My insides felt like I'd swallowed a grenade.

When my cell phone rang, I walked over to my desk, doing what I had done every day for the past week: hoping it was Scott.

"Hello?"

"Hello yourself," Rick said. "I'm outside your suite door."

"Okay, I'll be right out." I put on my coat and then gazed at myself in the mirror for one final assessment.

All I could see was sad Sara staring back at me—a gray film covering my spirit. "You'll be okay," I told my reflection, but we both knew it was a lie.

I opened the suite door, revealing Rick standing in the hallway. He wore a black tuxedo that must've cost more than most people's mortgage payments, his smile beaming. Even his cologne overpowered my perfume. Knowing that about him, I had taken enough cold medicine to prevent any sneezing fits. As I scanned his posh attire, a swollen cheekbone with a purple hue caught my eye. What was the deal? Were there boxing matches at the frat house?

"What happened?" My eyes homed in on the injury.

Rick smirked and brushed me off. "Oh, this is nothing. You

look beautiful." He reached his elbow out for me to take, which I did. "The party is about an hour away, in Richmond. I hope you don't mind the drive." We walked down the hallway, where he pushed the button for the elevator. "My dad insisted on getting us a driver so we can kick back and enjoy the ride."

I smiled, but it was artificial. Unless I was moping, everything I did was fake.

As we strolled through the lobby, I tasted Rick's cologne on my tongue, which didn't help my nausea. Outside, the fresh air was welcome, but I found myself searching for a pair of familiar blue eyes watching us. I wasn't doing anything wrong, yet the guilt overpowered me. Sue Anne and Mia shuffled past us near the entrance, each carrying a bag of takeout and a prayer book. We said our usual hellos.

When we reached the parking lot, a chauffeur popped out of a town car and opened the door for us. Once we were strapped in and were on the road, Rick reached forward and opened a small cabinet built into the seat in front of him. He pulled out a bottle of chilled champagne. From the console between us, he retrieved two flutes and a cloth napkin. The one thing missing was James Bond himself.

"We might as well enjoy ourselves ... compliments of my father." Rick smiled, then winced from the pain it caused.

"Are you going to tell me what happened to your face?" I also wondered if he knew what happened to Derek.

Rick wrapped the cloth around the neck of the champagne bottle. As he worked on the foil and the cork, he said, "I wasn't going to mention it, but if you insist."

I wondered why the secrecy. And then it struck me just before he said it.

"Scott found out I was taking you to the party, and he got a little upset."

I wasn't sure if I was flattered or horrified.

"I tried to tell him we were only going as friends, but he didn't seem to care."

I reached over and touched the wound as Rick closed his eyes.

He pointed in the general vicinity of his face. "Believe me. If I hadn't ducked, this would have been much worse. That guy is unstable."

Tell me about it.

"Is there ice in there?" I asked, gesturing to the cabinet where the champagne had been stored.

Rick nodded.

"Can I use this?" I tapped the napkin.

He undid the cloth and handed it over, his eyes inquisitive.

I draped the cloth over one hand and then reached into the cooler to pull out a small handful of ice.

"Well, aren't you resourceful?" Rick said in a playful tone.

After I had tied the cloth into a small pouch, I held it out for him to take. "Here."

"I'm fine, Nurse Browne." Rick pursed his lips, a grin forming.

"Don't be stubborn. You hold this, and I'll pour." I took the bottle from his hands and forced the chilled napkin into his.

It was a challenge to fill the glasses in a moving car, but I managed.

"Here's to new friendships." Rick tapped his half-full flute against mine.

We sipped our effervescent wine while a lingering question gnawed at me. "Can I ask you something?"

Rick shifted in his seat, facing me. "Sure."

"Amy told me she saw Scott the other day, and he looked terrible. How is he doing?"

Awful. He's miserable without you, Sara.

I cast the illusion out.

Rick lifted his glass to take another sip. "Don't worry about it. Enjoy your champagne."

I sat back and listened while Rick talked about the party and the political guests who would be attending. If he was trying to impress me, it was fruitless. I may have been there physically, but my mind was elsewhere.

Rick grew quiet, and the silence spoke louder than he did. "What?" I asked, self-conscious.

"I just told you we were taking a helicopter ride to Paris. I knew you weren't listening." Rick scratched at his eyebrow. "Okay. I see we need to talk about the elephant in the car and get it over with."

I dreaded what he was so reluctant to say.

"You asked me how Scott is doing."

I nodded, my pulse thrumming.

"He's been a little out of control lately. He was in Mindy and Charlene's room the other night, and I guess it got a little wild. I'm not sure, but I think the campus security was called."

"What, why?"

"From what I heard, they were partying pretty hard."

Gripping the stem of my flute so tightly I was surprised it didn't snap in half, I turned my face away, trying to hide my disappointment. Rick had crushed any hope I had that Scott was pining over me. However unpleasant, I *needed* to hear it.

It was obvious I was the *only* one still mourning our relationship. The man of my dreams was no man at all. He was a myth. He stole my heart and then left me devastated to pick up the pieces. How could I be so wrong about him? How could I love someone so flawed?

Chapter Twenty-Two

A few days later and with heavy eyes, I read a comforting sign on the side of the road: *Welcome to Vermont.* It was a relief when I finally crossed the border into the rural state I had always loved.

Snowbanks grew higher the farther north I ventured, while the temperature gauge on the dashboard display plummeted well into the single digits. The entire state had only two major interstates, so there was no easy way to get to Middlebury. The final leg of my journey consisted of secondary roads with lots of slow-moving traffic and stoplights. My back was beyond stiff, and my legs had red-hot pokers running through them. I had been in the car for over nine hours and still had another hour to go.

Since the party, Rick had sent me multiple texts. He said I had made a good impression on his parents and their friends.

I was surprised, considering I had spent a good chunk of the evening crying in the ladies' room. Deep down I wondered if Scott *wanted* me to find out about Rachael to give him the excuse he needed. What kept haunting me were those tender moments we had shared. I thought about the time he had given me that beautiful necklace, followed by his sudden bout of melancholy. "I know I'm not perfect, Sara, and I know I fuck up. But don't lose faith in me."

I had to believe deep down Scott had loved me, too. It wasn't as if he didn't *want* to be faithful; he just *couldn't*.

My cell rang through the car's speakers as Abigail's name flashed on the display.

"Hello?"

"How close are you?" she asked, a bounce in her voice.

"I'm just under an hour away." The searing pain down my legs made me question if I could make it that long.

Abigail repeated the news to Joel while I waited. "I can't wait to see you. I bet you're tired."

I let out an elongated yawn. "Yeah, I left at eight this morning, so I'm ready to get out of this car." Fatigue wasn't the only reason for my sedate mood.

"Well, we've got dinner waiting, and then you can lie down." Her enthusiasm consoled me. "We'll take good care of you."

Music to my ears.

An hour later, I rolled my window down for just a moment, allowing Otter Creek Falls to welcome me back home. Driving through Middlebury, the storefronts of brick and stone may have changed their names, but not their faces. As the winter sun dropped below the Adirondack Mountains, the restaurants and old country inns sparkled with Christmas lights. So little had changed here, yet the unmodified town felt different—no longer taken for granted. Memories of Mom and Dad remained on the sidewalks we had biked, in the restaurants we had frequented—even in Aubuchon Hardware, where Daddy and I had spent our Sunday afternoons. My memory popped like a pin to a balloon when I passed by the cemetery, a place I needed to go.

Love you, Mom and Dad.

Abigail and Joel lived in a small ranch-style house on the outskirts of town. As I pulled into the driveway, their Christmas tree stood aglow in the large picture window, paying homage to the home. Before I had a chance to get out of my car, Abigail had flung the front door open and would have been down the steps if not for Joel holding her back. He forced a coat on her defiant shoulders before she sprang like a racehorse out of the gate. Joel's eyes bugged out. In an instant, I got it. Abigail's lack of appetite in Newport News wasn't because of a diet after all.

Arms open wide, Abigail ran toward me, her shoulder-length auburn hair flowing in the frigid night air. "I'm so glad to see you." She pulled my cramped body into her embrace so hard I feared for her protruding belly.

"Wow, Abigail, you're pregnant." I pulled away and touched her stomach. "How far along are you?" I was shocked but in a good way.

"Five months. I waited until my last doctor appointment to make sure everything was okay. The doctor thinks it's a girl, and we're going to name her Melinda after your mother. Mel for short." Goosebumps ran up my arm. "And her middle name will be Roberta, after your father. If by chance it's a boy, his name will also be Mel." Her hazel eyes sparkled with tears.

Dressed in a vintage patchwork sweater, Joel approached from behind, his hand finding her shoulder.

"That's awesome news." I imagined a little sister in my life —an unexpected gift that made my heart swell. "I'm so happy for you. You're going to make great parents."

Abigail cradled my face in her hands. The smell of garlic

wafted off her fingertips. My stomach growled with anticipation.

As Joel carried my bags inside, Abigail and I followed with our arms wrapped around each other. With those bluish-gray eyes of his, the ones that embodied comfort and kindness, Joel glanced back several times, as if making sure his pregnant wife didn't slip. It was endearing.

"I made lasagna, your favorite." She pulled her head away. "You still like it, right?"

"Yes!" The scents of garlic, cheese, and tomato sauce drifting out the front door had my mouth watering and my stomach ordering my feet to hurry up. Except for a box of crackers in the car, I hadn't eaten anything since breakfast.

Wood beams and shiny wood floors, walls enriched in earth tones and local artwork, Abigail's home couldn't have been more inviting. Her fingerprint was everywhere, from the handmade curtains to the patchwork quilt that covered the back of the soft leather sofa. In front of the fireplace mantel, I admired three stockings, our names embroidered into the fabric—and one extra, smaller than the rest with a nickname already picked out: "Mel."

The sweet scent of balsam pine brought me to the centerpiece of the room. "What a beautiful tree." My gaze wandered over the multitude of tiny white twinkling lights before zoning in on several ornaments that were familiar.

Abigail rested her head against my shoulder. "I put on a few extra from your old home. The rest are packed away safely for when you have a place of your own." She nudged me with her elbow. "Maybe with Scott?"

I wanted to cry.

"So, we thought of having a small intimate party here on New Year's Eve. We can play charades and watch the ball drop." Abigail clapped her hands together. "You can have Scott come, and we'll all ring in the New Year together."

Her joy leapt into my heart and died a quick death. I wished New Year's was over so I didn't have to think about it anymore.

I sighed louder than I intended, my eyes watering.

Abigail stopped talking. She braced her hands on my shoulders, her face going slack.

"You look so sad. What's wrong?" As she pulled me into her arms, I had to hunch over to rest my head on her loving shoulders.

Joel cleared his throat from the doorway. "I put your suitcase in your room." His voice trailed off. "I'll check on dinner."

Abigail rubbed my back. It surprised me how much I needed her warmth and support. "Let's get you settled." She pulled away and laced her arm inside of mine, guiding me down a short hallway.

On my dresser sat the old jewelry box Mom had bought me for my tenth birthday. I walked closer and opened the lid. As I listened to a familiar tune, I picked up the old baseball glove I had used to play catch with Daddy. The smell of the leather brought my mind to another time. Pictures of me with my parents were on the dressers and the walls, surrounding me with love and a sense of loss.

I realized what a poor job I was doing hiding my emotions when Abigail took my hand and guided me to my bed. "Tell me what's got you down, sweetie." Her gaze scoured my face for an answer.

"Scott and I broke up."

Abigail put her hand over her mouth, the crease between her eyes deepening. "I knew something was wrong. I'm so sorry." She rubbed my back again. "When?"

"He was cheating on me, Mom."

Her eyes flickered.

"I'm sorry. I didn't mean to call you that."

Abigail grabbed both of my hands in a tight grip, shaking them for impact. "Sara, you *are* my daughter. I was hoping you'd call me Mom someday." Her face contorted with worry. "He was cheating on you? You two looked so in love."

I released a hollow laugh while holding back more tears. "I thought so, too, but I have proof he cheated on me twice. I saw it with my own eyes."

"Oh, that's awful." She patted my leg as we sat for several minutes in silence.

Finally, she took a deep breath. "Let's get some food into your belly, and then I'll make you a nice cup of tea while you get comfortable on the couch. You can tell me about it when you're feeling better."

* * *

When dinner was winding down, Joel pushed his chair back and stood. "Why don't you ladies get comfortable on the couch? I lit a fire, so it should be nice and warm in there. I'll bring you some hot tea." He tapped Abigail's nose. "Decaffeinated for you, Mommy."

Abigail rose and reached her hand up to meet all six feet of Joel. She ran her fingers down his cheek while landing a few kisses on his chin. As I walked out of the room, I caught Joel bending down to kiss her belly.

"How's my little angel?" he said.

"It may be a boy, you know." Abigail quirked an eyebrow.

Joel kissed the top of her head. "Boys can be angels, too, my love."

So sweet.

I changed into my flannel pants and a thick sweatshirt,

appreciating the softness against my chapped skin and tired muscles. When I walked into the living room, Abigail was already comfortable on the couch. She pulled the quilt back, inviting me in. I snuggled next to her and took a cup of hot tea from her hands. On the TV, a weatherman reported on an upcoming storm. I stretched my legs out over an oversized ottoman and let my body melt into the couch.

"If you're ready to talk about it, I'm here to listen." Abigail sipped from her mug with a Ben & Jerry's logo.

If she wanted to know, I was more than willing to tell her the whole sordid mess. When I was finished, Abigail looked at me as though I had just told her I had an inoperable brain tumor.

"Why didn't you tell me those girls were being so cruel to you?" She put her cup on the end table and grabbed my hand, her palms like little heaters.

"I didn't want to worry you." I set my mug down on the table closest to me.

Abigail bowed her head, and I knew why.

I had shut her out.

"I'm sorry. There's nothing you could've done."

The sounds of water running and plates clanking drifted from the kitchen, where Joel was cleaning up.

"You know, I feared this was going to happen and tried to stay away from Scott in the beginning. But he seemed so sincere." I rubbed my eyes, overwhelmed by it all. "I'm so tired, Abigail. Would you mind if I went to bed?" The drive, coupled with the breakup, had drained me.

"I understand." Abigail sat up, pulled the blanket back, and rose before taking our mugs to the kitchen.

I went to my room.

After brushing my teeth, I climbed into bed and inhaled

the scent of honeysuckle from the soft, floral sheets. I was reaching for the lamp when Abigail strolled in.

She sat on the bed. "I know this is a difficult time for you." She caressed my head in the same manner my mother used to. "Falling in love can be the best thing in the world, but losing love is the worst. Give yourself time, and you will heal." With a tender hand, she cradled my chin. "Scott may have been your first love. But he won't be your last. Your mother was the most beautiful woman I had ever seen." Her voice lowered, her eyes reflective. "I used to feel like a plain Jane next to her."

When I opened my mouth, she patted me off.

"My point is, you are even more beautiful, Sara. You have your mother's eyes and her porcelain skin, that wavy blond hair."

I could feel her love and support with every breath.

"Add in your father's strong cheekbones, and the combination is what I see here." She got up and clicked off the lamp. "You will never be alone for long, honey. Mr. Right is still out there waiting for you."

I wished I could take comfort in her words and believe better times were ahead. The problem was I didn't want Mr. Right. I wanted Scott.

* * *

Snow squeaked beneath my boots, sounding like pieces of Styrofoam as I arrived at the modest headstone with a curved top. The granite monument was dark gray with lighter gray boxes that included the birth dates of both my parents along with their dates of death. Shamrocks decorated the side where my dad was buried as a tribute to his homeland of Ireland. An apple with the words *World's Best Teacher* decorated my mother's side. Bridging the gap was a heart in the center from me—*I love you, Mom and Dad.* The symbol had been Abigail's idea.

"I'm ashamed I haven't been here sooner." I lowered my head. "You were the best parents a girl could ask for, and you deserved better treatment from me. My only excuse is that I was selfish." I used my gloved hand to brush a small pile of snow from the top of the stone. "It took me a long time to accept that you weren't coming back. I felt abandoned and alone." I glanced over at Abigail, who waited by her car. "I want you to know that Abigail was *always* there for me. She's done her best to fill your shoes. You'd be proud of her." I raised my arms and then let them drop at my sides. "As you can see, I'm grown up and in college now. I've met some good friends ... and—" I paused there. "I don't know how to say this. Although, I expect you already know. I feel you with me all the time. I had hoped to bring Scott here to see where I grew up. He made me happier than I ever thought anyone could. He brought me back to life." Talking to my parents like this made me want to cry as I would if they were here in person. "It wasn't real. And now I feel like I did when you died: abandoned. I wish you could tell me it will all be okay. But it won't, will it?" I dropped to my knees and welcomed the cold seeping into my skin and my heart. "I want to make a life for myself with a family of my own, but I worry that it's just not in the cards for me."

Abigail's footsteps approached.

"I don't know if I can try again. Sometimes I don't feel like I fit in this world and that frightens me."

Chapter Twenty-Three

The trip took eleven hours instead of ten to return to school. I dropped my bags on my dorm room floor, exhausted. I had spent the past month trying to put Scott out of my mind, with absolutely no success. During the day, the separation was tolerable; Abigail kept me busy shopping, cooking, and watching movies. That all changed when I was alone in bed at night. Scott occupied my every thought. What was he doing? Who was he doing it with? New Year's Eve was the worst. I hadn't expected to get any calls or texts from him, yet I was disappointed when none arrived. I knew he was an awful person, but I still loved him. I probably always would.

After a decent night's sleep, I stumbled over numerous suitcases and bags en route to the shower. Once I had finished blow-drying my hair, my stomach screamed for sustenance.

I texted Amy, hoping she was back.

My answer arrived a few seconds later when she knocked on my door.

* * *

"So, tell me about your break." Amy took a sip from her glass of orange juice. There were only about twenty students in the cafeteria. It was nice—like we had the place to ourselves.

She and I had texted over break, but we didn't get into anything too involved.

I swallowed a mouthful of waffles. "It was great. I spent a lot of time with Abigail and Joel. Did I tell you Abigail's pregnant?" Every time I thought about a little sister or a brother, my heart overflowed with joy—until the Scott train returned to the station. *Stay positive.* "We saw a couple of movies and went shopping in Burlington." I sat up straighter. "Oh yeah, we had dinner at this new place on Church Street—"

"Come on, Sara. It's *me*, remember?" Amy had snagged me with her Wonder Woman Lasso of Truth. "You don't have to sugarcoat it."

My posture slumped. Time to fess up. The artificial excitement left my voice. "Break was all right. I did do all of those things, and it *was* fun, but I couldn't stop thinking about—" Man, I hated how needy I was.

"Scott?" Amy lifted her coffee cup to her mouth.

I sank in my seat. "What am I going to do when I see him again?" By now, I imagined Scott's bachelorhood had reached celebrity status.

Amy put her mug down. "Maybe when you see him you'll feel differently."

I doubt it. "I hope so." Sitting forward, I used my fork to pierce a few roasted potatoes with a little added aggression.

"What did Abigail say about it all?" Amy stirred the contents of her yogurt. The scent and color told me it was blueberry. "You did tell her, right?" She stopped stirring, her eyes finding me.

"She was horrified. I should have told her sooner." I took a sip from a glass of water, hoping to wash down the guilt. "Everything happened so fast, I didn't think to call her." At least *that* part was true. In one week, my life had gone from total bliss to devastation.

Amy kept looking up at me until she cleared her throat. "Did you go to the cemetery?"

She knew so much about me. I put my fork down and slid back in my chair.

I nodded. "Before everything happened, I had this vision of bringing Scott to my parents' gravesite. For some reason, it seemed significant to me." From under my eyebrows, I stared up at Amy. "I know ... you think I'm pathetic."

Amy's face hardened. "No, I don't. Give me a little more credit. Sheesh."

I realized it wasn't Amy who was making me feel that way. It was me. "What *actually* happened when I went to my parents' gravesite was that I broke down and wept until Abigail had to drag me away." I wanted to cry now just thinking about it.

"It was your first time there." Amy placed her hand on my forearm. "Next time will be better." She blinked. "And as far as dudes go, don't stress over it. You'll meet someone better than ... some asshole who can't keep his dick in his pants." Anger flashed in her eyes, but it quickly dissipated. "Sorry."

Her comment reminded me of another development that had taken place over break. After a few minutes of contemplation and a few more bites of food, I wiped my mouth with my napkin.

"I also saw Rick over break." I lifted my mug to my mouth. The hot moisture tickled against my upper lip.

Amy halted a spoonful of yogurt halfway to her mouth. "Really?"

"Yeah. A couple of days before New Year's Eve he sent me a text telling me his parents were skiing at Sugarbush Resort. He asked me to join them. I said I wasn't much of a skier." *Understatement of the year.* "So, then he offered to take me to dinner."

Amy lowered her spoon in slow-mo, the strain on her face obvious.

"To be honest, it felt good to have one night off from thinking about Scott." That was only partially true. "The meal was great. Expensive."

"Don't tell me you had sex with him." Amy's phone rang, but she silenced it with one push of her finger.

I huffed. "No."

"Well, something happened, I can tell." Those moss-colored eyes of hers ran their own investigation. Amy prided herself as an artist, but she had the skills of a detective.

"Well, I *did* kiss him." I chewed on the inside of my cheek. "I mean, I didn't want to, but we had a few drinks, and he said something about wishing me a Happy New Year. The next thing I knew, we were kissing in his car."

Amy's face went into shock mode. "What kind of kissing? Was it friendly or was there tongue involved?"

My chest heated up and my cheeks right along with it. I peeled off my fleece jacket. "Well, the second one." I took a slow sip of tea, wishing it was iced.

"So, are you guys dating now?" With each question, Amy's lip curled a little higher. She looked like she could gag at any moment.

"No, but I think *he* thinks we are. He's been sending me texts every day since then, so I guess I need to talk to him."

She got a distant look in her eyes as she took a series of short sips from her coffee.

"Well. How was the kiss?" She put her mug down and glanced up. "Do you have feelings for him?"

"The kiss was weird, to tell you the truth. I like Rick, but not in that way."

Amy exhaled, her face returning to normal. She picked up her spoon, ready to resume eating, appetite back.

"I can't even think about dating someone right now." *And I'm not sure I ever will.*

My phone dinged. I tipped the screen to read, "Hi, Princess. How was the ride back?" Instead of answering, I set the phone back down.

"Was that Rick?" Amy stared at my cell.

"Uh-huh."

"Well, you better tell him sooner as opposed to later. He'll be planning your wedding soon if you don't." She pointed her spoon at me. "Just think ... you could be his first lady."

I rolled my eyes and grabbed a piece of toast off my tray. "No, thank you, and I plan to talk to him right away. Now, tell me about your break."

* * *

I sat on my bed with my cell phone in hand, dreading my next move.

I typed, "Can u stop by my dorm later? I'd like 2 talk 2 u."

A few seconds later, Rick replied, "Everything ok? Should I b worried?"

"Not at all, I just hoped we could talk a little."

His response: "Well, my mother wants to show me a property that she's considering buying for investment purposes (she's a real estate agent). It's the third time she's asked me, and if I don't go, she'll have my head. Why don't you come with me?"

I typed back, "Can we talk b4 u go?"

Another response: "Sounds serious! Well, I'm in Richmond right now and won't be back for a couple of hours. I told her I'd meet her there. If I leave here a few minutes early, I'd have just enough time to pick you up on the way."

I bit my lower lip and typed, "Are you free afterward?"

Somehow, I anticipated his answer: "I'm sorry, Princess. I'm swamped later today and tomorrow."

Not wanting to hang on to the stress another minute, much less two more days, I typed, "Ok, I'll meet you in the parking lot. What time?"

He replied, "Two. See u then!"

I spent the next several hours putting my clothes away and cleaning my room, which was no surprise, considering the condition I had left the place before break.

Just as I was finishing up, Amy came knocking on my door. "Want to order a pizza?"

I stuffed the last of my socks into a drawer and closed the wardrobe door. "Sure."

* * *

"So, have you heard from Derek?" I dropped the last piece of pizza crust into the box. We were sitting on Amy's floor, our backs against her bed.

Amy rubbed her full belly before letting out a burp that made us both laugh. "Nah, but he may be on his way here. I'm sure we'll hear from him soon."

We picked up the plates, napkins, and the empty pizza box, and then Amy lit an incense stick, replacing the pepperoni pizza smell with sandalwood. We stretched out on her bed, listening to music and zoning out. With my hands behind my head, I stared up at a map of zodiac constellations on Amy's ceiling.

"When I broke it off with Scott, I was so angry I didn't think about what to say." It was the second-worst moment of my life. "I'm not looking forward to this. How do you tell a person you're not interested in them without hurting their feelings?"

Amy sat up and leaned over to turn down the music on her Bluetooth speaker.

"It seems to me you've been telling Rick that from the beginning. I *knew* he wanted more than friendship." Amy used her fingernail to pick at some pizza crust stuck between her teeth. "At least you're telling him to his face. A few guys ghosted me or broke up with me over text. Dick move." She got up and dragged her desk chair over near the bed.

"Well, what about when *you* had to do the breaking up?" I sat up, ready to take mental notes.

"Well, that also bites, and you know me, I'm not one to tiptoe around the truth." She fiddled with her earring. "I just told them I wasn't feelin' it."

"Rick has been a good friend to me, and the last thing I want to do is hurt his feelings." He'd also spent a fair amount of time and money on me.

"Rick doesn't strike me as someone who's overly sensitive." Amy reached over and tapped the ash off the end of her incense stick. "So, where are you going again?"

"We're meeting his mother at a vacation property she's considering buying."

Amy raised both eyebrows. "Hmmm. That sounds awkward."

I blew out my cheeks. "I know. I figured I'd tell him on the ride back." The pizza in my stomach clenched. "I just want to put this behind me."

Amy raised her finger before standing. "That, I get."

Both our phones dinged in a simultaneous text, which turned out to be from Derek.

"R U guys back yet?" it read.

Before Amy sent a reply, she asked, "What time are you meeting Rick?"

"In an hour. Why?"

A light bulb went off over her head. "Let's tell Shag to come over here around six, and we can have a few drinks. You know, a late holiday party." Amy's eyes shined as she planned. "Sky's busy helping some friends in a band, so it will only be the three of us."

"Sounds good. I'll need a pick-me-up by then." I glanced at her clock and wished it would tick slower—or maybe much faster and I was already back. "I suppose I should go get changed."

* * *

An hour later, I arrived at the parking lot, where Rick's SUV sat idle. A light snow had developed—the sky a steel gray.

I climbed into the passenger seat.

"How's my princess?" Rick said, his enthusiasm over the top.

Your princess?

With a new level of presumption, he leaned over and kissed me on the cheek. "How was the rest of your break?"

I avoided his attentive eyes. "It was good. How about yours?"

Rick shifted the car into drive. "It was good. I went to a kick-ass party on New Year's Eve. I wish you'd been there." He cleared his throat. "Did you see anyone from school?" His question brought a new level of static to the air.

"No, only you." I glanced over as he smiled.

"Are you warm enough?" Rick adjusted the temperature controls, his voice carefree.

"Uh-huh."

"So, my shopaholic mother wants to buy this cabin and has been nagging me for weeks to check it out." Rick patted my leg. "Thanks for coming along. I brought us some drinks to enjoy while we're there."

In the back seat sat a small cooler. One thing Rick was proficient at was entertaining. He always came prepared and equipped to treat his guests well.

"It will be nice to see your mom again." I searched my mind, trying to remember her from the holiday party. Needless to say, I didn't remember much.

Rick turned on his wipers, adding washer fluid to clean his windshield from the road spray. "Oh, she called me right before you got in the car and said she couldn't make it. She had already given me the key in case this happened." He slanted his head, giving me a slight grin.

"Oh." I stared out the window, rethinking my strategy. Maybe this was better.

"I'm only going so she'll stop nagging me about it. Honestly, I couldn't give a shit whether she buys *another* place or not."

Rick didn't seem to respect his mother much.

"I enjoyed seeing you over break. I'm glad I made the trip up north." A noticeable shiver wiggled his shoulders. "That is one cold fucking state. I couldn't take that shit on a regular basis."

Rick was different today—more abrasive than I'd seen him. He reached over and rested his hand on my leg as though he had the right to. He didn't. One date did not constitute a relationship—unless it was with a tall blond ... on a beautiful hike ... nope, not going there.

I shifted in my seat, crossing my legs and forcing him to remove his hand. No need to start out sending the wrong message.

"Once the weather gets nicer, I'll have to give you a ride in my Porsche. It's a sweet ride. I saw a guy driving a Boxster in the snow the other day." He shook his head. "Amateurs. You wouldn't catch me taking my 911 out unless the weather was suitable." He glanced over. "Some assholes don't deserve nice cars."

I refrained from rolling my eyes.

Thirty minutes later, we turned onto a stone driveway that stretched up to an exquisite log cabin nestled in the woods. The A-frame mini-mansion featured enormous windows spanning across the front, acting as mirrors for the dense forest surrounding it. I counted six decks and balconies altogether, along with several smaller extensions flanking the impressive structure.

"This is amazing. Your mom wants to buy it for a vacation home?" With wide eyes, I climbed out of the vehicle while Rick collected the cooler from the back seat.

"I bet it's beautiful in the summer. You must feel like you're sitting in the woods." I imagined sipping hot tea while watching a bunny hop by.

"Always the best." Rick seemed more interested in his cell phone than he did the magnificent house in front of him.

Rich people.

As we climbed the porch steps, I ran my fingers over the massive logs interlocking with each other. The building looked solid and strong. While Rick used a key to open a padlock-shaped box that hung on the doorknob, I appreciated the impressive stonework, which, along with the natural wood, made the house appear as if it belonged to nature.

Rick placed his hand on the doorknob. "Well, at least the

key worked. I would've been pissed if she had made me drive all this way and we couldn't get inside."

As I stepped through the doorway, a chill hung in the air. I was surprised to find the house decorated with beautiful artwork, curtains, area rugs, and furniture.

"Does someone still live here?"

"No, they're selling it furnished. Vacation homes tend to sell that way. Why don't you look around, and I'll turn the heat up." Rick strolled through the living room, one hand gripped on his cooler.

While he was gone, I thought about what it would be like to live in such an extravagant manor. I opened every door as I wandered throughout the house. When I reached the second floor, I peered over the balcony at Rick standing next to an impressive stone hearth that reached all the way up to the top of the cathedral ceiling. He flipped a switch, igniting an instant fire.

"Wow, that's handy."

My comment caused Rick to gaze upward. "Have you finished your tour yet?"

"Yes, and I think your mother should buy it." I ran my hands along the polished maple railing.

"I'll tell her. There's a nice spa in the back. You'll have to return in the spring and use it with me." The glint in his eyes reminded me of my dilemma.

"I'll be right down."

After navigating the stairs, I walked past a grouping of thick leather furniture and a baby grand piano before meeting Rick over by the stone hearth.

"Have a seat." He sat and patted the area next to him.

The moment I sat, the warmth from the fire crawled up my back like a giant spider. My body was producing an overabundance of nervous heat on its own. I didn't need more.

"Look what I found." Rick reached beside him and picked up a tablet-sized electronic device. "This little box controls the temperature, TV, music, and lighting." He pushed some buttons, causing music to emanate from the walls and lighting to glow down upon us.

"Awesome." My head bobbled in all directions.

He put the tablet back down and smiled. "Yes, you are." He leaned closer and surrounded my lips with his. His kiss was hard and aggressive. I didn't like it much. When he moved in for a second one, I pulled away.

"Um, Rick. Can we talk?"

"Am I moving too fast?" He rubbed my back, driving the excessive heat from the fire into my chest. "You mean a lot to me, Sara. From the moment I met you, I knew you were special."

I turned my head away, remembering our first meeting at the tailgate. Considering how intoxicated he had been, I doubted Rick was being honest. I cleared my throat, readying myself for the speech I had rehearsed in my head.

"I'm so glad that I've gotten the chance to get to know you better. I think you're an amazing person." I slowed my mind down, gathering my thoughts.

"But ..." He stared at me, his brow lowering.

"No *but*. It's just that I'm not ready for a relationship with *anyone* right now." My cheeks flushed—even my ears were hot.

"We can take this slow, Princess."

Stop calling me that.

"I'm not going anywhere." Rick ran his fingers down my back in an unsettling way.

"When you kissed me over break, I was caught off guard." I glanced over to see his brow furrow even more, his dark eyes strained. "Don't get me wrong. The kiss was great, but if I let you believe I wanted more than friendship, I'd be leading you on."

Rick angled his head back, his eyes staring upward. "So, you don't want to go out with me at all?"

"Not at this point in my life. I'm still trying to get over Scott."

His eyes hardened and his jaw clenched. He didn't like Scott; that was obvious.

"It may be a while before I'm ready to date again." I wrung my hands. "It's not you. I mean, you couldn't be more perfect. You're good looking and kind, and any woman would—"

"Please. Don't." Rick pressed his fingers against the bridge of his nose. He closed his eyes with one long blink. "I don't need you to give me the speech. I get it." He took a moment. "It's okay, Sara. You can't blame a guy for trying." He inhaled through his nose before slapping his hands against his lap. "Well, let's have a quick drink, and then I'll take you back to school." Without another word, he rose to his feet and took off toward the back of the house.

"Want some help?" I was curious about what the kitchen looked like but knew it wasn't the time.

"No, I'll only be a minute."

A few minutes later, he returned with two glasses filled with what appeared to be white wine.

"Let's sit on the couch." He motioned with his elbow and head, holding the full glasses. "It's much more comfortable over here."

Still harboring guilt, I met him in front of the leather sofa.

"Is everything okay?" I gestured from him to me. "Between us?" It was hard to determine whether Rick was insulted or relieved. Men were weird.

His eyes shined with a hint of amusement as he sat. "Yes, Sara, we're good."

As I lowered myself onto the couch, he handed me my drink. A colossal weight lifted off my shoulders. Once again, Rick had surprised me with his kindness. He really was a good guy.

"So, I'll call my mom and tell her this place looks like a viable investment." Rick nodded as he sized up the room. "Maybe I can have a party here in the spring. There are enough bedrooms for everyone to crash." He paused. "Don't you like the wine?"

"Oh yeah." I took an eager sip. "I was just listening to you."

"I think there's a river nearby. It would be cool to get some tubes and float downstream. I also heard ..."

I sat there sipping on my wine and giving Rick my full attention.

"Two breweries and several wineries aren't far from here ...," He rambled on for several more minutes about the area before setting his empty glass down on the table. I put my empty glass next to his.

"Well, we should probably be heading back." I got up but a little too quickly, causing a massive head rush. Knowing my low tolerance for alcohol, I sat again, embarrassed. My body reacted quickly this time.

"Wow, I guess that wine went right to my head." I rubbed my forehead, a strange itch creeping over my skin like a rash. Allergic reaction?

I glanced over at Rick, who wore an odd expression on his face. I imagined *my* face puffing up. Even my tongue felt weird.

He let his head fall for a moment. "You got to me, Sara. Burrowed right under my skin."

I rattled my head. Why was he saying that? "Huh?"

"Do you have any idea how much effort I've put into you? I can't make you stay, but I'm not leaving empty-handed."

Focus, Sara. Was he saying strange things, or was I imagining it?

"I don't feel well." I put my hands over my face.

Rick turned in his seat. He pulled my hands away and lifted my chin, his eyes dark and foreboding.

"I only gave you half, so you have something to remember me by." Sliding his cold fingers around my cheeks like a slithering eel, he shoved his lips onto mine.

"What are you doing?" I shrieked, pulling away.

"I think you know what I'm doing." Rick's voice sounded distant, yet he was right in front of me. "You want me as much as I want you. Stop pretending."

That's not true.

Was I dreaming? My mind kept drifting as if it had taken flight from my body.

He moved closer, his mouth engulfing my ear.

"You've played with my emotions for long enough, Saraaaa." His voice echoed throughout my head. "You've given me no choice. If you won't admit your true feelings, I'll have to force it out of you." He shook his head. "This is so disappointing."

Chapter Twenty-Four

I never thought I'd see civilization again. Ever. But somehow I'd made it back to my room. Once I had the door to my room closed and locked, I sank to the floor and sobbed. Panting, I focused on stopping the wrenching pain in my gut. Small eruptions in my stomach had grown into explosions of burning acid that ran up and down my esophagus like a volcano. Could I make it in time? My knees burned against the industrial-grade carpet as I sprinted on all fours for the bathroom.

While I retched, Rick's beast of a voice seized my mind.

"This was your fault, Sara. I gave you months to come around."

I slammed my eyes shut, hoping to block him out. The dry heaves continued long after my stomach had emptied. How could I have seen Rick as anything less than the monster he was?

"I took pictures of you and that hot body of yours. Maybe the world would like to learn what a slut you really are."

His words shot into my soul, filling it with decay. The

pounding in my head had become intolerable. I braced my hands against my skull, trying to prevent my brain from exploding.

"If you tell anyone about this, I will ruin you, and then I will ruin your friends."

As my strength faded and my body weakened, a realization took hold: Rick had already ruined me.

* * *

"Sara, wake up!" I let out a gasp as my eyes flew open. It took me several seconds to make out Amy's face.

"What happened? Are you okay? I've been trying to call you."

I wiped my mouth with the back of my hand.

"I had to get the RA to let me in. Did he hurt you?" Amy emphasized every word, her speech measured.

She cupped her hands under my armpits and hoisted me up against the tub. It felt like she was pulling my arms from the sockets. With her hands braced on my shoulders, she gazed into my eyes as though searching for signs of life.

"Sara, what's happened to you? Can you hear me?" Her face tense, Amy turned to look at someone behind her.

Derek lingered in the doorway.

"I'm going to call the police." Amy straightened up and took her phone out of her pocket.

I fought to get the words through my charred throat. "No, I'm fine."

She knelt back down and stared into my eyes, barely blinking. "No, you're not fine."

"Rick brought shrimp, and I ate some and have been throwing up since I got back. I was too weak to answer the door."

Amy probed with her eyes.

"I feel horrible." I waved my limp hand in the air. "You guys should leave and let me rest."

"Sara, did Rick do something to you?"

I shook my head with all the effort my dehydrated muscles would permit.

"No. He was okay with being friends. Please, I'm too sick to talk." The bile in the back of my throat was unbearable.

Amy peered behind her at Derek, who kept his hands braced against the doorjamb as though preparing for an earthquake. After a few seconds, he lengthened his spine.

"Listen, I've gotta go take care of some stuff. Why don't you help Sara, and I'll see you later." Before Amy could respond, Derek had vanished.

"Thanks for the help, *Derek*." Amy shook her head and huffed.

I made every effort to keep my expression composed. "You should go, too. If this is a virus, I don't want you to catch it."

"Sara, don't bullshit me. What really happened?"

My throat, closing in on itself, made it nearly impossible to speak. "I'm not lying. Rick was cool." The words cracked inside of me like ice on a winter pond.

"Are you sure?"

"Positive. I think I'm going to be sick again, so you better go now." I motioned with my hand for her to leave.

"Alright. Call me if you need me. I don't care if I catch whatever you have." Amy's gaze darted around the bathroom. "Where's your cell phone, in case you need to reach me?"

I tried to remember.

She helped me remove my coat, then searched through my pockets. After she pulled out my cell, she watched me like a hawk.

"Well, that explains why you weren't answering. Why was your phone off?" More staring.

"My battery went dead." My strength was dwindling, and I knew I couldn't hold on much longer. *Please go, Amy.*

I lifted my hand, hoping she'd give me my phone. It was agonizing to watch her push the power button and wait.

"Your battery isn't dead. You have 60 percent power." She narrowed her eyes.

"I know. It went dead, and I charged it on the way back. Please, give it to me." I lifted my hand.

She made a noise in her throat, then set the cell phone in the palm of my hand. "Don't forget to call me." She pointed. "I'm taking your room key with me." When I didn't respond, she squatted down, meeting my eyes again. "Sara!"

"I will."

Once she was gone, I lay slung over the porcelain rim, remembering things I didn't want to remember, like waking up in that house of horrors. With his elbows resting on his knees and hands steepled, Rick had sat in a chair watching me sleep. I'll never forget how his eyes glowed in the dark like a wild animal.

Another round of uncontrollable vomiting resumed until I passed out again.

* * *

I awoke a second time, disoriented. When I realized where I was, I used every ounce of energy to lift my body off the bathroom floor. As though looking through water, my eyes struggled to focus, and I couldn't concentrate. The bitter taste in my mouth was sickening. After brushing my teeth three times, I peeled my clothes away as if I were ripping flesh. For several long and arduous minutes, I scoured every inch of my body until my skin burned. I wanted to scrub every cell, every fiber. Without drying off, I wrapped my robe tight around my body before stumbling back into my room and collapsing on my bed.

In the fetal position, shivering from a cold that came from the inside out, I drifted through the night like a kite in a thunderstorm. My skin burned underneath a robe that used to feel so soft and cozy. Whenever I dozed off, images of Rick violating my body continued to rock me to my core. "I only gave you half. I want you to remember this," he'd said. He had branded me for life, and I couldn't take the thought of it.

As darkness surrendered to the morning sun, a key went into the lock on my door.

Amy poked her head inside the room a moment later. "Are you feeling any better?"

At first, the words remained stifled in my throat, until I pushed them out. "Not really. You better go now." I stared at that same Vermont poster Abigail had bought me at the beginning of the year. I remembered how much she had wanted me to go to a school closer to home. I wished I had listened to her.

"Are you still throwing up? Maybe you have food poisoning." The side of my mattress sunk under Amy's weight.

"No, I'm not throwing up anymore. But I still feel weak." My voice, no longer my own, belonged to a woman who had just smoked a full carton of cigarettes every day for a year.

"Well, at least we don't have classes for another day." She put her hand on my shoulder, and I winced. "Do you want me to get you some ginger ale? That always helps me." Her tone was optimistic.

"No, I just need to rest." I closed my eyes, hoping she would leave me alone.

"Okay. I'm meeting Sky for breakfast, so I'll bring you back some toast." Her feet shuffled against the carpet as she crossed the room, opening the door and then closing it. An hour later, she returned with a drink and toast as promised. I pretended to be asleep, avoiding her questions and shortening her visit.

While college students returned to school or enjoyed their last day of winter vacation, I contemplated my life. *Alone* didn't come close to describing the hollowness I felt. How could I have put myself in such a compromising position? I wished I had never come to Commonwealth University, I had never met Scott, and I had never, *ever* met Rick. Both men had ruined my chance of having a normal life, and both men had shattered my heart.

"If you have any notions of telling Scott, don't bother. He's already attacked me once in front of several witnesses," Rick had said. "If he comes after me again, I'll press charges. He'll be expelled, and that is just the beginning. I can do far worse."

Rick knew as well as I did that Scott had moved on long ago. Why in the world would Scott go after him?

The scent of toasted bread riled the acids in my stomach. I imagined the effervescence of the ginger ale sliding down my throat and quieting the cauldron of turmoil in my gut. All I had to do was roll over—but I couldn't. I wanted to die and put an end to all this misery.

Dusk came and went, followed by a key clanking into the lock again. As the door squeaked open, a beam of light spilled in from the kitchen.

"Sara? Are you in here?" Amy spoke in a hushed tone.

Her coat rustled against her body as she clicked on the lamp, casting a piercing glow into the room.

"Jesus, you haven't moved all day? And you haven't even eaten or drank anything?" Amy perched herself next to me and tugged on my shoulder. "We need to get you to the hospital, Sara. Something is wrong here. You should be feeling at least a little better by now."

I yanked my shoulder free, resenting her audacity. "Can't

you just leave me alone!? How can I get any better with you constantly harassing me?"

As though it were on fire, Amy lifted her hand off my shoulder. "Well, excuse me for caring." She huffed and stormed out of my room just as I hoped she would.

Another long and sleepless night followed. By morning, every muscle in my body ached from atrophy. The first official day of second-semester classes had begun. I had no idea how I was going to get through them. One thing I knew for sure was that Amy would return soon. I dragged myself out of bed and searched my room for something to wear. I even took a few bites of the toast and sips of the ginger ale, causing the piranhas in my stomach to gurgle as they devoured every morsel I managed to choke down. I was weak and dizzy.

Before Amy had a chance to put the key in the lock, I swung the door open. She took a small step back, her gaze scanning over my appearance.

"Well, glad to see you're out of bed. You still look like shit, though." Amy fiddled with the frayed ends of her handmade bracelet.

What I did next was appalling.

"I didn't ask for your help," I growled. "Why don't you give me back my key and stop bothering me?"

Amy looked up and, with her mouth dropping open, handed over the key. She was *never* at a loss for words.

I closed the door in her face, hating myself for treating her that way but felt I had no choice. I was in a place where no one was welcome anymore, not even me. Everything was bad and ugly, and it would never change.

I skipped my first two classes but knew Amy would notice if I didn't go to my third, 2-D Art, the class we had decided to take together. I imagined our favorite teacher, Professor Adams, asking Amy questions about why I was absent. He would do it in his usual humorous way.

I bundled myself up in a dark wool coat and wound a thick black scarf around my neck until I was part mummy. My joints throbbed and my skin hurt. At least the cold temperatures would allow the disguise to pass without scrutiny. To avoid all possible eye contact, I added the biggest sunglasses I owned.

As I walked through campus, I tuned out the world around me. If the savage was lurking, I didn't want to know about it.

Class was already in session when I arrived. Amy watched me as I followed the wall to the back of the room.

Professor Adams came right over and put a syllabus down in front of me. "Hi, Sara. Did you have a nice break?"

I nodded with pain.

"Amy said you weren't feeling well?" He tipped his head lower, his tone soothing.

I took a moment to clear my throat, fighting for moisture to speak. "Yeah, just getting over a stomach bug."

"That's too bad. I hope you feel better soon. Do you want me to have Amy give you the notes so you can go lie down?" While bending over, he flipped his tie back and spoke in a tender voice. "It's only syllabus day. You're not missing anything big. And I'll still give you credit for attending class."

With her head turned a notch, Amy sat three rows in front of me. I knew she was listening while pretending not to.

"Thanks." I trudged back across campus, my body filled with what felt like cement. I sighed as my dorm appeared in the distance. And then I realized that someone was shadowing me. Terror ran through my body as I thrust my hands into my pockets, searching for my keycard. He couldn't touch me here. I'd scream. I'd fight.

"Sara?"

The voice wasn't *his*. It was Derek's.

The adrenaline subsided, allowing a new wave of lethargy to overpower.

"Are you feeling any better?" He was close, his breath visible. "Want some company?" He took my arm, sparking a fit of deep-seated anger.

I didn't want to be touched—ever again. *How dare you?*

"Get your hand off of me!"

In a flash, Derek released his grip.

I was mortified. My mind wasn't working right.

I faced him, my eyes struggling to absorb the image in front of me. One of Derek's eyes was swollen shut, a vertical gash marring his lower lip. Even the shape of his face wasn't right. Was I hallucinating?

I pulled my scarf down, releasing a pocket of moist breath, stale and unpleasant. "What happened?"

"It doesn't matter." Pale and with his posture stooped, Derek lowered his gaze. "I have something for you." He reached out and handed me a large opaque plastic bag.

When I realized the weight of it, I gripped the handles tighter.

"What's this?" I looked at him, bewildered.

Derek kicked at a few invisible stones on the pavers in front of him. "It's something that might help you." His voice was tender but purposeful. "Make sure you wear gloves when touching anything."

"Why?" A sudden wave of vertigo rolled through my body, trying to knock me over like a stack of bowling pins.

Derek touched my shoulder. "I am so sorry, Sara," he said, his face full of emotion. And then he walked off.

For a mere second, I contemplated following him but knew I didn't have the strength. Strange didn't begin to describe my life these days.

When I returned to my room, I dropped the bag on the

floor with a thud and fell onto my bed, exhausted. I awoke sometime later, losing my sense of time. What day was it? On my way to the bathroom, the plastic bag reminded me of Derek.

"Make sure you use gloves when touching anything." *Why?* I had to know. After putting on a pair of winter gloves, I reached into the bag and lifted out the heavy metal object. Not what I had expected. Embossed into the lining of a dark-gray metal strongbox were three letters—the same three letters that embroidered the handkerchief Rick had given me—R.A.S. *What is this?*

A startling knock on my door loosened my grip on the box. Placing the object down on my desk, I steadied myself, approached the door, and peered through the peephole at Amy on the other side.

I cracked the door open and did my best to disguise my sorrow with anger.

My wounded friend walked past me and placed a small paper bag on my desk, right next to the box. The scent of chicken stock hinted at the contents. "I brought you some soup and bread. Are you feeling any better?" She went behind me and removed my coat, which I hadn't realized was still on me.

I didn't deserve her compassion, not after the way I had treated her.

"You forgot your syllabus, and here's a folder with the class information. Dr. Adams said he hopes you feel better soon." She placed a hand on my arm and guided me over to my bed, where she sat next to me. "I have an aunt who counsels victims of domestic violence. On occasion, I've gone to some of the shelters with her. I don't know exactly what he did to you, but I do know a rape victim when I see one."

Chapter Twenty-Five

"Here, try and drink a little." Amy held a small cup in front of me. Although the juice was yellow, it didn't hide the vodka smell. My stomach revolted, and I flinched, trying not to convulse.

"I didn't put much in. Just drink it. It will relax you." Her hand went to my shoulder. "Are you still taking those birth control pills?"

"Yes. Why?" And then I stopped myself. My intestines burned all the way down to my uterus.

Like a mother bird, Amy stayed close. My hand trembled like that of a ninety-year-old woman as I brought the cup to my lips and forced what tasted like turpentine with a hint of orange juice down my throat. The second sip was a little easier, and by the third, my head was swimming.

Sitting next to me, Amy closed her eyes for a moment. "I'm an ass. I was such a shit to you." She rubbed her eyes with the heel of her hand.

"No. *I* was much worse to you." My words came out weird

as though my tongue was made of cotton balls. "He ruined me, Amy."

She pulled me into her chest. "Don't give that bastard so much power." Her voice rose with emotion. "He didn't ruin you." She pulled away and gripped my shoulders. "You *will* get through this. I promise."

I stared into her determined eyes, clinging to her resolve.

After a few minutes, Amy glanced over at the strongbox on my desk. I had already told her the circumstances behind it.

"So, Derek didn't tell you why he had a box with Rick's initials on it?"

"No." I wiped my face with a wad of tissues Amy had given me.

"And you're sure he said to wear gloves?"

I glanced over at the ominous box that threatened from afar.

"Yes."

"I have a pack of hair-coloring gloves in my room." Amy rose a few inches, then hesitated. "Will you be okay for a minute?"

I nodded.

She hopped to her feet and dashed out of the room, returning promptly with a box of gloves in hand.

"We need to find out what's in it." She put the gloves on.

When I stood, my body swayed like a tall pine in the wind.

Dashing over, Amy grabbed my arms so tightly she was sure to leave a bruise. "When's the last time you ate?"

Between the trauma, the fatigue, and now the alcohol, I couldn't remember five minutes ago, much less my last meal.

Amy ushered me over to my desk chair and sat me down. "Eat some soup and the bread." She also gave me a bottle of water.

I tried the soup, but my hand wasn't nearly steady enough,

so I went for the bread, which Amy had smothered in butter. With each bite, my stomach cried out for more.

While I chewed, Amy shifted her attention to the box.

"It's locked, but I can get it opened." She reached into her back pocket and pulled out a multitool device, which I'd seen her use to open bottles and clamshell packages. Inserting the screwdriver part of the tool into the lock, she concentrated, her tongue sticking out, just like she had done when she helped me with my makeup at the mall. A faint click caused my breath to hitch. Appetite obliterated, I put the rest of the roll down and scooted forward in my chair.

With her lips pursed and her brow wrinkled, Amy opened the box slowly as though it were wired with explosives. Before she went any further, she pulled out two more gloves.

"Here, put these on."

I did as she asked, then watched with trepidation as she reached into the box and sifted through the contents. The first thing she pulled out was a sandwich bag full of small, colorful pills. She dropped the bag on my desk. I imagined Rick putting one of those pills in the glass of wine he had served me. My blood boiled as I contemplated smashing the horrible poison against my desk and then flushing it all down the toilet. How many other women had fallen victim to Rick's alter ego?

Amy stopped working and stared me down. "Can you handle this?"

It took a few minutes, but I nodded. I had to pull it together.

She took out a pink window marker next. *The graffiti was even Rick?* What a sicko. My laptop? He was at the library that day. So was Derek. My mind struggled to make sense of it all.

"There's a camera in here." She reached her hand into the box again. "Hopefully it has those pictures he told you about."

She jiggled the camera in the air for emphasis. "If they're on here, we'll get rid of them."

I grabbed the camera from her hands. "What if he has more on his phone?"

"He may have, but I doubt it. Rick isn't stupid." Amy scowled as though regretting the compliment. "Pictures on a phone, even deleted ones, can be retrieved from the cloud, hence the need for a camera. He must know you can accuse him of this."

She took the camera back.

I rested my elbows on the desk, letting my head droop over my hands. "He made me shower."

Amy squatted down in front of me, her eyes round with sorrow. "What?"

"He made me shower in front of him. He said that if I didn't do a good enough job, then he was going to do it for me."

I called it a shower, but it had been more like a small room —a crypt, equipped with two sets of showerheads placed high and low on a wall covered in mosaic tilework. I remembered how the icy water had pierced my skin like tiny needles. "We need to clean you up, Princess." With his arms crossed, Rick watched as I humiliated myself in front of him. The memory smashed away at my soul like a car crusher at a junkyard. I wanted to crawl under my bed and hide there ... forever.

"After the shower, he gave me a towel to dry off and then threw it, along with the washcloth, into a garbage bag. He forced me to walk through the house naked while he followed close behind."

Amy looked down, her voice unsteady. "Where did he take you?"

"To the laundry room. He had my clothes in the dryer. I must have been out for a few hours." I shook my head. "I don't know exactly."

"Well, that's why I had the RA let me into your room. You had been gone for like six hours. I must've called you a dozen times, but your cell kept going right to voice mail. After a while, I got worried." She stared off into space. "That asshole really covered his bases."

She had that right.

"What I don't understand is how Derek got this box. I mean, if Rick was so careful, then how did Derek even know about it?"

Unable to grasp reality, I couldn't offer her much of an answer.

The warmth of Amy's hand slid under my chin. "Listen to me. Put all your energy into nailing that piece of shit to the wall. He's not going to get another chance to do this." She wiped a tear from her eye before returning her attention to the box. "Well, this is a surprise."

I shuddered to think what else lingered inside Rick's box of torture.

She pulled out several magazines, along with a few more cut-and-pasted letters, all intended for me. I had moved past being surprised or shocked by now. Just like before, each letter was ambiguous but threatening. Amy flipped through the pages of several magazines, stopping at the sheets with words cut out of them.

Her tone lightened. "Rick thought he was so smart." She held the address label in front of my face. "These are all addressed to his mother. What a fucking idiot." Amy put the magazines down and picked up the camera again. Then she cleared her throat. "Are you ready for this?"

"Yes." I sounded sure, but I wasn't—far from it.

A deep crease formed across Amy's brow as she scanned over several images. Her eyes, her mouth, her entire face was drawn. I wanted to die all over again.

"Let me see."

Rick using my body like a blow-up doll was the last thing I wanted to see. On the other hand, I didn't want Amy to see it, either.

When I reached my hand out, Amy slapped the camera against her chest like a poker player would a winning hand. "I don't think that's a good idea. Let me delete them, Sara. You don't need to see this."

"Please?"

Amy swallowed to gather herself. "I can delete them without even looking at them. You've had enough shit to try to forget; you don't need more. Trust me."

I slid back into my chair, hugging my legs into my chest and listening to an endless string of beeping sounds from Amy deleting the images. When the beeping persisted, I wanted to go to sleep and never wake up.

"I'm going to leave the less compromising ones." Amy looked up from the screen. "You know, in case we need them for evidence." After a few more beeps, she stopped. "Well, this is interesting."

What now?

Bent over, she placed the small screen in front of my face.

I snapped my head away, the muscles in my neck cramping from dehydration and strain.

"No, it's okay." Amy tugged on my arm.

With extreme caution, I pried my eyes open. She was right. I dropped my feet to the floor and grabbed the camera from Amy's hands. Filling the tiny screen was an image of Mindy and Charlene. Eyes glazed over and complexions washed out, both girls posed seductively for the camera. That wasn't what caught my eye, though. In the background, lying on an air mattress and *unconscious* was Scott.

Amy took the camera from my jittery hands to steady it.

She then scrolled through several more frames that were all similar.

"Rick isn't as smart as he thinks he is. Look at that." Amy was referring to a blurry photo of Rick's face partially blocked by his hand. "It looks like one of those skanks tried to take a picture of him. Mindy and Charlene look shitfaced."

Frame by frame, we watched as Charlene and Mindy pulled Scott's limp body to a sitting position. When they removed his shirt, my heart fell into my stomach. The final pictures were identical to the ones I had received in the mail. Scott wasn't enjoying Charlene's breasts; he was passed out in them. I never actually saw his face. Why hadn't I noticed that before? If only I had looked closer.

"What a dumbass." Amy's lips twitched. At the end of the string of photos was another revelation: a sequence of pictures of Rick with his family members posing at some tropical paradise. Holding umbrella drinks and with tanned skin, the Sweet family wore bathing suits and bright smiles—they epitomized the all-American family: dysfunction at its best.

"Scott didn't cheat on me, did he?"

Amy put the camera down. "It doesn't look like it. Scott wasn't even awake. I guess Jason was telling us the truth. Remember what he had said about Scott looking worse than he'd ever seen him? He said he couldn't even walk. But he was fine when he had left him just an hour before?"

I should have listened to him.

"The big guy doesn't strike me as someone who can't handle his alcohol. Somehow, Rick had drugged him."

The nickname had returned.

"They got him in a compromising position and then, by happenstance, Rachael took full advantage of it." She rubbed her chin. "I wonder how Rick got Scott to take the drugs."

"Rick was always making drinks for people." I rubbed my

eyes. "It would've been easy for him to slip something into his drink or a shot. Especially at a Halloween party."

"After he warned you about Scott's exes, he messed with your laptop and marked up your car, hoping you'd get the hint and stop seeing Scott. When that didn't work, he resorted to sending you those messed up letters. And when *that* didn't work, he did the one thing he knew would tear you two apart: He used Scott's reputation against him."

I didn't think my sorrow could sink any lower, but it did. I felt like a dirty piece of chewed gum, left behind on the bottom of a shoe.

"Poor Scott was victimized from the beginning." I wiped my nose. "I remembered him pleading with me to give him a chance. When I slammed that disgusting photo into his chest, he looked so stunned. I thought it was an act." I wanted to scream and never stop. "How could he ever forgive me?"

Amy knelt again. "Sara, I'm sure Scott isn't upset with *you.* Once he finds out what Rick did, he's going to tear him in half."

I peered into Amy's eyes, realizing the significance of her words.

"Then he can't find out."

"What?" Amy's head jerked back as if I'd slapped her, her mouth falling open.

"Rick will have Scott arrested, and then his future will be ruined. I can't let Scott go through that."

"But—"

I put my hand up. "He's not involved, and that's the way I want to keep it. Rick may have hurt me, but I won't let him hurt Scott." I wasn't sure Scott loved me anymore, and even if he did, what did I have to offer him *now?*

A message dinged on my phone, making us both startle. Before I had a chance to cross the room, another message came in, followed by several more. Ding, ding, ding. I grabbed my cell phone off my bed, anxious. All the texts said the same thing: "Sara, this is Jason. I'm standing outside your suite. Let me in. I have to talk to u. It's urgent!"

"Who the hell is it?" Amy walked closer to me, her brow tense.

"It's Jason. He said he's out in the hall."

We looked at each other.

"Do you think Rick could be playing a trick? Maybe he knows we have the box." I stared down at my phone and then up at Amy, who also examined the screen.

"It says it's coming from Jason's phone, but just to be safe, I'll go. Lock your door, and don't let *anyone* in." She set her jaw. "If you see Rick, call the police. Put your desk in front of the door if you have to."

"I can't let you risk your safety like this. I'll go." I took a step forward until Amy grabbed my arm.

"You're not exactly at 100 percent right now. If it's Rick, I can react quickly. Trust me. He won't get the jump on me. Your job is to watch from that peephole." She pointed. "If Rick comes into the suite, call 9-1-1. Don't. Let. Him. In."

She was gone before I could argue. As I focused and refocused my eyes through the tiny aperture, my heart raced and my mouth ran dry, my body covered in a cold sweat. Seconds passed like hours before Amy appeared with Jason in tow.

I swung the door open and stepped back as they dashed inside.

Jason spun around. He didn't hide his shock at seeing me so depleted and sickly. "Good God, Sara, I'm so sorry."

"Jason, why are you here?"

"I need your help." He paced back and forth like a tiger in a cage. "Scott knows what Rick did."

"What? How?"

"He's going after him, and there's no telling what he'll do. I tried to stop him, but he wouldn't listen to me." Jason headed for the door. "I'll explain in the car. We have to hurry. You're the only one who can stop him. We have to go ... now!"

Amy and I didn't hesitate. We were right on his heels.

* * *

As we pulled out of the campus parking lot, Jason's tires squealed. I gripped my cell and dialed Scott's number.

"It's going right to voice mail." Impatient, I waited for the recording to finish. "Scott, it's Sara. Please don't do anything to Rick. I'm so sorry I didn't give you a chance to explain. Whatever you're planning to do, please don't. I love you." I waited a few seconds to try again, but before I could, my phone flashed a battery symbol, and then the screen went black.

"My phone went dead." I was ready to lose it.

"Shit." Amy checked her pockets. "I forgot mine. It's in my room."

"We don't have time to go back." Jason handed me his phone, one much smaller in size. "Here, use mine. I broke my smartphone, so I'm using that old flip phone until I can afford a new one."

I dialed Scott's number. When it went to voice mail again, I repeated the same plea.

"How does Scott even know? Who told him?" I looked at Jason while thrusting my arm into the sleeve of my coat and then untangling my seat belt.

"Derek told him. He knew all along." Jason caused the car to careen around a bend so sharp, I had to grab the dash for support. Something tumbled across the floor in the back, which Amy did her best to catch. I clutched my hand to my chest to stay calm.

"Why wouldn't Derek have told me?" I double- and then triple-checked my seat belt.

"Because he's a pussy. He said he accused Rick of sending you those pictures of Scott with Mindy and Charlene. According to Derek, Rick didn't deny it. He threatened to have Derek's father fired from some job he apparently got for him, and if Derek didn't keep his mouth shut, he said he'd blame the letters on him."

I couldn't believe my ears. "I ran into Derek earlier today, and his face was bruised and swollen."

Each second that passed, Jason's shoulders grew higher. He kept his hands clamped around the steering wheel like a vice.

"Yeah, well, I'm sure that was Rick's handiwork." He slammed his horn at a driver who was inching along.

I gasped.

"He said he also confronted Rick about what he did." The darkness did little to hide the blood rushing to Jason's cheeks. "Derek said it was too late to warn you." Voice subdued, he glanced over at me. "Or some bullshit."

"We asked him at the snack bar if he knew anything, and he said he didn't. I never pegged Derek for a liar." Amy was fuming in the back seat. "When I see him again ..." She clamped her mouth shut, shaking her head and finishing her rant without words.

We flew through a stoplight that had just turned red before Jason pressed his foot harder on the accelerator. Recent snow had left a greasy film on the roads, and I was terrified we'd hit someone. *What if a deer crosses the road?* Panic was welling over.

"C-can you p-please slow d-down?" My heart was beating like jackhammer. I couldn't breathe.

It took a few seconds, but Jason finally eased his foot from the gas pedal, giving me a soft blink. "I'm sorry, Sara. I know you've been through hell already."

"Tell me more about Derek." I had to get my mind past the carsickness sloshing around in my stomach.

"Well, as I said, he confessed. If that asshole had told anyone about this sooner, we could have done something." Jason's tone was strong, unrelenting. "That's what Scott basically said before he almost choked the life out of him."

What?

Jason patted the air. "Don't worry. He didn't kill him."

"Scott must hate me." I stared into the void, realizing how wrong I had been.

Jason snapped his head in my direction, his eyes wide with shock. "Are you kidding? Scott loves you. You wouldn't believe what he's been going through since you two broke up. He confronted Rachael, and he tore up Mindy and Charlene's room looking for evidence. That put him on probation with the fraternity ... that and punching Rick."

The truth was so different from what I had imagined.

"If those girls planned to get Scott in this deal, they were mistaken. He fucking hates all three of them and let them know it. He even banned them from the frat house. He'd ban them from the school if he could. All he's cared about is finding out who caused your breakup. Although he partly blamed himself. He didn't know he'd been drugged until Derek told him earlier tonight."

Another ruse. Rick sat in that town car, so innocent, and he was the mastermind behind it all. That also explained why Mindy and Charlene had been avoiding me in class. Their plan had backfired.

"Why did Scott hit Rick before break?"

Jason didn't answer right away. Instead, he exhaled through his nose. "Because Rick said something to Scott that pushed him over the edge." He glanced over, sending my shivers into overdrive.

"What? Tell me."

"No need to hold out now, dude," Amy said.

Jason's shoulders stiffened. "He said … that *finally* one of Scott's hand-me-downs had worked out for him." It took three of us to hold Scott back, and he still managed to get in a swing at Rick."

Scott was still fighting for me. One moment continued to replay in my head: the night Scott had given me that beautiful necklace. "Don't lose faith in me." He had sounded so worried, his eyes brimming with sincerity.

What tormented me even more was what would have happened if he *had* told me the truth. What could he say? *I was out of it and may have slept with Mindy and Charlene?* Scott had no defense. He didn't even know he'd been drugged.

"We have to stop him. I'll never forgive myself if Scott ruins his life over this."

Jason kept pushing and then releasing the gas pedal, causing the car to jerk. We traveled along several back streets, avoiding as many stoplights as possible. I stared out my window, paralyzed with fear. Winter had crippled the earth, leaving the grass smothered and the trees in their dormant skeletal state—even the moon had been snuffed out by a thick layer of clouds. Tonight, the world was full of hate.

I kept trying to orient myself. "Where are we going?"

"The water tower. Derek told us about the evidence he gave to you." His eyes prodded. "Is that true?"

"Yes. We looked through it already. Where did it come from?"

"I guess it was hidden in Rick's SUV, and Derek broke the window and stole it."

Every new revelation was crazier than the last.

"He looked us right in the eye ... that fucking liar ..." Amy huffed.

When I glanced back, she came out of her reverie. With her lips pursed and her arms crossed, she stared out the window.

"Why the water tower?" I looked back at Jason.

"Scott told, well more like ordered Derek to call Rick and tell him that he had to meet Derek at the water tower in fifteen minutes to negotiate a deal or he was going to give all the evidence to the police. We didn't have a car, so Derek handed over his keys to Scott right before he made the call. I tried to stop Scott from going alone, but ..." Jason worked his jaw and then rubbed it with one hand as an injured person would do. "He's not himself."

Another bout of sadness slammed into my already troubled heart. Had Scott also hit Jason?

"Where the hell is Derek?" Amy said.

"I don't know or care." Knuckles stretched white, Jason's fingers strangled the steering wheel as though wishing it could get us there quicker.

"Don't you think Derek might warn Rick?"

I agreed with Amy.

Jason shook his head. "No, Rick is on the warpath for Derek. That's how this whole thing started. We were playing pool at a campus bar called Blue Ridge Break, and Scott went to the bar to get some drinks. He saw Derek and Rick arguing. Rick wasn't alone, either. He had two scruffy-looking dudes with him. Scott had to break it up. After that, Scott brought Derek back to our table. He kept acting all depressed, and Scott was trying to cheer him up. Anyway, on the walk back to campus, Derek finally confessed. He kept saying he'd do anything to fix things."

"Rick wasn't alone?" The insinuation wrapped itself

around my neck like a noose. "Do you think they went to the water tower with Rick?"

"I don't know." Jason's voice rose. He flailed a hand. "If I had had my car, I would've at least followed him there. I had to run back to campus as fast as I could."

"How could Derek let this happen?" Amy said.

"Derek kept saying he was sorry and that he never wanted any of this." Jason's tone mocked. "He said he didn't think Rick would take it this far."

"That's total bullshit." Amy unhooked her seat belt and scooted forward. "Rick had a camera in the box Derek gave to Sara. There were pictures of Scott with Mindy and Charlene, and from what we saw, it was obvious Rick had drugged Scott. Rick also had a shitload of pills and some of those fucked-up letters." She was spitting invisible fire from her lips. "Like the ones he sent to Sara. And there was a marker, which he used to mark up her car."

Jason shook his head and blew out his lips.

"He knew all along what Rick was up to. There's no excuse for him letting this happen." Amy shook her head, her jaw grinding. "He should've warned Sara."

"So, Scott knows everything?" It was so unbelievable. "Amy, put your seat belt back on."

Amy did as I asked.

Jason reached over and gripped my shoulder. "We'll find him."

Five minutes later, we reached the water tower. Jason's headlights gleamed off the chain-link fence that surrounded a structure that looked more like a lighthouse.

"I don't see Derek's car." Jason drove to the far end of the parking lot before skidding to a stop near an unfamiliar vehicle. A dark-maroon sedan.

Whose car is that?

We spilled from our car and spread out. A recent plowing had framed the parking lot in hefty snowbanks, making it difficult to see beyond the perimeter.

"Scott?" I yelled and then waited. No response.

"*Scott!* Are you here?" Jason and Amy joined in. After each attempt, the cold evening air returned nothing but my own fears.

"I have a flashlight in my trunk." Jason raced over to his car to retrieve the flashlight and returned.

"Where is everyone?" My head turned in all directions.

"I don't know," Jason said, his eyes dazed in confusion.

Amy and I followed him over to the dark-maroon sedan, where Jason tried the handle.

Locked.

Using his flashlight, he peered inside. "No one's in here, but there's a rental receipt on the dash." He then handed the flashlight over to me.

I moved the beam of light over to the edges of the parking lot, but nothing was out of the ordinary. A winter wind rustled the frozen branches, clanking them together like dried bones.

Amy's voice sliced through the darkness. "The gravel is disturbed over here, and there's something dark on the ground. Bring the flashlight over." She waved vigorously to Jason and me.

With my heart racing, I dashed over, the flashlight tight in my grip. The ground did look disturbed, as though someone had been dragging heavy machinery around. The dark red blotches implied something far worse. I was quaking in my skin.

Amy took the flashlight from my hand and used it to follow a trail of blood to the edge of the lot.

"Jason, aim your headlights over there." Amy pointed.

While Jason moved his car in the appropriate direction,

Amy and I followed the dark and ominous trail. Jason caught up with us just as we were stepping over the embankment, where we found even more blood. Between the tall fescue, the barren trees, and the near-complete cloud cover, it was difficult to see anything distinctive.

"Amy, give me the flashlight." Jason reached his hand out, and she complied. We needed more light, and I chastised myself for letting my phone's battery go dead.

We all walked in slow motion, Jason's flashlight beaming ahead. I stumbled on several fallen branches and hidden debris. I was a klutz when life was normal. Tonight, I was a bumbling mess.

Amy stopped, and I slammed right into her.

She glanced back. "Let's spread out a little."

"Are you going to be okay on your own?" Jason aimed his question and his flashlight in my direction.

Terrified beyond belief, I squeezed "Yyyes" from my distressed mouth.

I went left, Jason went right, and Amy stayed straight. Whenever I grew anxious, I glanced over at the flashlight, reassuring myself that friends were nearby.

The three of us continued to buffet the darkness, calling out the same question. "Scott, are you here?"

When something shot through the grass behind me, I shrieked and sprinted forward. By the time I realized it was most likely a small rodent, I had already tripped and fallen over a large mass on the ground. Even the darkness couldn't conceal the body beneath me.

Jason's voice carried through the air. "Sara, where are you?"

Directly under me, Rick's body lay stiff and unnatural. I was too late. Scott had killed him already. I looked around. Where were the guys who Jason had said were with Rick? Had they intervened? Had they taken Scott somewhere? Nothing made sense to me.

"Sara." A beam of light bounced up and down in my direction.

Before I knew what was happening, two hands grabbed hold of my shoulders, pulling me back. *Rick's thugs?*

"What are you doing? Let go of me." I clawed and slapped, trying to break free.

"Sara. Calm down." Wrapping his arms around my torso, Jason yanked me back as if he was in a game of tug-of-war.

The two of us landed on our backs in the snow. Jason scrambled to his feet and helped me stand.

We remained silent as Jason moved his flashlight over Rick's bloodied body, stopping on his face, mutilated and swollen. The brutal sight caused me to double over in pain. We hadn't gotten here in time. All the frustration, hurt, and anger screamed from my lungs in a full-on rage.

Jason cast the beam of light onto me next, causing Amy to gasp. I looked down at my hands and my clothes, all drenched with Rick's blood. Then the smell of it hit me—the acrid metallic odor—the smell of death.

I was cold beyond anything I had ever experienced before, and I couldn't stop shaking. I pulled my frozen fists into my chest and closed my eyes. I couldn't think.

"Robert, look out." My mother sat in the front seat of our truck, her face contorted, her eyes bugged.

Through the windshield, a pair of yellow eyes illuminated in the center of the road. My father's shoulders shot up as he steered the truck out of the path of the deer.

"Daddy, don't hit it."

Our truck careened sideways—carving up sheets of snow and ice in its path. When we hit the snowbank, my head slammed hard against the side window. Warm fluid trickled down the back of my neck. The snowbank, acting as a fulcrum, tipped us over sideways, sending our vehicle tumbling down a steep slope. The truck crumpled and crunched as if King Kong were turning us into a steel snowball. Shattered glass flew around the cab like confetti. Up and down lost all measure. When the truck tipped back and landed on its wheels, a metallic smell permeated—accompanied by burnt rubber and gasoline. The front passenger's side door was gone. That, and a gaping hole in the windshield, were all that remained of my parents. Red fluid dripping from the spikes of broken glass. I was paralyzed with fear.

"Mom. Dad. Where are you?" I had to find them. I had to try. My legs took off, searching, hoping, praying.

"Sara. Where are you going? Jason, she's freaking out."

Chapter Twenty-Six

I stared out the passenger-side window, watching my breath creep up the glass. Given the late hour, traffic was sparse—the storefronts vacant and the houses dark. Families were at home in their warm beds, most without a care in the world. Where was that promising life I had tried so hard to restart?

"How's your head?" Amy's question pulled me from my self-loathing. She drove her Volvo back to campus.

My fingers traced the bandage that covered my new lump. "It's okay. The doctor said it would heal in a week or so."

"I would have stayed with you, but Jason said he needed to go back to look for Scott, and I had to get my car." Amy's breaks squealed their age as she slowed for a stoplight.

"I know. You shouldn't have even brought me to the hospital. My head was fine."

Amy looked me over. It was difficult to avoid the worry pooling in her eyes. Once the light turned green, the car rumbled forward.

"We didn't want to take any chances. You ran into that tree

pretty hard." She glanced over her shoulder. "Oh, and I brought you one of my coats. Yours was covered in ... you know. I sprayed stain remover all over yours until we can wash it out later." She grabbed the coat from the back seat and handed it over.

I never wanted to see that coat again. It would go into the trash with the clothes I had worn to Rick's cabin of misery.

"Thanks." I couldn't stop the shivering, regardless of the heater blasting.

"It's a down parka, so it should do the trick. I also charged your phone. Here."

She grabbed my phone from inside of her console and gave it to me. The first thing I noticed: no new messages or texts from Scott.

I put on her coat, appreciating its sudden warmth. The puffy material smelled of sandalwood. Amy's incense.

We rode along for several minutes, Amy eyeing me but saying little.

"What happened to you earlier, Sara?" She turned down the radio, glancing over.

"What do you mean?" I wrapped her coat tighter.

Amy adjusted her rearview mirror. "Before you took off running, do you remember calling out for your parents?" She returned her hand to the steering wheel. "You said your parents had died in a car accident, but you never said you were with them."

Images shot back into my mind. The horror of it all. The blood. The loss. "I thought I had told you." Then I remembered I had shared that horrible detail with only one person: Scott. We were on the mountain at the time.

Amy's voice quivered with emotion. "Christ. You've had some tough shit happen to you, girl."

I wasn't sure how to respond to that, so I didn't try.

"So, I wonder who called the police and the ambulance for Rick," Amy asked changing the subject.

Even though I was out of it, I remembered Amy and Jason talking about it when we had left the water tower. "Do you think they saw us?"

"No way. I spotted the flashing lights when we were up on the hill, and by the time we had turned onto the main road below, they weren't in sight yet. Jason waited and drove slow to see if they were turning onto the road toward the water tower, and they did."

I envisioned Rick's limp body covered in blood. His face disfigured. The carnage. *Where are you, Scott?*

A dry cough escaped from Amy's throat. She pulled a roll of mints from her coat pocket and offered me one, which I declined, before popping one in her mouth.

"What's going to happen to Scott?" The thought of him going to prison for the rest of his life had me reeling. "This is all my fault."

Amy bit down hard on the mint with a *crunch*. "No, it's not. You can't control what Scott does."

I faced her. "Scott wouldn't have even been there if it wasn't for me. Now he's a murderer." Disturbing flashes of Scott, his family, and his future falling into ruin spun through my mind like a twister.

Amy gripped the wheel tighter, her speech rushed. "So, getting raped was *your* fault?"

I stared down at my hands. "I should have known Rick was dangerous."

Amy put on her blinker and turned right. "You know, most rape victims blame themselves."

I didn't speak. What was there to say?

"Fine. If you believe that, then I guess you think *I'm* stupid, too?"

I gazed over at her, perplexed. "Huh?"

Her face tightened as she glared at me. "Well, do ya? You think *I'm* stupid?"

What was happening?

"Answer me!" She was fuming.

"No, of course not."

"You weren't the only one who was fooled. I had no idea Rick was behind this whole thing. I thought for sure it was that Rachael bitch." Amy's cheeks burned red. "He's a sneaky bastard. He also spent a long time convincing *you* that he was trustworthy. This wasn't the first time you were alone with him. All those other times he acted normal, right? Plus, Derek vouched for him."

I made a noncommittal wave, unwilling to shirk the blame.

"So, how would you have known he was a psychopath? Stop blaming yourself. This wasn't your fault!"

Would she feel the same way if it were Luke facing a murder charge and a lifetime in prison?

* * *

Willy answered the front door of the frat house with sleepy eyes and a serious case of bed head. I skirted past him, making a few brief excuses for our visit, which he didn't respond to on his way back to his room.

When I reached Scott's door, I knocked a few times. No answer. I turned the knob. Unlocked. We rushed inside.

A stale odor reached out in the darkness. I clicked on the light to find his room in shambles. Whatever clothes weren't hanging out of open drawers were scattered over the floor, along with crumpled-up beer cans, cups, and even an empty whiskey bottle. That explained the stale smell, but not the metallic, pungent odor still haunting my sinuses—the same odor that had caused me to lose it at the water tower. I crossed the room and pushed open the bathroom door, and then I gasped. It was a scene right out of a horror movie, blood splattered over the sink and toilet. Scott's T-shirt, also covered in blood, sat in a heap on the floor. I covered my nose and mouth to stifle an overwhelming urge to barf.

"Holy shit." Amy's eyebrows shot up. "What the hell was the duct tape for?" She approached the sink, where a roll sat covered in bloody fingerprints.

"Do you think this is all Rick's blood?" I bent over, picking up the T-shirt soiled in red.

"I don't know. Maybe Scott was trying to wash it off?" Amy touched the base of her neck and swallowed hard.

My mind wanted to drift, but I wouldn't let it. I had to help Scott. "We have to clean this up. If anyone sees this mess, they'll call the police."

Amy knelt to search through the cabinet under the sink. She held up a spray bottle of tub and tile cleaner. "It's got bleach in it." She bent down and grabbed a tan hand towel off the rack.

"Scott's got a roll of paper towels in his room." I sprinted out of the bathroom and returned a moment later with a full roll. I also found a plastic shopping bag to use for anything we needed to take with us.

Amy was already scouring the surfaces, then rinsing the towel in the tub, before applying more bleach and starting over again. When the area looked clean, I added more bleach to my paper towels and finished the job. We even washed the walls until the paint started to peel away. Flushing the paper towels down the toilet was another hairy experience. I could only use a few at a time to avoid plugging the toilet. When there was nothing left to scrub, we returned to his room, looking for any other incriminating evidence.

"Was Scott this sloppy when you were together?" Amy's head panned back and forth.

"Not *this* bad."

She stared at me, and I knew she "got it" He had fallen—just as I had. I needed Scott, and he needed me. Without each other, we were broken. Lost.

I was about to fold a few articles of Scott's clothing when I spotted an object on his dresser.

"His phone is here." I powered it up and waited, anxious. Behind the swipe bar sat various missed calls and voice mails from one person: me.

"It looks like he didn't listen to any of my voice mails." I showed the screen to Amy just before it went black again.

"Why wouldn't Scott have his phone with him? And why hasn't Jason called us?" A thunderstorm raged in my chest.

With watchful eyes, Amy peeled the phone from my hands. "Deep breaths." She expanded her lungs while using her hands to exaggerate the motion—up and down—until I followed her example. After several conscious breathing exercises, my heart rate slowed.

"Maybe Jason found him, and he's trying to talk to Scott now." Amy rested her hand on my shoulder and spoke in a tranquil voice. "Jason is his best friend, and you know he'll call us when he can. Now, let's go back to your room and try and think of another place Scott might have gone."

Chapter Twenty-Seven

On our way out of the Kappa house, we crossed paths with Owen in the kitchen.

"If you're looking for Scott, he and Jason ran out of here earlier." Shirtless and wearing boxer briefs, Owen was at the sink, filling a glass of water. "Scott didn't look too good."

I halted. "What do you mean?" Although it was a relief to have a lead, his words were equally alarming.

"Jason was helping him walk. I couldn't tell if he was sick, hurt, or drunk, but I'm guessing one of the first two. You might want to check the hospital. I assume, at this hour, that's where they were headed."

Amy and I bolted for the door, a new mission in mind.

* * *

Fifteen minutes later, we parked at the same hospital I had left just a short time ago. Had Scott been here when I was? My cell rang. I fumbled in my coat pocket to retrieve it. "Jason? Why haven't you called me?" I mashed the phone against my ear. "I've been worried sick." I climbed out of the car and sprinted for the entrance, Amy at my side.

When the doors whooshed open, Jason spoke. "Wait, where are you?"

"We just walked into the hospital. Owen told us he saw you and Scott leaving the Kappa house. He thought Scott was hurt or sick, and said you might have brought him here. Is that true?" My legs felt like cooked spaghetti, my brain, soggy oatmeal.

"Yes, he's here." Movement on the line interrupted us. "I'll be right down. Don't go anywhere."

"Wait. What's wrong with him?"

It was too late. Jason had hung up.

Once again, Amy placed a calming hand on my shoulder. "Well, at least we've got the right place."

"What do you think happened to Scott?"

Amy opened her mouth to speak, but then spread her hands out and shook her head.

"What is going on, Amy? Has the world gone mad?" Unable to sit or stand still, I paced around the lobby until Jason appeared.

Without slowing his momentum, he walked straight toward the automatic doors, gesturing for us to follow him outside.

The late-night air had grown heavy with moisture, causing a hazy glow to form around the outside lights. It was like something out of a Dickens tale.

"Is Scott okay? Why is he here?"

Jason lifted his palm. "I *think* he's okay."

"You think?" The uncertainty of his words battered my nerves.

"Rick brought those two lowlifes with him to the water tower." His jaw flexed.

"I bet they were the ones who called the police." Amy stared at Jason, who nodded back at her.

"I think so, too." He hesitated. "One of them had a knife."

A knife? An image of Scott's bathroom stung my heart like a swarm of bees. My legs wobbled.

Eyes red with strain, Jason grabbed my arm and ushered me to a nearby bench.

"I had to force him to come here." He kept a firm grip on my arm, his tone unsteady. "He was pissed off that I brought you with me to the water tower." Jason rubbed his forehead in a way that indicated a headache might be brewing. "By the time we got here, he was losing consciousness."

The sky was falling. The earth was exploding. I sobbed into Jason's chest, wishing I could erase all the horrible things that had happened. I wanted to be angry with Scott for acting so impulsively, but I was too worried to go there.

I wiped my nose with my sleeve.

A pair of feet bounded up the sidewalk. "Jason," Heather said between pants. "I just got your text. How is Scott?" She came to a stop in front of us, wearing a mismatch of leggings, winter coat, and slipper-looking shoes as if she had grabbed whatever she could find.

Jason shot her a warning look. "I was just telling Sara about it."

Heather nodded and waited patiently.

Jason pulled his arm away from me. "They took him into surgery to close up the wound and make sure there wasn't any damage to his organs. They stabbed him in his abdomen. The doctor said it didn't look serious, but she wanted to be sure. The blood loss was her main concern." Jason made a tense face. "That's not all."

I stared at him, wondering what else he could possibly say to add to this ordeal.

"Rick was also brought here, and he is also in surgery. I don't know what his condition is, but judging by the gathering of doctors and nurses, I would guess that it's pretty serious."

"H-he's n-not dead?" *Damn it, why couldn't I speak?*

"Too bad." Amy scowled, her arms folded across her chest.

I wiped the tears from my cheek and glared at her. "If he dies, then Scott will be held responsible." *How can you not understand that, Amy?*

She looked at the ground and exhaled. "I know. It's just." She shook her head. "Never mind."

"When can I see Scott?" I rose, my legs like two twigs, weak and rickety.

Jason grabbed my forearm. "Wait. Some police officers are here. If they question you, what are you going to tell them?"

I stared down at him, searching my low-functioning mind for an explanation.

"She can say Rick attacked her and that Scott was trying to defend her." Amy nodded once with gusto. "If those pricks were there with Rick, then it was more like self-defense than murder."

Murder. That dreadful word twisted my gut.

Jason stood next to me. "I agree, but if Rick's thugs were the ones who called 9-1-1, then they may have already accused Scott of the attack. For now, we need to keep quiet. Think about it. Rick is a senator's son, so this is going to get some attention. Right now, it's only some guy's word against Scott's. They don't have any real evidence."

I tried to absorb everything he said.

"Until we can talk to him and corroborate a story, I think it's in Scott's best interest if we don't say anything." He looked to me for support.

"What if Scott's blood is at the scene?" I couldn't even

swallow. My mouth was *that* dry. "It was all over his bathroom."

Jason's eyebrows shot up. "Yeah, I know. That's where I found Scott. He was trying to close the wound with duct tape. I didn't realize you'd been to his room already."

I coughed out an explanation. "There was blood everywhere, but we cleaned it all up."

Jason covered his mouth with his hand. "Well, that was smart." He stared down at the sidewalk for a few seconds and then looked up. "There may be evidence at the scene, but right now we need to be careful about what we do. I'm sure the senator's got some high-powered lawyers, and if we don't play our cards right, we could ruin Scott's chance for a defense."

Not only was Jason a history genius, he was a level-headed thinker.

"Do you think I can see him?" I hoped and prayed he'd say yes.

"I don't know if you can see him, but I can take you to the waiting room on his floor."

* * *

The walk through the hospital was a blur of long, monotonous hallways, oversized elevators, and too many double doors to count, the walls gray and impersonal. The call of random pages floated through the air along with ringing phones and beeping monitors, the smell of disinfectant rampant. I would have been lost without Jason leading the way.

As soon as we arrived at the waiting room, Jason said, "I'm going to check on Scott."

I entered the small room lined with chairs and a few side tables loaded down with magazines. A TV hung high on the wall, playing a local station on mute. How close was Scott to me? I wished I knew.

A few minutes later, Jason appeared in the doorway. "He's still in surgery." He took a seat next to me.

For the next hour, we all sat around with nothing to say. I sipped on a cup of tea Heather had insisted on buying me and retraced all of the events that had taken place over the past several months. There were so many levels of betrayal for Scott and me.

After Amy ended a call with who I assumed was Luke, she dropped a *People* magazine on the table next to her. "Can I get you anything? Some crackers, maybe?" She looked up at the wall clock, which ticked four-thirty-five in the morning at her.

"No thanks. I was remembering when I went to that flag football game with Rick and Derek."

She leaned in. "Yeah?"

"Rick acted so generous, buying snacks and waters for the team. He even took credit for the uniforms. If he had done any of those things, the coaches would have known him ... or at least known *about* him." I swallowed another sip of tea. "Coach Brady had never met Rick before. He only talked about Owen." I shook my head. "I should have seen it."

Amy exhaled and dropped her head before looking up at me. "You've gotta stop beating yourself up. None of us knew."

"Derek knew," I said. "At that same game, Derek kept telling me terrible things about Scott. He said Mindy and Charlene had gone to his room the night before. He also told me Scott had threatened Rick. When I confronted Scott about it, he denied everything." I rubbed my swollen and dehydrated eyes. "How long was Derek lying to me?"

"Honestly, I have no idea. I'm guessing Rick only got Derek's father a job to make Derek feel obligated to him." Amy hissed through her teeth. "Not that it excuses what Derek did.

He had better hope he never runs into *me* again. Yeah, he came through in the end, but he should've told us the truth that day in the café or at least his suspicions. If he had, you never would have gone anywhere with Rick."

I cringed inwardly when I thought of all the times I had been alone with Rick—the night Rachael showered me with beer, the holiday party in Richmond, the dinner in Vermont, the times he met me for lunch or helped me study. On the surface, Rick acted like such a nice person. It was fake. He was a predator—one with influence and unlimited resources. "Do you have any idea how much effort I've put into you?" he'd said. I answered the haunting memory. "Yes, I do."

Amy's brow went up. "What?"

"Nothing."

On the other side of me, Jason shifted in his seat. "Derek *claimed* he didn't know what Rick was doing until after you received those photos."

"Did you believe him?"

"No. I think he knew Rick was obsessed with you." He rubbed his eyes. "He should have told you what he knew." With sloping shoulders, Jason stood. "I'm gonna see if I can find out anything."

"Can I go?" I looked up at him, hopeful.

Jason turned. "I told the staff I was Scott's cousin. They don't know who you are, and I'd like to keep it that way, for now."

I slumped into my chair. My eyes never left the doorway until Jason returned several minutes later.

"He's out of surgery," he said with a lift in his tone. "And the doctor said he's going to be fine."

Relieved, the vice around my heart loosened as did every muscle in my body. I went from stiff board to hot wax.

"He lost a lot of blood, but there was no damage to his

organs, major nerves, or blood vessels. He's resting right now and can leave as soon as the sedative wears off." He lowered his brow. "Unfortunately, those officers are wandering around outside of his room. I don't think we're gonna get to see him anytime soon."

My internal roller coaster had plummeted ... again.

Jason's eyes were firm. "I told you this was going to get some attention." He set his jaw. "We're going to fight this."

The next few hours crawled by while I walked up and down the hospital hallways, tallying the containers of hand sanitizer mounted on the walls. I repeated a silent prayer that Rick would live and Scott would be okay. Several times, Amy spoke, reminding me she was with me. When my feet grew sore, I returned to the waiting room with Amy to sit and wait.

The dawning light brought definition to the room just as Luke arrived. He sat next to Amy, who slept on his shoulder. Heather was also asleep on Jason's, whose eyelids were growing heavy as well. I watched shows and commercials on the muted TV, my mind in another place.

"Should we call Scott's parents?" I glanced over at Jason.

Jason gave his eyes a knuckle rub. "I'm not going to do anything until I can talk to Scott. He's angry enough at me right now." His eyes were red, his dark hair tousled.

I thought about Scott's family. How would they take the news? Scott had told me his father had acted so bothered by his grades last year. The situation was far worse than a couple of Cs on his transcript.

I bumped Jason's arm. "He's lucky to have a friend like you, Jason." Scott and I were both lucky to have incredible people in our lives.

At eight o'clock, the TV flashed a breaking news story about Rick. An attractive female reporter stood outside of the hospital entrance, an ambulance passing behind her. The headline read: "Senator's Son Clinging to Life." I followed the closed captioning with weary eyes. "Senator Sweet's son, Richard, was found at the Charlottesville water tower last night. He was severely beaten. When asked about possible suspects, the police said they could not comment since it's an ongoing investigation. ..."

The police standing outside of Scott's room told me they knew more than they were telling the press. I struggled to swallow. By ten o'clock, the same reporter had an update. She touched her ear as she spoke. "Doctors worked vigorously throughout the night to save Richard Sweet's life. A reliable source from inside the hospital has informed us that, although he's in critical condition, Mr. Sweet is expected to pull through."

My heart filled with hope. Luke, Heather, Amy, and now Jason were all asleep. Even though I had mixed feelings about waking them, I knew they'd want to know.

I nudged Jason's arm first. "They just said on the news that Rick is expected to pull through."

"What?" His eyes rolled open.

I repeated the news just as Jason arched his back, yawning at length.

"That's awesome." He lifted Heather's head off his shoulder to relay the news while he kissed her forehead.

I shook Amy's arm next. Her eyes slid open as she wiped a small pool of saliva from the corner of her mouth. Once she heard the news, she woke Luke up.

Like dominoes, the news spread.

"We're not out of the woods yet, but at least we're not dealing with a murder." I forced my optimism on them. It was all I had.

While I watched the TV, hoping for more updates, Jason, Luke, and the girls left to visit the restrooms.

Jason came back first. "I just walked by Scott's room and overheard some officers asking the staff if Scott is fit for travel. I think they're getting ready to move him."

Amy and Heather walked in to hear the tail end of Jason's update. Luke arrived soon afterward.

"If they're taking him to the station, I want to follow." I faced Amy. "Can I borrow your car?"

"Yes. But we can go with you."

Jason and Heather nodded.

"Let's do this together," Jason said.

"No, that's okay."

Four pairs of bloodshot eyes stared with unwavering loyalty.

"I promise to keep you all posted on what's happening. Go back to school and get some rest or go to class. I don't want you getting behind."

"What about you?" Jason fought against another yawn.

I squared my eyes. "He's my world, Jason. I'm not going anywhere."

He glanced at Heather, who rubbed his back and blinked softly.

"I doubt they'll take him out the main entrance. There's a smaller exit on the eastern side of the building. I'm guessing they'll use that to avoid the press." Jason rubbed the scruff on his chin. "I saw it when I was trying to find the emergency room last night."

"Yeah, I saw it, too." Luke ran a hand through his long hair.

Amy stretched her arms skyward, twisting her shoulders back and forth. "Okay, I'll move my car as close to the side entrance as I can. Sky, can you bring your van around?"

"Sure." Luke kissed Amy, and then walked out of the room.

Amy gave me a short hug, put on her coat, and disappeared out the door behind him.

Jason led the way while Heather and I followed. When we reached the side entrance, we waited outside until Amy pulled up and parked her car in a space nearby. Luke was already there, his van's engine rumbling. With dark smudges from her heavy eyeliner, poor Amy looked rough.

"Here's my keys." She placed them in my palm but kept a firm grip on my hand. "I don't need to leave, Sara. I don't give a shit about my classes."

I know you don't because you're awesome. I pulled her into my arms, letting her know how much I loved her. "No, I'll be okay."

After a bit more persuading, the three of them walked away, Heather pulling a reluctant Jason along beside her. Amy jumped in with Luke, who drove off. Once they were all gone, I found a nearby bench and sat. A warm front had arrived, causing the temperature to climb. Water dripped off the eaves and gutters, making puddles and tiny streams along the sidewalk. I rubbed my face, using every remaining brain cell to figure out a way to help Scott. Even though he wasn't a murderer, he was still in a lot of trouble. He would need a lawyer, and a good one. I was already going over our defense when the doors from behind me whooshed open.

I peered over my shoulder at a tall, dark-haired man who was pushing an elderly woman in a wheelchair.

Keeping his head low, the man spoke to the woman. "Are you sure you'll be okay?" He wore a name tag with the word *Volunteer* printed across it.

"No need to worry, Andrew." The elderly woman patted the volunteer's arm. "Henry will be here any minute."

Andrew ushered the woman over to the bench where I sat. He braced his hands under her elbow and forearm and then guided her down to the seat next to mine. "There you go." He straightened up. "You did well today," he said and then smiled. "Don't forget, I need that recipe for those lemon bars."

The sun peeked out from behind a dark, puffy cloud, casting a warm glow across my face. While the woman and Andrew carried on a conversation, I closed my eyes and tipped my head back. I wanted so badly to drift off to sleep, but I couldn't, not when Scott needed me. I fought back the fatigue.

"Well, it has certainly warmed up, hasn't it?"

I opened my eyes. Andrew was gone, and the woman sat staring at me. Her short, curly gray hair was so thin I could see through it. The message on her sweatshirt said "World's Best Grandma," flanked by two adorable kittens.

For the life of me, I couldn't remember what she'd said.

"Are you okay, dear?"

"Yes, I'm fine." My tone was less than convincing.

"Anyone with half a mind can see that isn't true. Do you have a sick relative here?" She placed her shaky hand over mine.

Something about her honey brown eyes and warm spirit pried open my floodgates

"The man I love is in trouble, and I don't know how to help him." My lips trembled, and my voice broke.

"Oh, there, there." She spoke with such kindness. "Sometimes when you lose all hope, a solution presents itself when you least expect it. Have faith, my dear; problems have a way of working themselves out." A lifetime of wisdom accompanied her advice, and boy did I need to hear it. I wanted to believe every word. "Find your strength." She took my hand. "It's in you. It's in all of us. Sometimes, we just have to dig deep to find it."

With its paint faded and spotted with an abundance of rust, an old red truck rattled up to the curb in front of us.

I wiped my cheeks dry and repositioned myself.

"Well, the man *I* love is here to collect me." She flashed me a winning smile.

After I helped the elderly woman stand, she crept toward the truck.

"Ethel, don't strain yourself." Donning a pair of oversized faded overalls over a red-and-black flannel shirt, Ethel's husband rushed over. A few wisps of hair remained on the older man's head, and his skin looked like a paper bag that had been crumpled and then flattened out. He reached out his knobby fingers to take hold of his wife's arm.

"This is my Henry," Ethel said with pride.

Before I could introduce myself, Henry whisked Ethel away. He may have even sneered at me.

From the passenger-side window, Ethel waved to me as the truck's engine sputtered and hiccupped. Off they went, passing two squad cars on their way in.

I swallowed what felt like a tennis ball.

Both cruisers parked along the curb, just a few feet away from me. In full uniform, two male officers sprang from the second vehicle and walked past me into the hospital. A man and a woman in the front car stayed put.

I rushed off the curb and over to Amy's Volvo, my feet trying to keep up with my heart beat. While I waited in the driver's seat, a group of uniformed officers came out with Scott, wrists cuffed, in tow. His blond hair a mess, his clothes loose and wrinkled, and his complexion washed out, he was the most beautiful thing I'd ever seen. My life was standing just twenty feet away. I wanted to run into his arms and hold him, assure him that everything would be okay. *We'd* be okay.

One officer opened the back door to the cruiser while the other cop braced one hand on Scott's arm and guided him into the back seat. I clamped a hand over my mouth to stop the words "Don't touch him!" from exploding from my mouth. *I'm here, Scott.*

If I was a nervous driver before, I was frantic now. Keeping my car close, I worried I'd lose them every time we hit a stoplight. When we pulled into the precinct, the lead cruiser parked out front while the second car, containing Scott, proceeded to another lot surrounded by a chain-link fence. I parked Amy's car outside the fence as they escorted Scott through a side entrance.

Eager to do something—*anything*—I grabbed the door handle and then Jason's cautionary words echoed in my head: "If we don't play our cards right, we could ruin Scott's chance for a defense." Like a sandcastle hit by a wave, my confidence crumbled. Would my being here make matters worse for him? I contemplated my options. I even considered going to the press and telling them what Rick had done. But how many times had women accused prominent men of rape and lost? Plus, that wouldn't excuse Scott's actions. One crime wouldn't cancel out another. If anything, it would make him appear guiltier. I needed a way to save him. I needed a miracle.

I fell over the steering wheel and begged for guidance. "Mom, Dad, I need you. Please tell me what to do!"

Chapter Twenty-Eight

"Find your strength, Sara."

My eyes fluttered open. *What?*

I sat back and gazed around the interior of Amy's car. No one was there. Outside the precinct, flags flapped in the wind. People and police cars came and went. It was business as usual out there—but not in my world, although something had sparked in my mind.

As if a light had turned on, the solution became clear to me. I started Amy's car and raced toward campus. My cell rang on the way.

"Hello?"

"It's Jason. Have you found out anything?"

"Yes, I was going to call you. I need you to go to the police station and try to talk to Scott." I stared up at the street sign. "The one off of Lauderdale Avenue."

"So, they brought him to the station?"

"Yes, I just left there. I have an idea for a way to help him, but I need to make sure Scott doesn't confess anything to the police."

"I'll do whatever I can. What's your plan?"

"I'm headed to see the senator."

Right now, he was the only one holding the cards to Scott's fate. If I could convince him to drop the charges—or *force* him if I had to—then maybe we had a chance. The evidence Derek stole gave me an advantage, and I had to use it.

"I'm going to use that evidence against him. But it's important that Scott doesn't confess. And if you talk to Scott, tell him I'm going to get him out ... and that I love him." I couldn't wait for the moment when I would tell him myself.

"On my way ... and Sara?"

"Yeah?"

"Be careful."

The warmer air chiseled at the snowbanks, diminishing them into streams of dirty water greasing the roadways. My windshield needed a near-constant stream of washer fluid to wipe away the road spray. Fatigue, dehydration, and anxiety compromised my ability to drive, or at least to drive well. I sat up straighter, opened the window, cranked the radio, and did everything short of jumping jacks to stay alert.

* * *

As I unlocked the door to my room, Amy came bounding out into the hall. Her hair was wet as were her gray T-shirt and yoga pants. If she had just showered, she had bypassed the towel.

"I didn't expect to see you so soon. Has something happened?" It was unusual to see Amy without makeup on. She looked so different—even more beautiful and yet innocent.

"I was going to come get you. Come in."

Once inside, my eyes homed in on the strongbox on my desk. I was thankful it was still there.

"They took Scott to the police station." My throat was too dry to carry words.

Amy kept her eyes pinned on me.

I crossed the room to grab a bottle of water and downed it, then spoke. "Jason is going there now to try and talk to him."

After drinking half the bottle down, I dashed into the bathroom, splashed water on my face, and brushed my teeth. I expected to look haggard, but when I lifted my face to the mirror, I was far worse than that. If my plan was going to work, I had to make myself presentable. I fumbled with my makeup container, attempting to cover the dark purple rings and blotchy skin tone.

"Did you see Scott?" Amy's voice brought me back to the moment. "Here, let me help you." She took the foundation from my hand and sat me down on the toilet lid.

"No. After what Jason said, I was afraid that I'd make the situation worse for him."

Amy applied a thick layer of foundation, then she moved on to mascara and liner.

My mind kept drifting in and out.

When she was finished, I darted back into my room to search through my wardrobe.

"So, what's the plan?" Amy sat on my bed watching me.

I pulled a white eyelet lace top off a hanger, then my black dress pants, and put them both on. It was alarming how loose the pants were.

Amy slapped her hand on my comforter. "Sara, what's going on?"

Before I could answer, another thought took over. "Where are those gloves?"

With her brow furrowed, Amy stood and searched the room. "We threw them off so quickly they're probably somewhere on the floor." She squatted down and looked under my desk. "Fuck it, just grab a new pair." Standing, she took the box of gloves from my desk and held it out for me.

"I used to have a bunch of plastic bags under my bed." I got down on my hands and knees and peered underneath. As I pulled out a crumpled-up plastic bag, a shoebox containing all my photos of Scott, along with every loving note he had ever written to me, caught my eye. A day ago, I had wanted to burn that box. Now, I wanted to clutch it to my heart and cherish it. There wasn't time.

I climbed to my feet, put the gloves on, and crossed the room in two strides, where I reached into the strongbox. I pulled out one of the magazines, along with one of Rick's disturbing letters, and placed them both in the plastic bag.

"Here, put them on." I peeled off the gloves and gave them to Amy. I also handed her the bag containing Scott's bloodied T-shirt, the soiled hand towel, and the duct tape.

With her mouth pinched defiantly shut, Amy did as I asked.

"You need to take all this stuff out of here and hide it. Somewhere no one can find it. Do you understand?"

Amy leaned closer. I sensed she was ready to shake the information out of me. "Are you going to tell me why?"

"Because we're going to need it."

"Good, let's nail the bastard." She spoke with conviction in her voice and resolution in her eyes.

"No, it's not what you think. The only way I can get Scott released and the charges dropped is to hit Rick right where he lives ... literally."

Amy grabbed my arm. "Sara, you need to tell me what you plan to do. You're dealing with a very dangerous person here. You can't do this alone."

"I don't have time to explain it all." In truth, I was afraid she'd try to talk me out of it. "If Scott confesses to attacking

Rick, then it's going to make things worse for him." I bit my lower lip. "I can't lose any more people I love. Not when I can do something to stop it." I touched her shoulder. "Thank you for letting me use your car." I handed her keys back and then grabbed my own from my desk drawer.

"Go ahead and take the box and bag now. Don't leave them here. Find a place no one would think to look for them. I don't know what Rick's father is capable of."

Amy's face froze, and then went slack. *She knew.* "Oh. You're going to try to talk to *him? Why?"*

"Because I have something on his son, and he's the only one who can stop this."

"But how is that going to help you with *your* case?" She picked up the box and bag and released a heavy sigh.

"That doesn't matter right now. Scott put his life on the line for me, and I'm going to do everything in my power to help him." If Rick paid for what he'd done to me, then Scott would pay, too. That would mean Rick won, and I couldn't accept that.

Amy tried to speak, but I cut her off. "I'll call you if anything changes."

I opened my door, and we stepped out into the kitchen. No sound came through Sue Anne and Mia's closed doors. A lucky break.

En route to her room, Amy stopped and turned.

"Good luck, Al." For a moment, she was back to my take-no-prisoners Amy—full of wit and humor. "You got this."

An unspoken exchange followed, one that reflected how much we meant to each other. "Thanks, and I love you, Amy."

Her face softened. "Yeah, me, too."

I took a breath and forged forward.

When I reached the parking lot, I jumped into my car, started the ignition, and hit the gas. Speed wasn't an issue for me. Not anymore. By the time I had reached the hospital, I'd played out every possible scenario in my head. My nervous system was running on overdrive.

At the hospital information counter, an elderly woman with short silvery hair and glasses halfway down her nose, sat working on a crossword puzzle when I approached. Ingrid, according to her volunteer name tag, told me what floor to find Rick. I rode the elevator to the fourth floor, then walked down a long hallway, across a smaller lobby, and past another set of elevators. Outside a pair of ominous-looking, seafoam-colored doors, the words "Intensive Care Unit" had my heart spasming. A stocky young man with a shaved head, wearing scrubs, sat behind a small desk shuffling papers.

"Can I help you?" the man asked. His ID badge with photo indicated Trevor Beckerman.

I wiped a tacky palm down my coat. "Yes, is Rick Sweet here?" I held my breath awaiting his answer.

"Are you family, or are you part of Senator Sweet's staff?" Trevor picked up a clipboard to examine it.

"Uh, no, I'm a friend." The word *friend* violated my body all over again.

Trevor put the clipboard down. "Only family is admitted into intensive care. Unless you're with the senator. I can see if a family member can come out and talk with you. What's your name?" He waited.

"Sara Browne." I tempered my nerves. "I'm actually here to see Senator Sweet. Could you see if *he* is available?"

"I can ask." Trevor called into the unit while I practiced a speech in my head. I hoped the senator would be available, but regardless, I wasn't leaving until I spoke to *someone* from that family.

"You're free to have a seat." With the phone propped between his jaw and shoulder, Trevor motioned with his hand to a short row of chairs against the wall. "It may be a few minutes."

I sat in a chair, my back rigid. Every time a doctor or nurse came out of the intensive care unit, my heart skipped a beat. By the time Senator Sweet appeared thirty minutes later, my armpits seeped with sweat, my pulse doing a hundred-yard dash.

Dressed in a black, expensive-looking suit, crisp white shirt, and dark-blue striped tie, his salt-and-pepper hair slicked back, the senator approached the volunteer. Holding his cell phone in one hand, he scanned the area, his gaze sliding right past me.

"Who requested to see me?"

Trevor pointed in my direction.

I sucked in as much oxygen as my lungs would carry and stood, taking a tentative step forward.

Senator Sweet's eyes warmed. "Oh, are you a friend of Rick's?" He reached out his hand, which I took, hoping he didn't notice the clamminess of my palm.

Just like Rick, he smelled expensive.

"Could we go somewhere to talk for a moment?"

"This isn't a good time." The senator's gaze shifted between me and the door. "We're getting ready to move my son out of intensive care."

More good news.

"It's about what happened to him," I said, trying to sound persuasive while maintaining eye contact. "I promise to be brief."

"Have you spoken to the police?" The senator kept looking

at the doors. He didn't seem to notice the basket case in front of him.

"Not yet. Please. It's important."

The screen on the senator's phone flashed. He stared at it for a few seconds, and then extended his arm in the direction of the hallway. "There's a break room at the end of the hall. We can talk there."

We were halfway down the hallway when one of the senator's staff members stuck his head out the door. He had a cell phone to his ear. "Senator Sweet, we need to discuss the press conference."

Once again, I held my breath.

Mr. Sweet raised a palm. "In a minute. I'll be right back."

Together, we walked to the end of the hallway, where the senator stopped and pushed open a door to the right, gesturing for me to go ahead of him. I entered what appeared to be a small kitchen equipped with an ice machine, a fridge, and a multitude of cabinets. I hoped for chairs to support my shaky legs, but there were none.

As soon as the door swung shut, the senator spoke. "I need to get back out there. What do you want to tell me? Do you know more about what happened?" He leaned against the counter and crossed his arms. His phone flashed again, but he ignored it.

I prepared myself for battle. "There are a lot of things you don't know about your son. Things I'm sure you wouldn't want the police or the press learning."

The senator uncrossed his arms and straightened his back, dark clouds rolling into his eyes. "My son has been brutally beaten." He bared his teeth. "His jaw is wired shut, and his injuries are so severe it will take months before he fully recovers. What is this?"

"Your son raped me a few days ago." It was out of my

mouth before I had a chance to stop it. "When I told him I only wanted to be friends, he slipped a drug into my wine and then raped me." Tears welled up in my eyes, but I refused to succumb.

For a second, he flinched. Then the senator huffed at me and walked toward the door. "That's ridiculous. I don't have time for this." He stopped and pointed at me. "If you don't leave right now, I'll have security throw you out." He glared at me with those same menacing eyes his son had inherited.

"I have proof."

He stopped in his tracks.

"Your son has been stalking me for months. He even sent me anonymous letters in the mail." My lips twitched as I spoke, my body vibrating with tension. "He wrote all over my car and ruined an expensive laptop."

"What are you talking about?" He faced me.

"Rick cut words out of magazines and pasted them onto blank sheets of paper, making these strange letters. I have some of them and also pictures of what your son did to me." I'd opened the geyser. Only one way to go now.

The senator rubbed his chin, his face flushing before his eyes widened. "Wait. I remember you. You were Rick's date at the holiday gala."

I nodded, shameful.

"I remember him telling me that you might be the one. Did you two fight? I know he has issues, but—"

"Issues?" *Was he for real?* "I only liked your son as a friend and told him that from the beginning. A few days ago, he took me to a log cabin that he said your wife was interested in buying."

The senator looked down and then up from his cell phone that had been flashing in his hand.

"I have a witness who will testify that he knew Rick was

stalking me and that he drugged my boyfriend. I also have evidence that proves he raped me."

"What evidence?" More blood rushed to the senator's cheeks.

I cleared my throat. "Rick's camera. It contains pictures of everything I just told you."

He blinked. "How do you know it's Rick's camera?"

"Because on that same camera are pictures of your family."

He touched his chin again, his gaze searching around the room as if looking for an answer. "That doesn't prove anything. Someone else could have used his camera." His voice was weakening.

"No, Rick was in one of those compromising pictures. I also have a bag of pills he used to drug me."

The senator whispered something that sounded like "Damn kid." He regained his composure. "That doesn't prove anything. Maybe your boyfriend *wanted* him to take those pictures, and the pills could be anyone's."

"Oh, really?" I sounded confident. I wasn't—but I *was* angry. "I also have the magazines he used to cut the words out of, and even a few sample letters. Your wife's name and home address are on the mailing labels. Plus, Rick's fingerprints are all over everything." That was a bluff—I didn't know that for sure.

"Where did you get this supposed evidence?" He ridiculed me with his dark, hooded eyes.

"It doesn't matter where I got it. But I will say that it was in a strongbox with Rick's initials embossed into the metal."

"Does this have anything to do with my son's car being vandalized? I could have you arrested for that."

The conversation wasn't going the way I had hoped it would.

"I didn't have anything to do with that. The evidence was

given to me by someone who knew what Rick was doing." My chest filled with frustration *and* sadness. "And if you want to talk about illegal acts, then let's get real here. Your son drugged and raped me. You want to file charges? Go right ahead." I wasn't sure where my strength was coming from, but I was grateful for it.

With nothing left to say, I held the bag out in front of me.

"What's that?" The senator flinched as though something might leap out and bite him.

I wish.

"Take it."

The senator took the bag but didn't look inside. "Let me guess. Your boyfriend is Scott Williams?"

"He used to be. He meant everything to me, and your son destroyed our relationship."

"Well, I have an eye witness that says Scott attacked Rick."

"Scott found out what Rick did to me, and that's why he went to the water tower. It wasn't a fair fight. Rick had two other men with him. One of them stabbed Scott. My guess is that it was the same person who called 9-1-1 and who also pointed the finger at Scott. Sounds more like self-defense to me."

Beads of sweat dotted the senator's brow. With eyes downcast, his face revealed more than he may have realized. He had to know this about his son. How could he not?

"Scott could have just as easily been the one in that hospital bed." I pushed the image from my mind. "If you refuse to drop the charges against him, I will take all my evidence to the police *and* the press. Scott may go to jail, but so will your son. Judging by the number of pills in his possession, I'm guessing I'm not the only person he's done this to. I'm sure having a son who's been convicted of rape doesn't play well for your political career, now does it?"

For a moment, the senator's shoulders crumpled, and his gaze returned to the floor. Then he straightened up to his full form. "You're bluffing."

He knew I wasn't. I was sure of it.

"If I have to lose the man I love, your son is going to be held accountable. No one should have the right to destroy people's lives without consequences. Scott was only there to defend me. He's been through hell and back, and it's all because of *your* son. What would you do if someone did that to your wife?"

He grimaced as though my words had caused him physical pain.

There was more to this man than I had realized. *Family secrets?*

"Give me a few hours. I need to check into this."

"No, we need to go to the police station right now and get him released."

My heart was weakening. I needed this resolved. I needed Scott.

He tilted his head. "How do I know you're not lying in an attempt to get your boyfriend off the charge? I need to confirm some things."

"Look in the bag." I motioned with my hand.

With fear in his eyes, the senator opened the bag slowly, and without removing anything, he closed it again.

"I'm not lying to you. I wish none of this had happened. There's no reason that everyone's life has to be ruined here. If you drop the charges, I won't come forward."

"You say that now, but what if I drop the charges and then you come forward anyway?"

"If I did, then you could still file charges again. My silence doesn't only help *you*, it also prevents Scott from going to jail."

The senator grew silent, staring right through me while I counted the seconds.

"You say Rick's fingerprints are on this?" He held the bag in the air.

"Yes." I hoped I was right.

"I can have this confirmed in a few hours. If my son's fingerprints are on this letter, then we can talk. I also want to check into a few other things." He looked at his Rolex. "Do you know where Hubbardton Park is ... near campus?"

"Yes." *Did I?*

"I'll meet you there at the fountain in two hours."

I looked at my cell.

The senator reached for the door and stopped. "If I find out you are lying or that this is a trick, you will regret it," he said.

I was certain he meant every word, but so did I.

Chapter Twenty-Nine

I found Hubbardton Park, where I sat on the edge of a small fountain, its water turned off, and waited for the senator to arrive. The winter sun hung high in the sky, filtering glimmers of light through the enormous oak and maple branches, all devoid of their leaves.

The sounds of laughter caused me to peer across the lawn patched in snow where two young men played a game of basketball. They laughed and teased each other, each trying to steal the basketball from the other, reminding me the earth was still spinning.

I was sick, I was unsure, and I was beyond nervous. Terror ran through my veins. How in the world was this going to work out? I ran the "what ifs" through my mind: What if the senator didn't find any fingerprints on the note? What if he went to the police? I could almost picture the headline: "Senator's Son Blackmailed by Girlfriend of Attacker."

Just when I was about to run into the bushes and barf, my cell rang.

"H-hello?"

"It's Jason. They won't let me in to see him." Distortion on the other end told me he was on the move.

Just then, a large and very shiny black SUV pulled up to the curb—no police cruisers accompanying it. The door to the back seat opened from the inside, sending a spark of dread through me. *The lion's den.*

"I have to go, Jason. I'll call you later."

"Wait ..."

I walked around to the other side of the car, where a window rolled down, revealing the senator's angry face.

"Get in," he said in a clipped tone.

"No, I think I'll stand right here." I crossed my arms.

"Fine, then. I'll just tell you right now. I can't help you." His eyes were cold and unwavering.

Tears stung my eyes. "Why? I'm not bluffing. I will take all my evidence to the—"

"Don't bother threatening me, young lady. I've already spoken to Scott." This time he sounded almost fatherly in a settle-down-young-lady sort of way.

He'd spoken to Scott? "You what?" My mouth gaped open. "What do you mean you've spoken to Scott?" My thoughts jumbled. "Why would you do that?"

The senator looked away.

I should have known I couldn't trust him. The whole family was rotten.

"You've given me no choice." My cheeks fired, my stomach boiled. "We'll fight you, and we'll win." I wasn't sure who I was trying to convince, him or me. "This is your son's fault, and he will pay for what he did to me."

I took a step away.

The senator opened his door and stepped out of the car, shading me from the sun. What was he planning to do? I backed up and clenched my hands into fists.

The senator's posture relaxed, his brow shining with perspiration. "Young lady, I'm not going to hurt you." He lifted a palm of surrender.

I stopped but remained ready for … whatever.

"I need you to listen to what I have to say. I talked to Scott, and he wasn't willing to agree to my terms." The senator pulled out a white handkerchief from his suit jacket and wiped his forehead. His hand trembled. I took comfort in that.

"What terms? You never mentioned terms." *What was he talking about?*

"I told him I would consider dropping the charges."

Hope sprang to life in my chest.

"But he had to agree to stay away from Rick." He continued to dab his brow. "It's obvious how much Scott still hates my son. I'm not going to help that animal get free just so he can finish the job. I don't care what you do to my family. My son's life is more important than anything you can do to us." He returned the handkerchief to his pocket.

I stared at the senator, absorbing the details of this new development. His loyalty was admirable, but it posed a greater challenge for me.

An idea hit me square in the head. "Let *me* talk to Scott."

"It won't do any good."

"Please. It's worth a try. If I can get him to agree, then we both get what we want." I implored him with my eyes.

The senator let out a long sigh and looked at the driver. "We can try. Get in."

"I have my car. I'll meet you at the precinct. I know where it is."

As he climbed back into the car and his window rolled up, Rick's father dialed his cell.

I ran to my car and sped toward the police station. When I arrived, the senator met me on the front steps.

"I don't think this is going to work." His voice was stern. "If anything more happens to my son, I promise you I will make it my life's mission to destroy Scott *and* you."

His words did little to hide the alarm in his voice. We weren't so different, him and I. Both of us were desperate to protect the ones we loved.

"I give you my word that if Scott is released, he will *not* be a threat to Rick." In truth, I wasn't sure what this experience had done to Scott. And I didn't know if I could sway him. All I knew was that I had to try.

* * *

As I walked through the precinct, I felt like a teakettle ready to blow its lid. I had been on a near-constant adrenaline rush to the point where a chair scraping across the floor or the radio chatter on the dispatcher's intercom had me jumping out of my skin.

We reached the back of the main area, where the senator shook the hand of a brawny man with grayish-red hair. The fluorescent lights gleamed off a sheriff's badge, pinned to his brown uniform, a firearm holstered on his right hip. "Thanks, Lenny."

Wide gray sideburns framed Lenny's round face, meeting a jawbone that looked like it could bite through steel. Given the man's height and broad shoulders, I guessed he was a force to be reckoned with. Perfect for a sheriff.

The senator looked at me. "This is Sheriff Murphy."

"Lenny, this is Sara Browne." He motioned with his hand.

The sheriff gave me a scrutinizing once-over.

I swallowed hard. *What did he know?*

Together, the three of us continued down a cinder block

hallway, where I hoped Scott would be. For all I knew, they were going to lock me up instead.

We approached an ominous-looking door, where the sheriff pushed a button, igniting a loud buzzing noise that cracked through my bones. The door swung open, metal grating against metal. *Nails on a chalkboard.*

While I tempered my nerves, the senator bent down and whispered in my ear. "I'm going in with you, but I'll wait by the door. If he agrees, then I need to hear it with my own ears." His tone was bold and determined. "I need to be sure."

I had to agree. What choice did I have?

It felt like an eternity since I had seen Scott, and deep down I was terrified to face him now. He used to look at me with such loving eyes. After everything he had been through, what remained of the man I knew? Had anger and resentment replaced the love in his heart?

I took a step and then another one, my feet knowing what to do.

The moment Scott came into view, I nearly lost my nerve and my footing. He was lying on a cot, one arm draped over his forehead. I had trouble squeezing his name out.

"S-Scott."

Moving his arm, Scott sprang up and winced, clutching his side. "Sara, what are you doing here?"

I looked at him and he looked at me. Regardless of how he felt now, I had enough love in my heart for the both of us. I had never stopped.

"I'm so sorry all of this happened." I grabbed the bars with both hands and leaned my head against the iron barrier that separated us, tears pouring from my eyes.

Scott jumped to his feet and crossed the cell, one hand glued to his wound. "You have nothing to be sorry for. I should never have let this happen. I should have protected you."

"How could you have known?" I swallowed my tears. "I'm sorry I believed you would cheat on me. I couldn't see the truth. Can you forgive me?" My heart was about to shatter into a million pieces.

"There's nothing to forgive." His eyes glistened with heartache. "It wasn't your fault. You had nothing to do with my decisions. I couldn't bear it if anything else happened to you. I love you more than anything in this world."

There it was. Scott's love coming back to me.

"You don't need to worry about me. I'll be fine." Scott put his arms through the bars and stroked my hair the way he used to. His eyes zeroed in on the bandage on my forehead.

"It's just a scratch." I stared at the laceration on his lip.

With our foreheads touching, we sobbed in each other's arms for several seconds. The smell of iron and corrosion taunted my nostrils, reminding me of how far we had fallen.

Scott pulled his arms back and brushed the hair away from my face.

"It kills me to know that he hurt you, Sara. I'd give my life to make that go away for you."

He *had* given his life. Our current location only proved it.

I took a deep breath. "I need you, Scott. I can't make it without you. You have to agree to the senator's terms. Please do this for me ... for us." I gripped the bars so tight, my knuckles throbbed right along with my heart.

Scott pressed his lips hard against my forehead and stayed there. Then he backed away, his expression fallen. I was petrified of what he was going to say next.

"I'd do anything for you, but I already told him I wouldn't cooperate." He bowed his head. "It's too late."

The senator cleared his throat before stepping into Scott's view.

Scott moved back, his shoulders stiff and his hands

clenched, rage riding up his spine like an inferno. He was in combat mode, his cheeks, two hot coals.

"What are *you* doing here?" No longer tender, Scott's eyes burned.

The senator swallowed, probably thinking *holy crap*. "It's not too late." He kept his tone even. "If you give me your word that my son will be safe and you are no longer a threat to him, I will help you."

Scott glared at the senator, his neck corded. Even his hands were shaking. I had never seen him so angry.

I squeezed my eyes shut and waited for Scott to decide our fate.

"Rick needs to pay for what he did to her." I opened my eyes to Scott pointing his finger as though it were a sword at the senator's head. Heat continued to fill his cheeks, his eyes fueled with hatred.

"Please, Scott," I said.

When his gaze shifted to me, he melted, his voice almost a whimper. "Don't you want to make him pay? Rick shouldn't get away with this." I could see the conflict within him, the self-lessness.

I reached my hands through the bars. "Yes, Rick should pay, but if I lose you, then he wins." I lowered my head and wept. "I can't lose you again."

Scott stormed the bars. "I only want justice for you." He wiped my tears away.

"If I lose you, then there will never be justice for me ... ever." I shivered, as though a gust of wind had swept through the room.

It dawned on me that it wasn't only anger that had made Scott attack Rick; it was guilt. He felt responsible for what had happened to me. He wasn't to blame. No one was, except Rick.

My life and my sanity waited for Scott to decide.

He lowered his voice. "I'll agree."

My entire body released a mountain of tension, my muscles going limp.

"If you mean it, then let's shake on it. In my day, that's how we did things." The senator reached his hand through the bars and waited for Scott to reciprocate. I knew in an instant why the senator had done it. If Scott couldn't shake his hand, then how could he be trusted to keep his word?

The revulsion on Scott's face sent me reeling again. When he stepped forward, I wasn't sure if he was going to shake the senator's hand or wring his neck. He chose the first option but with a warning. "I will agree to your terms, but if Rick ever goes after her again, or I even hear he is thinking about it, all bets are off."

The handshake ended.

With tight lips, the senator nodded once. "You don't know me as well as you think you do. When I was a boy, my mother ..." He clamped his mouth shut, his jaw fighting to stop him.

Neither Scott nor I spoke.

I *knew* there was a secret. I just didn't suspect something so dire. His mother was raped and his son was a rapist? I actually felt sorry for the man.

"I don't take this lightly." Senator Sweet's voice dipped lower as he walked behind me. "My son will *not* be a problem." He took a breath. "If you love this girl, then you need to focus on taking care of her."

Scott stared down at me. "I intend to. Now, get out."

* * *

I had to leave the precinct. The walls were closing in. I waited outside for Scott, letting the fresh air rejuvenate me. Soon, Amy, Luke, Jason, and Heather came, supplying hot tea, a scarf, a pair of gloves, and more importantly, their support.

A call came in on my phone. It was Derek.

I wanted to answer, but I couldn't. It was too soon, and I wasn't ready.

A few seconds later, he left a voice mail, which I listened to right away: "I'm so sorry, Sara. I'm leaving school today and wanted you to know that I never wanted any of this. I wish I could go back and make better choices. I knew Mindy and Charlene didn't go into Scott's room that night, and Scott never threatened Rick either, not then. Rick had talked a lot of shit about Scott, and I worried that he wasn't right for you. I knew Rick really liked you, but I never suspected that he'd take things as far as he did. I suspected he sent those letters, but I wasn't sure until I stole the evidence from his car. If you need me to testify, I give you my word I will do it. Anyway, take care of yourself, and I hope someday you can forgive me." My heart felt heavy, my throat finding a new level of pain.

Poor Derek.

"Was that Scott?"

Amy's question caught the attention of the group, who all stared with inquiring eyes.

"No, it was Derek."

Amy huffed and rolled her eyes. "What did that asshole have to say?"

"He said he was sorry and that he's leaving school. He hopes someday I will forgive him."

"Good riddance," Jason muttered.

"This wasn't all his fault, and if it weren't for him, Scott wouldn't be getting released right now." My arms hung slack at my sides.

Amy's face became full-on angry. "Can you *not* ... if he had told you the truth when he first suspected anything, then Scott wouldn't be here in the first place."

I hated how they felt about Derek. I hated that Derek wasn't strong enough to warn me. I hated *everything* about this situation. Most of all, I hated Rick. Scott felt that Rick had gone unpunished, but in reality, Rick had paid for his crimes—Scott had made sure of it. Whatever scars or trauma Rick suffered, or would suffer, were his cross to bear, just as my scars were mine.

As the next hour passed, darkness descended around us. The streetlights clicked on, illuminating a flurry of snowflakes, drifting like tiny feathers through the air. I tipped my head back and let the speckles of moisture refresh my skin. I had been through hell over the past several weeks, but Scott was back in my life again. It was nothing short of a miracle—one I would not take for granted. Inside my battered heart, a tiny flicker sparked to life.

To the open air, to my parents, and to anyone who would listen, I whispered, "Thank you."

Just then, the station's door flung open, and Scott emerged, a free man.

Wanting to keep my hands free, I slipped my phone in my coat pocket, ready to embrace the love of my life.

The instant his eyes met mine, he held his side and jogged down the concrete steps. All I could think was *Please don't slip.* Despite his rumpled clothing, obvious exhaustion, and painful injuries, he was beaming as if he'd just won the lottery. Because he had, we both had. We'd won the chance to be together again.

I stumbled forward and threw myself into his arms, holding on as tight as my grip would allow. He hugged me so hard I could barely breathe. Like pieces of a puzzle, our bodies came together, Scott's heart pounding against my cheek and mine drumming its own rhythm back to him. *I love you. I missed you. I'm sorry.*

"My God, I love you." Tears rolled down Scott's stubble as he cradled my face in his hands. His eyes drank me in, his heart wide open. "I can breathe again. I've been so lost without you, Sara. Don't ever leave me again." He pressed his lips against mine, and I could feel his desperation for me.

When he pulled away, I stared at him through my own wall of tears. He was a gift, a miracle in my life, and I never wanted to be without him again.

"I'm not going anywhere." I ran my fingers through his disheveled hair. "You're stuck with me, handsome." I hugged him with everything I had and everything I would ever be. I was home.

Reviews ...

If you liked *Flickering Heart*, I'd be grateful if you would leave me a review on Amazon, Goodreads, or BookBub (no spoilers, please). For Indie authors, reviews are immensely important.

Also by Tricia T. LaRochelle

Sara Browne Series Romantic Suspense:

Flickering Heart - Book 1

Revive - Book 2

Handfast - Book 3

Bleeding Heart - A Holiday Romance - Book 4

Stand alone Contemporary Romances:

Sun in My Heart

Coming soon ... A Collision with Love

About the Author

Since she was a little girl, award-winning author, Tricia T. LaRochelle, has been obsessed with tragic love stories. No beach reads for her. Bring on the grit with a double side of turmoil. She likes to *feel* the character's anguish as they fight to overcome obstacles to be together. Growing up in central Vermont, she has seen her share of tragedy but remains a hopeful romantic. She now lives in central Virginia where she continues to foster the possibilities of how love can conquer all.

Flickering Heart, the first book in the *SARA BROWNE SERIES*, won first place for romance in the 2022 Incipere Awards. The sequel, *Revive*, received an honorable mention in the same category.

Stay tuned for updates and announcements on Instagram, Facebook, and Twitter, or sign up for her newsletter at www.-TriciaLaRochelle.com.

Acknowledgments

Where to begin. I started *Flickering Heart* many moons ago when I was dipping my toes into the literary pool. I've rewritten this story too many times to count. (The title used to be *Flickering Star*.) What started as a coming-of-age tale, transformed into a love story ripe with turmoil, passion, and bravery. I am grateful to so many who have helped me along the way. From Melissa Shelton Harrison's expert and extremely helpful advice at the beginning of this venture, to Michelle Wallace, who advised me that one point of view worked better than two did, to the amazing Liz Kracht, who showed me that one chapter didn't work, which paved the way for a new stronger chapter to emerge—and to Olga Jackson for her beta read, which helped me polish toward the end. I am grateful to them and their trained eyes.

My husband, Bob, kept me off the ledge on more than one occasion. My sons, Ryan and Sean, offered their unyielding support and encouragement as well as great material about how college-age men think and speak. Hattie Firebaugh has not only been a great proofreader, she's offered valuable input for the story's age group and encouraged me to keep going.

My incredible editor, Kim Catanzarite—a brilliant writer— offered not only great editing and developmental advice, she's been my confidant, sounding board, and friend for many years. I truly couldn't do this without her. *We're in this together!*

My ARC proofreaders Cheri Gravett, Bob LaRochelle,

Ryan LaRochelle, Kim Catanzarite, and Hattie Firebaugh were immensely helpful at finding any hidden typos that lurked within the forest of words.

Writing and pursuing a dream of this nature requires a village of support, and as I've shown, my village is pretty awesome. I remember reading my initial chicken scratch of a story to my friend, Cheri, who boasted over every word. It was just the boost I needed to pursue this crazy dream of mine. My family and friends stuck by me, and I couldn't be more appreciative. Thank you all, and to those who I didn't mention, for your support and kindness. I will never forget it.

9 798986 175614